Volume 23

Secrets

Satisfy your desire for more.

The Sex Slave

Jaci Coe needs a hero and th- ⏐⏐⏐⏐⏐ ll the criteria, even if he does walk ⏐⏐⏐⏐⏐ ; a second
time that first night, the opp ⏐⏐⏐⏐⏐ ..zarus
Stone's commandingly prote ⏐⏐⏐⏐⏐ ..c two together, their
flaws and strengths blending, ι ⏐⏐⏐⏐⏐ ..v to live free... and love freely.

Forever My Love by Calista Fox

Professor Aja Woods is a sixteenth century witch... only she doesn't know it.
Christian St. James, her vampire lover, has watched over her spirit for five
hundred years, waiting for her to fulfill her destiny. When her powers are
recovered, so too are her bound memories of Christian—and the love they
shared half a millennium ago.

Reflection of Beauty by Bonnie Dee

Artist Christine Dawson is commissioned to paint a portrait of wealthy
recluse, Eric Leroux, a man shrouded in mystery. It's up to her to tear away
the briars and scale the symbolic wall to reach the heart of this physically
and emotionally scarred man. For his part, Eric must learn to open himself
and trust after a lifetime of rejection. Can love rescue him from isolation and
restore his life?

Educating Eva by Bethany Michaels

Striving to make her mark as a serious academic, Eva Blakely attends the infamous Ivy Hill houseparty to gather research for her book *Mating Rituals of
the Human Male*. But when she enlists the help of research "specimen" and
notorious rake, Aidan Worthington, she gets some unexpected results. Can
Eva achieve the recognition she's worked for all her life, or will her irrational
desire for the bad boy put her academic aspirations on the shelf for good?

Roxi Romano

Calista Fox

Bonnie Dee

Bethany Michaels

Volume 23

Secrets

Satisfy your desire for more.

SECRETS Volume 23
This is an original publication of Red Sage Publishing and each individual story herein has never before appeared in print. These stories are a collection of fiction and any similarity to actual persons or events is purely coincidental.

Red Sage Publishing, Inc.
P.O. Box 4844
Seminole, FL 33775
727-391-3847
www.redsagepub.com

SECRETS Volume 23
A Red Sage Publishing book
All Rights Reserved/July 2008
Copyright © 2008 by Red Sage Publishing, Inc.

ISBN: 1-60310-164-0 / ISBN 13: 978-1-60310-164-6

Published by arrangement with the authors and copyright holders of the individual works as follows:

Book typesetting by:
Quill & Mouse Studios, Inc.
www.quillandmouse.com

Contents

Roxi Romano
The Sex Slave
1

Calista Fox
Forever My Love
69

Bonnie Dee
Reflection of Beauty
165

Bethany Michaels
Educating Eva
243

The Sex Slave

by **Roxi Romano**

To My Reader:

The Sex Slave will take you into a future that is not so alien from our present. There are still the haves and have-nots. Still politics, secrets and power struggles. Most importantly there is still the human condition.

    Meet Lazarus Stone, a species of human with special powers that condemn him to the life of a sex slave. Just when he gets the opportunity to escape, a free-spirited girl stumbles into his path with secrets of her own. Now they both face slavery if they don't escape.

Chapter 1

Lazarus Stone's sort had been bred for sex, hardwired to respond to the dictates of lust, which was why his cock twitched at the crude invitation issued from the dark alley. But he passed the street sexer, his step measured rather than faltering. He was thinking with a more evolved head tonight. He had to. He needed to find the one man who could get him off this foul outpost of a moon before someone figured out what he was and sold him to the highest bidder.

That was why he'd come to the underbelly of this goddess-forsaken moon in the dead of night. Men who did business on the edge of the law did their business in places where even the law didn't venture after sundown.

He turned up the collar of his greatcoat and strode through the smog hanging between the buildings, his target the faint glow of a streetlamp that marked the corner. There were a half-dozen more dives yet to check, three of them on the next block. He hoped to find Marco in one of them.

The debris rustled ominously where it was gathered against the curbing of a street built in an era that accommodated wheeled vehicles, and Laz's greatcoat billowed around him. Nice as it was to have his heated body cooled, any time a breeze blew across this barren moon, it meant a storm was brewing.

He lowered his head as he stepped into the dim glow of the corner mounted streetlamp, letting his hair fall around his face like a dark veil. Sometimes light wasn't a man's friend. The thought had barely crossed his mind when a girl with wild ribbons of blonde hair skidded around the corner, stutter-stepped to a halt just short of running into him, and grabbed him by his coat front.

"You gotta help me," she demanded.

"I don't have to do anything," he said, tugging at the hold she had on him.

Footfalls echoed off the buildings lining the side street, muffled by the smog bank that hung over the city night and day. He glanced over her head at the corner. From the sounds of those rapidly falling feet, there were at least two of them and one of them sounded decidedly large. They were fast closing on the corner. Laz scowled. He didn't have time to play the rescuer. Hell, his own freedom was at stake here.

"If you don't help me," she panted, "they're going to catch me."

He looked down at the girl, her forehead barely reaching his chin, well short of the women whose company he kept. A pair of huge waif-like brown eyes pleaded up at him. Maybe she was younger than he thought—a child even. The feet of her pursuers pounded closer. He groaned.

By the Goddess's blood, he was going to regret this.

But before he could take action, she yanked him by the lapels into the nearest empty doorway. He stumbled against her, flattening her against the door with his own body. High, firm, developed breasts pressed back against his chest. Definitely not a child.

She settled him back on his heels with ease. Strong, too, for such a bit of a female.

The next thing he knew, she was on her knees, her mouth level with his crotch. Cloaked by his greatcoat, they no doubt looked like any other couple having street sex. He silently conceded it was a better plan than the one he'd had... which was to fight her assailants while she ran.

Two men rounded the near corner and skidded to a halt behind them. One of them stepped up close.

"You see a little blonde run by here?" the man asked, his foul breath snaking over Laz's shoulder and slithering across his nostrils. Laz winced.

"Hey, I asked you a question, Dick Brain." The man dropped a thick hand on Laz's shoulder. This is what good deeds got a guy. Laz tensed, readying himself for the inevitable fight.

"Wait yer turn, gents," the blonde on her knees at his crotch said. "I'll be done with this one in short time."

The foulmouthed hood's fingers flexed on Laz's shoulder, diverting the flow of blood to his groin where a hot wet mouth breathed promise of release against his cock. It had been two days since he'd released. Not long for a normal man. But he wasn't normal.

Laz growled over his shoulder, "Back off."

The thug growled back, "I could pop your head like a fat pimple."

Laz's muscles coiled for the fight. But the blonde's teeth slid open over the cloth covering Laz's shaft and her breath bathed his cock in heat. He groaned, sagged against her mouth and caught himself with flattened hands against the door above her to keep himself upright. Though bred and trained to be ever on the ready for service, he'd also been taught restraint... and he had a reputation for phenomenal restraint. Yet this girl all but brought him to his knees.

The hand on his shoulder tightened, dragging his attention from the mouth heating his cock. Laz stiffened. The mouth on his cock moved up and down, slid-ing its teeth lightly the length of him—making him swell against the chamois-like microfiber of his britches. He bucked and groaned.

The other man, the one not touching him, snorted. "Leave 'em be, Dickie. A nuclear blast could go off and that guy wouldn't notice."

The beefy hand lingered a moment longer on his shoulder, then slid away ac-companied by a snarled, "Just a couple filthy street-sexers."

Then they were gone, nothing more than two sets of heavy footfalls fading off in the direction he'd come. Almost immediately, the girl kneeling between his legs released his hips and started to her feet.

Lazarus's knees gave at the sudden withdrawal of the girl's mouth. He stag-gered, caught himself and demanded, "What the hell was the blow job through the pants about?"

"To get you to sound like a man having sex," she snapped, fumbling around inside his coat.

He felt a tug on his OxyCan.

Snagging her by the wrist, he hauled her out from under his long coat.

"You weren't thinking of stealing my oxygen canister after I helped you out, were you?"

She scowled and rubbed her temple with her free hand, her hair streaming over her hand and down past her shoulders like pale ribbons. "Is that what whacked me in the head?" She fingered his coat open. "What all ya got in there?"

He released her and took a step back from her prying fingers. "Nothing that is any business of yours."

She drew a ragged breath. "I could use a hit off that OxyCan. I breathed in a lot of this bad air running from those guys."

He eyed her short tight skirt and the stacked platform shoes she'd been running in... and the shapely legs that stretched between shoes and skirt. The overall package didn't fit with those waiflike eyes that had pleaded for help. Street whore or party girl?

"What'd those guys want with you?"

She shivered and rubbed her arms through the slick fabric of a red blouse. "They wanted to party and I didn't."

There was something about her answer that didn't quite ring true. Maybe it was the way her eyes didn't quite meet his as she'd answered. Or maybe it was the fact the lipstick-red blouse had been unbuttoned far enough to expose the upper edge of a red lace bra and a plump cleavage that didn't match with the youthfulness hinting from beneath the heavy makeup.

Then there was the scent of her, a sweet, musky fragrance of female sex, strong even through the metallic odor that clung to this ore-laden moon. Yet, there was also the rancid scent of fear about her. Working girl who knew how to barter or kid in trouble?

"So do I get a hit off that OxyCan or not?" she asked, head cocked to one side and all-too-knowing eyes slanting a challenge his way.

"It'll cost you a couple of credits," he tested.

She frowned then glanced down at his crotch. "I could finish that job for you. A hit of oxygen for a hand job."

He twitched involuntarily. No working girl had ever tempted him beyond control.

He studied her more closely. Without her platform heels, she had to be a full head shorter than him. Was that it—her unusual short stature? Most grown women on this moon hovered around the six foot mark, not much shorter than the average man's height and he was average in height. This one wasn't much bigger than... *Goddess's blood, please tell me you didn't allow some early-developed child to do this to my body.*

"I usually get a hundred credits for that," she said, obviously misreading his hesitation.

She sidled close, the scent of her sex spiking, and stroked him with the palm of her hand. "Help me get off this rock and I'll even blow you."

So much for her being a kid in need of help. Stature aside, she wasn't anything the word *girl* conjured for him.

He resisted the urge to lean into the warm curve of her palm. "I just saved your ass, kid. If anyone owes anybody anything, it's you who owes me."

"Okay," she all but purred, giving a head toss that made her ribbons of hair bob around her shoulders. "I'll do the hand job as a thank-you. Then I'll blow you for a hit of oxygen and fifty credits."

He laughed.

She snatched her hand away from his crotch, her coyness fleeing. "I'm not blowing you for a lousy hit of oxy—"

She started to cough, the dry kind resulting from poor oxygen absorption. "Go to hell," she hacked out, stumbling toward the corner on coltish legs.

He groaned. Goddess's Blood, he was a soft touch.

Plucking the OxyCan from its inside pocket, he called, "Wait."

She paused beneath the streetlamp and looked back at him. He held out the OxyCan. She hesitated.

"What do I gotta do for it?" she asked, her voice raspy.

"Nothing. You can have a hit."

She eyed him suspiciously.

"Now," he commanded, advancing on her. "I've got places to go."

He held the OxyCan up in front of her. She closed her hands over his on the can and fit her mouth to the inhaler. Simultaneously, she hit the trigger and inhaled.

Her eyelids drifted shut and her head lolled back as she held the oxygen in her lungs. Directly below the streetlamp, he took the opportunity to look her over more closely.

No telltale dark roots. A natural blonde. That was an oddity in this world, an oddity that could make her a sexual commodity on this dark moon. She could well have been telling the truth about why the two thugs were chasing her.

Then there were the tear tracks furrowed through the makeup on her cheeks. Apparently she wasn't as tough as she pretended to be. Or maybe she was more scared than she let on. She was young, though not as young as the wide eyes she'd lifting pleadingly to him had suggested.

She blew out the breath, opened her eyes, and tottered. He caught her by the upper arm. "Steady there. You took a pretty big hit."

"Yeah," she dreamily sighed. "It sure was good."

She blinked up at him, her eyelids at half mast and a loopy little smile on her plump lips. "I could still thank you."

She flexed her fingers in the air by way of explanation. His dick strained at the offer. But, between her unusual petite size and the mane of blonde hair flying about her head, this girl stood out like a laser beam. Even worse, somebody wanted her bad enough to send a couple thugs into this hell hole of depravity in the dead of night to chase her down. He had enough trouble of his own without being seen with a fugitive temptress.

Or seen at all, crawled the thought up the back of his neck.

He muttered a curse and glanced up at the tiny camera fastened high to the light pole and aimed down the street. Big Brother liked to keep an eye on all its neighborhoods, and Laz had been careless. If his face had been seen out in the world after curfew....

He took out his laser and shined it up at the lens of the camera. No reflection. Someone had painted over it. His luck had held. But he wasn't taking any more chances.

He shook his head, released the girl, and stepped around her. "You're on your own, kid."

Chapter 2

Jaci Coe watched the man who'd rescued her disappear into the fog, his black greatcoat billowing back on a gust of wind like a superhero's cape. She really should stop looking for hero qualities in men, especially after what she'd experienced tonight at the hands of her current boyfriend. Make that ex-boyfriend.

Then again, she shouldn't rule every man out. This guy who'd given her a hit off his OxyCan—*given*—had acted more like the superhero of her vintage comic book collection than any man she'd ever encountered.

Correction. Her former vintage comic book collection. She'd lost everything she owned the minute her jerk of a boyfriend handed her papers over to that creep with the two goons. That was enough to punch any lingering bravado from her. Without papers, she had no identity in this world, and without an identity she had no apartment, no job, and no currency. She'd ceased to exist. Hell, she didn't even have clothes except for the party outfit on her back.

"Damn you, Rex Brody," she muttered into the air hanging heavy with pollutants. "If I ever get my hands on you, I'm selling *you* into sex slavery... after I string you up by the balls for a while."

Which was not at all what she'd liked to have done with her superhero. He sure had himself a pants' full of cock... just like her leotard clad vintage comic book heroes. Her palm tingled with the lingering imprint of it and her pussy contracted. She suspected he knew how to use his equipment well to satisfy a woman.

A gust of wind stirred the litter in the gutter at her feet and pressed the thin cloth of her shirt against her skin. Goose bumps prickled up her arms, but not from the breeze. She was paperless and alone. She could have used the help of OxyCan Man. He knew his way around this hellhole, as any good superhero would.

She glanced up at the disabled surveillance camera. She'd noticed it and its painted lens when he'd pointed his laser at it. She'd always depended on the native inhabitants of the worlds she visited to teach her survival techniques on their streets. Better than the trial and error methods her mother had used in the early days. The Goddesses be damned, she hadn't even gotten her hero's name. Like his name was of any use to her.

She sighed and stepped out of the ring of light cast by the streetlamp. She was on her own, and the first thing she had to do was change clothes to make herself less noticeable. But without a single credit at her disposal, thanks to her weasel of an ex-boyfriend, she didn't know how she was going to go about doing that.

She was halfway across the street when she heard the whirr of an approaching hovercraft. She raced for the nearest building and ducked into its recessed doorway.

Please let it not be a police cruiser, she silently chanted. If they shined their flood-lights her way, they'd be sure to spot her pale hair. Given the rampant corruption on this rock, they'd as likely sell her into sex slavery themselves as give her back to the guy who'd paid her slime-ball boyfriend for her.

The hovercraft whirred past, and Jaci let out a relieved breath. Now, how to cover her hair? There wasn't an extra inch of fabric to be had off her skirt, thanks to Rex who'd told her they were going partying. She was going to eviscerate that creep when she got her hands on him.

She fingered the slick, red fabric of her blouse. Not a color that blended well into this gray world, but it would draw less attention than her blond hair. If she wrapped it up turban-like around her head, she could hide virtually every strand. Besides, it wasn't like she'd be the only female running around this neighborhood wearing a bra as an outer-garment, and hers was a sassy red lace number. It covered more than most street-sexers wore.

She'd just tugged her shirttails from her skirt when her mother's warning echoed between her ears.

Never cut your hair and never ever wear it up off your neck.

It was the one thing her mother had pounded into her before she'd over-dosed on psychedelic drugs and croaked. She touched the mark on the back of her neck beneath her thick mane of hair. Given the events of tonight, she was beginning to understand why her mother had obsessed about keeping that mark hidden.

So much for wrapping up her hair turban style. If only she had coin enough to buy a nice mousy-brown hair rinse. She bet there'd been more than a few coins in the many pockets of her hero's great coat. She shook her head. She was slipping, or she wouldn't have come out from under that coat empty-handed.

She glanced up and down the dark streets. Like if she had even pilfered a coin or credit or two there'd be any place to spend it. No salon or even a necessities shop was open after dark on this side of town.

She ripped the bottom off her blouse, tucked the raw ends up under her bra and fashioned a scarf out of the remainder. The ends of her hair still hung below the scarf, but it was better than nothing. Now all she had to do was figure out a way to earn enough credits to get back to her rental so she could get what she needed to restore her identity... if it was even safe for her to return to the government-owned dormitory.

But nobody was going to hire her without papers... at least not for any legitimate job. Not that she thought there was much call for a file clerk in this neighborhood. Not that many folks sought boring filing clerk jobs. But the prospect of a filing job in the Department of Building Licensing where the blue-prints of every building on the colony were filed put a smile on the face of a cat burglar.

Picking pockets was still an option. Again she thought of her tall, dark superhero—of the bounty between his legs that had distracted her from his coat pockets.

He'd smelled like pure sex, all musky and primal. Her mouth watered with the thought of tasting him... and her vaginal walls flexed with the notion of doing more. Like climbing his hot bod and seeing how much of that big rod of his she could take inside her. She could have ridden him into the next millennium. And if she'd gotten him to pay for it as well....

Hell, why not? She liked sex. She liked it a lot. Why not get paid for it? It had to be safer than picking pockets in this neighborhood.

Laz elbowed his way through the crowd and slapped his OxyCan and credits card down on the bar. "Fill her up. Give me eight ounces of water, too."

"Bottled, premium filtered, or regular?" the barkeep asked.

He thirsted for a glass of premium. Cold and sparkling, tasting the way water was meant to taste. But it wasn't wise for a man to flaunt wealth on this side of town.

"Regular," he said.

"You want something in that water?"

Why anyone would ruin a perfectly good water with alcohol, he didn't know. He shook his head.

The barkeep moved off to process his card and fill his order. Laz made a half-turn and leaned one elbow casually against the bar, trying to blend in as he scanned the crowded room. He'd checked out three gathering places since his little run-in with the leggy blonde.

He shook off the memory of her fingers sliding up his hard cock. He didn't need a woman. Especially not now. He needed Marco.

The barkeep slapped down his OxyCan, credits card, and glass of water. "You sure you don't want something in that water?"

Laz eyed the mineral crusted glass at his elbow. A bit of alcohol would help sanitize the glass and kill any bacteria in the water... had he needed such protection.

"I'm sure," he said.

The barkeep shrugged and moved off. Laz pocketed his card and can. Over the rim of the crusty glass, he gave the room another scan. Marco had a knack for blending in. But then, a guy in his kind of business needed to keep a low profile.

A female voice caught his ear. It sounded unnervingly familiar. But when he surveyed the direction it had come from, all he saw was a cluster of burly mineral drillers. He needed to get that girl out of his head. At best, she was distracting. At worst....

A scowl pulled across his mouth. She spelled trouble, and he already had enough trouble of his own to get himself dissected ten times over.

He turned his attention to the back of the tavern, squinting into the shadows that were a perfect cover for anyone conducting illegal business. He didn't see Marco, but he caught an exchange of a generic credits card for a vial of psychedelic liquid. He recognized the iridescent green of the drug. He should. He'd bought enough of the stuff since landing on this rock to give half its population a permanent high. Laz winced and tipped the water glass to his lips.

A guy standing next to him with his back to the bar chuckled and elbowed the guy slumped over his drink against the bar to his far side. "Looks like Scurvy Stanley got himself some fresh blood."

Scurvy Stanley. *Fresh blood.* The hairs at the back of Laz's neck prickled. The rampant infestation of sexually transmitted disease on this mineral mining colony cut to the core of why Laz needed to get off this rock ASAP. As much as it didn't sit right with him that another *clean* woman—whore or not—was about to get herself infected, he had his own troubles. Besides, he doubted any sexer would appreciate him losing her a client.

The second guy peered over his shoulder in the direction the first one looked and gave a low whistle. "A blonde, too."

Blonde? Laz closed his eyes, clenched his jaw and pulled a steadying breath into his lungs. *Please let it be some other blonde.*

He opened his eyes and lifted his gaze to the cluster of burley mineral drillers. The cluster of drillers had thinned and there, in the midst of them....

"Damn."

The better part of her hair was covered by a red scarf and she had her back to him, but he knew she was *his* blonde girl-woman. Even without the ragged edge of the midriff-baring blouse that had slipped from under the back strap of her bra telling him where she'd gotten the slick, red scarf that covered her head, even without recognizing the legs climbing from the floor to eternity, he knew it was her.

"Goddess's blood," he muttered. She was all but surrounded by a crew of drooling, horny miners. He cursed again.

She's not your responsibility.

Besides, she might get lucky. She might only have to service the one driller she currently hung on, the youngest and least motley looking of the bunch. The younger miner might be clean.

"She must be new," one of the men to his side said, "to go with that disease-infested pup."

Scratch that bit about her being lucky. Someone should warn her what she was about to get herself into. A spasm of guilt shimmied up his spine.

She's not your responsibility.

He turned his back to her and the drilling crew. He sipped at his water.

She's not your responsibility.

In a patch of mirror above the back-bar that hadn't yet been frosted over with grime, he saw her arch her body into Scurvy Stanley's as he squeezed her ass with a grimy hand.

"Goddess's blood," Laz muttered, downed his water, pivoted on his heel and headed straight for her. Reaching over her shoulder, he plucked the bills Scurvy Stanley had given her from her fingers and handed them back to him.

She wheeled on him, protesting. "Hey, what do you think you're doing?"

"Taking my *sister* home," he growled, grabbing her by the elbow and hauling her away from a stunned Stanley and his fellow mineral drillers before she blabbed that she wasn't his sister. He was in no mood to fight for her ass, sweet as it looked in her tight scrap of a skirt.

"I'm trying to do some business," she hissed through her teeth.

"That kind of business is going to cause you a lot of hurt, little girl," he muttered as he shoved the tavern door open and stepped out into the damp night.

By the time the bar door closed behind them, he'd hauled her beyond the reach of the sputtering neon light marking the bar's entrance and kept going. He wanted as much distance between them and that dive as he could get, just in case her mineral drillers weren't of a mind to let a *brother* take his *sister* home.

"He had money. Not just credits, but real money," she argued as she stumbled along beside him.

The pace he set didn't give the woman in platform heels any chance to fight. But she kept flapping her mouth.

"How am I supposed to get the funds to get myself out of this hole if you keep playing Sir Lancelot with me?"

Lancelot? Not many of the girls selling sex on the street were well enough educated to know the ancient legends. He grunted. "I might remind you that it was you who begged for my help."

"Yeah, when I was being chased," she snapped. "In the bar, I didn't need anyone's help."

"Like hell you didn't."

"Like hell I did."

He hauled her down a side street and hopefully out of earshot of any trailing drillers. "Your buddy Stanley is diseased."

"I wouldn't have caught anything off him," she muttered.

He snorted. "You kids. You think you're invincible—that nothing can touch you."

"I'm not a kid," she fired back at him. "And I haven't caught anything up to now and I've partied plenty."

He stopped and faced her. "You have unprotected sex?"

She cocked her chin at him. "Sure. The johns pay more for barebacking."

He eyed her narrowly. Barebacking wasn't a term generally used by heterosexuals. Street sexer or party girl, which was she? Whichever she was her pheromones wound a sweet musk up his nostrils.

"They do, huh?" he said, testing her.

"Yeah," she answered, holding his gaze. But her eyes had gone hard, the truth walled behind their defiant glare. She was lying about being a pro.

"Goddess's blood," he muttered, starting to walk again. "You're coming home with me for the night."

"I charge a thousand credits for an all-nighter," she said as she trotted along with him.

Chapter 3

Why this girl was pretending to be a pro, he didn't know. But she was going to get herself diseased or dead if she wasn't more careful. He could at least get her off the street for the night, and if it took letting her think he was taking her home for a night of sex, he'd play along with the act. And in the process, maybe he could impress upon her how dangerous was the profession she seemed hell-bent to take on.

He popped on his night-vision goggles as he hauled her into the blackness of an alleyway. To his left, a street-sexer gave head to a driller. Just past a dumpster to his right, a woman was bent over while another driller hammered his dick into her from behind. He led his pheromone over-loaded girl-woman down the unoccupied center of the alleyway well away from the noses of the johns. She was problem enough without him having to fight off an alley full of horny men.

Jaci couldn't see a thing. But she smelled heightened pheromones among the garbage and unwashed bodies and heard plenty. Grunts. Slurps. Groans. Dirty talk. Her nipples hardened and her clit tingled. But there was also the fetid stench of rotting garbage and the rank musk of unclean sex. Is this where he intended to make her spend the night with him?

She balked. He tightened his grip on her wrist, giving her no choice but to continue forward through the blackness with him. Something skittered across her feet. She squealed and stumbled into her superhero.

He released her wrist and caught her by the upper arm, his knuckles brushing the side of her breast. Hard, masculine... large. She imagined those hands cupping her breasts and his long, thick fingers sliding into her vagina. Vermin and garbage aside, the crotch of her panties grew damp.

Almost as though in response to her flood of juices, a surge of pure maleness blasted her nasal cavities. Every pore in her skin opened itself to the explosion of hormones. Every nerve drank in the nectar of his testosterone. She no longer cared where they were going to do it, only how soon she could take his promising cock inside her.

Jaci shifted into a trot, no longer fighting his lead, and panted out, "Is this where we're going to do it?"

"Does that bother you?"

His voice rumbled back at her, low, more vibration than sound. It should have frightened her. But she detected a goading edge to his tone that made her smile. Besides, this guy was a hunk and she was a girl who liked adventure. "Doesn't bother me if it doesn't bother you," she parried.

He grunted and picked up the pace.

"Hey, platform shoes weren't made for running," she groused.

"We're not running," he growled.

"Maybe you're not. But to keep up with you, I nearly have to."

There was a commotion to her right. Shouts of protests. Curses. The sharp sound of flesh slapping flesh and a scream.

"Shut up, bitch," a male voice snarled, "or I'll cut off your tit."

Maybe this was more adventure than she wanted. Maybe she should have made a break for it when he'd changed his grip on her arm. Maybe she should be grateful he hurried her along. She shuddered.

"What's the matter," he muttered. "Don't like the sounds of paid sex?"

"It didn't all sound like that last one," she fired back at him, pride overriding good sense. It wasn't the first time her bravado got the best of her. Not even the first time tonight.

"The Goddess's blood on you, Rex," she muttered through her teeth.

"What's that?" her superhero asked.

"How can you even see where we're going?"

A low, patronizing chuckle drifted down over her. More out of temper than fright, she dug her heels in.

It didn't even slow him. He kept walking, his fingers tight on her upper arm keeping her upright as she stumbled forward with him.

She was about to lambaste him when her superhero propelled her out of the alley into another street. The smog hung just as heavy here and the streetlamps were just as dim. But there wasn't quite as much debris in the gutters.

He moved them across the street so fast, she almost didn't catch the night vision goggles he flipped down over his eyes as they entered the next alley. Okay, so he didn't have superhero vision and they weren't going to have sex in that Goddess-awful alley. They were also heading away from the underbelly of this rotting rock of an outpost.

They cut through another alley. She was wheezing now. He stopped in the shadows short of the next street and handed her the OxyCan. She took a hit of oxygen and handed the can back to him. He took a small hit, slipped the can back inside his coat, and hustled them across the street into yet another alley. This one seemed empty... at least of human beings. There was still the skitter of multi-footed vermin among the garbage bins.

Just short of where this alley opened to yet another street, he stopped them. There was just enough ambient light for her to see him reach into his pocket. A second later she heard the low whir of a hovercraft descending on them.

"What's going on?" she demanded, straining against his grip.

"You said you'd spend the night with me. You backing out?"

She eyed the hovercraft floating in front of them, awe over-riding her trepidation. "Is that an SG-12?"

"Yup," he said, pointing his keycard at the craft.

"That's a high-end machine."

"Yes, it is."

The interior lights popped on and the doors swung open. The light spilling out hit him, scoring his high brow and square jaw, detailing lips that begged for a woman's touch and reflecting off dark, wounded eyes that touched something familiar deep inside her.

"Get in," he commanded, the light snagging on the frayed cuff of his greatcoat as he motioned her forward.

She raised a dubious eyebrow at him. "This is yours?"

He met her gaze, his eyes almost challenging her as he answered. "More or less."

He docked the hovercraft and helped her out onto the private deck of the apartment tower.

"You're above the smog," she murmured.

He knew what she was thinking. *High-rent district.*

He positioned his eye in front of the cornea-reader, disarming the security systems, and let her into the apartment. Instantly, the lights came on, revealing the stark whiteness of the great room before them. She sucked in a breath. He suspected that deep breath had less to do with the fresh oxygen continuously pumped in the space than surprise at what panned out before her. She tilted her head back and up as she took in the room from floor to vaulted ceiling two levels above. The first time he'd walked into a room like this one he'd had the same awed reaction... and gotten an electrical jolt from the slave chip implanted at the base of his spine for revealing too much of what he felt. Since then, he'd well learned how to mask his emotions while letting others reveal theirs to him.

As he reset the security shields, she roamed the room surveying the erotic art adorning the walls, trailing her fingers along the upholstered backs of the white chaises. His hand hesitated over the control panel. He'd swear, for the briefest of moments, his fingertips could feel the plush fabric her fingers stroked. Impossible. Watching her likely just prompted his own memories.

He punched in the final code just as she stroked the cut abs of a full-sized, naked, white marble Adonis. The skin across Laz's abdomen tightened. Wishful thinking?

He cursed under his breath and shook off the sensation. His freedom—his life depended on his escaping this rock. He shouldn't have brought her here. The last thing he needed right now was some lost, over-sexed girl.

Damn him and his misplaced sense of chivalry. This was not a world in which playing hero paid off.

Nor a safe place for a man to allow himself the distraction of sexual attraction... even if sex had been that man's sole purpose.

Had been.

He stepped from the foyer into the sunken great room. She'd paused by a side table, its glass top supported by statues entwined in an erotic pose. She turned, her eye dipping over the rest of the glass-topped tables scattered about the room, all likewise braced. Her gaze stopped on the largest and lowest of the tables. Centered among the chaises, she circled the clear surface of the tabletop supported by the hand and knee of the life-sized figure in semi-recline serving as its base, its phallus fully and proudly erect. Did she recognize him?

The pulse throbbed in her neck. He wanted to close his mouth over that pulse point. He wanted to strip the make-shift scarf from her head and press his cheek to her blonde hair. He wanted to inhale her essence, pull her back against his chest, and feel her gasp as she discovered how very accurate that statue was.

She raised an eyebrow at him. "I take it this place is yours, too, more or less?" He willed his rebellious body back under control as he met her gaze. "Uh-huh." One corner of her mouth lifted. "What do you want to do first?"

So that was the way it was going to be. As long as he'd made the mistake of bringing her here, he might as well play along, see just how far she would take her charade. After all, there was nothing else for him to do about his situation until night fell again.

He motioned toward the massive spiral staircase that climbed to the balconied upper level. "That way."

She scampered up the steps ahead of him, her scrap of skirt revealing legs that seemed far longer than what should be found on a woman of such slight stature... long, shapely, flawless. He could almost feel them wrapped around his waist as his cock stroked her silky channel.

"Which way?" she asked at the top of the stairs, snapping his attention back to the business at hand.

They were standing in front of the middle of the three doors off the balcony, the *playroom* full of sex toys and aids. He could take her in there. It might be enough to scare some sense into her.

Then again, maybe not. She'd demonstrated an advanced sexual knowledge by the way she'd pressed her mouth over his crotch in the dark doorway with the goons chasing her, and he meant to teach her a lesson.

He took her by the elbow and steered her toward the door on the right. He hit a pressure pad, the door slid open and the room lights popped on. She hesitated. He could guess why. The midnight blue of this room served a sharp contrast to what she'd so far seen of the apartment. Then there was the lack of adornment. Not a scrap of artwork, erotic or otherwise softened the space. Nothing personal in sight, either.

Unless one counted the king-sized platform bed filling the space, its linens as dark as the walls and ceiling. Everything else was recessed into the walls. Drawers, cabinets, lights. Her reality... if she pursued the sex trade and was lucky enough to be privately used.

Laz shrugged off his greatcoat, popped open a wall panel, and hung up his coat.

"Not much of a wardrobe for a man who drives an XG-12 and lives above the smog," she said, peering around his shoulder into the closet.

He closed the panel and met the challenge in her eyes. "Some of us don't need much by way of clothing."

Her eyes narrowed as though she were adding up the incongruities between him and his surroundings. Time to get this game back on his terms.

Fully clothed, he flopped backwards onto the bed, folded his hands behind his head and commanded, "Show me what you can do."

He expected a little hesitation, a comment about the brightness of the light at the very least. What he got was a broad smile as she climbed onto the bed. Maybe he'd misjudged her. Maybe she was a sexer.

No. He'd have seen her around. That blonde mane stood out in this dismal world like a laser beam. Besides, the guy in the bar next to him had referred to her as *fresh meat.*

She nudged his knees apart, knelt between them and grinned. "What's your name?"

"You don't need to know my name," he replied.

"But what if I want to scream it in the throes of passion?"

"Street-sexers don't scream in passion."

In spite of the ominous tone of his voice, she sat back on her heels and planted her hands on her thighs. "You think you know everything, don't you?"

"Not everything. But a lot."

"I know a few things myself," she purred, leaning forward and planting her hands on either side of his shoulders.

Her upper leg pressed against his cock. He resisted the urge to press back against her—resisted the desire to stare at the lovely breasts dangling in front of his face from the deep opening of the scrap of blouse, breasts full and ripe, barely contained by a red lace bra.

She dipped low over his chest, peered up at him through heavy lashes and closed her lips over his nipple. Even through the sturdy cloth of his heavy cotton turtleneck, the heat of her mouth instantly bathed his skin. Hot. Moist. Unexpected. His nipple tightened and she rolled her tongue around the taut peak.

How many times had he done the same to his sexual partners? How seldom had they paid such homage to his body, his needs?

And here he was, demanding from her what all those who'd come before her had demanded of him—taken from him. This was freedom. The realization sent a shockwave of panic through him and he blurted, "Lazarus."

She rose over him, her eyebrows raised in question. A cool dampness spread over his abandoned nipple and, for a split second, he thought of giving in to his need. It would be so easy to relieve himself on this girl—to slake his lust on her. But, could he do to another being what had been done to him all his life?

"My name," he said, willing the blood back to his brain. "My name is Lazarus Stone."

"Like the guy who was raised from the dead?"

She had no idea how close her statement was to the truth. But of more interest to him was the fact that she knew who the historical Lazarus was. This was the second time she'd revealed a hint of education.

"I'm Jaci," she said, grinning. "Any requests?"

Strip me naked, press your hot lips to my skin, trail that talented tongue down my stomach, my abdomen, all the way down and swallow my cock to the hilt.

"Yeah," he said.

She licked her lips in anticipation.

"Take off the scarf."

Her grin slipped. Had she been hoping for something else? Might she truly want his sex for sex's sake?

She reached for the scarf; the skin across her bared midriff stretching over her ribs. The girl could use a meal or two as well as the reality check he was determined to provide her, though he was beginning to suspect she had already experienced a lot of reality in her young life.

She pulled off the scarf and honey-hued hair sprang out around her face and down over her shoulders. He preferred a softer style, but the color... golden like honey caught in sunlight. He wanted to run his fingers through those gleaming tresses. He wanted to press his face into them and inhale their sweetness.

She tossed the scarf aside and tugged at the fastenings of his pants, reality invading fantasy. Who was this girl who'd demanded his help? Who had she been running from? What would happen to him if they were caught and the authorities discovered what had happened here?

He needed to keep his wits about him. He needed to focus on finding Marco and getting himself smuggled off this outpost.

He needed to remember why he'd brought her here. Lessons.

His pants flap fell away, cool air whispered across his bare skin, and his unwanted houseguest drew back as though she'd found a mouse in his pants instead of a limp dick.

"You're not hard."

"Making me hard is your job," he said, wondering if he'd made a mistake by trying to rescue this waif of a girl.

She sat back on her heels and stared at his flaccid member.

Maybe teaching her a few survival lessons wasn't a mistake after all. "You act like you've never had to make a john hard before."

She blinked and met his gaze. "Men are usually already hard by the time I get their pants open."

"Consider this lesson number three."

She eyed him narrowly. "Lesson three? What were lessons one and two?"

"You haven't figured them out yet?"

She gave him a go-to-hell grimace and touched the head of his cock with one fingertip. His cock jumped. The corners of her mouth curled upward, and she closed her fingers lightly around his semi-flaccid shaft. He drew a sharp breath.

"You like that?" she purred.

Oh, yeah. Not that he had any intention of encouraging her in any way and replied instead, "Your hand is cold."

"Sorry." She lifted both hands to her mouth and blew on them.

He could tell her how he'd like to warm them up. Hell, he could tell her that sometimes a cool touch against hot flesh was an explosive combination. But that wasn't the sort of lesson he intended to teach her. She needed to learn that, when sex was turned into a commodity, it provided little pleasure to the one giving it.

"Use your mouth to make me hard," he said.

She lowered her hands, her eyes twinkling. "Eager devil, aren't you?"

He was neither a devil nor eager for what she thought.

She bent over him, those ribbons of honey-blonde hair brushing forward around her face and over his hips, a whisper of a touch across his naked groin. Blood careened toward his shaft even before she touched the tip of her tongue to the head of his cock. But it was nothing he couldn't control.

She rolled her tongue around his expanding shaft, taking her time licking and nibbling her way down. She pressed the tip of her tongue into the slight indentation at the base of his cock. He barely caught the groan before it escaped his throat.

One at a time, she sucked his balls into her mouth, bathing them in her moist heat. She ran a tight tongue up the underside of his dick, every ridge, every vein, every nerve ending throbbing for release. He hadn't expected her to be horrified by his command—to leap off the bed, refusing to put her mouth on him. She was no innocent. But neither had he expected her to wield her tongue so skillfully he found it difficult to contain—to control himself.

"Enjoying yourself?" she said, her pink lips inches from the head of his cock slick with her saliva, and her eyes twinkling with a cat-in-the-cream smugness.

"You have some good technique," he said with deliberate reserve.

"Some good technique?" She reared up between his legs and planted her hands on her hips. "I give great head."

"But you're no pro."

"I got you hard, didn't I?" She started to go down on him again.

He caught her by the hair and hauled her up. "Any woman can get me hard if I let her."

"But not every woman will take you down her throat and milk you for all you're worth. Now, you going to let me finish you off or not?"

He damned near exploded at the mere promise of her words. He was long over-due for release and, for a guy used to getting off at least once a day, he was more than ready to blow. Good thing he'd been well-schooled in the art of holding back.

"Not," he said in answer to her question.

"Fine," she said, tugged her arm free and scrambled off the bed. "But you still have to give me the thousand credits."

Braced up on his elbows, he met her hot gaze. "Lesson number two. Always get payment up front."

She glared at him. "You were going to let me blow you and fuck you and then kick me out?"

"On the contrary. I'm a man of my word."

"Then give me my credits."

"When you fulfill your end of the bargain."

"You won't let me."

"All I asked you to do is spend the night. I said nothing about sex."

"Go to hell." She spun on her heel and headed for the door.

"Where you going?"

"Back to the street where I'm sure I'll find someone who'll pay me *up front* for my services."

"You know how to get back to where you came from?"

Her hand stopped short of the pressure pad opener. She stood framed by the por-tal with her back to him, shoulders hunched, hands balled into fists at her side.

"Lesson number one," he said. "Never let a john take you anywhere that you don't know how to get back from."

Chapter 4

She pressed her forehead against the cool metal door. *Shit! Shit! Shit! Can things get any worse?*

Behind her eyes loomed the image of her supposed boyfriend handing her papers over to that slug of a slave trader flanked by two hulking goons. *Hell. Things have already been a whole lot worse.*

She faced the bed, her hunky *hero* still up on his elbows. "Fine. You've got me for the night. I'll take my thousand credits now."

The corners of his lips lifted ever so slightly. Desire pinched at her stomach. Why did he have to have such kissable lips… and such a fuckable cock? She eyed his crotch. Even at half-mast, it was a beauty.

He got up and stuffed himself back into his pants, loosely refastening them as he strode to the closet. Ever since she'd seen his full glory immortalized in the stone base of the coffee table, she'd wanted to know what that baby would feel like sliding between her lips. Hell, the scent of him the instant she'd planted her mouth over his crotch in that dark doorway along that darkened street in the pits of this hellish colony had nearly made her forget about the goons chasing her.

Now he opened the closet panel and reached for his coat, his hair shifting around his shoulders with each move, a smoky mahogany that her fingers itched to touch, along with his broad shoulders and narrow hips… and muscled thighs… and long, thick cock. She'd bet every inch of the guy was superhero hard. The problem, it seemed, would be to get him out of his clothes. Not that the close fitting turtleneck didn't nicely hint of well-sculpted abs. But how much fun would it be to strip his long legs of those black cargo pants, to free his feet of the black combat boots, to run her tongue the naked length of his body?

Her vaginal walls flexed and fresh juices drenched the crotch of her panties. Why did she have to be such a horny wench?

He dug into one of the inside pockets of the coat.

"What's with all those pockets?" she asked.

He said nothing, just continued rummaging around inside the long, dark coat. Maybe if she pushed him a little harder….

"And what's with this plain, dark blue room when the rest of the place is white and sterile?"

She waited for an answer. But none came. He just kept searching coat pockets, a scowl pulling at his luscious lips.

She expelled an exasperated breath. "Am I going to get in trouble if I'm caught hanging with a guy who *sort of* owns a high-end transport and *sort of* lives in a high-rise?"

He straightened from the closet, a credits card in hand, and looked her in the eye. "You're the one on the run. Am I going to be in trouble if I'm caught with you?"

Good question. What would happen to him if he was caught with her? In the eyes of the law, was she just a girl without papers? Or a fugitive?

Still, there was something not quite kosher about her superhero. Maybe he was more trouble for her than she was for him. She folded her arms high across her chest, cocked her chin at him, and tested that proposition. "If we're caught together, you'll be in no more trouble than me."

His eyebrows edged up onto his forehead and the corners of his mouth lifted a couple of millimeters.

"What's so funny?" she demanded. "You some sort of spy?"

The slight upward tilt of the corners of his mouth vanished, and he held up his credits card. "Give me your card, and I'll transfer the credits to it."

Scrap the spy theory. A spy would be more observant, she decided as she answered, "My card is in my purse."

"You don't have a purse," he stated.

Neither would a spy risk his cover to rescue a girl on the run. Superheroes, on the other hand, were well known to rescue damsels in distress. And superheroes were protective of their identities. Superheroes also had bodies of steel and wore uniforms. She scanned his trim, hard body clothed all in black, before meeting his gaze and responding to his request.

"And you didn't even need X-ray vision to figure that one out."

"X-ray vision?"

"Yeah. An old form of seeing into matter."

"I know what it is," he retorted.

So he was a student of past technologies as well. Not that she was in any mood to discuss antiquated equipment, ancient legends or superheroes with some surly hunk.

She waved him off and muttered, "The short of it is my purse is now in the possession of the boss of those two goons who were chasing me."

"And their boss is...?"

"Some slug who apparently deals in the sex-slave business."

Something changed in her hero's eyes, some involuntary reaction that, for an instant, carved lines into the corners of his eyes. Did he have issues with sex slavery?

Before she could search further for tell-tale signs of emotion, he dug a small case out of another coat pocket, punched open the door and headed across the balcony. She followed him past the middle mystery door to the one on the far end of the balcony. There was a keypad to get into this room, and he punched in the numbers without hesitation.

The door slid open and the cloying scent of lubricating lotions, sex and something she couldn't quite place hit her, something that reminded her of the alley on the cheap-side of town. Otherwise, it was another white room opulent as the great room below. But the gauzy fabrics draping the bed gave this space a softer, more intimate air.

Her host headed around the bed to a wall covered in artwork. She hung back, eyeing the bed that dominated the room, and the fleece-lined shackles hanging from its bedposts. They gave a whole new meaning to the label *master*suite.

"This isn't your place, is it?" she said.

"This is where I live," he replied, deactivating a holographic painting of a naked Aphrodite and revealing a wall safe.

Security. Simple device, she absently noted, her attention more focused on how superhero Lazarus answered her questions. He either ignored them or gave an indirect answer. But he didn't lie. He chose his words carefully. Semantics. She filed away the information for future use.

She turned her attention back to the bed, expecting the scent of sex lingering among the rumpled sheets. She didn't expect it to be stale. And there was that other odor, the one that reminded her of the day her mother died.

And the way the sheets were twisted as though whoever had last occupied the bed had left in a hurry or not on her own power. She sniffed, trying to identify that troublesome scent.

Through the sheer drapes, she spotted a tray on the far side of the bed. It wasn't the tray but what appeared to litter its surface that drew her. She brushed aside one of the sheer drapes. Syringes, all but one empty.

"Don't touch the bed." He hadn't spoken the command loudly. But the words— his tone held an edge, an urgency that made her jump.

She came down on a rhinestone-studded slipper and sent it skidding. He gave the shoe a pointed glance.

"In fact," he continued from where he stood in profile in front of the wall safe, "don't touch anything."

"Sorry," she said, folding her arms over her her bare stomach. All that skin between her low-riding skirt and skimpy red bra reminded her how little she had left to her. She looked at the man who was about to give her a thousand credits. Her hero.

The little case he'd taken from his coat now sat open in his raised palm. He removed from it a rubbery membrane, fit the membrane over the tip of his smallest finger and pressed it against the safe's fingerprint-pad security device. The safe door swung open.

Her superhero might not lie, but he wasn't above a little larceny. She snorted. Neither was she. But then she had few qualms about lying, either.

After returning the membrane to its case, he removed a stack of credits cards from the safe. She moved to his side and caught sight of some hefty numbers as he shuffled through the stack. There was also a pile of hard cash still inside the safe. Her fingers itched. Just half that cash would be enough to buy her a ride off this rock.

He handed her a card loaded with a thousand-credits. She turned it over in her hands, examining it. "I won't get in trouble when I try to spend the credits, will I?"

"No. It's a generic card."

She slipped the card into her bra. His gaze dropped to her cleavage. Now that was the reaction she was used to getting. "We could still finish what we started in your bed."

His gaze came back up to her face. "You're determined to sell your sex, aren't you?"

She shifted closer to him, close enough that the electrical charge off his body tugged at the tiny hairs on her arms and drew her huskiest voice. "On the contrary. You paid me to *spend the night*, as you pointed out." She patted the breast against which the card lie and shifted even closer to him. "Any sex we have would be for fun." She drew her fingertips down the center of his chest, stopping where his pants tented over his beautiful cock. "What d'ya think?"

He plucked her fingers from the front of his pants. "I think you'd rather take a shower."

She yanked her hand from his and scowled. "You telling me I stink? You'd stink too if you'd just had to run for your life."

"You want a shower or not?"

She folded her arms over her chest, prepared to resist anything he suggested. But the truth of it was her sweaty clothes scratched at her skin, and the grit of street grime seemed to have ground into her skin.

He caught her by the elbow and ushered her through a sitting area and around a changing screen that hid an opening in the near wall, muttering, "Relax. You'll like this shower."

"I thought you didn't want me to touch anything in the room," she retorted.

He steered her past a chrome rack piled with thick, white towels and a row of ornate hooks from which hung several white terrycloth robes and one of a slinky pink fabric. "You can touch whatever you want in here."

She eyed him narrowly. "Just not the bed, huh?"

He guided her around a bend in the short tiled wall, grumbling, "You don't need that bed."

Her attention turned from him to the shower stall in front of them. The alcove was big enough to accommodate three, four, maybe even more people at one time. And, like the bedroom with the off-limits bed and the great room on the lower level with the naked statues, white predominated. But here it was broken by flesh-colored mosaics of men and women in various poses of copulation.

She regarded the shower. "This doesn't look like any of the exfoliant stations that blast a person with grit, air and a mist of some questionable liquid."

"It's not. It's a real water shower."

"Real water," she crooned. "I haven't had a full body shower with water since before I came to this hellhole."

"Told you you'd like it."

She stroked one of the half-dozen penis-shaped showerheads pointed in various directions. She bent, eyeing a labia-shaped relief encircling a water jet. The only thing that would have made the experience better was if her superhero had joined her. But he'd taken her clothes and left her naked and alone.

She sighed and straightened. "What the hell."

She passed her hand in front of an on-off detector. Instantly, she was doused by a tropical-forest warm downpour. She played with the motion detectors until she got herself a comfortable combination of spritzers, sprayers, and one wickedly placed water jet.

She backed toward that jet, bent at the waist and spread her legs. Her labia swelled beneath the friction of the water and she exhaled an approving, "Oh, yeah."

She rocked her clit against the pulsing stream and gasped. "Oh, yes."

A real water shower alone was enough to make a girl come. Mix in the fact she seemed always primed to come and that the taste of a hunky stud's thick, hard cock yet lingered on her tongue—a cock she could only fantasize about sliding in and out of her and—

"Yes! Yes! Yes," she cried out, grabbing a low-placed penis showerhead to keep from collapsing to her knees, taking the jetting water against the mouth of her vagina as she rode out the orgasm.

When it was over, she slid to the floor and she slumped against the wall, panting. It had been a good orgasm. But it wasn't enough. She wanted to be filled by a big, hard cock, and she knew right where to get one.

She appeared at the edge of the changing screen separating bathroom and bedroom, the slinky pink robe clinging to her damp curves. He folded down his soft-panel and secured it to his wrist. He wasn't about to expose Marco or any other space pirate to a girl on the run, even one running from slavers.

He started to rise from the chair he'd taken facing the shower room to insure she couldn't sneak up on him. Grinning, she hurried to him and pushed him back in the chair, her palms like firebrands on his chest. She braced her knee to the chair seat between his legs and leaned into him.

"We could still finish what we started earlier in your bed."

He looked into her freshly scrubbed face. Her skin glowed without the heavy makeup, her lips a plump, burnished pink in their naked state, and her eyes—

Her eyes were striking without the dark lining of a coal pencil and the glittery wings of eye shadow. Striking and young.

"You're determined to sell your sex, aren't you?" he said, hoping his bluntness might yet jolt some sense into the girl.

"I believe we already established that the credits were for me to spend the night, not for sex."

He looked deep into her eyes. He'd been wrong about them being young. There was an oldness to them, like she had experienced a lot in her young life. What gave them the illusion of youth was the hope in them. What was it like to live with hope?

"Besides," she continued, "what difference does it make whether I get paid for sex or just plain enjoy having it?"

"People for whom sex is a job don't necessarily enjoy it. They just act like they do."

She leaned closer, her damp hair tumbling over her shoulders. Goddess, she smelled good.

"I assure you," she all but purred, "I enjoy licking, sucking and fucking. I enjoy it all very much."

"Good for you," he said, closing his hands on her upper arms, intending to set her back from himself before the wet circles of her knotted nipples became too much for him to resist.

"Aah, come on," she pleaded, nudging his balls with her knee. "Don't you want to help out a horny girl?"

The scent of her freshly washed sex wafted up from the hem of the short robe... and the lingering musk of a recent orgasm. He wasn't surprised she'd indulged herself in the shower. He'd enjoyed the amenities of that chamber more times than he could recall in the past three years. Goddess's blood, he'd been sorely tempted to join her in the shower, knowing she was naked and wet and exploring the stall's erotic offerings.

"It'll be fun," she urged, shifting closer.

When had he last had sex for the fun of it? Had he ever?

She traced a fingertip down his chest, past his abdomen and over his hardening sex.

"I feel your interest," she purred, leaning in and tonguing his ear.

As if of its own volition, his hand slid up her arm and over her shoulder to the nape of her neck. His fingers closed on the hair at the back of her neck, capturing her, tipping her face to his. His lips closed over hers, and she welcomed his tongue into her mouth.

She was as sweet to the taste as she was hot to the touch. And eager. She sucked his tongue deep. The hint of a memory niggled at the edge of his consciousness. Or was it a multitude of memories of countless women suckling him in the same way. He started to draw back. She rolled her tongue around his, entangling him in the kiss, drawing him back to the present, to the sweet nectar of a hot mouth, the siren call of a fresh body and the slick heat of a woman's sex pressed to his thigh.

His cock throbbed. He was free to fuck her or not.

Free. For the first time in his life he actually realized what freedom meant. In the past twenty-four hours, he'd been so focused on how to escape he hadn't really thought about what the change in his status really meant for him. Or was he free at all? He hadn't yet escaped this world where one of his species would never be allowed to live free. And given what his species had been bred for....

He drew a deep breath, forcing air into lungs that felt as though a fist had suddenly gripped them. Was he turned on merely because of how he was hardwired, or did he really want this diminutive seductress? He needed time to figure out what he wanted.

He rose from the chair, breaking her hold on him and sending her stumbling back from him. "I've got just the place where you can scratch that itch of yours."

Chapter 5

He led her to the middle door on the balcony, the one at the top of the stairway. This room also had a keypad entry system. It seemed only his door lacked a lock. Before she could ponder what that meant, he punched in the code, the door slid open and the room lights popped on.

The place looked like a workout gym except instead of weight benches, recumbent stationary bikes and treadmills, the mirrored room housed all sorts of sex apparatus. Her clit twitched.

"You must have every sex toy ever made."

"Just the good ones."

She gave him a sidelong look, a smile stretching across her lips. "All personally tried out by you no doubt?"

"Not all of them," he said, nodding her ahead into the room.

Hot damn, she didn't know where to start. Then she spotted a sex chair off to one side. She scrambled onto it and tried several of its positions, letting the silk robe fall open. His gaze traveled over her breasts and down her stomach to her pussy. She spread her legs wide, revealing the pink lips framed by her lush bush. The bulge in his pants pushed at the fabric confining it, and his breathing grew shallow and quick. But his expression remained steely. She clearly had more enticing to do.

She hopped out of the chair, enjoying the flash of surprise in his eyes. She all but skipped over to where a fucking sling hung from the ceiling in the back corner. "We might just have to start with this."

His eyes narrowed at her.

"But not until I check out a few other apparatus," she said, putting a little extra swing into her hips as the strolled to a shallow, plastic-lined pit in the middle of the floor. She peered over her shoulder at him and raised a questioning eyebrow.

"Wrestling," he said, "in oil, mud or whatever your horny heart desires."

"Aaah," she sighed with approval, her gaze rising to the clear orb above the wrestling pit. It had to be at least ten feet in diameter. "And what's that?"

"An anti-gravity ball."

"Be still my heart," she murmured. "A fucking anti-gravity environment."

"The operative word here being *fucking*."

She dropped her gaze over him, stopping on the massive hard-on now pushing the limits of his trousers. Pussy juice gathered on her nether lips. "Shall we start with the anti-gravity ball?"

"We?" he questioned.

Her eyes snapped up at his. There was a hint of smugness in their darkness.

It confused her.

"You're the one with the itch that needs scratching," he said.

She glanced down at the outline of his hard-on. "And your itch doesn't need scratching?"

"No."

"What the hell are you, a cyborg?"

He snorted. "No. I am humanoid. Cut me and I will bleed."

"Then how can you deny yourself? You're throbbing for release, and I'm willing to give it to you."

"And if I accept your invitation, what guarantee have you that I won't just use you to service myself?"

She glanced around and said pointedly, "Look, if you didn't intend to fuck me, why'd you bring me into a room full sex toys?"

⁂

He took her by the shoulders and turned her toward the toy in the far corner.

"A fucking machine," she said through an awed gasp. "An honest-to-goodness automated fucking machine."

Zombie-like, she strode toward the apparatus, her shoulders sliding out from under his hands. His cock ached. Hell, he'd wanted to bend her over the fucking chair, push that robe up her back, and ram into her cunt. He could have taken his release in two or three strokes and the woman be damned. He had the freedom to do that now.

Then again, it was doubtful he could get off that fast. He'd been well-conditioned. Besides, he wasn't so sure he wanted a one-sided fuck.

"How does it work?" she asked as she circled the bench-mounted contraption.

He moved to the action mechanism. "You pick out the dildo of your preference, attach it to this arm and make yourself comfortable on the bench."

Her gaze lifted to the dildos displayed on the glass shelf along the back wall. She paused at the one cast from his own dick. Her tongue slipped out between her lips. His shaft twitched with the memory of how that tongue had curled around it.

"How about this one?" Her fingertips stroked the length of the silicone-molded shaft and she gave him a lingering look from beneath heavy lids.

So she recognized him. Observant girl.

"I'd recommend something smaller for the first time on the ram."

She snatched a modest-sized dildo from the shelf and handed it to him. She stripped off the robe, her eyes riveted on him—challenging him. Without breaking eye contact, she climbed onto the padded platform and settled on her back.

"Now what do I do?" she asked.

"Do you need lubricant?"

She spread her legs and parted her plump, pink lips. "What do you think?"

She was glistening.

He fit the dildo to the machine's arm. "It'll spin as well as move back and forth in you. You want to take it in—get a feel for it before I turn it on."

"Sure." She skidded down on the platform and impaled herself on the dildo. "It's a little cool," she said.

"It won't be for long," he said.

She rotated her hips around the fake dick. His very real dick twitched.

"Ready for me to turn it on?"

Her eyes met his. "Yeah. Turn this baby on."

He passed his hand over the sensor and the arm of the machine began to move.

"Oooh," she said, sounding a little surprised.

"Too deep?" he asked.

She shook her head and lifted her hips to meet the next thrust. It wasn't long before her eyes drifted shut. She didn't seem to mind him standing there watching her.

And he did watch. He watched how she slid her tongue over her lips as the machine stroked the dildo in and out of her—how she arched her neck back with her rising arousal and parted her lips over throaty sighs. He watched her color heighten. He'd watched a thousand women climb towards orgasm. Yet he could remember none that had done it with such eager abandon—such freedom.

There was that word again. Freedom. *Free.* What did it feel like?

He shook his head. This wasn't the time to contemplate something he hadn't truly attained yet, something he might never know.

The scent of sex jerked him back to the present. He focused on the woman being fucked before him. Jaci. He'd never smelled a woman with such potent pheromones. Would she taste as appealing? He could easily dip a finger between her legs and catch a little of the juice oozing out around the pistoning dildo.

Her mews of delight rippled along his nerve endings. Her gasps punched him in the gut. He found himself breathing faster, matching the increasing pace of her breaths.

Her back arched from the platform. Her fingers clawed at the thick padding beneath her. She was breathing through her mouth now, her blonde hair spilling across the platform, her skin glowing with a sheen of sweat. It would be so easy to lean in and touch his tongue to one of the beads of sweat forming between her breasts, her beautiful, high, round breasts—to lave his tongue across each of her knotted nipples.

A flush of color blossomed between her breasts and climbed toward her throat. She was close to coming.

And he wanted… *wanted…* to be part of her orgasm.

He ran a hand lightly over her abdomen. She rose to his touch and mewed. He wanted to pull her off the fucking machine and plant himself between her legs, but she was on the brink of release and the interruption might ruin it for her.

But what about what he wanted?

He wanted to see her come. That's what he wanted.

He ran his hands up her body, spreading his fingers over the outer points of her hips, closing them on the dip of her waist, and then palming her breasts. She arched into his touch, her nipples hard and urgent against his palms.

He closed his thumb and forefinger around one plump nipple and squeezed. She cried out, the stain of color climbing her throat.

He slipped his index finger through the nest of curls at the apex of her legs and found a throbbing clit. He tapped it, and watched the color flush up her cheeks. One more tap and she threw her head back and bucked hard against his hand and the dildo. Her mouth fell open with a silent cry. He slowed the speed of the mechanized fucking arm. Little mews escaped her and her body shuddered and shuddered and shuddered. Her orgasm shuddered up his arm from the hand he cupped over her pubic mound. He felt the power of it through his chest and down his legs. He felt it everywhere but where he most needed to feel it… around his cock.

When the shudders began to subside, he shut off the machine and gathered her into his arms. She still shook all over, and he hugged her close and kissed her temple.

When she quieted, she smiled weakly up at him. "Wow."

"The ram fucks a woman better than any man," he said.

"Next time I'd like to try out that thick, nine-incher."

He'd expected her to say she wanted to try out the real thing next. He'd expected an invitation to drink of her sweet juices and sink into her hot, wet pussy. He wasn't prepared for the disappointment twisting through his hot body.

"That'll do it for you then?"

"No," she said, a twinkle in her eye. "I'd prefer the real deal. But you're not cooperating."

Every ounce of testosterone-laden blood flew toward one point in his body and he growled, "The hell I'm not."

Chapter 6

He'd shed his clothes so fast she'd had no time to check out his naked body. But now, as he free-fell toward her in the anti-gravity ball, steering himself with extended arms and legs, she could see he was every bit as magnificent as the statue of him holding up the tabletop downstairs depicted. Better even. Beautifully muscled without being bulky, his skin taut and tan. His big, thick cock like a rocket coming at her.

She groaned and spread herself even though she doubted he'd last long enough to give her another orgasm. The man was too hot, too ready. But even a few strokes from that beauty, right after the incredible double orgasm she'd had on the fucking machine, would feel heavenly.

His missile hit its target dead center, in a single stroke filling her channel. She gasped and her vaginal walls clamped onto him. Joined, they slammed into the soft wall of the orb and bounced back out into space.

She wanted to come around that rocket of a cock. She wanted it moving back and forth in her until she came and came and came. But she felt him throb against her clinging walls and was certain he'd never last long enough.

Free-falling in the anti-gravity ball will be enough. It'll be fun.

Resigned, she closed her eyes and waited for the imminent explosion of semen against her cervix. He shifted, his cock sliding back from her.

Heaven. If only she didn't have to return to the hell of reality. But she couldn't expect a man driven to the brink as he'd been to last more than a stroke or two more.

One stroke, two.

He felt like liquid fire gliding in and out of her.

Three, four.

She rocked against his delicious cock, itching for more.

Five, six.

Her vaginal walls twitched.

Please don't stop.

"I won't."

She blinked. She hadn't said that out loud.

Give in to the sensations.

The words ricocheted around inside her head, more solid than a thought. Before she could examine their source further, he tucked their bodies into a ball and they rolled.

He was beneath her, pumping up into her. They were upside down, pumping against each other. He was her superhero. He was a sex slave doing her bidding.

No. Not hers. He was servicing a dark-haired woman.

He growled and rolled them wildly.

He was looking for a man named Marco.

Get out of my head.

I'm not in your head.

Had she just answered him without speaking?

He pushed them hard off the wall of the ball, propelling them across the sphere. His anger crackled through her, aimed at the dark-haired woman even as he fucked the living daylights out of her.

What the hell was going on? Who was the dark-haired woman? What was this talking between heads business? But his every stroke urged her closer to climax, making her care only about the glide of his long, thick cock in and out of her, across her G-spot. Close. She was so close to coming.

Don't stop now, she cried out inside her head, her body floating, tumbling, climbing towards climax. Maybe it was the fact that nothing touched her body except his. Maybe it was the weightlessness. She'd never fucked in a weightless environment before.

Or maybe it was his skill that sent the shock wave of her orgasm through her body—that made her clench and gush around him. He kept moving, finished her before he let himself come. Hot, pelting cum made her scream with completion.

They collapsed in each other's arms, their bodies still linked—still floating. Bliss until...

The dark-haired woman. Jaci saw her again inside her head, like a memory. But this time she wasn't in the throes of passion. She was in a flash-freezer. Dead.

⁂

Laz pulled back from Jaci at the same moment she let go of him, both simultaneously spewing accusation.

"What the hell did you do to me?" she demanded.

"What the hell are you?" he demanded.

"I saw a dead woman in the freezer," she howled.

"I know what you saw. I felt you inside my head. Tell me you're not Astartian."

"Fine," she said backpedaling from him. "I'm not Astartian. Tell me you didn't put that woman's body in the freezer."

He hung in the weightless air half the globe away from her, surveying every alabaster inch of her. "Right. You couldn't possibly be Astartian. Astartians are a dark race. Tall. Statuesque."

She huffed and planted her hands on her hips. "Excuse me for not measuring up to your standards."

"I'm not talking standards. I'm stating facts," he went on, dismissing her combative stance, focused on reasoning away the doubts prickling up the nape of his neck.

"Like the fact the woman in the flash freezer is dark and statuesque? Like maybe you don't like Astartians."

"I'm Astartian," he growled.

"You wouldn't be the first species to hate its own kind," she countered, her chin sweeping a challenging arc in the air between them.

He looked her in the eye. Any retort he might have offered was lost by what he saw behind her defiant glare. He saw the sharp watchfulness born of street-smarts… or from being born into a slave race that relied on a keen sense of observation to anticipate a master's pleasure.

He shook his head. It couldn't be. She couldn't be. "You were walking the streets freely."

"Excuse me," she muttered through tight lips, "but when we ran into each other, I was neither walking nor was I free."

"If you are an Astartian of unique color and unusual size…"

"Is that another reference to me not being statuesque?"

"Goddess's blood, woman, don't you know what it means to be Astartian?"

She shrugged and a bit of the combativeness fled her posture. "Astartians are reputed to be exceptional lovers."

"And?"

Her eyes narrowed. "And what?"

He pulled his arms and legs in enough to let him drift through the weightless air toward her. "How was it your boyfriend was able to sell you into sex-slavery?"

"Wasn't hard," she countered, her fingers flexing against the points of her hips but holding her position. "He got his hands on my papers and handed them and me over to a dealer."

"Who'd have had little trouble smuggling you off the colony and into any of a number of sex slave rings," he pondered aloud, still troubled by that nagging suspicion in his gut. He hung just beyond reach of her, His gaze locked on hers. "Who was this dealer?"

Her chin cut a battle-ready angle. "He was introduced to me as Otto Galt."

"Galt." The name escaped his lips on a low growl.

"You know the man?" she asked, her chin now tilting a wary angle.

Oh, yeah, he knew Galt. Galt was among the sleaziest of sex-slavers and he specialized in Astartians.

"Goddess rot that slimy slave-dealing thug," he growled through clenched teeth.

"Yeah," she said. "That's him."

Lazarus studied the blonde hanging in the air before him. She couldn't be one of his. Her skin was pale. She was small. But she had the brown eyes of an Astartian. She fucked like an Astartian. She'd fallen into mind talk as easily as any Astartian.

She'd been purchased by a slaver specializing in Astartian sex-slaves. Without DNA testing, he knew of only one definitive way to find out if she was Astartian.

"Show me the nape of your neck."

She dropped her hands from her hips and backpedaled. "Like hell. I'm not turning my back on you until I know what happened to the woman in the freezer." *And likely not even then.*

He heard her thought easily. Astartian telecommunication or just some other humanoid species evolved enough to mind speak?

Her fingers gripped the soft walls of the anti-gravity ball behind her. Fear tangled with the combativeness in her eyes and scented the musk of their sex. He needed answers.

"What did you see inside my head besides the woman in the freezer?" he asked.

"That's all I saw," she said, struggling to hang onto the soft wall near the escape hatch.

She was lying. He'd known it before she'd uttered a single syllable.

"Goddess's blood," he growled, tucked his limbs in close to his body and rolled toward her.

A squeal escaped her and she flailed at the gravity-free environment, trying to reach the hatch. Maybe he didn't need to touch her to probe her thoughts and memories. He stopped, hung in the air above where she frantically tugged at the hatch, and concentrated.

"What are you doing?" she cried out, her hands flying to her head, pressing at her skull, digging into her hair. "Get out of my head!"

He wished he wouldn't be able to get into her mind. He hoped she would turn out to be just some other humanoid with highly developed telecommunication skills. He wished he didn't need to probe every memory fold of the girl's brain for any Astartian knowledge to be sure.

In her head, he found none other than what a non-Astartian would know. It should have relieved him. Yet that niggling sensation that she was something even she didn't know she was wouldn't subside. That left him no alternative but to search the back of her neck.

He dove to where she huddled, sobbing, against the orb wall. He caught a fistful of her hair, that silky golden hair that had lured him in, and lifted it away from her neck.

There it was, the sunburst with its raised corona. The mark genetically implanted onto every Astartian. He let loose with a string of curses.

"Leave me alone," she sobbed.

"By the blood of the Goddess, I wish I could."

✽⟡⟨ʚ◌ɞ⟩⟡✽

She woke in the bed in the blue room in Laz's arms. Damn, he felt good spooned against her back, one arm cradling her head, the other draped protectively over her hip. He made her feel warm and safe. He shouldn't. Not after she'd found the memory of a dead woman inside his head. So much for him being anyone's super-hero, let alone hers.

She suppressed a shudder before it could ripple to the surface and alert him she'd awakened. She needed to get away from this guy.

The arms all but encircling her remained slack. Okay. Still asleep. Next question. How sound a sleeper was he?

She lifted her head from his arm. The steady, shallow breath of deep slumber whispered across her shoulder. So far so good. Then again, if they'd been asleep a long time, he might be closer to waking than she thought. It felt like eons since she'd tumbled weightlessly with him into that mind-blowing orgasm. Heat blossomed low in her groin.

No. Do not go there. She needed to get herself out of his bed—out of this apartment. Hell, she needed to get off this rock.

Cautiously, she inched away from his side. The smooth sheets blanketing them slipped across her skin, soft as a lover's caress. But there was nothing soft nor gentle about this man entrapping her beneath his hot, heavy arm—an arm that had held her firmly to him as they'd fucked their way around the anti-gravity ball. Hard and hot, he'd pushed into her, then pulled away before pushing back into her.

A dampness gathered between her legs. Now was not a good time to get her juices flowing. She closed her eyes and willed the memory away. She was only inches from escaping his hold, inches from slipping out from under that possessive arm when it tightened around her waist and hauled her back to her captor's side and deposited her on her back. He braced himself up on one arm, watchful eyes gazing down on her.

She swallowed hard. "Am I going to wind up like the woman in the freezer?"

His fingers flexed against the tender skin at her waist, hard as brands and twice as hot. "Only if you let yourself become a slave to drugs and overdose."

She narrowed her eyes at him, wondering what memories he might have stumbled across while rummaging through her brain.

"Like your mother," he added as though reading her mind. Oh, wait, he had read her mind.

She snorted. "Didn't your mother teach you it's not nice to snoop around a person's brain?"

"I don't remember my mother. I was taken from her when I was very young."

She didn't know what to say to him about being raised motherless. She'd had a mother and it hadn't done her any good. Okay, maybe some. Her mother had taught her how to take care of herself, if not by outright lesson then by the process of her drug-induced neglect.

Except for that mark on the back of her neck. The importance of hiding that had been the one thing her mother had actively, vehemently, sometimes corporally impressed upon her. Otherwise, she taught by neglect.

What had the absence of a mother taught Lazarus Stone? She studied his face, the tense lines etched around his full mouth and into the corners of his dark eyes. It was a sharp contrast to the light touch of his fingers on her waist, and she ventured to ask, "You saying the dead woman overdosed when she happened to be in the freezer?"

"You need to go back inside my head and see my full memory."

She grimaced. "You mean do to you what you did to me?"

His thumb traced tiny circles against her hip. "Untrained as you likely are," he murmured, "you won't be able to probe that deep."

Aah, the not-so-sweet reality.

"Nor will you have to," he continued. "I will open my mind to you. I ask only that you keep your probing to the pertinent details."

She snorted. "Respect your privacy like you did mine?"

"These are dangerous times. I cannot afford to be careless about who I allow into my confidence."

"That's something I discovered tonight."

"Another lesson well learned," he said almost gently.

"Number four," she murmured, thinking about how simple the troubles of her life had been before tonight. Would she have been better off living oblivious to what the mark on the back of her neck meant, a mark her mother had not shared?

That meant her father had been the Astartian. It was his blood that made her the same breed as this man.

Would she have been better off not knowing she was Astartian?

Yeah. Probably. But it hadn't happened that way, and odds were she wouldn't have escaped that knowledge forever. In a way, it was her good fortune that the end of her freedom came on a night when an Astartian male happened into her path.

A hero who might well have killed his mistress… yet had rescued Jaci. Murderer or hero? Which was he?

She met his gaze, and he answered her unspoken question. "You want to know the facts of Simone's death?"

"The woman in the freezer?"

"Uh-huh."

She hesitated, wondering if he could manipulate his thoughts, wondering if she could trust what she found inside his memories. But then she remembered how he'd used semantics to avoid lying, and how, when they'd been mind-linked, she'd seen things he hadn't wanted her to see. She remembered how those true memories had felt to her. Armed with a gauge she could measure the truth against, she consented.

"How do I do this?"

"The more fully you touch me, the easier it will be." He hitched himself up against the headboard until he was sitting and hauled her across his lap so she knelt straddling him.

Her labia spread over his cock, slick with her juices. Her clit twitched. She wanted to lean forward and press that sassy nub against his awakening cock. She wanted to impale herself on its hard shaft and ride him until they were both mindless with orgasms. The hell with mind probes and dead women.

She rocked against his cock. He caught her by the hips, stilled her.

"We start fucking, and someone is bound to find us here joined like a couple dogs in heat."

Her vaginal walls yawed, begging to be filled by the throbbing cock wrapped up in her tingling labia. She wanted to ask him if that prospect would be so bad? But the reality of the danger she was in nagged her and she retorted, "At least they'd find me alive."

A muscle at the hinge of his jaw popped. "Just probe my mind, and you'll get your answers."

She let him place her fingers on his skull behind his ears. "Now close your eyes, open your mind, and follow my voice."

She hesitated ever so briefly before complying. She was still alive. That had to count for something. But the instant she heard his voice inside her head, her eyes sprang open.

Close your eyes. I'm inviting you in. That's all.

She closed her eyes to his command. The next thing she knew she was tumbling through a tunnel, the walls blurred with images. Disjointed images. Some were erotic and familiar. Some made no sense to her. Some made her skin crawl. He called her back from those.

When she found the memories of the dark-haired woman, the tumbling slowed. As though she watched the scenes through his eyes, as though his thoughts were hers, she followed the sequence of events he'd lived the past twenty-four plus hours. The woman had died as he'd said she had. But it was the reason he'd flash-frozen her body that brought it all together for her.

Her eyes popped open and she looked him in the eye. "You are a sex slave. You were *her* sex slave."

"Yes."

"You serviced her, kept her disease-free."

He nodded.

"Your ejaculate released into an orgasming partner cures the sex diseases. That's your value. Your curse."

"And yours," he replied.

Chapter 7

"That's what my boyfriend sold me into?" she howled. "That's what would have happened to me?"

"If you were lucky."

"I am going to flay every inch of skin from that creep when I get my hands on him."

He found her reaction amusing and couldn't help but tease, "Such big plans for a little girl."

She thumped him in the shoulders with the heels of her hands. "And you, Mr. Thinks-He's-Got-All-the-Answers. I suppose you think you're some sort of hero for rescuing me."

"Hero?" He snorted, long unused muscles pulling at his lips.

She swatted at him. "Do *not* laugh at me."

Had he laughed? He couldn't even remember when he'd last felt like laughing.

Anger tightened her mouth and pulled her eyebrows together above her nose. "I'm not feeling funny right now."

His thumbs slid over the points of her hips. "I agree. You don't feel the least bit funny."

"And now you're making jokes?" she demanded.

He was. How about that?

He let his hands slide higher, his thumbs bumping over her ribs until they nudged the undersides of her breasts. "In fact, I'd say you feel decidedly hot, female and—" He shifted beneath her, his hard cock slipping between her labia and finished with— "And wet."

She rained blows down on his shoulders. "Damn you, damn you, damn you and all your sex."

He caught her by the wrists, stilling her hands even though he was enjoying her fight. But there was something else he wanted to hear more about and he drew her against his chest. "What happened to my being your hero?"

"I never said you were my hero," she said through clenched teeth. "I said you probably thought yourself a hero."

"But you want me to be your hero."

She shook her head hard. "Na-ah. I'm through trying to find a hero. They don't exist."

Goddess, but she had spirit, this girl who'd just been sold into sex slavery, escaped and chased by a pair of goons, abducted by a man she likened to a hero and discovered she'd been born into a species of sex slaves. He wanted to be her hero.

He brushed his lips across hers, whispering, "Give it one more shot."
For the first time, tears gathered across her eyes. "Go to hell."

Though she stubbornly held back those tears, he felt them sure as they burned in his own eyes. He couldn't let her lose that wonderful spirit born of freedom and he murmured, "I'd rather go to heaven and take you with me."

He released her wrists, clamped his hands over her hips and lifted her just enough to allow his cock to spring upward. Then he lowered her, her creamy sheath gliding down over him. Of the thousands of women he'd fucked, none had had a channel more liquid, more instantly ready.

She sucked a quick breath. "I thought you said we couldn't fuck."

"I said, if we did, someone would find us here like two dogs in heat."

The tears evaporated from her eyes. "And that's no longer an issue?"

"On the contrary. It's highly dangerous," he said, noting how her pupils flared. Danger excited her. It fed her spirit. He slammed his hips up against her bottom.

She threw her head back, her lips popping apart around a gasp. An animal growl rumbled up his throat.

She raised herself over him and met his next thrust with equal need. He sucked a breath. Her inner muscles pulled at him. He groaned. She rolled her hips, free to move at will above him while he pumped up into her.

Aah. To know such freedom. To be unfettered by any demand but that of the body seeking pleasure. Even Simone and her friends didn't fuck for pure enjoyment. There was always an ulterior motive lurking among the act, even if only to claim a more thorough fucking than anyone else.

But he felt none of that in this girl. No competition. No seeking of notice, prestige, or power... or cure. Just pure abandonment to the act of fucking, to its pleasure. That's the kind of freedom he wanted.

Her inner muscles rolled up and down his shaft, pulling at him. It was enough to make the average man come. But he wasn't the average man.

Not even as she found his rhythm and rode him with the ease of a practiced paramour, her hips rolling to meet his every thrust, did he lose control. From beneath heavy lids, sex-drugged eyes watched him. Her nostrils flared as her body called for more oxygen and her breasts rose and fell with her increasing breaths, those beautiful, high, full breasts. He cupped them with his hands and rolled his palms over the tight knots of her nipples. She threw her head back with another gasp and a rosy hue flushed upwards from the valley between her breasts.

Her pulse throbbed against the thin skin of her throat, beating a rhythm that underscored their undulating bodies, beckoning him. He leaned forward and fit his lips over that hot, pulsating point of life's blood.

She moaned deep in her throat, the sound vibrating across his lips, into his mouth and down his throat. He wanted the moment to last forever. He wanted her gasping and panting and throbbing for eternity around him.

He slowed his pace, rocking into her now instead of pumping. A whimper of protest escaped her. He touched his tongue to the throbbing pulse in her throat and her body quivered around him.

She tasted of salty sweat, fragrant soap and aroused woman. He wanted more.

He nibbled her shoulder. He kissed a path along her collarbone. He nipped her earlobe. He brushed his lips along her jawbone, across her cheek... pressed his lips to her temple... to her eyes.

He closed his mouth over hers and drew her sweet breath into him. Their tongues touched. She moaned.

She was his. She belonged to him.

No. That was wrong. No human being should own another.

Her muscles rolled up and down his shaft. A primal growl vibrated in his throat, obliterating all rationality.

He reached down between them, flattened his hand low across her abdomen and pressed as he stroked hard in and out of her. Her groans mounted, filling his mouth with their vibration. She slung her arms around his neck and clutched him close. And she came.

Too late he realized his mistake. Her muscles tightened around his shaft, gripped him, captured him. Captured. If he wasn't careful—if he allowed himself to feel too much for this woman, he would never be free. He needed to get back out in the world. He needed to find Marco. He needed to escape.

Her vaginal walls pulsed around him as Laz pulled out of her. She fell back against the mattress beside him. He swung his legs over the side of the bed.

"Not much for cuddling in the afterglow, are you?" she huffed.

"I've got business to tend to," he muttered, rising and heading for the clothing bay.

She raised herself on her elbows. "What just happened?"

"We fucked. Now I've got places to go."

"What time is it?"

"Time," he called as he punched open the clothing bay panel.

A recorded male voice with a decidedly sexy timbre replied, "Twenty-three hundred hours."

"You're going back out on the streets to find Marco, aren't you?"

So she knew about Marco. She must have picked that up when he let her into his mind. Laz winced and retrieved a fresh shirt and pants. That's what he got for letting her inside his head.

"Have I time for a shower?" she asked, the bedclothes rustling behind him with her movement.

He tossed the shirt over his shoulder and stepped into the pants. "You have all the time you want."

The sounds of movement behind him stopped. "Let me get this straight. You're in a hurry, and I have all the time I want. You're not taking me with you, are you?"

"I need to find Marco before the next solar flare, and you draw too much attention." He pulled his pants up his legs.

So my superhero prefers commando style.

The words sounded so clearly in his head, she could have spoken them aloud. He turned and found her on her hands and knees, her naked breasts swaying between her arms, her gaze fixed just below his beltline.

That easily, he slipped inside her mind—inside her. Her hormones did a clog dance that hammered their beat clear to the tip of her clitoris. A drop of their mingled love juices rolled from her vagina down her quivering clit.

His cock began to swell. He scowled, turned away and gathered the shirt over his head.

"The deal was a thousand credits if I stayed the night here. I've more than fulfilled my obligation. If you won't take me with you, I'll search out my own way off this rock." She skidded off the bed. "Where are my clothes?"

He tugged the shirt into place, sat on the end of the bed and picked up a boot. "I threw that get-up in the demoleculizer."

She stopped in front of him, her naked legs drawing his gaze up her sinfully sculpted form. "You had no right to eradicate my clothes!"

In spite of the hunger still clawing at him for more of her body, cynicism tugged at his mouth. "You're a slave on the run. You have no rights. Get used to it."

A shadow crossed her eyes, so fleeting most would have missed it. But, he felt the reality of her circumstance prickle through her veins as surely as if they were his own. The girl was a fast learner, maybe even faster than he'd thought. From the outside, she looked all tough and sure of herself with her hands on her hips and her chin cocked.

"Guess I'm going to have to borrow something from your girlfriend," she said, wheeling for the exit panel. "It's not like she's in any position to miss anything."

"Simone's not my girlfriend."

"Excuse me," she simpered, facing him again. "Your mistress, er, master."

"Help yourself," he muttered, rose, reached around her and punched the opener pad. Her heat pulled at him. He forced himself to move past her, to keep going.

He was halfway down the steps when he heard her shout from the balcony. He glanced up at her. She'd wrapped the sheet off the bed around herself. He shook his head and continued down the stairs into the foyer.

Just as he raised his hand to the security panel, he heard a distressed squeal, a thump and an oomph. He turned and found Jaci sprawled belly down at the bottom of the stairway, the sheet formerly covering her now trailing up her leg and the last few steps from one of the phallic-like banister scrolls.

He strode back to her and squatted in front of her. "You okay?"

She scowled and started to push herself up. "How nice you care enough to ask."

His gaze came back to hers. Astartians tended to be a somber breed, people of few words. Sarcasm was too much emotion for them. Yet sarcasm fired from this half-Astartian woman's mouth quick as a sky sled's thruster. It made him want to smile. Surely a little humor didn't threaten his freedom... unless it interfered with his search for Marco.

He snagged her by the arm and stood, hauling her to her feet. What indeed was he going to do with her, he asked himself even though he knew the answer.

"Let me go," she demanded, tugging at his hold.

"Goddess's blood, you are a stubborn wench."

He released her with a suddenness that left her swaying in his wake as he strode past her to the scroll snagging the sheet. He yanked it free and returned to her. "Raise your arms."

"The hell I will."

"Raise your arms, or I'll wrap them against your sides and you can stay wrapped up like a mummy until I get back."

"You would bind me up in a funeral shroud?"

"No civilization binds or buries its dead anymore."

"Thank the High Lord Chancellor for decreeing all things dead and worthless be demoleculized," she said grimly.

He saw in a memory flash, as clear as if he were remembering it himself, how her mother's body had been wrapped in a shroud and buried in the ground to rot. That she'd experienced the barbaric ways of old squeezed at his heart and unnerved him. He actually felt her anguish. Was this typical between Astartians, this linking of mind and body? He didn't like it. It was an invasion of privacy, especially for a man whose mind had been his only refuge, the only part of him no one had ever enslaved.

"Raise your arms," he repeated with an ominous note.

"You think I'm not resourceful enough to get myself out of your shroud? Out of this apartment?"

"You haven't proved yourself very resourceful at anything so far."

She snorted. "I was resourceful enough to pick you to help me when those goons were chasing me. And we both know now that I wouldn't have caught any disease off Scurvy Stanley. In fact, I might have cured him."

"Only if you'd orgasmed, and I doubt that lowlife would have bothered satisfying you." A knowing gleam twinkled in her eye. He shook his head. "Then again, easy as you come, maybe he'd have gotten lucky."

She hitched her chin a notch higher. "Hot and always on the ready. That's the Astartian way, no?"

He frowned, reminded of all he knew of the Astartian way and how very little that now seemed to be. If this girl's mother had been impregnated by an Astartian, had it been because some clinic personnel had failed to block the man's reproductive ability? Or had the man been free? Free Astartians. He'd never thought it possible.

Yet he had been seeking to escape his slavery when he'd run into Jaci, a half Astartian woman, a free Astartian who was no longer so free. What had he thought was going to happen to him then? Had he really expected to escape or had he expected to be shot down running? It would be a far more merciful eradication. A low growl rumbled up his throat.

"Fine," she said and raised her arms. "You don't have to go all caveman on me. Wrap me up."

"Caveman?" he questioned as he began wrapping the sheet around her.

"Yeah. You know. Prehistoric man."

He raised an eyebrow at her, wondering how a girl raised in the streets had learned such ancient, useless history.

She huffed, apparently misreading his reaction. "It's a species of man who lived like animals in caves."

"There are some who still live in caves yet are advanced as us," he retorted as he drew the sheet around her, his arms encircling her, her heat mingling with his, tempting him. She drew a deep breath and he knew she inhaled his sex as surely as he did hers.

"The cavemen I speak of didn't know how to make tools. They were ancient. Crude."

He trailed his knuckles across the half moons of her breasts exposed above the wrap. "Have I been crude?"

A pink stain spread up her chest. "No."

He drew the last corner of the sheet over her shoulder, paused as he examined the rug burn on the rise of her breasts. "A shame to damage such beautiful skin."

"A shame to escape this rock only to be captured on the next," she retorted.

He blinked at her, unsure where she was going with that comment. "I have done well moving among all sorts on this world."

"Buying your masters drugs—moving among the freemen of this moon—is not the same as real freedom on other worlds. You need me to teach you how to live free, Lazarus."

"You need me to get you off this moon."

"I can get myself off this moon. You and your access to a safe full of currency are just a means to a quicker escape."

"You believe your instincts will keep you out of the hands of the slavers?"

She tossed her head. "If I didn't go with my instincts in that doorway last night and plant my mouth over your cock," she said, "I'd be in chains by now. That's what saved me last night. I acted on instinct."

"You acted on street smarts—on what you learned living on the streets."

"Exactly. And those street smarts that honed my instincts are what have kept me free for twenty-three years."

"But they're not going to keep you free on this moon for long."

She stuck her face in his and spoke through her teeth. "You need me to teach you how to stay free."

He saw the defiant hope in her eyes. Why the hell were they arguing? Because she was desperate. Because she wanted to prove herself useful to him so he wouldn't abandon her. Because he'd never before had anyone reliant on him for her freedom.

Goddess's blood, if he failed her, she could wind up in a clinic servicing an endless stream of infected males. He couldn't picture the spirited girl giving in to that fate. More likely, she'd end up on a dissection table, experimented on in search of the element that gave Astartians the power to heal.

His blood ran cold.

She thumped him solidly in the chest with her fist. "Dammit, Laz. I need to get off this rock."

He tucked the corner of the sheet into the wrap toga style, his hand lingering against the side of her breast, and sighed. "You are a trial, woman."

She squared her shoulders and, though tears pooled in the corners of her eyes, asked in a steady voice, "What do I need to do to get you to arrange passage for two?"

He knuckled her chin up, brushed his lips across hers and whispered, "You already did it."

He truly was her superhero. Jaci smiled at the panel through which Lazarus had exited, hugged the toga he'd wrapped lovingly around her and twirled. At last, the emptiness in the pit of her stomach was gone.

But then, she always got a giddy feeling in her stomach when she fell in love, something she did far too often. And it hardly ever worked out. Look what the last love of her life had done to her.

She plopped down on the bottom step, braced her elbows on her knees and propped her chin in her hands. Was Laz like all the others? Had she fallen in love with him merely because she loved being in love? Because she desperately wanted to be loved? She had wanted it so much she'd substituted lust for love over and over. Had she done it again?

But he'd rescued her.

Rescue didn't mean love.

But Lazarus had aided her in her orgasm on the fucking machine, with his hand and fingers making the orgasm bigger, stronger, more powerful. Yet he had taken nothing for himself. Well, almost nothing.

Sex didn't equate to love.

What about his letting her inside his head? He had trusted her with his secrets.

But trust didn't prove love.

He was taking her with him when it was going to be hard enough to smuggle himself off this rock. He cared enough for her to risk his own freedom. That had to be love.

She smiled. Lazarus Stone was the real deal after all. She had finally found true love.

Lazarus Stone. Super Stud. Man of Black. Her smile stretched. Superheroes always wore a costume and Lazarus's was black.

She popped to her feet, gathered up the trailing sheet and bounded up the steps. She would shower and then eat. Eat. Yes. She was ravenous. She hadn't eaten since before Lazarus had rescued her and brought her to the apartment.

Come to think of it, she hadn't seen him eat, either. That was something she could do for him, have food ready for him to eat when he returned.

Then she would ready herself for their escape… together.

❧❀❦

She'd prepared a feast of cold-cuts, cheese, and grapes, and had eaten her fill. The rest waited for Lazarus in a chilling cube beside his bed. Now, she stood in the middle of Simone's dressing room surrounded by hangers of clothes, racks of shoes and shelves of lingerie, all suspended on a moveable track system.

She started with the lingerie chest with its narrow drawers. She touched the flat front of the top one. It slid open and then the thinness of the drawers made sense. Panties weren't folded and stacked. They were laid out, three to a drawer, every pair of them silk.

"Be still my heart," Jaci murmured, fingering the rare fabric. Laz's Simone must be richer than the fabled Midas. Moderately wealthy people in possession of silk never hid it under their outer garments. Then again, given Simone's hedonistic lifestyle, perhaps French-cut panties and thongs constituted outerwear.

Jaci slipped a pair of panties from each drawer and tucked them into her backpack. Never empty a drawer, a case, or a safe, so the victim won't immediately see the theft. That was something she'd learned in the arms of a very accomplished burglar. For now, she'd wear the one and only black pair, in deference to Laz's penchant for black.

She examined a couple of bras. Definitely too small for her. Score one for the slave girl.

A neighboring cabinet contained hairpieces, most a deep brunette like Simone's hair. She and Lazarus with his mahogany mane must have made a handsome couple. Jaci frowned and moved on with her inventory.

The closet also contained wigs ranging from pink to ebony and styled from Pixie short to Godiva long. Aha. Simone liked variety.

A thought scampered across Jaci's mind. Maybe Simone liked variety in men as well.

"Of course she did," Jaci muttered, thinking of the sensual décor of the apartment. This woman was all about sex. Lazarus was simply a means to keeping her free of sexual disease.

Jaci winced. No wonder Lazarus was so somber. He was used, not loved.

"I'd love you, Lazarus Stone," she murmured, her fingers tenderly stroking one mahogany hued wig. She knew what it was to live without love, knew how it ached in her soul even as she partied with her body.

She curled her fingers back from the wig and closed the cabinet. One of those wigs could come in handy later as a disguise.

Next came the shoe racks. Dozens and dozens of them on a rolling system of clear boxes. Black, red, silver, gold, pink, blue, and every one of them with fuck-me high heels.

"Be still my heart," she sighed and retrieved a pair of blood-red sequined four-inch heels.

Too big. She sighed. Then the shoes molded to her feet.

"Skin shoes," she gasped, her mouth hanging open in awe. Only the richest could afford shoes made of living organisms that molded perfectly to one's foot.

Jaci turned to the garments on the track-mounted hanger system and studied the abundance of expensive fabrics. Just how rich was this woman?

Images she'd gleaned from Laz's memory flashed through her mind, memories of power brokering. Riches came in many forms, and Simone's wealth was power.

"Damn," she muttered. Just how highly ranked was this woman?

Jaci commanded the hanger system into motion. Flowing loungewear, shimmering evening gowns and skimpy party-wear floated before her eyes. But she didn't pause to admire their fabrics or contemplate slipping into anything just for the fun of it. The hairs prickling at the back of her neck warned her that she searched out something more telling. Why hadn't that early warning system given her a clue about her ex-boyfriend?

Because of her damnable habit of looking for a hero in every man she met. She grimaced. What if she'd made the same mistake with Lazarus? He could this very night be bargaining away her freedom in exchange for his own.

Clothing swayed passed her, a blur of rich colors and costly fabrics. Maybe she should find something among Simone's clothing that would fit her and get the hell out of this apartment ASAP. There were more ways to escape besides the hovercraft bay.

And after she escaped, then what? All she had were the thousand credits Laz had paid her for staying the night. If only she'd thought to slip that case with Simone's fingerprint from Laz's pocket before he'd left. As a series of pressure-equalizing suits for travel swung by in protective sleeves, she thought about the stacks of currency she'd seen in Simone's safe. And she thought about Laz handing over a credits card to her. If he intended to betray her, he'd have given her nothing.

Nor did the man lie. Semantics was his game. And he really needed to be off this planet before anyone found out his master was dead. That's what he'd been doing last night when she'd run into him. The fact was folded into the lobes of his brain. She'd seen it when he'd opened his mind to her. Of course he'd gone tonight to search again for Marco.

In front of her a section of skin-fitting jumpsuits shuddered past. Something beyond their high grade composite fabric and perfectly tailored design caught her attention. The braiding around the neck and cuffs, the embroidered insignia on the upper left chest, the epaulettes on the shoulders.

Jaci halted the track system, one of the uniforms swinging to a stop squarely in front of her. Her eyes locked on the insignia of the Federation of United Star Systems. That Simone was in the employ of the governing body was bad enough. But it was the color of the epaulettes that sent a shudder through Jaci. They bore the color code of The Department of Intergalactic Enforcement.

Jaci's chin dropped to her chest. Of all the men on this Goddess-forsaken rock of a moon, why did her freedom have to rely on a slave owned by an officer of DIE, and, judging by the number of stripes on her sleeve, a very high ranking one?

"Goddess's blood," she muttered. It wouldn't matter that Simone's overdose was self-inflicted. The Federation would need a scapegoat, and Laz might have been the last person seen in her apartment before she was found dead.

Escaping this moon would be the easy part. Staying free would be the hard part. And tomorrow was Monday, the start of a new work week. No, it was a long weekend. Some holiday.

But Simone would be expected in her office on Tuesday, and if she didn't show up, someone would check in on her. They'd find her dead and turn their focus on Lazarus Stone. They'd hunt him to the furthest reaches of the galaxy. Laz would never be free.

Over the intercom came three tones, a signal of a weather alert followed by the same voice that had earlier announced the time. "Solar flare alert. Prepare for a solar hit just before sundown this evening."

Jaci grimaced. She needed a plan, and she needed it fast.

.

Chapter 8

Laz docked the SG-12 in the bay outside Simone's apartment and shut down the transport. He'd spent most of the night tracking down Marco. Then, when he'd told the smuggler the job included a woman, that lizard-toed son of a troglodyte had negotiated a ridiculously high price.

Wearily, Laz climbed from the transport, face lowered from the security recorder. It was a useless habit for many reasons. Anyone monitoring or reviewing the optical screener would have known it was him anyway. He'd been inventoried like every other piece of property Simone owned, recognizable by any number of identifying points.

But what of Jaci? Would anyone viewing the security recordings see her as just one more of Simone's sexual playthings, or had he implicated the girl in Simone's death? It had been foolish of him to bring her here. Even more foolish of him to succumb to his sexual urges. But most foolish of all to learn too much about her, to find her amusing, to feel too much toward her. It all made him feel responsible to get her safely out of this mess.

He raised his face, the security scanner reading and matching his cornea to those allowed admittance. The security recorder above now got an unobstructed view of his face, the number one reason his attempt to hide his face was useless.

He shuffled into the foyer, the entry panel whispering shut behind him. He had to hope no one figured out his mistress was dead before the rendezvous with Marco tonight. Marco wouldn't blast off until sundown when the next solar flare scrambled tracker beams. Space pirates had to plan their departures around things like that.

He punched in the security code. He didn't like waiting. Every extra hour they spent on this Goddess-forsaken moon made them more vulnerable to capture. Sooner or later, someone was going to come looking for Simone. The woman rarely spent more than twenty-four hours incommunicado unless she was partying. He could only hope her assistant would assume the latter.

He slumped against the wall. Maybe he and Jaci should get out now before anyone came looking for Simone. But, going out in the world with all its surveillance would make them more vulnerable. The apartment was the safest place to wait out the day… he hoped.

His head spun with debate over where they would be safest and reeled with the details of the rendezvous with Marco. Before sundown. Just the two of them with only what they could carry on their backs. So this was freedom.

Not quite yet, he reminded himself and rubbed his gritty eyes. He needed sleep but he was too wired to relax. Maybe snuggled up next to Jaci he could unwind enough to get some sleep. For some reason, that girl had a calming effect on him. Odd, considering their circumstances and her penchant for arguing with him at every turn.

He thought of how eagerly she'd joined him in the anti-gravity ball, how readily she opened her body to his. Okay, she didn't argue every point between them.

Two at a time, Laz took the stairs, and his long stride ate up the distance across the balcony to his room in little time. With a swipe of his hand the entry panel opened and, just as he'd hoped, she was in his bed.

Curled up on one side and eyes shut, she looked like a sleeping wood nymph. But the bare, coltish legs angled toward him definitely described her more accurately than any wood nymph. Or maybe she was an angel as the halo of golden hair fanned across the pillow suggested. The worries of the night began to melt away.

His let his gaze wander over her torso, each curve detailed by the light weight tunic she wore. Red, like the blouse she'd been wearing when he'd first seen her. Most blondes favored softer colors, baby blues and pale pinks. Not this one. She favored red and red favored her.

His fingers itched. His cock twitched.

Not now.

For now he wanted only to feel her beside him as he slept. Why that was enough, he didn't comprehend. Not now at least, weariness dragging at his body.

He tossed his coat across the foot of the bed. She stirred and blinked sleepily up at him.

"Didn't mean to wake you," he said quietly, sitting on the end of the bed and reaching for his boot closures.

"You didn't wake me," she murmured, sitting up. "I set the security system to alert me to anyone entering the apartment." She held up her arm, showing him Simone's soft-panel attached to her wrist.

"Clever girl," he said, slipping off his boots. Maybe it was having someone else watching out for him that made her a calming influence, a partner with a like goal.

"I need to talk to you," she said.

"We need to sleep," he muttered, crawling up the bed to her side.

"But—"

"I've secured passage off this rock for us both," he murmured, the weariness tugging hard at his eyelids. "That's what you want to know, right?"

"There's a solar flare—"

"We leave just before it strikes."

He flopped onto his back and gave her a sleepy smile. "Space pirates smuggling sex slaves need all the cover they can get when making a run for it."

"Great. That works."

Of course it did, he thought as his eyes drifted shut.

"But I still need to talk to you."

The bed shifted beneath him, and he peeked under a low-hanging eyelid at her. She held a cool cube in her hands.

"I put together something for you to eat," she said and set a platter of meat, cheese, and fruit between them.

No woman had ever fed him, other than as a form of sex play. A foreign sensation squeezed at his heart and, more than anything, he wanted to pull this woman who thought to feed him into his arms and fall asleep curled up around her warmth.

He held out an arm to her. "Too tired to eat. Just need you."

"What you need is to eat, and while you eat, I'll talk."

He groaned and closed his eyes.

"I have a plan," she said.

"So do I, and it's working just fine," he mumbled.

Fingers featherlight brushed a path along his jaw.

"Need sleep," he murmured.

"Need food," she said, her knuckles brushing his lips.

"Sleep," he repeated, nipping at her fingers only to find a grape between his lips. He bit down and sweet juices flooded his mouth. Would her juices taste as sweet? They smelled as sweet. His stomach growled.

"Good boy," she said.

He squinted up at her, seated cross-legged beside him, the food platter now in her lap. He was suddenly hungry, but for the food or what lie beneath the platter in her lap? He knew which would better serve him.

He sighed and hitched himself up against the headboard. "Okay, I'll eat."

She fed him a rolled up piece of beef, talking as he chewed. "Now, about my plan."

The last thing he needed right now was to have to think. He opened his mouth to protest and she shoved a pickle wedge rolled up in a slice of ham into his mouth.

"If DIE believes you were the last to see Simone alive, they'll never stop hunting you."

"I was the last to see her alive," he managed to get out as he chewed.

"You'll always be on the run."

Never free.

Didn't he know it. Apparently so did she. Was that her true concern, that she'd be in the same danger as he as long as she stayed with him? An ache heavier than weariness throbbed in his chest. Through clenched teeth, he offered, "You'll be free to go off on your own once we escape this rock."

"That's not my concern," she whispered, pressing another sweet grape between his lips.

Truth or lie? If only he weren't too tired to probe her mind.

"DIE will put a bounty on your head so high your own mother would turn you in."

The ache tightened, pulling at his gut, wrenching his heart.

"I can help you, Laz."

But help him how? She fed him. She'd eased the ache between his legs, but what of the one knotted in the center of his chest? Would she also help him right into the hands of DIE and collect herself a hefty bounty?

"Laz—"

He shoved the food tray out of the way and rolled on top of her, his mouth covering hers before she could speak another lie. Or disturbing truth. What if all she wanted was that bounty? Maybe she seduced his body and mind to distract him. Her own freedom might depend on his capture. He'd been witness to Simone's dealings so long, he had to question. He had to be wary.

He swept her mouth possessively with his tongue. This wasn't how he wanted to travel the sweet path to the heaven known as Jaci. But he could not face what it was he truly needed, at least not until he knew her truth.

He pressed his knee against her hot, wet center. Her body quivered.

Truth or lie?

He opened his eyes and found hers staring up at him.

What about me do you fear? Is it the bounty? Do you fear I'll turn you in for the bounty?

He sent a growl into her mouth, ground his knee against her mons, and pinned her wrists above her head. Her tongue touched his, softly, gently, lovingly even as a tear rolled down her cheek.

Come into my mind. Find your truth, Laz.

He winced and loosened his grip on her body.

I can make it look like you were not the last to see Simone alive.

No way.

Hear me out, Laz.

I'd rather love you.

For an instant, they both went still. Fuck. He'd meant to say he'd rather fuck her, right? He tore his mouth from hers.

"Laz—"

Roughly, he shoved the red tunic up her pale torso, her skin soft as rose petals against his fingertips. He shook his head. He couldn't afford the distraction of any sweet thoughts right now. He wanted no thoughts at all.

He shoved the tunic higher, exposing her full, ripe breasts and the pink knots of their nipples. Naturally pink, not rouged. These unfashionably large breasts were made to pillow a man's head. Their nipples strained to be touched, suckled.

Worshipped.

No! There could be no worshipping of bodies. Not now. Not when a seductress he'd known barely more than twenty-four hours made him drop his guard far too easily.

He spotted a scar on the underside of her arm he hadn't noticed before, the sort one might think a defensive wound. Under her chin was another shaped like a miniature crescent-moon. Her nails were trimmed to a functional length, just long enough for their sharp tips to inflict injury without breaking. She wasn't the polished, manicured type of woman to which he'd become accustomed. This woman was a fighter, and a good one. She'd escaped a slave trader's goons. She'd lived free all her life in spite of being half-Astartian.

My plan will show Simone alive after you leave.

He shook the words out of his head, closed his mouth over Jaci's nipple and swirled his tongue around the taut little peak. Jaci squirmed beneath him. Goddess but she felt better than any woman ever had beneath him. Another of her defensive talents?

If she's seen after you leave, DIE might not come after you. At the very least, it'll buy you time before they do.

How? He fought the question forming in his head, concentrating instead on nipping a trail down to her bellybutton.

I can put on her clothes, her hair pieces, her makeup—

He circled the deep dimple of her bellybutton with his tongue as he had her nipple, making her suck a breath, making her stop thinking.

Yeah. That's the way. Let your guard down. She wasn't the only one who knew how to wield sex as a weapon.

He nipped her abdomen hard. She jumped but groaned in ecstasy. He captured the thin strap of her panties between his teeth.

An image of Simone popped into his head. No, not Simone. Jaci dressed as Simone. He gnashed his teeth, shredding the panty strap between them.

I can do it, Laz. You just saw it in my head.

The strap released, he rose to tear the rest of the panty away. The black triangle covering her pale curls made him pause. He didn't understand why the sight of the black panty made him stop. He didn't want to understand anything at this moment.

"I'd have thought you'd have chosen red to match the tunic."

"I chose black to match my man of black," she replied in a quiet, level voice.

A groin muscle jerked at his testicles, but he felt the pull on his heart. How he wanted to believe her.

"I open my mind to you, Laz."

Emotions flooded through him, things he hadn't felt in years, things he'd never felt. They weren't his feelings, though, they were hers. Every raw moment of her life, she opened to him. Total trust. And he saw she was genuine, real.

Emotion gripped his stomach and shot through his chest. Suddenly, all that mattered to him was she smelled like heaven, tasted like sin and could take him to a world where a man was free to love as he pleased.

His fingers gentled against her body. He rose to his knees and slowly, reverently peeled the black panties she'd chosen for him from her body. Then he knelt between her legs, lifted them to his shoulders and worshipped her with his mouth.

❧🙂❦

She'd awakened in his arms, naked and sore in the most delicious places. No other man had ever made such all-consuming love to her. How tempting it had been to stay in the cozy cove of his arms, or to wake him with tender kisses and worship his magnificent body as he had hers.

But he was exhausted. He needed sleep. And she needed a few things if she was going to carry out her plan. So, without having explained her entire plan to him, she'd slipped unnoticed from his bed, donned one of Simone's skin-suits and a pair of her boots, made a few adjustments to the security system and made off in the SG-12.

Grit blasted the cruiser, bouncing her about a bit. A precursor of the major solar flare to come. Her heart tightened in her chest. Laz's freedom depended on her plan working.

Laz who had made love to her more thoroughly than any man ever had. Love. He'd even called it that. She suspected he'd never made *love* to any other woman. Oh, he'd wielded that artful tongue and practiced fingers to service many women, but… loved?

A blocky building, dead gray like all federation buildings, rose through the yellow haze of daylight. Jaci blinked back to the present, reminding herself to concentrate on the business at hand. Dangerous to let herself be distracted by memories of Laz's sweet lovemaking, of his calling it making love, of how contented he'd looked in his slumber as she slipped from his side. She'd wanted nothing worse than to stay snuggled beside him. But she had a plan, and that plan was the only way she was going to be able to keep that contented look on Laz's face.

She cruised the SG-12 three times around her old dormitory building before assuring herself there were no guards, thugs, or rotten ex-boyfriends waiting for her. She glided to a halt in front of a broken third floor window she'd noticed on the last pass. Repairs on dorms for menial jobbers didn't get priority.

Giving the back of the building one last appraising scan, Jaci locked the SG-12 in place below the broken window. Hot, dry air hit her as she opened the hatch. Sweat dampened the spine of the borrowed skin-suit as she plucked the remaining shards of glass from the window frame and climbed through. The hall was empty, and half its lighting source was burned out or broken. Home sweet home.

She took the stairs to the second level, cracked open the fire door and checked to make sure the hall was empty before heading for her dorm room. Her key card was in her purse, which was probably still in possession of her ex-boyfriend or that slug of a slave-trader. But another charm of federation-built group housing was its low level of security.

One well-placed kick with the flat of her borrowed boot and the door flew open. The space she rented consisted of a metal-framed cot and locker in a room of six such configurations. The bedding had been stripped from her cot and the mattress left cockeyed as though someone had searched beneath it for valuables.

"Amateur," she muttered and eyed her open locker. It too had been stripped clean. Surprise? Not.

No high-tech keypad security for the menially employed. Just a good old-fashioned combination padlock that invited thieves with deft fingers and sharp ears, or a laser cutter. Good thing she'd learned that lesson back in the days she and her mother lived in flophouses. One never locked up valuables. Valuables were hidden.

She shoved the cot away from the wall, its legs leaving tracks in the dust. Jaci smiled. No evidence anyone had found her hiding place.

She slipped the edge of the credits card she'd earned by spending the night with Lazarus into a seam in the wood-patterned composite floorboards and pried up the loose panel. The backpack was nestled between floor joists just as she'd left it. She reached for it. But a noise from the hall stopped her.

She cocked her ear toward the open door and listened. Nothing but the creaking of an old building. She scooped the pack from its hiding place and approached the doorway with caution.

She stuck her head into the hall, scanning first in the direction of the stairway. But as she started to turn her head, something flashed in the corner of her eye. Her attention snapped to the near end of the hall. Had there been someone there?

No open doors. No occupied warning light burning above the freight lift. Maybe she'd imagined it.

Flinging the pack over her shoulder, she speed-walked to the stairway at the far end of the hall, her ears honed for movement. She gave the hall one last glance, slipped through the fire door and bolted for the third floor. She heard the footsteps on the stairs below her just as she hit the third floor fire door.

She ran to the broken window, activating the SG-12 with the remote keypad and vaulted over the sill into the seat. She barely paused to secure the hatch before taking off. One last backward glanced as she barreled away, and she spotted a man in the broken window. No, not a man, a rat fink of a former boyfriend. Leave it to that scumbag to stake out her room. But, as usual, he couldn't keep up with her.

Jaci smiled, the yellow smog closing around her and the cruiser as she veered for the condo.

Where the hell was she?

Lazarus stalked from room to room, their empty air pressing against his naked skin. Suffocating. A vague memory of her talking about some plan of hers raised the hairs on the back of his neck. Finding the XG-12 gone had turned his insides to liquid. What did she think she was doing?

The foyer door slid open and, for an instant, he thought it was Simone walking in. But of course it wasn't. The mahogany wig had never warmed Simone's skin as it did Jaci's. And Jaci didn't quite match Simone's height, even with the high-heeled boots. Even with breasts clearly bound, she remained far curvier than was fashionable. His cock swelled.

Jaci let loose with a long, low whistle as her gaze slid the naked length of him, settling on the vicinity of his hard on. "Now that's the way to greet a woman."

It was the wrong thing for her to say, in spite of his aroused state—in spite of how her hips swayed as she moved toward him. Desire didn't erase the worry, the threat of danger. Even relief eased a man only so far.

"Where in the Goddess's name have you been?"

She stopped inches in front of him and held up a backpack. "I needed a few things to pull off my plan."

"My plan is working just fine."

She lifted her mouth and brushed her lips across his. "Mine is better."

In spite of how heavenly, how inviting her lips were, he scowled. "How'd you fool the security system?"

She brushed a lock of hair back from his brow, her eyes dreamy as they met his. "I made an adjustment to the security system. My cornea for hers."

He eyed her narrowly. "Where the hell did you learn to alter a level five security system?"

She settled back on her heels and the dreaminess melted from her eyes. "I'm surprised you didn't glean all that information from my head when you burrowed around in there the first time."

"My search back then focused specifically on Astartian information."

She sighed. "Confession time. You want to do your own rummaging through my brain, or should I just 'fess up?"

"Just give me the short answer."

"You know how I grew up. You know I lived on the street most of my life."

"Uh-huh."

"A girl can learn a lot from people living outside the law."

"Get on with it."

"In short, I am a cat burglar."

"You're a file clerk."

"I'm a file clerk for the Department of Building Licenses where the blueprints for nearly every building on this moon are stored."

He winced. It made sense. "And you know how to alter high level systems, too.

You're a very clever cat burglar."

"So I've been told."

He shook his head, still bewildered. "How does your being a burglar make your plan better than mine?"

She sighed as though she were about to explain something he should already know. "Like I told you last night, Simone needs to be seen alive after you leave."

"A lot of good that'll do if someone out there saw you sneaking around and recognized you. What if they tracked you back here?"

She blinked and stepped around him, heading for the dining room off the great room. "No one followed me."

She was hiding something from him. He saw it in that blink, felt it prickle off her skin just before she stepped away.

"You're sure no one followed you?" he pressed, trailing her.

She plopped the backpack on the glass tabletop and faced him, but her eyes were shuttered. "You doubt whether or not I'd know if anyone followed me after I made it in and out of this fortress without setting off any security alarms?"

Whatever she was hiding she wasn't revealing to him. He either pushed more or trusted her. He pulled her into his arms and held her close. "I'm just relieved you're back and safe. So what was so important you had to risk your freedom to get?"

Her fingers played across his shoulders. "I need certain equipment to implement my plan."

He pressed his lips to her forehead. "Refresh my memory of this plan I don't recall agreeing to."

She threaded her fingers through his hair. "Basically, it will throw the focus off you where Simone's death is concerned."

He traced her spine with his fingertips as though they were memorizing each perfect vertebra. "And we do that how?"

She pressed her body the length of his and nibbled at his ear. "First, you are recorded driving me away and returning alone. Then you are recorded driving away with Simone, me dressed like her. Simone, me, returns alone."

He drew his arms across her back as though holding her would keep her safe. "And how do you get back in the apartment to play Simone without being seen, then leave as yourself in the end, again without being seeing?"

She nodded at the backpack on the table. Reluctantly, he released her and she opened the pack. On the top was an old comic book. "This is what you risked your freedom for, old comic books?"

"Vintage comic books," she retorted, prying the brittle copy from his fingers and returning it to the dog-eared stack she placed beside the pack. "I didn't go back to my dorm just for them."

She pulled out a quartet of spider-cups and dangled them in front of him. "This is how I'll climb the inside of the incinerator shaft to get in and out of the apartment unseen."

He snorted. "This apartment isn't connected to the central incinerating system."

"Yes, it is."

"Simone has a personal demoleculizer. She was adamant about security."

Jaci's eyebrows hitched a dubious angle. He scowled. "Okay, you broke the code to her security. But there's still no shaft to—"

She took him by the hand and led him into the kitchen where she opened a lower cabinet, emptied it and removed a panel from its back. He stuck his head through the cabinet and looked down a long shaft.

He pulled back and looked at Jaci. "The blueprints from the D.B.L.?"

She nodded. "It seems all the newer construction on this moon was done by the same few contractors, contractors who paid their bribes on time and cut corners where they could. Or maybe the government just wanted to make sure every apartment had an unguarded way in."

He shook his head. "If Simone had known her apartment was still attached to the central incinerating system, she'd have gone supernova."

He climbed to his feet, frowning. "There's nothing you can do to alter the security system so we can just walk out of here without risking your neck climbing some shaft?"

"Even I have limitations."

"Okay. Say we go with your plan, can it be completed before sundown."

"Before the major solar flare," she said. "Easily."

"Marco won't wait for us. He'll leave without us if we're late."

"I understand."

He frowned. "You're still not as tall as Simone."

"I've got that covered."

"Okay, so we thaw Simone and put her back in bed."

"As per your initial plan," she said.

He grimaced. His plan had been simply to outrun DIE. "There's still a problem. I'm listed among Simone's inventory. Sooner or later, they're going to realize I'm missing and come looking for me."

She took him by the hand and led him back to the dining room where she retrieved a data tube from her pack. "This contains just about any legal document a person might need. In your case, you need a transfer of ownership document."

"Lot of good that does if Simone can't sign it and we can't get it notarized. Not to mention, any purchaser's name we put on it, DIE will verify."

"Oh, ye of little faith. My magic capsule also contains the program to duplicate signatures and supply a notary's stamp. I think I can come up with a buyer's name even DIE won't pursue."

"Someone so powerful DIE won't fuck with them. This might actually work."

"Relax," she said, one stroke of his cock bringing the buzz of blood back to it.

"How can you think of sex at a time like this?" he asked.

She laughed, hitched herself up on the edge of the table and spread her legs. "We're Astartians, love. We're always thinking about sex."

Her fingers glided up and down his shaft, feather light, teasing him until he couldn't resist parting the convenience opening at her crotch. The scent of her sex flooded his nose, an aphrodisiac that pulled at him. He licked his lips and bowed toward the pink lips glistening from the suit's opening. But she stopped him with one hand to his cheek and the other tightening around his throbbing cock, guiding it to that gloriously wet, ripe point between her legs.

"I want you in me," she said, her voice husky, her eyes sultry.

Like a Javelin-class transport riding a tractor beam into a docking bay, he slid unerringly between her swollen lips and glided into her well-oiled channel. She hooked one leg around his waist and the other over his shoulder and took him to the hilt. Few women could.

How many more ways would this woman surprise him?

She rotated her hips, her slick heat gliding around him and heating his cock. He stood still, letting her do her thing, letting his cock get hotter and hotter. It became a wick that soaked up her heat, a fuse feeding fire up his shaft and into his groin.

He groaned, wanting badly to pull back and pump hard into her. But the muscles of her slick tunnel rippled up and down his shaft—tightening and releasing over and over again.

He clenched his teeth against the desire to move. The heat spread up his flanks, burned through his chest and popped beads of sweat out on his forehead. She rotated her hips and, like molten lava, the fire flowed into his arms and legs and he became what he was born to be.

He threw back his head and howled. Then, he drew back his hips and slammed them forward. Again and again, he plunged into the undulating waves of her hot, drenching channel.

She was an ocean in which he wanted to drown. She was a volcano of molten rock to which he wanted to sacrifice himself.

She was his mate, swallowing him into her soul.

Sharp pants of pleasure escaped her parted lips. Her hands gripped the edge of the table holding her in place against his thrusts. Her pelvis rose to meet his every stroke and her vaginal muscles began to tighten around him.

She was close to coming. So was he.

He slowed his stroking, his shaft rubbing over her G-spot. Short, slow strokes.

Her body arched, color flushed her cheeks and she cried out, a sound that came from the core of her. Simultaneously, her muscles clenched around him, rolling up and down his shaft, squeezing and pulling at him like a milkmaid's hands.

One last stroke into her body and he gave himself up to the ecstasy—let her body milk his of every last drop of his cum.

For a long time, he lay bent over the table in the embrace of her arms and legs, linked in their lovers' embrace. Their chests butted together with their panting breaths. Their sweat mingled as did the life-giving fluid bathing vagina and cock. Their hearts beat a complementary rhythm, then, as those beats slowed, they fell into synch with each other. He could have spent the rest of his life like this.

"Laz," she whispered in his ear. "We need to get ready."

For what, he almost murmured before reality slapped him out of his stupor. Escape. Freedom.

The fear of failure.

He hugged her close and slid his mouth to her ear, croaking out, "You could have been caught while you were out there, and I wouldn't have been able to do a thing about it."

Her cheek stretched against his as she quipped, "Watch it, Super Stud, a girl might get the idea you like her."

He straightened, taking her with him, settling her on her feet, and hugging her close. "Goddess's Blood, Jaci. You're Astartian. Do you know what they do to Astartians?"

"They become sex slaves like you," she purred against his chest and circled one alert nipple with her tongue.

He caught the groan in his throat. "Few get the luxury of private service like me. Most end up in clinics, servicing an endless stream of clients."

She chuckled and wiggled against him, her breasts swollen yet from their lovemaking. "Endless sex, huh? What's the downside?"

He pulled back from her, held her away from him by the upper arms. "This is no joke, Jaci."

Her eyes were all dreamy and her smile a little loopy. "You really do care about me."

"The end of the line is dissection," he continued, giving her a little shake, trying to force her to understand the danger she was in. "They'll cut you open and slice through every inch of you in search of the magic cluster of cells that enables you to heal others. I could never leave behind another Astartian to face that fate."

⁂

So this wasn't about her. His concern was for the Astartian in her.

At least now she knew the truth before she made a total fool of herself. Even a good fucking on the dining room table hadn't wiped away that fact. And when they were done, she'd pulled one of Simone's tunics over the skin suit, tossed off the wig and kicked off the boots. A little fluffing of her own hair and she was ready for security to document Laz returning the girl sex-toy to the street where she'd come from.

In reality, Lazarus had dropped her off on the backside of the building nearest the delivery bay and the incinerator shaft, where the security recorder was fortuitously malfunctioning. The plan was for him to circle around for a while to make it look like he'd dropped her off some distance from the building.

She crawled out of the incinerator shaft and through the kitchen cabinet to find Laz pacing the cubicle. *I could never leave behind another Astartian to face that fate.*

"Where have you been?" he demanded, pulling her to her feet.

She waved the spider cups attached to her hands in his face. "Low tech means slow going."

"Whatever. We better get moving with the next phase of this plan of yours."

She removed the spider cups, tossed them into the low cabinet and closed the door. "My Simone outfit is laid out."

Fifteen minutes later, she stepped out of Simone's dressing room, her curves and one of Simone's pressure suits covered by a draping tunic, lounge pants and a full-length, flowing overlay. One of Simone's long, dark wigs and a thick layer of her makeup topped off the illusion... topped it off successfully judging by Laz's dropped jaw.

She strode up to him on a floating gait and looked him level in the eye. He'd caught the one unseen transformation, judging by the pinch of his eyes as he processed it. "How'd you make yourself as tall as Simone?"

She lifted her foot to the chair beside him, hitched up a pant leg and revealed a curved titanium prosthetic modified to fit her foot. "These were also in my backpack. Once science got the hang of growing body parts, a gal could pick and choose from the thousands of prosthetics tossed away, provided she got to them before the compactors did."

He grunted. "There's a lot you didn't let me see inside your head when I probed you, isn't there?"

"More like you just didn't search those memory folds. I don't think I would have been able to hide any memory from you."

They stood there, looking at each other, both wanting to explore the other's inner thoughts, both afraid of the truths they might find there.

"Let's get on this plan of yours," Laz finally said.

"Yeah. Time's a-wastin'"

Chapter 9

Jaci, dressed as Simone, dropped Lazarus off at Marco's launch bay, mentally ticking off the shortest foot route from there to the apartment. She wouldn't have the transportation of the XG-12 when she next left Simone's. *Simone's* journey ended in her apartment, alone.

Jaci stepped up to the cornea scanner, raised one lens of her sunshades. The entry panel slid open, and she hurried into the foyer and reset the alarm. Flipping open the wrist-mounted soft panel, she started restoring the original security setting as she strode toward the stairs. The springy prosthetics bounded her up the stairs three and four at a time. She was on the balcony before she'd finished putting Simone's cornea profile back into the security bank and deleting her own. But all was restored to normal by the time she reached Simone's room.

"Time," she called out as she unfastened the soft panel from her wrist, getting a prompt answer from recorded voice.

Jaci smiled. Her plan was running right on schedule.

She placed the soft-panel on the tray on the bed containing Simone's syringes, all empty but one. She avoided looking at Simone on the far side of bed and moved to the safe. She was suffering enough guilt without being reminded of how they were using Simone's body in their escape plot, and guilt was an odd emotion for her. Especially when it came to picking pockets.

She took the case with Simone's fingerprint from beneath the skinsuit's wristband where she'd tucked after lifting it from Laz. When he found out what she'd done, he'd have a whole different perspective on that deep, up close and personal kiss goodbye she'd given him at Marco's launch bay. But Laz still didn't grasp how much it would cost to stay a free man.

The safe door swung open. Laz had taken only a few of the generic credits cards. She took the rest as well as the currency. Neither of those items could be traced, unlike the jewelry deep in the safe. Her fingers itched. If this was a normal burglary, she'd have taken them. But the idea was to leave the place looking as normal as possible.

She closed the safe on the jewelry and the data disk that contained Laz's forged transfer of ownership document. Then she reactivated the holographic painting and gave the room one final appraising glance.

Her gaze stopped on Simone, thawed now but no less dead. She looked as though she'd fallen into a deep slumber, except for her deathly pale skin and the lack of any breath lifting her chest. Jaci shivered and headed into the dressing room.

She tossed off Simone's wig and dropped her slacks down her legs and kicked them off the prosthetics. Nothing was creepier than being with a dead body.

"So that's how you managed the extra height," sounded a voice from behind her.

She spun toward the voice, facing something creepier than Simone's dead body. "Rex."

He gave her a lazy smile and leaned against the doorframe. "Didn't know I spotted you back at your barracks, did you?"

"I saw you," she said through clenched teeth. "I just didn't think you could keep up with me. You were never able to in the past."

"But I did get ahead of you once, babe."

The night he sold her into slavery. Every epitaph, every vile name she'd ever called him, every promise she'd made to get even with him bubbled to the surface.

One bounding step on the prosthetics, and she was in the air sailing towards him. She hit him solid in the chest and sent him reeling backwards into the bedroom.

"I'm going to beat the living crap out of you, Rex Brody!" she growled as she advanced on him.

At the foot of Simone's bed, he braced himself up on one elbow and rubbed his chest. His smile was gone and his eyes had gone slitty. "And if I don't get you back to Glick, he'll kill me. So I got nothin' to lose."

He popped to his feet. She took another run at him. But this time, when she soared feet first at him, he caught her by the prosthetics and flipped her onto the bed beside Simone's dead body. Instantly, he was on top of her.

She shouldn't have used the same attack method on him twice in a row. But anger drove her actions and all she wanted to do was decimate Rex. Maybe Laz was right. She didn't think.

Rex kneed her legs apart. "How about a farewell fuck for your old love?"

"Go to hell, Rex Brody."

He bared his teeth, pinned her by the throat with his forearm, spread her legs painfully far apart with his knees and probed her crotch for its convenience opening.

She swung at him. His forearm pressed into her throat. She swung again. He pressed harder on her throat. She gasped but took in no air. She tore at his arm until dark spots swam before her eyes. It couldn't end this way!

Oh, Laz, I'm sorry.

❧ ⋆ (ʕ•ᴥ•ʔ) ⋆ ❧

In mid-pace, Laz stopped dead. Something was wrong.

"Finally," Marco's voice echoed off the bay walls. "I was beginning to think you would pace a groove into the floor."

"Something's wrong," Laz said. "She called out to me."

"She's still got a few minutes," Marco muttered as he continued his pre-flight check.

Laz shook his head. "No. Something is wrong. I can feel it."

Marco straightened and faced Laz. "You? Feel something? No fuckin' way."

But Laz wasn't listening to Marco. He'd turned to the open cargo bay and was scanning its contents. There, magnetically locked to the inner wall was just what he needed.

A string of curses followed him as his shot past Marco on the slider bike along with one pointed reminder of how tenuous was his freedom. "I fuckin' won't wait for you!"

The darkness closed on her and her arms fell like lead to the bed either side of her. As though spoken through a tunnel, Rex's words echoed distantly in her ears.

"Now you're getting the idea."

He lessened the pressure on her throat and she sucked in oxygen as he fumbled with the convenience opening in the crotch of her suit. Bitter bile rose in her throat at the idea of Rex fucking her in the same way Laz had last made love to her. No way could she allow it. She needed leverage. She needed a break. She needed a weapon.

The syringes on the tray!

If she stabbed him with one of them, she could startle him. It would be enough to give her the break she needed to throw him off. But if she stabbed him with the one full syringe, she could disable him.

He tore open the crotch of her suit. She bucked and squirmed. In the seconds between when he released her throat and pinned her hips, she went for the syringe.

Just as his cock butted against her crotch, she stabbed him in the neck. He yelped and reared back, his eyes wild with rage. Maybe she hadn't gotten the full syringe after all. Maybe she'd stabbed him with one of the empty ones. Maybe she should shove him back while he was stunned and make a run for it. Then he dropped like a load of blaster balls onto her.

With a mighty heave, she dumped him off herself and scrambled from the bed. She'd done it. For a moment, she stood there stunned. Then—

"Solar flare, level one," reported the weather warning system.

The storm had begun.

"Time," she shouted.

The answer sent chills up her spine. Marco had to be firing up his blasters by now. She'd never make it to the ship. A tear slid down her cheek.

She stared at Rex, face down across Simone. If it was too late to run, she could take all the time she wanted to take her revenge on Rex. She could string him up by the balls. She could flay the skin from his body. She could make him wish he'd never so much as thought to sell her into slavery.

But none of that seemed to matter to her, not when she was losing Lazarus. Unless Laz had convinced Marco to wait just a little longer. The storm wouldn't be impassible until it reached a level three.

She grabbed her backpack, bounded from the room and down the stairs into the kitchen where she crawled through the cabinet into the incinerator shaft. With shaking hands, she closed the cabinet door, replaced the panel at the back of the cabinet, and slung her pack over her back. She fit one set of spider cups to her hands and climbed into the shaft. She made her way downward between her spider cupped hands and the brace of the rubber-padded bottoms of the prosthesis to the opposite wall. This was going way too slow.

She loosened her grip on the walls of the shaft and plummeted. She could only hope the cups and prosthetic pads would slow her descent enough to keep her from breaking her neck. Half way down, the scent of burning rubber trailed past her nostrils. The rubber pads protecting the feet of the prosthesis. She closed her eyes and sent a plea to the Goddesses to get her to the street in one piece.

She hit bottom with a bone cracking twang that vibrated up through her body. The curvature of the artificial legs rebounded, lifting her a few feet. With the aid of the spider cups, she settled herself to the ground.

The instant she stepped into the street, wind-whipped sand blasted her. With the aid of the prosthetics, she bounded across the street and into an alley. The sand blasting diminished considerably. But the debris in the alley swirled and slapped at her. Another level higher on that storm warning and the wind would pitch her around the alley with the rest of the debris. Maybe she should find herself a place to hunker down until the storm passed. That was what reason dictated. But her instincts urged her to keep running, and instinct had served her well more times than not.

The high whine of a slider came up fast behind her. She ran harder even though she knew she couldn't outrun a slider. They were fast as an XG-12 and, with their narrow frame, nearly as maneuverable as a human.

The slider kept coming. Her sides ached, her lungs burned and her ears hummed.

The slider came up beside her. An arm snagged her and deposited her belly down over the lap of whoever was driving this thing.

"You were supposed to be at the ship fifteen minutes ago."

At the sound of Laz's voice, she relaxed. "I got company."

"Who?"

"The old boyfriend."

"If we don't get to the ship before Marco takes off, I'm going to hunt that boy down and beat him silly."

They crossed a street, momentarily blasted by the full brunt of the storm. It was reaching level two velocity. Even back in an alley, there was too much debris whipping around to risk opening one's mouth to talk.

You didn't have to come back for me. You could have left. You could have been free.

Laz pulled her up until she settled her legs over the seat in front of him. *I could never have left you, Jaci.*

And she knew precisely why he couldn't leave her behind. Her heart ached and she pulled off the backpack so she could lean back against Laz's chest, his solidness, his warmth. She could have at least this much of him.

You're a good man, Lazarus Stone. Few would risk their freedom to rescue someone just because she was one of his kind.

I rescued you because it was you.

Her heart stutter-stepped. Could he mean it?

They shot out of the alley into near level three force winds. The slider bucked its way down streets that grew narrower and dirtier. Launch bays loomed on either side, stacked like windowless warehouses, all doors battened down against the storm… except one. But that one open door, Marco's, was closing. Lazarus gunned the slider.

Duck!

They barely cleared the launch bay door before it clanged shut, and now they hurtled toward a decrepit ship, its cargo bay doors closing like a clamshell. If they didn't get inside before Marco launched, they'd be vaporized by the heat from the ship's thrusters. Lazarus laid the bike on its side and skidded through the narrow opening and slammed into a freight box.

"You break it, you pay for it," boomed a voice from the intercom system.

"Go fuck yourself," Lazarus responded, helping Jaci to her feet.

Laughter echoed through the cargo area, then, "You two better get yourselves into a cargo net, or you'll splat against my cargo door like a couple of juicy bugs. And you know how I hate to clean bodies off my walls."

The engines roared to life, and Marco added, "This is going to be a close one, folks."

Laz and Jaci climbed into an anchored cargo net just as the blasters shot the freighter out into space.

Laz's arms encircled her, holding her tight against his body as the g-forces pressed them into one another. Every hard angle of him, every adrenaline-pumped muscle, every corpuscle of blood that pumped into his groin she felt as though it was part of her body. Even now, he desired her. That was clear.

But she wanted to know what he'd meant by *I rescued you because it was you.* But the pressure of hurtling into space squeezed the air from her lungs and the blood from her brain. She couldn't even manage a word of mind speak to him.

The ship dipped and bucked its way through the solar storm. Marco had said they were cutting it close. What if they didn't make it? She couldn't die without letting her hero know how she felt.

Mustering all the breath she could, she whispered against his chest. "I love you, Laz. I love you."

After what seemed an eternity, the ship began to settle down. Laz's arms loosened around her, his hands spreading down her back and cupping her backside. She lifted her head from his shoulder where she'd tucked it and lifted her mouth toward his. His lips closed on hers and his tongue reached deep into her. She wanted to climb his body and take every inch of him inside her. She wanted to drop to her knees and suck him down her throat. She wanted—

She broke the kiss. "Why'd you come back for me, Laz? Why chance your own freedom to rescue me?"

His fingers flexed against the small of her back. "I felt your danger. It was as though you called out for me."

"I did call out for you. But you didn't have to come for me. You could have stayed here, could have guaranteed your escape."

His fingers traced a path up her spine, a world of uncertainty swirling in his eyes. "I couldn't leave you behind."

"Why, Laz? Is it just because I'm Astartian?"

He began plucking the pins from her hair that she'd used to anchor it beneath the wig, his eyes shifting with each falling lock. "I could never leave behind—"

"—another Astartian. I know."

"It was that instinct thing you use." His eyes focused on hers. "Where is your boyfriend now?"

"Ex-boyfriend, and he's back at Simone's apartment."

Laz frowned. "He'll tell DIE about us."

"I doubt anyone will believe anything he has to say at this point."

"What makes you think no one will believe anything he says?"

"He's going to be found face down between Simone's legs with his pants around his ankles."

A small smile stretched across Laz's lips."

"It's not that funny."

"I know."

"He was lying in wait for me. Nearly scared me out of my skin."

The smile on Laz's lips stretched.

"I thought it was all over."

The smile faded. He stroked her bruised neck and frowned.

"Guess I got the bastard in the end," she said.

"That's one of the things I love about you, Jaci."

Her heart did a two-step at the sound of the word love. But she kept a lid on it. He didn't actually say he loved her. "So you love that I get my bastards in the end?"

"I love that you are ingenious and capable. I love that you know how to take care of yourself."

"Told you I'd be an asset to you if you took me with you."

"I need you, Jaci. I need you to teach me how to be free and…"

She gaped up at him when he didn't continue. She felt the uncertainty well up inside him and heard the question forming in his mind.

"Yes," she said. "I meant what I said in the cargo net. I love you, Laz."

He shook his head. "I've never had anyone love me. I don't know what it should feel like."

She pressed one of his hands to the side of her head and placed the other over her heart. He closed his eyes and, for several moments, he took in everything she'd opened to him.

He opened his eyes and met her gaze. "Is this it? Is this what love feels like?"

She nodded.

He took her hands and placed one to the side of his head and the other over his heart. His heart thumped beneath her palm and all the emotion buzzing through his brain and body were familiar.

Tears gathered across her eyes as she gazed into his. She'd gotten her answer even before he put it into words.

"I love you, too, Jaci."

About the Author:

Roxi Romano's Midwestern neighbors probably think her most wicked vice is her love of chocolate. They'd be wrong. An avid reader of just about any genre, it was simply a matter of time before Roxi discovered erotica... as a reader and a writer. Visit RoxiRomano.com *to read more about Ms. Romano.*

Forever My Love

by Calista Fox

To My Reader:

One of my favorite things about writing fiction is that I get to create imaginary worlds and populate them with people I love... or love to hate! Playing in the land of powerful witches, sexy vampires, and evil demons is all the more fun when I get to build in an ultra-steamy romance like the one Aja and Christian share. I hope you enjoy their adventure as much as I enjoyed creating it!

As always, special thanks to Alex and Cindy.

And to JT—thanks for supporting my passion for writing every step of the way!

Chapter 1

Aja Woods teetered on the ledge of the seven-story brick building and fought to steady herself. A mystical force worked against her, keeping her dangerously off balance. She wobbled precariously, trying to maintain her footing. The large gold-and-sapphire medallion dangling from a sturdy chain around her neck grew impossibly heavy. An invisible hand seemed to tug at the pendant as though trying to pull her over the edge.

Thick, gray clouds filled the night sky and concealed the harvest moon. Thunder rumbled in the distance, low and ominous. A flash of lightning startled her, the glowing rod striking close, causing her body to pitch forward, then backward. She was losing the battle to stay upright.

Terror seized her heart. She feared nothing could stop her from falling.

The silk nightgown she wore swirled around her, tangling between her legs. The chill of the evening air made her teeth chatter as much as her perilous predicament did. As the wind picked up, her long, curly hair whipped all around her, the auburn strands slashing across her face, impeding her vision.

Finally, the weight of the medallion became too much for her small frame to bear. She had no choice but to accept the inevitable. She gave a quick, silent prayer to the heavens above before she tumbled over the edge of the tall building.

Aja cried out as she fell.

Suddenly, a large hand pierced the thick blanket of fog and reached out to her, grasping at her own hand. The heavy, wet mist surrounding her made it impossible for her to see any farther than the hand stretched toward her and the sinewy forearm attached to it.

She felt long, strong fingers entwine with hers. Her body was lifted out of the dense fog and her feet touched solid ground. Powerful arms wrapped around her, warming her instantly and making her feel protected.

"You're safe." The deep voice and the strong embrace she remained in helped to abate her fear. "You will always be safe while I watch over you."

His warm lips pressed to hers, chasing away the eerie chill that had besieged her earlier. Her arms tightened around his neck as her body melded to his. Large hands skimmed over her backside, pressing her more firmly against him. She felt his strong muscles all around her, felt his erection against her belly. Her heart thundered in her chest and her pulse raced as erotic sensations consumed her, replacing the terror and dread she'd felt before he'd saved her.

And he truly had saved her. In every way possible. His hot, possessive kiss stirred her passion, bringing her to life. His tongue delved deep inside her mouth, caressing and teasing hers, pleasuring her in the most enticing way. The pangs of loneliness that had been so acute of late began to ebb as other sensations overpowered the emptiness she'd felt for so long. Desire built quickly, coursing through her, hot and bright.

As her fingers tangled in his silky hair, she realized suddenly how much she needed this man... Needed him not only to save her from a terrifying fate, but to save her from her isolated existence. She felt an innate connection to him. Intimacy and warmth flooded her veins. A sense of familiarity swept over her. It was as though she knew him well.

As though they belonged together.

Forever.

When the kiss ended, she was breathless, but filled with a sense of belonging and eternal love. He eased her down onto the rooftop, gently guiding her until she lay on her back. He settled between her parted legs. The storm had passed, and the night was quiet, the air calm. The large moon shone bright and full overhead. The stars twinkled and glittered in a clear, black sky. There was nothing left to fear.

"I've waited so long for you," he whispered. His deep, sensual voice was strained, telling of his own desire and need.

"I've waited for you, too." Though she hadn't realized it until this very moment.

Her fingers plowed into his long, silky hair again. She arched her back and pressed her body against his, desperate to feel every inch of him, desperate to drown in his heat and his passion. His hands clawed impatiently at the silk around her legs, pushing the hem of her nightgown up until it was bunched around her waist. Anticipation seeped through her veins, warm and molten. She longed to feel him inside her, longed to have him buried deep, fulfilling all her fantasies and darkest desires.

"Soon," he said in a soft voice. As though he'd read her thoughts. "We'll be together soon, Aja. I promise."

As his mouth sealed with hers again, her eyelids fluttered closed. His kiss was long and sensual, stirring her soul, heightening her arousal. One large hand covered her breast as he rubbed his hard cock against her mound, making her painfully aware of how much she needed him. Her legs tangled with his, keeping him on top of her, melded to her. He gently squeezed and caressed her breast as he deepened the kiss. His touch was familiar and titillating. Aja felt as though she'd waited her whole life for him to find her, to make love to her.

When he ended the kiss, she whimpered a soft protest. He smiled down at her, his emerald eyes glowing in the moonlight.

"Make love to me," she whispered.

He nodded. "I will. As soon as you wake up, Aja."

Panic suddenly seized her. "No. I don't want to wake up. Every time I do... you're gone."

"Not this time."

"Please don't leave me."

He brushed strands of hair from her forehead as he looked deep into her eyes. "Never, Aja. I've never left you. I never would. You belong to me. Forever."

His hand slid down the length of her body. Long fingers pushed aside the elastic of her panties and grazed her swollen lips. Aja gasped, the touch jolting her to the core.

"Yes," she whispered as her eyes closed. "Touch me. Please."

His fingers stroked her wet flesh until she was panting loudly. Then they plunged deep into her throbbing pussy. Aja cried out as the erotic sensations tore through her like a raging fire. He bent his head to her breast and licked a hard nipple through the silky material of her nightgown. As his fingers pumped in and out of her, Aja surged toward the kind of fulfillment she'd only dreamed of but had never experienced before. A love that would fill the empty cracks within her, a climax that would make her whole. She wanted it. More than she'd ever wanted anything in her life.

She gripped his rigid biceps as he continued to stroke her pussy and tease her nipple. Aja inched toward that elusive sensation... more than just an orgasm, it was an all-consuming emotion that would finally complete her.

"You will always be safe while I watch over you, Aja." His voice penetrated the passion-induced fog that filled her head. "Always."

He stroked her faster, plunging deep.

"Oh, yes," she cried as the sensations inside her collided and exploded. "Oh, God, yes!"

"*Ooohhh!*"

Aja woke with a start and sat bolt upright in her bed. The breath escaped her as the powerful orgasm pulsed inside her. She squeezed her inner walls tightly to prolong the intense sensation, savoring every second of the erotic abyss that consumed her. Her legs pressed together and they trembled slightly. Her stomach quivered and her breath returned in sharp pants.

"Oh, God," she whispered as the wonderful feelings began to ebb. She fell back against the pile of pillows on her bed. She squeezed her eyes shut, concentrated on drawing in a full, steady stream of air. She could honestly say she'd never experienced such a strong, all-consuming orgasm. Its intensity startled her, but more bewildering was the fact that a dream had sparked it. No one had touched her, not in reality. She had simply dreamed of being touched, dreamed of being driven to that beautiful, erotic place. And then it had happened. In real life.

Aja's hand slid over her body. Her nightgown felt cool to the touch, but her skin burned with a sexual fever she'd never experienced before. Her eyes drifted open. She pushed strands of damp hair from her face and neck as she stared into the shadowy depths surrounding her, suddenly searching for any sign the dream had been more than that.

It had seemed so real to her. She'd felt the fear in her heart and the cold evening air on her skin as she'd fallen. She'd felt the strength and warmth of her savior as he'd rescued her from a doomed fate. And she'd felt his hands on her body, his lips on hers... Those sensations were real. They lingered still.

The sheets and comforter she'd tucked around her before she'd drifted off to sleep were now strewn about the bed, indicating she had thrashed restlessly during her dream. She climbed out of the large bed, her bare feet hitting the cool hardwood floor. She rushed to the tall french doors, pushed them open and stepped onto the balcony. She had no idea what she expected to find. She only knew something waited for her.

A shiver crept up her spine at the eerie thought. She rubbed her bare arms with her hands to ward off the chill that slid over her, not just because of the late night air, but because she felt a peculiar presence lingering close by.

However, as she looked about her, Aja found nothing to confirm her suspicion that someone had been on her balcony, watching her. Nor had anyone been in her bedroom. Unfortunately, the lack of a physical being did nothing to quell her nerves. She returned to the warmth and safety of her house, locking the doors behind her.

It was only a dream.

But it was one she'd had before, which made it all the more unsettling.

Aja crawled back into her bed and pulled the covers up around her. She stared into the darkness and tried to reconcile the dream. For four nights in a row, she had been spared a terrifying fate. Each time, the same man rescued her.

Tonight was the first time he'd touched her so intimately.

What did that mean?

Aja shook her head and tried to form coherent thoughts. Though the man in her dreams was difficult to see, his features undiscernible, she recognized his piercing, emerald-green eyes. Aja simply couldn't fathom why Christian St. James, a man she barely knew, continued to save her. Or why he always whispered the same words.

"You will always be safe while I watch over you."

Chapter 2

"I'm sorry, Miss…?"

Aja stared at the young secretary and tried to keep her temper in check. Her jaw clenched. "It's Professor Woods. Aja Woods. Pronounced 'Asia.' You know, like the continent?"

If she had to give this woman her name one more time—or pronounce it yet again, for that matter—Aja feared she'd reach across the desk and strangle the ditzy girl.

"Oh, yes," the perky blonde replied with a soft laugh. She waved a manicured hand in the air in a dismissive manner. "You said that before."

"Look." Aja mustered a calm voice. No easy feat. She was tired and wound a bit too tight for this nonsense. In fact, she felt like a caged animal, ready to pounce—and the pretty little secretary was about to become her prey. "I've been waiting for nearly an hour. When may I see Professor St. James?"

"I'm sorry. I just don't know."

Aja's patience wore dangerously thin. She knew St. James kept odd hours. He only taught evening classes and his office visits were limited to the hour before class and a couple of hours afterward. If Aja didn't get in to see him this evening, she would have to wait an entire day to meet with him. That simply wouldn't do. "I really need to see the professor. It's urgent. Perhaps you could buzz him or step into his office and let him know he has a visitor."

The young woman let out what sounded to be a very exasperated sigh. "Miss— I'm sorry—*Professor* Woods, I don't know how long he'll be. And I make it a point never to interrupt Professor St. James. No matter how urg—"

"Oh, to hell with it," Aja said as she moved past the secretary's desk and stalked toward St. James' office.

"Professor Woods!" The young woman shrieked in apparent shock. "You can't go in there!"

"Why on earth not? I doubt very seriously that he's conducting top-secret research in there. He's a history professor, for Pete's sake." Aja gave one quick rap on the door before she flung it open and marched inside.

Christian St. James stood behind his massive Louis XVI desk, his large hands planted on lean hips. He'd been talking into the speakerphone on the corner of his desk, but he stopped abruptly. His dark gaze shot across the room and speared Aja.

She drew up short and gulped audibly. He didn't look pleased to see her. Not that she'd expected him to welcome her with open arms. Despite the sensual dreams she'd had about him recently, they scarcely knew each other.

Aja shut the door behind her, then gave her colleague a tentative smile, to which he cocked a dark eyebrow. In a heartbeat, she was filled with guilt over her rude intrusion.

How utterly unprofessional.

Yet she'd had no choice but to barge in, she assured herself. She had serious issues to reconcile, and this man, she felt certain, could help her find some of the answers she sought.

St. James returned his attention to the phone and said, "Gentlemen, I'll have to call you back. I apologize for the inconvenience." He punched the disconnect button with such force it echoed in the quiet room.

Aja gnawed her bottom lip for a moment, feeling uneasy. She'd forgotten how imposing Christian St. James could be, particularly given his tall, broad frame and dark features. He was handsome in a brooding, devilish way, with chiseled cheekbones and a slightly squared stubbornly set jaw. His emerald eyes were hypnotic. He had hair as black and shiny as an obsidian stone, and a strong, powerful physique.

Christian St. James looked like a man ready, willing and able to ravage any woman he fancied.

The wicked thought made Aja's stomach clench. Tiny pinpricks of desire targeted the juncture between her legs, causing her to squeeze her inner walls tight in hopes of staving off the prickly sensation.

Memories of the dream she'd had the night before suddenly flooded her mind. Last night, Aja had inspired Christian to save her, *and* to ravage her. But that had just been a fantasy. She suspected that, in reality, she was much too compact and certainly much too studious to fully engage his passion. Despite their mutual profession, she had no doubt a man as gorgeous as St. James preferred statuesque beauties to petite scholars.

Yet despite the fact that he hadn't made love to her in her dream, he had been incredibly possessive. Determined to make her feel as though they belonged together.

What did that mean?

She frowned. Where Christian St. James was concerned, she simply couldn't form any conclusive, or even fully coherent, thoughts.

Not that she blamed herself. She suspected every woman who came into contact with the enigmatic professor lost her head around him, no matter how worldly she might be. Aja was fairly certain every one of his female students and fellow faculty members were secretly—or perhaps not so secretly—infatuated with him. Aja most definitely understood the attraction. Even glaring at her as though she were an unwanted distraction, he still made her heart flutter and her insides quiver.

Wearing a pair of black pants and a dove-gray dress shirt, he looked refined and dangerous at the same time. His dark hair was a tad too long. The ends of the glossy, thick strands dusted the collar of his shirt, adding yet another element of intrigue to him. His face may as well have been sculpted by an artist, so perfect were his features.

The mysterious-looking man standing before her crossed his arms over his expansive chest as he presumably waited for an explanation for the unannounced interruption. Aja had yet to find her voice to provide that explanation.

Good God, the man is sexy.

She felt a sigh of longing tickle her throat, but she tamped it down.

Christian St. James was exactly the type of man Aja would want to rescue her from falling several stories, protecting her from all things evil…

Remembering the first—and most terrifying—part of her dream brought her around. She needed to find out what this devilishly handsome man had to do with her falling off a building. One that looked disturbingly similar to the faculty building they were currently in, as a matter of fact.

Aja crossed the room in quick strides. Forcing some verve into her voice, she thrust her hand out and said, "I'm Professor Aja Woods from Pembrook. Across the river. We met last spring at the Sixteenth Century Historical Symposium."

"I remember."

She still held her hand out to him. He didn't accept it. Heat tinged Aja's cheeks, but she refused to slink off. She dropped her arm to her side. She recalled he hadn't shaken her hand at the symposium, either. Perhaps the thought of touching her repulsed the eccentric professor.

Pushing aside the disturbing thought, she said, "I'm terribly sorry to interrupt your call. I'm not usually the sort to burst into a colleague's office unannounced and without consent, but I'm afraid I'm embroiled in a rather complex, potentially dire situation." She knew her expression was compelling as she added, "In other words… I need your help."

He appeared to be completely unmoved by her apology—or her precarious circumstances.

Aja rubbed her slick palms against the material of her black skirt. She licked her lips and tried to compose her thoughts. Damn, the man was intimidating. His handsome features looked practically chiseled in stone as he stared at her, wholly disinterested.

"Well?" he finally inquired in his deep tone. It held the sort of sensual tinge to it that made her nerve endings stand up and take notice.

Aja's insides clenched in a curious way; a way she'd only ever experienced one time before in her life—when Christian had spoken at the symposium. Her heart thumped hard and strong in her chest at the sight of the mysterious, aloof professor. His dark, sinful looks were enough to make her weak in the knees—and to make her almost forget the reason for her unexpected visit.

Luckily, she found the mental faculties to focus on the business at hand. She concentrated on keeping her voice steady—and also did her absolute best to keep all erotic thoughts involving Christian St. James at bay.

Summoning her inner strength again, she forged on. "Tell me, what do you know about the orphaned gypsy Ajana?" She asked the question without preamble. Without a hint of explanation as to why she would broach the topic, when discussing this particular subject matter wasn't the least bit commonplace.

An ebony eyebrow lifted again. So far, that seemed to be the only indication that he intended to listen to her, rather than have security toss her out.

He was silent for several seemingly endless moments, and Aja felt the consternation swirl around in her belly, building into full-blown panic. Maybe he really was contemplating having her forcefully removed from his office.

How humiliating would that be?

Finally—almost to her surprise and certainly to her relief—he said in a frank tone, "She's a myth. As is the lost Corte Terre *Roma* tribe of the sixteenth century from which she was supposedly orphaned."

Expelling the breath she'd been holding, Aja mimicked his stance. Folding her arms over her chest, she innately slipped into debate mode. "It sounds as though you're quite knowledgeable on this subject." As she'd hoped he would be. "And yes, some will argue she's a mythical being. Although jewelry passed down for several generations, bearing her mark, suggests otherwise. The pieces were handed down until there were no more descendants of her bloodline. At which point, they simply... vanished."

"Then how can it be proven they existed?"

"I've seen sketches of her medallions in a number of books."

St. James nodded. "Books on mythology."

"Yes."

"Mm-hmm." A look of amusement crossed his handsome face, as though he'd just proven his point that Ajana was, indeed, a mythical being. "I fail to see why you had to burst into my office and interrupt my phone call to debate whether or not Ajana and her jewelry existed."

Aja found herself irritated over his indifference. She'd thought she could engage this man in an enlightening conversation about the infamous gypsy who'd become one of the most powerful witches of her time. That clearly wasn't the case.

His disinterest unnerved her, but she fought to keep her frustration at bay. "I've sought you out, Professor St. James, because you are the only one in this country who knows more about the myths and legends of sixteenth century Europe than I do."

Christian acknowledged the accolade with a slight nod of his head. But he did not pursue the conversation further. "I was in the middle of a very important call, Professor Woods."

"Please, call me Aja." Anything else seemed too formal for the man she'd dreamed of rescuing her for the past four nights. And, following that incredible orgasm he'd managed to deliver without even laying a hand on her in reality... Well. She had to admit, she did feel an intimate connection to him now.

"Fine. *Aja*." He said her name as though it pained him to do so. "I have work to do. So if you don't mind—"

"I do mind, actually," she interjected, albeit on a nervous note. "This is important."

St. James looked surprised by her audacity. Yet he also seemed to be intrigued by it. "Well, then, by all means. Sit down." He gestured to a tall leather chair.

Aja studied him for a moment. Was it her imagination or was he merely trying to *appear* vexed by her unexpected visit?

Confused, she sank onto the supple cushion. She tried to rein in her riotous emotions. It was bad enough she was holding onto her sanity by a thin thread; it didn't help matters that Christian St. James was so sexually alluring she could barely think straight.

He waited for her to continue. He eased into his own chair, folded his arms over his chest again and gave her a challenging look. One that conveyed a clear message: whatever she had to say better be worthy of her unprofessional interruption.

Aja offered him an apologetic smile, hoping to soften him up a bit. She couldn't tell if it worked or not. His look remained impassive, at best.

She had hoped St. James would be as enthralled with the mystery of the lost artifacts as she was, but no... He remained apathetic.

Aja let out a soft sigh. Trudging on, she said, "I can prove the existence of her jewelry isn't a myth."

"How so?" he asked in a dispassionate tone.

Damn it. Did nothing pique this man's interest?

Fighting the urge to grind her teeth together in frustration, she said, "Someone has been sending me pieces from Ajana's collection. The medallions are extraordinary. And they all bear her mark. I've had a renowned gemologist at Pembrook authenticate the jewels and confirm the marks were made when the jewelry was forged, not afterward."

"Forged in the sixteenth century?"

She nodded.

St. James gave her a dubious look. "Professor Woods... Aja," he corrected. "The story of Ajana was invented centuries ago, likely by a frustrated father who couldn't get his daughter to go to sleep one night. The *Romanies* of the Corte Terre tribe—and Ajana's jewelry—never existed."

Aja stood her ground. "Treasure hunters have searched for the missing pieces from her 'mythical' collection for centuries. Five pieces, in particular, are of the greatest importance. Alone, each of the five medallions is worth a small fortune. As a collection, they're considered to be priceless antiquities, particularly because the pieces are rumored to hold mystical powers that can only be evoked when they're joined together."

"Well, then. You can sell the pieces being sent to you and retire a wealthy woman." He reached for the receiver of his phone and lifted it from the cradle. He cast a quick glance in her direction. "Are we quite through with this conversation?"

Aja wanted to throw something at him. The man was insufferable. "No, Professor St. James. We are *not* quite through with this conversation."

He set the phone down and sighed. "Call me, Christian. I insist." Though his tone suggested he'd prefer it if she simply went on her way.

Aja gnawed her lower lip for a moment. She sensed his curiosity, so why was he feigning boredom over the entire discussion? It disappointed her greatly not to have piqued his interest further.

Hers had certainly skyrocketed the past several days. Something mysterious had transpired this week. Aja had pieces of an intriguing puzzle that only needed to be fit together to solve a curious mystery.

She had received four of the five medallions rumored to possess mystical powers. Each night following the receipt of the medallions, Christian St. James appeared in her dreams to save her from a terrifying fate. Most intriguing of all, her name was a derivative of Ajana's, a fact that had mystified Aja since the first time she'd read the tale of the gypsy from the Corte Terre *Roma* tribe.

All of these factors added up to one thing: Somehow Aja was connected to the sixteenth century witch.

Was Christian?

Chapter 3

Christian studied Aja as she fidgeted in her seat, looking unsettled and anxious. It took all his willpower not to go to her and comfort her. She looked like she could use a strong arm around her shoulders to steady her.

But Christian maintained his distance, as always.

It was pure torture.

Aja stimulated his senses on every level. Intelligent, strong and beautiful, she possessed all the traits in this lifetime that had made him fall in love with her five hundred years ago.

She was young in this current life. She'd turned twenty-eight on her last birthday. This was her fourth reincarnation, and Christian found her to be just as alluring as she'd been centuries ago. Striking, in fact, in the most basic, natural way.

Her long, curly auburn hair was streaked with strands of gold. Her large amber-colored eyes were crystal clear and mesmerizing. And her body...

Christian bit back a groan of desire. Although Aja was small in stature, she had the kind of tight, curvy body that inspired erotic fantasies. Her shapely legs, slender waist and plump breasts were enough to make him hard, whether she was naked or not.

But Christian knew he wasn't allowed to touch her when she had no idea of her true identity, so his desire for her was moot. His charge was to protect her from evil, to keep her safe until she was called upon to fulfill her destiny.

The time for that drew near.

The beautiful professor sitting before him in a classic black suit had sought out his expert advice much quicker than he'd anticipated. But Aja had no idea it was almost time for the past to collide with the present.

"I'm confused as to why you're not taking me seriously." Her soft voice penetrated his thoughts.

Christian sighed. He did take her seriously. But only she could unravel the mystery of her existence. In the meantime, he had to play along, as though he didn't know her. As though they hadn't loved each other desperately five hundred years ago.

"What would you like me to say to you, Aja?"

Her amber eyes clouded. She was a brilliant woman, he knew. She'd written several intelligent papers on sixteenth century Europe in this current life. She brought a fresh, insightful approach to her work, though she had no idea the reason she was such an expert on the subject was because she'd lived during that time period.

She was also quite persistent. She reached into her small purse and extracted an intricately designed medallion. She set it on the desk before him.

"This is one of the pieces I've received," she explained. "As you can imagine, I'm rather surprised such a valuable antique has made it into my possession."

"Why?"

She stared at him, a look of incredulity on her pretty face. "For starters," she said, speaking in a tone she might reserve for a small child. It amused Christian. "This medallion alone is worth a small fortune. Second, Ajana's pieces are rumored to pass only to her descendents or those of the Corte Terre *Roma* tribe."

Christian wanted very much to tell Aja she was just that—a descendent of the "fabled" gypsy tribe. He alone knew there was nothing mythical about the Corte Terre. But she wouldn't believe him if he told her the truth of her existence and why she was the recipient of such invaluable antiques.

Instead of offering truths she was not ready to accept, Christian picked up the gold-and-sapphire medallion and pretended to inspect it closely, as though looking at it for the first time. He already knew it was authentic.

"How did you receive this?" He posed the question, despite the fact that he'd been the one to leave it for her.

"It was at work when I arrived on Monday. Four of the pieces have appeared in my office—one each day this week."

"Hmm. Perhaps you ought to consult with security at Pembrook. Seems there's a breach, if people can come and go so easily from your office."

"I don't keep it locked," she admitted. "I keep my valuables at my home office, including my old volumes and anything of historical value."

Christian was quite aware she didn't lock her door. He'd slipped in and out of her office enough times this week to know first hand. Not that a lock could deter him…

"Bit trusting of you," he commented in a soft tone.

Aja merely shrugged. "It's a small campus. Mostly honor students. I've never encountered any problems. And with finals over this week, the place is nearly deserted."

Her eyes shifted from him to take in the shelves full of books and scrolls lining his office walls. "If anyone were interested enough in sixteenth century European history to steal literature and artifacts, I imagine they'd hit your office, not mine."

He nodded. "I do have an extensive collection." Most of which were first edition works, but he didn't mention that, lest she question how he'd acquired such rare and priceless items. He couldn't exactly tell her that he'd kept them with him through the centuries he'd existed. Besides, the less he had to lie to Aja about his past, the better. The situation was complicated enough as it was.

Christian's very existence hinged on his belief that someday Aja would recall the memory of her past life, and her destiny in this new one. She would know he had watched over her for centuries, protecting her from those who wanted to harm her. But the realization was something she must come to on her own.

"So tell me," she said as her amber eyes dropped to the medallion he still held in his hand. "Am I right? Is it authentic?"

"What makes you think I would know?"

She merely scoffed at him. As though she knew *he* knew the myth of Ajana and the Corte Terre tribe was no myth at all.

But that was ridiculous. She couldn't possibly know that.

Christian studied the piece a moment longer before setting it back on the edge of his massive desk. "If it were real, Aja, why do you believe someone would leave it for you?"

The question appeared to take her aback. She stared at him a moment, her large eyes full of surprise. And something else... Hope?

"I read Ajana's story in junior high. Not exactly common reading material, I realize. But I had an affinity for myths and legends since the day I learned to read, I think."

She reached for the medallion. "Ajana was born to one of the *kris*—a tribunal leader of the highest order. His wife died during childbirth. From the first day his daughter came into the world, the gypsy leader knew she was special and destined for something beyond his comprehension."

Her thumb eased over the enormous sapphire as she spoke. Her voice held a distant tinge to it, as though she'd been transported back in time. "Ajana possessed mystical powers, the likes of which the *Roma* had never experienced. Believing it to be the right thing to do, the gypsy leader offered his daughter to the deities worshipped by the *Roma*. He believed only the Higher Beings, who have controlled the realm of *magik* since the beginning of time, could teach Ajana to harness and control her powers. And only they knew why she'd been blessed with such rare gifts."

Christian listened intently as she continued, though he knew the story well. He'd lived it, after all. And he'd been the one to pen it, immortalizing the tale for all of time.

"After much tutelage by the Elders, Ajana returned to her tribe, who resided in this—the material—world. Her charge in her first lifetime was to protect innocents from the demons roaming the countryside. The mysterious deaths of travelers and villagers were continually blamed on gypsy tribes. Ajana was tasked with vanquishing the demons before they murdered more people and created greater hatred toward the *Romanies*, who were already distrusted by society."

With a soft sigh, she set the medallion back on the desk. "Unfortunately, the demons also sought her out. They slaughtered anyone in their path as they searched for her. No one was safe. She learned that dreadful lesson first-hand, when her father was murdered."

Christian knew how great the pain had been for Ajana when demons had slain her father. She'd been so young, and she'd blamed herself for his death, believing she should have been able to protect him. But not once had she wavered from her duty, no matter how difficult it had been to continue on, following her father's death.

"Tell me about the medallions," he said in a quiet voice, wanting to know exactly how much of the tale Aja knew. He sensed she was close to the truth, close to realizing her destiny. It took all the willpower he possessed not to solve the mystery for her. Revealing her destiny to her—and before it was time—went against the restrictions imposed upon him by the deities that ruled the mystical realm Ajana had been raised in.

A world Christian had never known existed until he'd met Ajana. A parallel universe where the medieval past still existed and old-world *magik* was the reigning power; a world governed by all-powerful deities—known to Christian and Ajana as the Elders—that maintained the balance between good and evil. Unfortunately, the demons spawned in the realm of *magik* often found their way into this world and wreaked havoc on the humans' existence.

Christian was a demon, born of one of the vampires that had escaped the Elders' realm. But he had sought immortality. It had not been forced upon him. And because his purpose was a noble one, he did not prey upon the humans. He coexisted peacefully with them, protecting them, as he protected the woman sitting before him, still struggling with the peculiar situation she'd suddenly found herself embroiled in.

Aja looked lost in thought, as though carefully considering her curious predicament. And her next statement.

Christian all but held his breath, desperate to hear words she hadn't spoken in five hundred years. If only she could embrace her fate and set it in motion... then they could be reunited. Something Christian longed for above all else.

Her voice was soft, yet full of passion as she spoke. "Each medallion represents one of the magical elements—earth, air, fire, water, and spirit. When brought together in the cone of power by a witch of Ajana's strength and expertise, they'll release awesome powers."

"Yes," Christian murmured, mesmerized as always, by this bewitching woman. "Ajana risked her life to save innocent people. When she learned she had an even greater task to accomplish than that, she allowed the Elders to capture her powers in the medallions so they would not abate or weaken over the centuries. She was continually reincarnated so her spirit and essence could live on until the deities summoned her to fulfill her true destiny."

Aja eyed him with what Christian recognized as hope. "You believe in the tale, don't you?" she asked. "Despite what you said earlier about her existence being a myth."

Christian shrugged noncommittally.

"Tell me," she said in a breathless, compelling tone. "Do you believe Ajana is now trying to reclaim her medallions so she may fulfill her destiny?"

Yes!

Christian forced himself to hold back the truth. He could not reveal that he was trying to help reunite Ajana with her medallions.

It was almost time to set the spell in motion that would return Ajana's powers to her. He had sensed the change coming, knew the time drew near.

"The question, Aja, is do *you* believe it?"

He could see by the quick rise and fall of her chest that she was caught up in the story, swept away by the mystique of it. Not just because of her interest in mythology, but perhaps because she now had four of the five medallions in her possession.

Christian wanted to prompt her further, to help her bridge the gap between the past and the present. But he could do no more than wait as patiently as possible for her to make the correlation herself.

In his mind, he urged her to seek and find the truth. To accept what was inconceivable to her, but which was, in truth, a blatant fact. She was so close... he could feel it.

But then Aja's eyes dropped to the medallion, and a frown slanted her plump lips. "I'm not her," she whispered. "Nor am I a surrogate. This is all a bizarre mistake. Or a terrible prank."

The words and the certainty in Aja's voice took Christian by surprise. He let out his breath, not even knowing before that moment he'd been holding it, hoping she'd accept the truth.

Damn it.

His gut wrenched. He'd thought she was so close to making the discovery. But, of course, she couldn't fathom being the heroine in the immortalized tale. She was much too sensible in this lifetime to comprehend the extraordinary past she'd once lived.

Christian sighed despondently. He was back to playing the disinterested, unmoved history professor. "Well, then. I guess that concludes our conversation."

"I understand." But she looked disappointed. Christian couldn't tell if she was merely disenchanted with him, or if she had held out hope she was somehow connected to the fabled witch, only needing confirmation from him to reconcile the issue.

She stood to go, her gaze remaining on him. Her beautiful eyes searched his for Lord only knew what. "I thought you'd be intrigued by all of this."

"I am, but I still fail to see the point of this debate." Faith drove him to prompt her further.

Aja continued to look dejected. And irritated. "You're reputed to be fascinated by European myths and legends, despite the fact that you often renounce their validity."

"I'm a historian," he said simply.

"As am I. Yet..." She shrugged her slender shoulders and sighed. "That doesn't mean the impossible doesn't intrigue me."

Christian had to know why she was so compelled to continue this discussion, why the topic piqued her interest so. "What if the tale of Ajana were real?" he inquired. "What if the jewelry being left in your office were real pieces from her collection? What would it mean to you?"

Aja's beautiful face lit up when she smiled. "It would mean she lived."

Again, Christian's breath caught in his throat. "And what significance would that bear?"

Her amber eyes shimmered in the soft glow of his desk lamp. "I suppose, above all else, I always found Ajana to be very heroic. Without her powers, she became defenseless against evildoers. Yet she willingly put herself in grave danger, and sacrificed her first lifetime, because she cherished the deities she served. I admire her strength, her selflessness, and her loyalty to those she considered to be her family. She was fiercely protective of those she loved."

She dropped her eyes, seemingly unable to continue holding his gaze. "I'm not exactly a risk-taker, myself. I've led a very sheltered, conservative life. I really can't imagine doing anything quite so brave, experiencing such wild adventures." She paused a moment, before continuing in a quiet voice. "Nor have I ever experienced the kind of love Ajana knew in her lifetime."

Christian came forward in his chair as he studied the beautiful woman before him. Aja had no idea of the inner strength and loyalty she possessed because she'd never had to call forth her true essence. But the last comment she made, and the hint of loneliness that crept into her soft voice, caught his interest above all else. "You found the part of her story, regarding her companion, to be...?"

"Terribly romantic," she said on a sigh.

Christian felt something deep inside him come to life. For so long, he'd kept his love for this woman buried deep. To hear her speak of the passion they'd shared was both tormenting and encouraging at the same time. "How so?"

Aja let out a soft laugh, as though embarrassed. "Her companion was strong enough to help her vanquish demons. He was neither threatened by her powers nor fearful of them. Later, he became her protector. He sacrificed all that he possessed and all that he could come to be in that lifetime, so he could ensure no harm would come to Ajana over the centuries. The deities allowed him to seek immortality. He lived day after day, year after year, century after century, following Ajana's spirit each time it returned to earth, keeping her safe. But he was never able to tell her of the love they once shared."

"He lived with nothing more than the memory of that love," Christian added, speaking as though the story had a conclusion, when it did not. "He could not hold her, he could not divulge to her the love they had for each other. His duty was to stand guard over her spirit and protect her from evil, until the Elders summoned her."

"But the deities could not guarantee she would remember her past life. Or him, for that matter," Aja added on a sad note. "And there was no guarantee she would be able to reclaim her powers or that she would even survive the spell to restore them."

Christian swallowed hard. He knew all of this. Yet he had sacrificed his present and his future to be a part of something greater than anything he could fathom. To help Ajana fulfill her destiny… it was worth any consequence.

"And so the tale ended," Aja said. "With her protector watching over her spirit, never knowing if they would ever be reunited."

"You're a hopeless romantic," Christian said in a low voice.

Soft pink patches stained Aja's otherwise perfect complexion. "Yes, I suppose I am." Her hopeful smile returned. "Have you ever loved a woman so much, Christian, that you would make any sacrifice to protect her?"

The question jolted Christian, as did the interest in her large eyes. He stood and turned away from Aja. Crossing to the far wall, he mindlessly selected a book. He feigned great interest in it. "No, Aja," he lied to her, though he hated to do so. "And I can't imagine a woman could trust a man so much that she would literally hand over her spirit to him."

"He wasn't just *any* man, Christian," she argued in a defensive tone. "He was the man Ajana loved with all her heart and soul. She loved him more than any material possession she coveted during her lifetime, and she trusted him beyond all doubt to protect her and watch over her."

Christian couldn't help but smile, though he didn't reveal his pleasure to Aja.

So, her soul had survived the centuries. She still possessed the loyal heart he'd come to love and cherish for all of time.

"Well," she said, her voice strained. "I've taken up enough of your time. I apologize, again, for the intrusion."

He kept his back turned until he heard the soft click of the door as it closed behind her.

Christian returned to his desk and dropped the book on top of it. He sank into his chair, still grinning.

His Ajana lived.

Chapter 4

Really, it shouldn't bother her.

Aja knew she was being ridiculous, yet the mere fact that Christian St. James thought so little of true love irked her.

What does his opinion of the subject matter, anyway?

Perhaps, Aja reasoned, she'd conjured up some sort of knight-in-shining armor fantasy, starring Christian St. James, because she'd found him intriguing when she'd met him at the symposium. Perhaps it was because he shared a mutual passion for sixteenth century history that she'd selected him as her dream savior.

It all became very clear to her as she stalked down the cobblestone pathway leading from the faculty building to the parking lot. She'd invented an invisible, terrifying force to torment her and a hero to save her.

A classic fantasy.

She rolled her eyes as she passed under the dim lighting of the antique lamp posts that lined the walkway. Aja's subconscious mind found the brooding professor attractive, and she was now fantasizing about him.

She nearly laughed out loud at her own foolish behavior. He probably considered her to be a complete loon. She'd gone on and on about a myth and told him she'd been receiving antiquities he barely even believed in, if at all. She had yet to determine whether he'd simply been humoring her toward the end of their conversation.

So much for having a professional conversation or a working relationship with a worthy colleague. She'd be lucky if he ever spoke with her again. In fact, she wouldn't be surprised if he steered clear of her at the next symposium. Why shouldn't he? She'd sounded like a sappy romantic in his office, not an intelligent scholar.

Unfortunately, she'd only barely scratched the surface of what vexed her. These damned antique pieces, she thought as she considered the one she'd stuffed back into her purse, where the other three were ensconced. She couldn't stop thinking about them. Or wondering when the fifth one would arrive—if it arrived at all.

Aja crossed the parking lot to her car. She searched in her purse for the keyless remote, but drew up short before she reached her SUV. The silence surrounding her was deafening, to the point of being eerie.

She lifted her eyes and glanced about her. There wasn't a soul in sight. Nor was there a breath of wind. The air was still and cool. Much more so than it should be on a balmy, late-spring evening.

Aja sensed something evil lurking nearby.

A shiver raced up her spine. She'd never felt so chilled to the bone. Yet there was nothing tangible to alarm her. No snapping of twigs from booted feet, no heavy breathing from a crazed stalker. She felt no human presence, no physical threat. But Aja knew she was being watched.

She turned to stare up at the tall brick building she'd just left. It was dark, save for a few dim lights burning in faculty offices. Her eyes lifted to the rooftop. The building was historic and elegant. Oddly, it felt... familiar.

Without knowing what possessed her, Aja retraced her steps, heading back to the entrance of the building. A peculiar sense of desperation and intrigue gripped her. She had no idea what propelled her forward, but she took the elevator to the top floor nonetheless. Powerless against whatever force drove her, she located the stairs to the roof and ascended them. She pushed open the heavy metal door and stepped out onto the rooftop.

Panic seized her.

She'd been here before. In her dreams.

This is the building.

The one from which she'd continued to fall the past several nights.

Reality hit her hard, bringing her around. She bolted for the door and pulled on the lever. It was locked. Aja bit back a desperate cry of fear.

What had compelled her to come up here in the first place? What mystical force had made her ascend those steps?

She had no idea. But she did know she was in danger. She could feel it, raw and palpable.

Her throat felt tight and swollen. She wanted to scream, but somehow she knew no one would hear her. Or rescue her.

Aja turned from one direction to the next, taking in the immediate area, searching for an escape.

She gasped loudly when a large hand clasped her arm. But she'd expected something like that to happen. She knew some sort of demon would force her to the edge of the building.

Fear and panic welled inside her, but Aja fought for control. "Who are you?" she demanded.

The man holding her captive was... handsome. Shockingly so. Aja shook her head, trying to clear the muddled thoughts now racing through her mind. He was no demon. He was an attractive, well-groomed man, who appeared close in age to her.

But he must be a demon, she rationalized, for he was dragging her across the roof to the ledge.

The non-existent wind suddenly made its presence known. A gentle breeze swept across the rooftop. The cool air seemed to build in strength with every step that drew Aja closer to the edge of the building. Within seconds, a violent gush of wind tore across the night sky, whipping all around them. A flurry of leaves and other debris filled the air as a violent storm suddenly rolled in.

The man holding her, dragging her across the rooftop, paused to relish the spectacle. His white teeth gleamed in the moonlight. "Ah, yes," he said with obvious delight. "The time is now."

Terrified, Aja tried to wrest her arm from his tight grasp. "Please let me go," she begged.

His attention turned back to her. "You must not struggle."

He forced her to step up to the concrete lip encompassing the top of the massive brick structure. He snatched her purse from her and dumped the contents onto the rooftop. Then he extracted another medallion—the fifth one, Aja realized—from his pocket and added it to the collection.

"You've found your destiny," he said to her as he gripped her shoulders and spun her around, so she faced the small campus and the river beyond it.

What she'd *found* was the ledge of the building, which she teetered on. She stared seven stories down at the ground where she would land if he let go of her.

Aja cried out.

"I'm not going to hurt you," he said in a calm voice.

Aja nearly choked on her fear. "What do you want?"

"I want you to trust me," he implored in a compelling voice. "The way you trust *him*."

"Him, *who*?" She couldn't even begin to fathom what this man spoke of... what bizarre, terrifying game she had suddenly, unwittingly become a part of.

One of his powerful arms slid around her waist. "You just need to stand here a moment longer."

"If you want my wallet, just take it."

"I don't want your money."

"I have a really nice car," she said in desperation. "Keys were in my purse. It's the silver SUV in the visitor's parking lot."

The man chuckled. "You amuse me. But I don't drive."

A crackle in the air made her gasp. Then a peculiar sense of calm crept over Aja, chasing away her fear and settling deep into her bones. She was able to pull in a full breath and her body suddenly stopped trembling and swaying.

Something very strange was about to occur. She could feel it in the air. It prickled her skin and made the hairs on the back of her neck stand on end. Yet, she felt... ready for it.

"Who are you?" she asked again.

"My name is Draken."

And, as if his name alone evoked mystical spirits, the early-evening moon disappeared behind a patch of thick, ominous clouds, which had filled the night sky in the blink of an eye. Lightning speared the darkness and thunder crackled loudly.

"Holy Christ." Aja gasped.

Draken chuckled again. "Trust me, your Christ has nothing to do with this. Now, hold still."

"Like hell." Whatever was about to happen, she really didn't want any part of it. Aja struggled against Draken, but he had a powerful body and a strong grip on her.

"Don't fight me," he warned again. "I need to concentrate." He began to chant in a strange dialect Aja had never heard before, nor could she decipher any of the words he muttered.

The wind continued to whip all around them. Thunder clapped in her ears and flashes of light all but blinded her. Hazy streaks of purple, gold and pink filled her vision as a three-pronged spear of lightning pierced the clouds and struck her and Draken.

Aja cried out from the sizzling pain that lanced through her body. One long, seemingly endless scream echoed in her ears as her body vibrated from the electrical jolt.

When the flash of lightning dimmed and the vibrations in her body eased, she realized Draken had released her. Aja swayed unsteadily. She felt woozy and dizzy. Her breathing was abnormally slow and her heart seemed to be barely beating.

She was dying. Slowly, from the inside out, she guessed.

The man who'd called himself Draken had collapsed onto the rooftop. Aja assumed he was dead, as she should be. She'd just been struck by lightning, after all.

Several minutes passed. She regained her footing, felt steady on the ledge. The wind died down. The clouds retreated and the thunder no longer roared in the quiet night.

The storm had passed.

Slowly, the burning inside Aja abated until she no longer felt singed to the core. A peculiar sensation began to seep through her veins, making her feel rejuvenated. Reborn. Every nerve ending danced and her skin tingled with life. A curious sense of renewal flowed through her, warm and wonderful.

She pulled in a full breath, then let it out slowly. She felt strong. Powerful, even.

Suddenly, a second burst of lightning penetrated the darkness, scaring the hell out of her. Aja jumped out of its path just as the bolt struck the very spot in which she'd been standing. The flash of light temporarily blinded her again. Aja stumbled backward as the heat from the lightning rod seared her skin. She lost her footing and swayed on her tall heels. She scarcely had the breath to scream as her body pitched over the edge of the building.

She fell fast, her arms flailing helplessly, her legs making scissor-like slashes in the cold night air.

Her dream was coming to fruition. Only this time, there was no one to save her. Christian's strong hand did not penetrate the thick fog. He didn't reach for her. He didn't rescue her.

Aja's body hit the cobblestone path alongside the faculty building and she lay there, breathless, wheezing, darkness descending fast.

She was going to die.

Chapter 5

"Aja!" Her name escaped Christian's lips on a painful rush of air. He sprinted across the courtyard in several lightning quick strides and dropped to his knees beside the limp, broken body of the woman he'd been destined to protect.

He cradled her in his arms and felt the life begin to drift from her. Christian's entire being responded to the sight of Aja, dying in his arms. His insides constricted and it felt as though a powerful hand gripped his very essence and squeezed it tight. Fear racked his body as he watched the blood ooze from Aja's parted lips.

Her eyes were narrowed slits as she stared up at him. She gasped for air, but wasn't able to draw in a full breath.

Christian felt rage and sorrow mingle within him and course through his veins. He stared up at the ledge of the tall building and found Draken standing there, a triumphant grin on his face. Christian cursed his name, but Draken merely laughed. A moment later, Draken teleported himself to the courtyard, standing mere yards from Christian, his arms crossed over his chest.

Draken's victory would be short-lived, though.

"What the hell where you trying to do?" Christian demanded on a low growl.

"I invoked the spell to return her powers. I now possess half of them," Draken's confident voice echoed all around Christian. "She belongs to me now."

"*Never*," Christian growled.

"We are joined in a way you will never understand, vampire."

"No! She's not yours." His gaze returned to Aja. Her lips quivered, her eyelids fluttered. She was fighting to stay alive, but he could feel her strength diminishing. "The spell isn't complete."

Draken scoffed. "I felt the change."

"You fool," Christian spat. His words were soft, but he knew Draken could hear him. "If it were complete, she wouldn't be lying in my arms, dying."

Draken's gloating ceased instantly. "She can't die," he insisted, his voice full of panic. "I can't rule without her. I need her!"

Christian cast a menacing look at him. "You'll have her over my dead body. Which, by the way, will never happen."

"Give her to me," Draken implored. "Let me complete the spell."

"Returning her powers to her was a one-shot deal, you dolt. You've ruined her chances to fully reclaim them." Christian's gaze returned to Aja. Her eyes had rolled upward. Blood spilled over her lips and across her jaw. Her breathing was shallow and her body lay limp, almost lifeless in his arms.

Christian would make Draken suffer for this. Of all the sinister, greedy things the sorcerer could do, taking Aja from him was the worst. He'd make Draken pay for the rest of eternity.

"You can save her."

Christian bit back a groan of pain and angst. "I can do nothing now. She's only partially changed. And her powers are too weak right now. She can't survive."

"She can!" Draken insisted on a harsh breath. "And you know it. You alone can save her. Damn it! Why are you even hesitating?"

Christian shot the greedy sorcerer a menacing look. "I won't even entertain the idea." Shock and dismay pierced his soul.

"Would you prefer she die?"

If Christian weren't cradling Aja in his arms, he'd have caused bodily—albeit temporary—harm to Draken. Instead, he ground his teeth together for a moment before he growled low and deep. "And damn us for all eternity?"

"*You'll* be damned for all eternity for going against the wishes of the Elders. She won't. Only partial eternity."

Christian closed his eyes and cursed his own fate. He didn't want to consider the possibility of which Draken spoke. Yet when he opened his eyes and gazed down at Aja, he saw her golden skin turn a pale, dull gray. He knew he had no choice. He couldn't let her die.

He *refused* to let her die.

"You've got about thirty seconds left, vampire. Do it!"

Christian wanted to scream with maddened rage that he was even considering turning Aja. She wasn't as strong as Ajana had been centuries ago. She was young and fragile—a woman of the modern world, not the less civilized world they'd known half a millennium ago. Plus, it went against the rules imposed upon him by the deities that ruled her realm.

Christian's fingers grazed her cool skin. He could feel the breath and the life and the spirit leaving her.

He couldn't let her go.

So he did the unthinkable. In the centuries he'd followed her spirit, he'd never turned her, never infected her with the vampire virus.

Tonight, he would do just that.

He tilted her head away from him, exposing the long graceful line of her neck. His fangs sank into her cool flesh before he gave himself a chance to think twice. He drank her blood, pulling it into his mouth, swallowing it down. When he'd nearly drained her, he released her flesh.

Her limp body slumped against him. He would feed her now. Give her strength. Make her a part of him.

But Aja would never be just a vampire. What coursed through her veins was a mystical power that would mingle with his vampire blood. She would be part witch and part vampire. Neither fully immortal nor all-powerful, because the spell was not complete. Nor would it ever be.

One day, Aja would die. As she always did.

The only difference was that after her next passing, she would never return to him.

Chapter 6

Aja felt like hell. Every inch of her body ached. Even her brain hurt. Her eyes, shrouded behind her lids, stung. An obnoxious ringing filled her ears. Her throat was dry and swollen, and her heart felt odd. She lifted her right hand from beside her and dropped it over her chest. She frowned, even though that simple motion pained her. The beating of her heart was faint and much too slow to be normal.

She eased onto her side and forced her eyes open. Her vision was blurred. She could see no farther than a few inches in front of her face. She heard voices, but couldn't make out any words. She had no idea where she was, how she'd gotten here or—more importantly—why she was still alive.

She'd fallen off the roof of a seven-story building and landed on a cobblestone path. And though her body ached, she knew innately not a single bone was broken.

But how could that be?

She slumped back against the pile of pillows on the bed and closed her eyes. It was too painful to try to focus on anything. Too painful to think.

⁂

The next time Aja awoke, she was ravenous. An overwhelming hunger consumed her like never before. Her eyes flew open and she let out a low growl. Without even assessing her immediate surroundings—she still had no idea where she was—Aja left the room and prowled the hallway, an acute sense of smell and keen gut instinct guiding her. She stepped into a large kitchen and the scent of fresh blood filled her nose. Her stomach clenched in a tight knot of need.

Aja lifted a mug from a coffee warmer. Without a second thought or a moment of hesitancy or reservation, she drained every last drop of warm blood that had filled the cup. Within seconds, a heady, euphoric sensation coursed through every inch of her. Her skin tingled and her insides vibrated from the wicked pleasure shimmying through her veins.

For a moment, Aja experienced the most erotic, sensual feelings washing over her, consuming her, making her insides throb and pulse with life.

But then realization dawned. Her body began to reject the blood as violently as her mind did. Her eyes widened as her hand flew to her mouth, covering it. Something vile and unholy welled inside her. Her stomach clenched tightly, her throat constricted. Aja rushed to the sink as she began to gag. Painful, body-racking convulsions took over her body.

She gripped the edge of the counter and leaned over the sink, eager to expel the contents inside her. But the blood didn't come up. Instead, it flowed through her veins, searing her insides, making her hot with fever.

Choking and sputtering, Aja tried to cry out for help. But no sound escaped her lips. Her eyes burned and large tears pooled in them before seeping out the sides and sliding down her scorching hot cheeks.

Oh God! Please help me!

She screamed in her mind, over and over again, because she had no voice to plead out loud. Her throat had seized up and she could barely pull in a shallow breath. She wheezed and coughed.

What the hell had possessed her to drink *blood*?

The mere thought of what she'd just done evoked the most wretched sensations inside her. But emptying the contents of her stomach was clearly not an option.

As Aja tried to process everything that had happened to her since her visit to Christian St. James' office, another mysterious shift occurred deep within her. Images and voices from the past suddenly assaulted her mind. A near-blinding stab of pain pierced her brain and made her cry out as she fell to the floor, momentarily paralyzed by the violent throbbing in her head.

Squeezing her eyes shut, she tried to force all thoughts from her head, but they invaded every crack and crevice of her being. In her mind's eye, she saw several lifetimes flash like a movie trailer. She heard the voices of the people she'd once loved... Her father. Her tribe members. The Elders. Christian...

Aja gasped as her head thrashed from side to side on the kitchen floor. The sensations that suddenly flooded her body overwhelmed her. Pain, joy, heartbreak, fear, anger, elation, ecstasy. One moment she was screaming with maddened rage, the next she was laughing hysterically. Finally, she broke out in body-racking sobs. Heaped on the cool tile floor, she wept for all of her past lives and the people she'd loved.

While she still lay crumpled on the kitchen floor, the intense sensations slowly ebbed and the vividness of the memories abated. She struggled to pull in a full, steadying breath. Her eyes stung from her tears, her throat was sore from her screams. Her mouth quivered and she sniffled loudly as she pushed strands of damp hair from her face and swiped at the wet patches on her cheeks.

The sound of bare feet on the tile caught her attention.

Aja lifted her head. Christian stood before her, dressed only in a pair of black jeans. The rest of his body was gloriously naked. Her sore eyes took in every inch of his hard muscles, long lines, and golden skin. He had a perfectly sculpted chest, with solid, well-defined pectoral muscles and small, enticing nipples. His skin was smooth and tempting. His rigid abdominal muscles and flat stomach gave way to lean hips and powerful thighs. He was breathtaking.

Aja's lips curled slightly, though she was too weak to manage a full smile.

Christian knelt down next to her and lifted hair from her face, pushing it away from her cheeks and forehead.

"Are you alright?" His voice was full of concern and uncertainty.

She gave a slight nod of her head. "Yes. I think so. I... I remember you," she said in a soft voice. It hurt to speak, and the soreness of her throat was audible in her raspy tone. "I remember..."

"Everything?" Christian asked as he inched closer to her. He studied her carefully for a moment. "Do you remember everything, Aja?"

"Yes." She reached a shaky hand out to him, placed it on his cheek. "I remember my father. The Elders. You." She stared at him, shocked and relieved at the same time. "It worked, Christian. My memories returned to me, along with my... *Oh.*" A sharp breath escaped her as a dark chill worked its way up her spine. "Oh, Chris. Something's not right." She searched her memories and quickly hit upon her sudden source of consternation. Her gaze lifted and locked with his. "I don't possess my full powers, do I?"

Christian's jaw tightened. "No, sweetheart. You don't." His dark eyes reflected his dismay. "Draken stole half of them."

"Oh, Chris..." Her hand dropped from his cheek. She tried to make heads or tails of what had recently transpired, but her thoughts were still a bit fuzzy. Knowing the past and the present would all fall into place when the throbbing in her head subsided, she forced herself not to worry about anything just yet. The spell to return her powers had worked. Her memories had been unbound. And now, she was with Christian. Her beloved. She smiled up at him. "I had dreams about you this week. As though I subconsciously knew you were trying to reach me."

His fingers smoothed over her flushed skin, gently caressing her forehead and cheek. "I've waited so long for this moment."

Aja's smile faded. "I know. Christian, I'm so sorry for all you've been through." She leaned toward him and flung her arms around his neck. He held her in a tight embrace, and Aja finally felt whole again. Her loneliness and the uncertainty of her place in the world instantly vanished. She knew exactly where she belonged. With Christian.

"I've missed you so much, Aja," he whispered, his voice strained. His arms tightened around her, holding her close to him.

Emotion welled inside Aja. Tears filled her eyes again. The joy of being reunited with Christian mingled with her remorse that he had spent centuries waiting for this moment.

"I'm here now," she said. Working her way out of his strong embrace, she looked deep into his beautiful green eyes. Her hand rested on his cheek again. "Christian, I love you. I have always loved you. I always will love you. It's an emotion I hold deep in my soul. Nothing will ever change that."

A fine mist clouded his eyes. "Aja..." His head dipped and his lips brushed over hers. Softly at first. Almost tentatively. She felt the emotion that he briefly held back. They knew each other intimately, though, and the gentle kiss quickly turned to something darker. Desire welled within Aja as Christian gathered her in his arms again and held her to him. Their lips parted in the same instant and their tongues sought each other, tangling, twisting, teasing. Heat seared her insides as Christian drew out her passion, commanding it with his own desire.

Though her memories had lain dormant for five hundred years, her love for Christian was an inherent part of her. Their souls were connected. They belonged to each other.

Aja's heart swelled with love as the passion arced between them, like an invisible stream of energy. Everything inside Aja sprang to life. Though she knew there were many unanswered questions she ought to ask, so much that she needed to concentrate on in order to better understand her destiny, the only thoughts that consumed her mind—her entire being—were of Christian.

She felt raw with need and an intense yearning to get as close to him as possible, closer than she was, even now, in his tight embrace. The desire gripping her was stronger than anything Aja had ever experienced. Fire roared through her body as lust and longing welled inside her to an almost unbearable degree.

Her fingers tangled in his glossy, obsidian hair and she held his head to hers, not wanting their impassioned kiss to end. Ever.

The familiarity of his touch warmed her heart. She knew this man, intimately. She'd known him for longer than she'd existed in this particular lifetime. She'd known him for centuries.

She didn't question how she'd ended up at Christian's house tonight. The last thing she remembered about the evening was falling seven stories, after Draken had stolen a good portion of her powers. She didn't even question the changes she felt inside her body, including her newfound appetite for warm blood.

She simply gave herself over to the desire building inside her.

Aja longed to feel Christian's mouth and hands on her body.

As though she'd spoken the words out loud, his hands slid around to the front of her and his fingers worked the buttons of the crisp white shirt she wore—Christian's shirt. It fell open and he broke the kiss. His eyes lowered, taking in her naked body for several long moments. A soft groan escaped his lips. The sound—and Christian's reaction to her—heightened her arousal.

Aja shimmied out of the shirt and let it drop to the floor beside her. She wanted no barriers between them. Christian stood and held a hand out to her. Helping her to her feet, he continued to gaze at her, his eyes filled with lust and love. Aja stood before him, naked, her skin flushed with heat from his smoldering gaze.

His large hands smoothed over her flesh at the curve of her waist. He eased her toward him, until their bodies melded together. He let out a long breath. She could feel his body tremble as the tips of her breasts rested below the hard ledge of his pectoral muscles. His hands moved over her body, up her ribcage, across her back, down to her bare bottom.

"Oh, yes, Christian." Aja sighed against his chest. "Touch me."

Christian's fingertips pressed into the delicate flesh of her bottom as he cupped both cheeks in his hands. He pulled her tightly to him, so his erection nestled against her belly through the thick material of his jeans. She could feel his heat and the hard length of him, despite the clothing he wore.

"It's been forever," he whispered into her hair. "Too long since I've touched you, Aja."

She knew what he was saying to her. His need was great, his desire overwhelming. The thought sent a delicious jolt of pleasure chasing through her thrumming body. The rapacious need inside her intensified.

"I need you just as much," she assured him.

She felt Christian's muscles tense all around her. He bent his head to hers and captured her mouth in a possessive kiss. He took several steps forward until he'd pushed her up against the edge of the granite counter. His tongue delved deep into her mouth and tangled with hers. His hands swept over her body, to her full breasts. He filled his palms with her flesh and teased the hard centers with his thumbs.

Aja wrenched her mouth free of his and gasped for air as desire tore through her.

Christian growled, low and deep. "You want me, don't you, Aja?"

"Oh, yes," she said on a heavy breath.

He lowered his head and flicked his tongue over a puckered nipple. Aja felt the room tilt. Her insides burned with need and desire. The sensations racing through her grew more powerful with every quick stroke of Christian's tongue on her tight nipples. Her fingers curled into his strong biceps and her head fell back as he began to ravage her body.

Aja wanted him to have full access to every inch her. She wanted him to feast on her flesh and drive himself deep inside her body.

But she knew Christian would take his time pleasuring her before he sought his own release.

She felt her body go into sensory overload as Christian's mouth worked its way over her hot skin. His lips and tongue skimmed her belly, his teeth nipped at the rim of her navel.

Aja tried to focus. He desperately wanted her, she could sense it. But he was trying to keep his passion in check, she could feel his restraint.

"Don't hold back," she whispered. "Please. It's been so long, Christian. We both need this."

He dropped to a knee before her. Christian's firm lips and moist tongue slid up her inner thigh until his mouth reached the juncture between her legs. Aja let out a sharp cry as he licked her swollen flesh. His thumbs parted her outer lips and his mouth covered her. He stroked her clit with his tongue before drawing the sensitive knot against his teeth.

Erotic pleasure consumed Aja. Her hips bucked against Christian as she pressed herself to his mouth.

Christian pushed two long fingers deep inside her as he continued to lick and suck her swollen nub. Aja cried out as a powerful orgasm rocked her body, quick and unexpected. The waves of sensations flooded her veins, making her tremble and vibrate from the inside out.

Christian did not let up. He pushed a third finger into her throbbing pussy, filling her. His tongue pleasured her clit as his fingers pumped in and out of her. Aja's heart slammed into her chest. She'd barely felt its beat earlier, but now it thundered inside her and her pulse raged in her ears. She whimpered and cried as the sensations built again, so much more powerful and consuming than anything she'd ever felt.

She wanted more. *Needed* more. The desperation gripping her terrified and thrilled her at the same time.

She fought for a full breath. All the while, Christian lifted her higher and higher.

He stroked her faster, harder, obviously fueled by her response to him. Aja felt the shattering inside her again as another climax tore through her body.

"Oh, yes!" she screamed. Her body clenched violently, her inner muscles contracting around Christian's fingers as he continued to plunge deep inside her, drawing out every last bit of pleasure.

As she gasped for air, Christian stood to his full, imposing height. Her sex begged for more.

Reaching out for Christian, she gripped his strong arms to help steady herself. Her trembling legs threatened to give out at any minute.

It seemed to take a short eternity for Aja to catch her breath. Finally, she said, "I think that's the quickest you've ever made me come."

Christian's handsome face was a mask of hard angles. He was holding back his intense need for her; it seemed to war with his tender side. Aja smoothed a finger over his furrowed brow. "Don't fight this, Chris. Don't treat me like I'm fragile. I want you," she said with conviction. "Please make love to me. And for God's sake, don't hold back."

Chapter 7

Christian scooped her up in his arms and carried her down the long hallway to his bedroom. His house was an elaborate work of art, decorated with sixteenth century artifacts—relics from their time period.

He placed her carefully on the bed, then stood over her, once again taking in every inch of her naked body. Excitement hummed through her. Her gaze dropped to his hand as he flicked the button at his waist. He slid the zipper down its track and then pushed the jeans down his hips and legs.

Aja's pulse raced. Her eyes drifted slowly up his powerful thighs to his sex. Her mouth watered. The man was more glorious than she remembered. Fully erect, his thick cock brought back too many erotic memories to process at once. In her mind, she heard their moans of ecstasy, saw their twisted, tangled limbs, felt their two hearts beating as one.

Aja lifted her gaze to Christian's. He saw it, too. Everything in her mind, he saw. He had the gift, she only had to allow him to use it on her. Aside from the Elders, she and Draken were the only ones capable of blocking Christian from intruding on their thoughts, though Aja had only ever used her ability to shut him out when she wanted to surprise him.

Christian's chest rose and fell sharply. "Christ," he mumbled. "Where do I start?"

Aja grinned up at him. "So many positions, so little time?"

Christian's jaw clenched. "We have time."

Aja's gaze returned to his erection. She licked her lips longingly. She came up on her knees before him. "In the old days, you never denied me anything I wanted."

"I would never deny you now." His voice was low, thick with desire.

"Good. Because I am dying to taste you, Christian." Her palm smoothed over the tip of his penis and he jerked violently from the intimate contact.

Christian's eyes narrowed on her. "Don't make me come, Aja. I intend to make love to you for a very long time."

"Promise?"

A tight grin touched his lips. "Oh, yes. I've waited much too long."

"I know." She could feel his tortured soul. It was a part of her. She knew his every want, his every desire... his every pain. They were joined in the most intimate, intricate way. Two hearts that beat as one when they were together, two souls tormented when they were apart.

Aja's fingers wrapped around his thick shaft. She felt a familiar shock of excitement rush through her body from head to toe. She'd missed this man. For five hundred years they'd been apart. For her, the longing only intensified now that they were reunited.

For Christian, she knew, the torment went on and on, century after century. For half a millennium he'd had to wait for this moment. Though The Powers That Be had allowed Aja to return to this world after each of her passings, always in the exact same form, her memories of Christian and their past life together had always been locked away, out of her reach.

Christian, however, had carried their love with him all this time.

Aja knew what loomed on the horizon for her now. Why the bound memories had been released. She had a job to do. The Elders called on her to fulfill her destiny and secure the legacy of their people. A destiny she would rightfully execute.

But not tonight. Tonight, she belonged only to Christian.

She leaned toward him and slid her tongue over the tip of his cock, eliciting a low growl from her sexy vampire. His fingers twined in her curly hair and he closed his eyes. Aja sighed happily. Pleasuring Christian was a gift unto itself. It filled her heart with joy and made her feel whole.

She took him deep inside her mouth and sucked hard.

"Aja." He said her name on such a lustful groan it made her inner walls clench.

She released him from the warm depths of her mouth and lay back on the bed, her legs spread in anticipation of joining with him.

Christian stared hungrily at her. They shared an insatiable lust for each other. Even before Christian had become a vampire, he'd had a monstrous sexual appetite. Aja's own passion had equaled his. She was strong because of her people, and more than capable of meeting Christian's demands. He could be rough, she knew. Sometimes she purposely sparked the dark side of his lust. It excited her to have him crazed with desire and in desperate need of her.

Aja couldn't take her eyes off of him as he settled between her parted legs. "The moment I saw you at the symposium, I fell a little bit in love with you," she admitted. His tongue laved a tight nipple and she let out a low sigh. "And then yesterday, in your office, my desire for you deepened." She considered her innate response to him, then let out a soft laugh. Her fingers twined in the silky strands that brushed her bare skin. "How could I not fall for you? You are devastatingly handsome, Christian. And so intelligent. Do you remember the first time we met in this lifetime?"

He lifted his head and stared at her. "We both spoke at the symposium, and afterward, Dean Albright introduced us."

She nodded. "He was in awe of you, I could tell. I was a bit jealous because I was the resident expert on European history until you came along. Albright was very disappointed you didn't join the Pembrook faculty."

"Pembrook didn't need me on staff. They had you."

Aja smiled. She pushed long strands of obsidian hair from his face and said, "I was disappointed, too. I thought it would be nice to have an office down the hall from you, rather than across the river."

"Oh?"

Aja thought about the lifetimes she had experienced. She had met Christian in all of them. "I've fallen in love with you in every lifetime I've lived. Don't you know that?"

"I couldn't read your thoughts when your memories were locked away, Aja. But now that you mention it, you always did have sort of a dreamy expression on your face when you looked at me."

"I'm not surprised. But you never tried to win my heart. Why is that?"

Christian's head dipped again. His lips glided over her skin, teasing her areola and then the outer swell her breast. His mouth moved over her stomach and his tongue delved into her naval, causing an erotic jolt to pierce her between the legs. He glanced up at her with a satisfied look.

In a breathless voice, she asked, "Why didn't you try to be with me, Chris?"

He shook his head. "I couldn't. It's forbidden, Aja. My job is to watch over you, to protect you. The Elders required me to keep my distance. Stand guard over you at night and keep evil spirits and demons away." He shifted so that his mouth could move lower, across her hip, over her pelvic bone.

His breath teased her sensitive flesh as he said, "Really, Aja. How could I have engaged in a relationship with you in this world? In every life you live, you grow older, but I don't age a day."

His tongue swiped her swollen, slippery flesh.

Aja let out a sharp gasp. "Good point."

Once again, his head lifted and his lustful gaze connected with hers. "I'm never far from you, Aja."

Her fingers twisted in his long, silky hair again. "It must be so difficult for you."

"To not be able to touch you, make love to you, hold you? Yes," he whispered. "But I've always held the hope that one day we'd be reunited."

Her head dropped to the pillow. She let out a long breath. "This may only be temporary, Christian," she said as she stared up at the ceiling. "Once I fulfill my destiny, my memories may be lost to me again. You'll continue to watch over my spirit, never knowing if the Elders will summon me again."

"Let's not waste a single minute," he said. "I can't take another breath without feeling you all around me."

Aja's pulse raced at the mere thought of joining with Christian. It had been so long. And she'd wanted him all this time, even though she hadn't known how important he was to her, how much they loved each other. "Make love to me, Christian."

His mouth covered her. His tongue speared her tight opening before slowly circling her throbbing clit. Aja let out a soft whimper. He responded to her plea by lapping erotically between her lips. One long finger eased inside her and pushed deep while his mouth devoured her clit.

"Chris." She moaned, low and deep.

His finger stroked her, his tongue toyed with the over-sensitized nubbin between her legs. He pushed her closer and closer toward another powerful orgasm. Her body rose off the bed, her hips thrusting upward as she pressed herself against his mouth. Erotic words slipped from her parted lips, unbidden. When the wave of ecstasy hit, she cried out his name. Aja held fast to the pleasure that consumed her body, her very being.

"I hope you're well rested, Aja. It's going to be a very long night."

Chapter 8

Christian had yet to tell her he'd altered her fate when he'd sucked her blood. But that would have to wait. At the moment, all he could think of was making love to her. It had been five hundred years. He couldn't stand another second.

He dropped a soft kiss on her luscious lips, which slowly deepened into an erotic, soul-baring kiss. He felt her love for him as intensely as he was sure she felt his. "You are so beautiful, Aja."

She smiled at him. "Not bad for someone who's been reincarnated four times, huh?"

"No," he said as his lips trailed over her collarbone and down to her plump breasts. "Not bad at all. In fact, you're just as perfect as you were the day we met."

Christian's hands smoothed over her warm skin. He drew a puckered pink nipple into his mouth and sucked it slowly, languidly, eliciting a deep moan from Aja. Her back arched, pushing her breast against his mouth. His tongue continued to tease the tight bud.

"I want you inside me, Chris. Please. I can't wait another minute."

Neither could Christian. He eased himself between her parted legs, coming up on his knees. He spread her thighs wide and hooked his forearms under her knees. He held her open to him and pushed the tip of his cock against her warm, dewy flesh. His eyes devoured every inch of her, stretched out on the bed before him. Her nipples were hard and her golden skin was flushed with heat. Aja's eyelids fluttered closed and her plump lips parted slightly as sharp breaths of air escaped her.

His entire being swelled with his love for her, and his cock throbbed with desire. She was the only woman who could satisfy his hunger.

"Please, Christian," she begged him. "Please, take me. Now. Please…"

"Yes, Aja."

He eased inside her, oh-so-slowly. It was agonizing and painful to carefully inch into her. She was wet and ready for him, but Christian wasn't so sure he could keep his composure. Though he wanted desperately to thrust himself deep inside her and bury his cock in her warm depths, he knew he'd come the instant he did it. And he wasn't quite ready to give up his control just yet. He wanted to savor the moment. He wanted to bring Aja as much pleasure as he could before he let go.

A soft whimper fell from her lips. "Oh, Chris. This is better than I remember."

He pushed deeper, reveling in the intensely erotic sensations that consumed him. When he was finally buried inside her, they began to move in a slow, steady rhythm. He released her legs and they immediately wrapped around his waist. His upper body hovered over hers, the tips of her breasts barely grazing his skin, teasing him, driving him half out of his mind with wanting her.

Aja's hands traveled all over his body. Up his arms, down his back. She cupped his ass with her hands and pushed him down into her as she raised her hips. Christian let out a low growl. Beads of sweat broke out on his forehead and at the base of his neck.

"I told you not to hold back," she whispered. Her legs tightened around his waist. "I know you want more than this, Christian. I want it, too."

Her inner walls clenched around him, holding him in a vice grip. Christian's breath escaped him in a harsh puff of air. "Oh, sweet Jesus," he groaned.

She was so damned tight. Hot and wet and clinging to him as he moved inside her.

Aja arched her back and rocked her hips against him, forcing a faster tempo.

"No." He let out a low growl. "Don't. Christ, Aja. This is too much."

"I know. Oh, God. It feels so good." She forced him to move inside her with her grinding hips and writhing body.

Unable to contain his desire, Christian let his restraint go. He needed her as much as she needed him. They had all night, and he recovered quickly. One of the many advantages of being a vampire.

"Take me, Christian. Make us both come."

He thrust deeper into her, causing his passion to spike. With great vigor, he pumped his hard cock in and out of her, making Aja moan and whimper and beg for more.

He felt her reach the pinnacle, felt her body tense all around him. Her body began to tremble and vibrate as it always did at the first sign of climax. He pushed deeper inside her, stretching her. Her inner walls clenched around him, holding him so tight it stole his breath. And then he felt her muscles quiver around him and she cried out, screaming his name as she came.

Christian couldn't hold back his own release. He surged inside her as she milked him, and he exploded with such intensity it shook him to the core. His body vibrated and hummed, making Christian feel... alive.

For the first time in five hundred years, he felt complete.

"Oh, God," Aja groaned as Christian slowly withdrew from her body. "That was simply too amazing for words."

Christian merely grunted as he collapsed beside her.

Aja sighed happily. She rolled onto her side and plopped her head against his hard chest. Her breath still came in hard pulls and her heart beat abnormally fast. "I've really, really missed you."

Christian's arms slid around her. He held her in a tight embrace. "I've missed you, too, Aja. More than you'll ever know."

She squeezed her eyes shut, fighting back the wave of emotion that threatened to bring tears to her eyes again. "I *do* know, Chris. But for the time being, I'm here. With you. And the Elders will want you to stay close to me and watch over me while I do whatever it is they've summoned me to do."

She felt Christian's muscles tense. She pulled away slightly and stared down at him. She searched his beautiful emerald eyes, sensing immediately he was keeping something from her. They'd never kept secrets before.

"Christian?"

She watched as he worked down a hard lump in his throat. He lifted a hand to her face and smoothed a long, tapered finger over her cheek.

With regret in his voice, he said, "I've altered your fate, Aja."

"How so?"

Christian's dark eyes clouded. "I've made you partially immortal."

Aja's stomach lurched. She sat up and moved out of Christian's reach, the implication of his words striking like lightning in her heart.

"What are you talking about?" she asked, though deep in her soul, she already knew the answer to that question. She'd simply ignored it all this time.

He'd made her a vampire.

Christian looked stricken. "I had no choice, Aja. You were dying."

Tears instantly sprang to her eyes as realization dawned. The knowledge of what he'd done had been with her all this time. She'd simply suppressed it, not wanting to acknowledge or believe what he'd done. Aja knew the exact ramifications of Christian's actions. She knew he'd invoked an irreversible curse. He'd altered the course of their lives. Now their paths, once split, could never be reunited.

She stared down at him, the shock and horror of what he'd done piercing her heart. She knew her destiny, knew she'd been summoned to fulfill it.

And now she knew their doomed fate.

The Elders had allowed Christian to become a vampire so he could protect her. He'd willingly agreed to become immortal so he could follow her throughout the centuries. But the Elders had warned Christian that he must never try to make her immortal. It went against the laws set forth in the book of prophecies.

Though Aja retained the powers that had been restored to her, she was now neither full witch nor full vampire.

She would die, eventually. Problem was, because of her altered chemistry, this next passing would be her last. Her spirit would not return to earth. She would not be reborn. She and Christian would never be reunited.

Large teardrops pooled in Aja's eyes. One crested the rim and slowly slid down her cheek.

"Christian," she said on a heartbroken sigh. "We'll never meet again."

He sat up. Reaching a hand to her cheek, he brushed away the wet drops on her face.

"I had no choice," he repeated. "You were dying. And if you died, Aja, you wouldn't be able to fulfill your destiny. You wouldn't have the chance to save your people. And..." He shook his head and let out a tortured sigh. His voice was strained when he spoke. "We wouldn't have had tonight. I wouldn't have had one moment with you when you remembered me, when you remembered how much we've loved each other from the first moment we met. I couldn't live the rest of eternity without having one more night with you, Aja. I *had* to save you."

She nodded in understanding. Still... "You're going to have to watch me die, Christian. And know this time I won't come back to you."

Chapter 9

Although she lacked her full powers, thanks to Draken's greed, Aja managed to teleport herself to the Elders. When she reached them, she felt a peculiar sense of exhaustion. It took the majority of the energy she possessed to enter their realm.

She closed her eyes against the blinding golden light surrounding her and sank to the cold, hard floor. She panted heavily. *Damn Draken.* The sorcerer had gone too far this time.

"You look terrible."

Aja opened her eyes and lifted her head to find Cassius and Vassar staring down at her. Dressed in their flowing robes of gold and sapphire, they looked every bit the majestic deities they were.

Vassar had spoken to her. He stood with his arms crossed over his wide chest. He cast a disapproving look her way.

"What a lovely greeting, Vassar. After all this time…"

The look on his face softened and the corners of his mouth twitched, as though a smile threatened his lips. "I didn't mean to hurt your feelings, Ajana. I've just never seen you so—"

"Drained?" She let out a low sigh. "I know. But with only partial powers, I can't teleport so easily. Frankly, I'm shocked I made it here."

"Draken," he said on a low growl. "We couldn't stop him while he was in your world. He invoked the spell and there was nothing we could do to stop him from taking your powers. We're lucky you retained half of them, Ajana. Otherwise…"

"Yes, I know," she said, understanding that if Draken had succeeded in taking all of her powers, she wouldn't have made it back to the Elders. She would be useless to them.

Cassius studied her for a moment before kneeling beside her and reaching a hand out to her. He pushed the strands of hair off her neck. He frowned. "Christian's marks."

"Surely you understand why he did it?" For a moment, she worried that Cassius would punish Christian for going against the laws imposed upon him. She glanced from Cassius to Vassar and back.

But Cassius nodded in response to her question. "You would have died otherwise. He did the right thing, for the people of this realm."

"Yes. Just… not for us."

Cassius stood. He helped Aja to her feet. "You'll have a long life with him, Ajana."

Her insides coiled at the thought of the long life Christian would have *without* her.

Cassius turned away. He and Vassar walked to a tall, arched doorway and passed through it. Aja followed. She entered the Elders' private chambers. She'd been here many times before, long ago.

As a child, she'd been sent for to stand before the Elders and account for why she'd used her powers in a reckless manner. It had taken awhile for Aja to learn her powers weren't meant for her own personal gain or amusement. Cassius and Vassar had been the ones to help her cultivate the special abilities she possessed. Magical powers passed to her that were beyond the comprehension of her father, the tribunal leader of the Corte Terre gypsy tribe.

The Elders had taken her under their collective wing, in part because she was invaluable to them, and in part because her quest meant she could belong to no tribe, and because she'd been orphaned at a young age, when demons had slaughtered her father.

Aja knew that, as a small child, the Elders had found her amusing, though they'd rarely ever cracked a smile at her practical jokes. She'd endeared herself to them by making many sacrifices to help her people, as well as other innocents.

The last time Aja had appeared before the Elders, they'd told her about her destiny. And Christian had volunteered his services to protect her. Aja planned to ask him about the demons he'd fought off while watching over her, when they actually got around to talking about the past five centuries. As it was, they'd spent all of last night and most of the morning making love.

The thought of Christian made her smile. She loved him even more today than she had five hundred years ago, she was sure. Their bond seemed even stronger, perhaps because she had known him in other lifetimes, had a link to him for half a millennium, even when she hadn't known its significance.

Now, as Aja stepped before the Elders, who had taken their seats on either side of the prophecy book. She knew better than to try to sneak a peek at the book. She had done so once as a child, and the book had slammed shut, her fingers stuck inside. The Elders had been forced to pry the book open to release her.

"Draken may possess half of my powers, but I'm still powerful in my own right, yes?"

The Elders nodded. "You will regain your strength as time passes and your powers will intensify."

"Good." She pulled in a deep breath, knowing it was time to get down to business. "What is it that I'm supposed to accomplish for you? What is my destiny?"

The Elders exchanged looks. Vassar said, "You're tasked with locating the source of all evil."

"*Oh.*" The breath escaped her on a hard rush of air. "That was rather unexpected."

"It is a very serious charge, Ajana. A task of the utmost importance."

Well, what had she expected, really? The Elders hadn't kept her spirit intact for five centuries for a frivolous mission. Of course it was going to be something extraordinary. She just hadn't considered anything quite so... dark and ominous.

"Is there some sort of homing beckon I'm to follow?"

Vassar almost cracked a smile. Almost. "It's not quite that simple, Ajana."

"I know. Otherwise you wouldn't have locked my powers away and kept me around all this time."

"We knew there would be a threat in this century," Cassius said. "The time has come, Ajana. You must locate Maylar and keep her safe."

Aja's stomach took a violent tumble. "What do you mean, *her*? The source of all evil is a *her*?"

"Maylar is a six-year-old girl," Vassar explained. "She's not evil, herself. But within her lies the worst demon to ever live. He intends to destroy this realm—starting with Cassius and me."

Aja's blood ran cold. "How?" she asked, a chill working its way up her spine.

"The demon Kabore is a culmination of evil spirits joined together over the past half millennium. Maylar teleported Kabore inside herself to keep him from unleashing any evil. But he continues to collect powers and grow stronger. Eventually, he'll find a way out."

Aja's mind reeled. "She *teleported* him inside herself? I didn't even know that was possible."

Cassius nodded. "Maylar is a very gifted child, very powerful. She is a distant descendent of the Corte Terre *Roma* tribe. Her mother, who was an immortal witch and a member of the tribe, lived in this realm for centuries."

"I didn't know I had any ancestors left. I thought they were all dead."

Cassius gave her a solemn look. "They are now. After Kirin gave birth to Maylar, she died. She was slain by a demon, one more powerful than anything we've ever encountered in this realm. He is capable of killing immortals, Ajana. We were lucky we were able to save Maylar."

"The two of you are the last of your people," Vassar added.

Aja felt the familiar tightness in her heart that always accompanied thoughts of her slaughtered tribe. A sense of loneliness crept up on her. She'd been orphaned at a young age, and the pain of losing her father had never diminished.

Vassar continued. "Even as a baby, Maylar possessed powers that rivaled ours. She knew of the danger Kabore posed to Cassius and me—and the people of our realm. She tried to stop him the only way she knew how. Years later, Maylar is aware of the evil that has built inside her, which continues to grow. She went into hiding, hoping to keep Kabore away from us."

Aja's mouth gaped open for a moment, but she recovered quickly. "Brave girl," she said in a quiet tone. "Clever, too." Aja looked forward to meeting her, provided she could find Maylar.

"Once Kabore is released from Maylar," Cassius said, "You must destroy him before he enters our realm."

Aja said, "I'm confused as to why he'd pose a threat. You and Vassar are the most powerful beings in this realm. How could a demon harm you?"

The Elders exchanged looks again, concern etched on their homely faces. "From the beginning of time, we've been able to overpower demons," Cassius said. "But change is upon us, Ajana. We cannot explain it all to you at this time, but a shift has occurred. And there is now a powerful force working within this realm that makes Kabore's mission to annihilate us possible."

Aja swallowed hard. "*Draken*," she said on a harsh breath. "With half of my powers, Draken is incredibly strong now. He's the force working against you, isn't he?"

Vassar nodded. "And with Kabore's capacity for evil building at a rapid rate, Draken is all the more powerful. This threat is real, Ajana. It is more deadly than anything Cassius and I have encountered in the millennia we've ruled this world. You must find Maylar. And you must stop the evil demon from entering our realm."

Aja shifted nervously from one foot to the other. The thought of anything happening to the Elders caused her anxiety and panic. She would do everything in her power to protect them. Still... "You realize it's been five hundred years since I've vanquished a demon."

"It'll come back to you," Vassar assured her.

Aja swallowed down a lump of emotion—and dread—as she debated the dilemma. She didn't like that the Elders' lives were at stake, and that their realm was in jeopardy. If all of this rested on her shoulders... It was one hell of a task.

"What about Christian?" she asked. "Will he be able to help me?"

Cassius nodded. "He is powerful enough to work with you, Ajana. But Christian's destiny is different than yours. He is your protector. He is strong, but you will have to find the power to defeat Kabore."

She let out a long, slow breath. Aja didn't feel powerful. She felt tired and weak. Confused, too. Her charge was a matter of life and death, the existence of an entire realm hung in the balance. And she was still reeling from the knowledge that she was now part demon.

When the Elders had granted Christian the right to seek immortality, they'd suggested he become a vampire. It had been a means to an end; imperative, in fact. He could not have fought off the evil forces hunting Aja through the centuries if he were merely immortal. He also needed extraordinary strength and speed. Though he had become what Aja loathed and what she had risked her life in the sixteenth century to destroy, she had not thought of Christian as a demon.

But now that she was part vampire, there was a certain sense of self-loathing that lingered within Aja. She had become what she despised, what she had worked so hard to destroy.

She didn't blame Christian. She understood why he'd turned her, though she was still disheartened by the turn of events. Not to mention the fact that she and Christian were now living on borrowed time.

Thinking of their doomed future, she asked, "Can my fate be reversed?"

"You wish us to take away the partial immortality you have gained?" Vassar eyed her with a good deal of speculation.

She nodded. "You told me long ago that you would continue to reincarnate me every century and summon me when you needed me. Consequently, Christian and I would be reunited each time that happened. Since he's made me partially immortal, he's altered my fate."

"You want to continue to die and be reincarnated?"

"Yes, Cassius. Even though my memories will be locked away, at least I will remain in Christian's life. And I can continue to serve you when you need me."

Cassius and Vassar conferred telepathically.

Endless minutes passed until finally, Vassar, ever the staunch one, said, "I'm afraid that's not possible. We are incapable of returning you to your previous state. You have vampire blood in you, Ajana. You are partially immortal. And that partial immortality will serve you well when you fight Kabore. Even if we could reverse your fate, it wouldn't be in our best interest to do so."

Cassius added, "Only a demon as powerful as Kabore could threaten your existence now, Ajana. But you won't live the eternity that Christian will. Your body will continue to age, though at an incredibly slow pace. So much so that even you won't feel it."

"But eventually, age will catch up to me."

"Yes," Vassar said.

"We cannot change what you have become, Ajana."

She nodded in understanding.

"We will not punish Christian for his actions," Cassius continued. "We know how much he will suffer when he eventually loses you, Ajana. And though it pains us to know he will suffer, after all he's done for us, and that we will also lose you, we are bound by certain laws. Rules we must follow in order to preserve this realm."

"We placed restrictions on Christian because it was necessary to do so," Vassar added. "He went beyond the bounds of those restrictions. And though he did it to save you so that you could, in turn, save this realm, he also had selfish motives, Ajana. And that cannot be overlooked."

Aja had broken many laws herself when she was younger, and she'd had to suffer the consequences and atone for her actions. She understood the deities could not let Christian be an exception. To do so would disrupt the order of their realm and undermine the Elders' authority.

Draken would be punished for the rules he'd broken, if the Elders could manage it. But with the new powers he possessed and his ability to hide in the world in which Aja and Christian lived, it was possible he could escape the Elders' wrath.

Aja knew she had to find Maylar quickly, destroy Kabore, and return Draken to this realm so the Elders could deal with him accordingly.

She had no idea where to start, but this was her charge and she would fulfill her destiny.

She left the Elders to return to Christian.

Chapter 10

Or so she thought.

Aja awoke on the cold concrete floor of a cell. She stared at the tall, steel bars surrounding her and almost laughed out loud. As if steel bars could contain a witch of her magnitude. Even without her full powers, she was still a force to be reckoned with.

She'd find a way out.

If she had the strength, she'd simply teleport herself back out. But with her abilities at only half capacity, she'd need a while to recover before she did that. As it was, teleporting herself out of the Elders' realm had left her so exhausted she'd passed out when she'd landed here.

Which was where, exactly?

Aja rose to her feet. She was still too disoriented to free herself, but she would. Eventually.

"Well, this is a fine mess you've gotten yourself into."

Aja crossed to the front of the cage and gripped the bars before her. She smiled at Christian, happy to see him. "Is this some sort of sexual game you've invented?"

"I wish." He examined the steel rods for a moment and frowned. "These bars are pretty thick. They'll be tough to bend, but..." He reached for two in front of him.

"Wait," she said. "Let me help. I need the practice."

Christian stepped aside and Aja summoned the powers deep inside her. Chanting softly, she lifted her hand in the air, holding it outstretched before her. A flash of light formed into a multi-colored orb, hovering just above her upturned palm. The energy lingered for a brief moment before splitting into two rays of light that shot across the room. The energy connected with a pair of steel bars and lanced right through them.

The surge of power that emitted from Aja echoed all around her and the force of expelling the energy from inside her hit her so hard, she went sailing backward as though she'd been kicked in the midsection. She landed on the hard floor and winced out loud.

Unfortunately, the energy she'd projected also speared the wall across the corridor, leaving a gaping hole in the concrete. The lights immediately went out as the electrical wiring in the wall was severed.

"Wow." She lay sprawled on the floor, drained physically.

Christian quirked a dark brow at her. "Bit rusty with those powers, I see."

"A bit."

Christian eyed the steaming hole across from him and whistled under his breath. "You may want to work on that control, sweetheart. Although I do admire your gusto."

"Imagine what would have happened if my powers were at full capacity. I could have blown this whole building up."

"You'll get the hang of it. You haven't had your powers in five hundred years," he reminded her. "It's no surprise you've got control issues."

"It's good to know I'm still pretty powerful, though. No thanks to Draken."

Christian gripped the two seared bars and pulled them apart with his vampire strength. Aja hauled herself up and slipped sideways through the narrow opening.

"My guess is we can also blame him for this little trick," Christian said.

Draken had redirected her teleport? The thought shook her to the core.

Christian wrapped a comforting arm around her. "Are you okay?"

She nodded. "A little confused by Draken's intentions." She knew the sorcerer was up to no good by amassing a large source of evil and bringing it into the Elders' realm. But what did he want with her?

She shook her head and asked, "How did you find me?"

"You're kidding, right?" He looked at her askance. "I've played the vampire-bodyguard bit for centuries, sweetheart. I follow you everywhere."

She stared at him, quizzically. "But you didn't possess the ability to teleport when you became a vampire in the sixteenth century."

"It came afterward. With the bodyguard gig. The Elders were able to get away with a few tricks to help me." Christian cast a serious look on her. "I won't be able to follow you when you perform astral projections, though. With teleporting, your physical form moves between realms. When you astral project, it's just your essence that leaves. I can't protect your body if I'm gallivanting about in different planes, following you."

She nodded. "I'll keep that in mind." Still unsettled about Draken's ability to command her so easily, she asked, "Can you get us home? I'll feel safer there."

⁂

Back at Aja's apartment, Christian helped her to undress and slip into bed. She was still weak from using her powers and teleporting herself in and out of the Elders' realm, despite Christian's help with the last journey.

He started a small fire in the fireplace in Aja's bedroom before he stripped down to his briefs and climbed into bed next to her.

She snuggled close to him. "I'm worried about this exhaustion," she told him. "I'm not performing well."

"Give it a few days. Maybe you just need time to adjust. It's been a long while since you've practiced witchcraft."

"True," she conceded. "It's just that… I'm terrified to cast spells. After five hundred years of inactivity, hell. I might turn you into a frog."

Christian let out a low chuckle. "That would certainly put a damper on things." He stroked his hand down the length of her spine.

Aja sighed contently, basking in the warm touch and the sensations the very nearness of him called forth from deep within her.

But dark thoughts lurked in her head.

She explained the task set before her by the Elders, and also told Christian she feared encountering Kabore when she barely had the strength to teleport herself. "How am I supposed to protect the Elders and the people of their realm when I can barely take care of myself? If Draken can redirect my teleport… What could an evil demon like Kabore do to me?"

Christian kissed the top of her head, then her temple. "You've always had extraordinary powers, Aja. Now you're part witch and part vampire. You possess incredible strength, in addition to your magical powers. You just need a little time to get used to your abilities again."

"I don't think I have a lot of time, Chris," she told him. "I've got to find this kid before Kabore finds some way to escape her body and go after Cassius and Vassar." The mere thought of anything happening to the Elders made Aja shiver in panic.

Christian's strong fingers caressed her cheek. His gentle touch and steady presence reassured her and soothed her frayed nerves. For the moment.

"We'll find her, sweetheart. In the meantime, I'll keep any other demons away from you."

She splayed a hand over his hard chest, stroked his warm, smooth skin with her fingertips. "You've been doing that for centuries."

"They know you, no matter what lifetime in which you exist." Christian was silent a moment, as though lost in thought. When he spoke again, his voice was dark and tight. "I should have been closer to you when you left my office the other night. I should have sensed Draken lurking about. Instead, I got back on the phone and tried to secure the fifth medallion."

"Oh, Chris! I completely forgot about the medallions. Draken must have all of them."

Christian groaned. "He managed to collect the last one, unbeknownst to me, so he could set the spell in motion."

"Which is why the spell wasn't complete. That last medallion never made it into my possession. I'm not the one who unleashed my powers."

"Plus, you stepped out of the way of the second lightning bolt. That additional blast would have restored more of your powers. They couldn't all return at once. You'd never survive it. If only I'd secured that last medallion before he got hold of it, Draken would not have been able to take any of your powers."

She gently stroked her fingers over his chiseled cheek. "You're being too hard on yourself. None of this is your fault. You're a good protector, Christian. I owe you my life. All five of them."

He shook his head slowly, not falling for her quip. "I should have been with you. I could have stopped Draken from taking part of your powers."

Aja lifted her head from his chest and stared at Christian. She could see the guilt and torment reflected in his dark eyes. "Please don't torture yourself over this. It was my fault. I let him lure me up there. My insatiable curiosity got the best of me. I knew—" She let out a low groan of despair. "I knew an evil presence lurked on that rooftop. I'd had dreams about it. I knew something waited up there for me. And I knew somehow I'd end up falling from the building. But I went up there anyway."

Christian's jaw clenched. "I should have been there to save you."

"You *did* save me," she reminded him.

"No." He untangled himself from her and sat up. He dropped his powerful legs over the side of the bed and hung his head between his shoulders. "I should have been on the roof when Draken was there. I could have reached you before you hit the ground. I could have saved you without altering your fate and your biological chemistry."

A thought suddenly occurred to Aja. "Chris, if you hadn't bitten me, I'd be dead. And even if I'd somehow, miraculously, survived on my own, I'd only be part witch because the spell wasn't complete. I'd have less strength than I do now. I may not have been able to teleport myself to the Elders today."

Christian glanced at her over his broad shoulder. She hated the tortured look in his eyes. She scooted closer to him and wrapped her arms around him. She rested her head against his. "You saved me. And maybe the Elders, too."

"I hope you're right."

"I think I am." She held him for a moment longer, then said in a suggestive tone, "I'm feeling revived now."

Christian let out a soft chuckle. "Is that a fact?"

"Mm-hmm. What do you say, sexy vampire-bodyguard. Wanna make love to me?"

Christian turned, forcing her to relinquish her hold on him. He gave her a devilish smile, which ignited her insides. "I've wanted to make love to you again since you left my bed this morning."

She threaded her fingers through his silky, black hair. Her lips grazed the thick column of his neck. "Take me, Christian," she said on a lustful moan. "Love me the way only you can."

He pressed her down onto the mattress, his large body covering hers. His hands roamed over her flesh, inciting a riot of sensations inside her,

"I love how you touch me," she said in a soft voice. "You know every inch of me. And you know exactly how I like to be touched."

Christian let out a low growl. He hauled himself up and in a swift, fluid motion, flipped her onto her stomach. Aja let out a soft squeal. Christian's big hands slid to her breasts as his body curled around hers. She arched her back, lifting her backside and pressing it against him. Christian's erection pushed against the cleft of her ass. She could feel his heat through the thin material of his briefs.

His mouth was on her neck, his lips and his tongue searing her skin. His teeth nipped her flesh, making her gasp. She felt the sharp edge of his fangs graze her throat, sending an electrifying jolt of excitement to the heart of her as he teased her with his soft biting.

His fingers plucked at her hard nipples before his hand eased down between her legs. He rubbed and pinched her clit until she came, crying out his name. Then he divested himself of his briefs. He hooked an arm around her waist, hoisting her slightly upward until she was on her knees, her forearms braced against the pillows on the bed. Her bare bottom was fully exposed to him now, and a wicked thrill worked its way through her body at the thought of how decadent Christian could be.

She loved that he didn't treat her as though she were fragile. He knew she possessed the same desire and passion as he. He understood her true nature. In this lifetime, Aja might have been a bit more tentative and reserved than in the past, but she'd been a product of her environment. She'd been raised by prominent parents who were also scholars. She'd cultivated different characteristics in this lifetime, but there were certain behaviors that were inherent in her. Her passion was one. It was fierce, strong for Christian.

As his fingers eased inside her already wet pussy, Aja felt that familiar, overwhelming need to have him make love to her without restraint. He stroked her sensitive flesh, slowly at first, igniting a small fire inside her. Then he pushed deeper and used longer, quicker strokes until the fire turned to a raging inferno.

He pumped his fingers in and out of her throbbing pussy until she was just about to come. When she teetered on the verge, he withdrew his fingers and thrust his hard cock inside her, making her come instantly.

Aja let out a sharp cry that filled the quiet room.

"Oh, yes," Christian groaned. "I like it when you scream, sweetheart."

"More, Christian," she panted. "I want more."

His cock surged and pulsed inside her, filling her, stretching her, searing her with heat and desire. The feeling was so erotically exquisite, she never wanted it to end. She wanted to keep Christian buried inside her, joined with her for all of eternity. She wanted this wonderful, wicked feeling to go on and on and on.

He continued to thrust long and deep, making her body hum and vibrate with life. He rode her hard, until she could feel them both reach the pinnacle of desire. He pushed himself deeper inside her, until her body clenched around him, squeezing him tightly, making him come at the same time she did.

"Aja!" His low growl echoed around them, mingling with her scream of pleasure.

On and on it seemed to go, their bodies joined, her inner walls clutching him, drawing out every last bit of pleasure until he pulled away from her and collapsed beside her, breathing as hard as she.

Aja fell onto the pile of pillows surrounding her and dragged in sharp pulls of air. The blood in her veins flowed hot and thick, her sex throbbed with pleasure, and her pulse raced.

She was wonderfully satiated. "I love the things you do to me," she said. She let out a contented sigh. "Only you can make me this happy, Christian."

His silence caused her to prop herself up on an elbow and gaze down at him. His jaw was set in a hard line, his eyes were dark and clouded. "Christian?"

He stared up at her. "Only me?"

Aja heard the slight edge to his tone. Her gaze locked with his. She knew the direction in which his dark thoughts had suddenly gone.

"There have been others," he said in a tight voice.

She couldn't deny it. She'd taken two lovers in this present life. Aja suddenly felt as though she'd deceived him. Her insides coiled at the thought. "They were before I knew about you, Christian," she reasoned. "Before the spell was invoked and my memories of you returned."

He continued to stare at her, seemingly not finding the words he sought. Aja wanted desperately to quell the haunted look that had crept into his eyes, but she didn't know what to say.

Christian's jaw worked vigorously. She could tell he was struggling to rise above the jealousy he felt. Other men had touched her when he could not.

"Did you... watch?" she asked. She heard the tentative note in her voice. The dark look in his eyes provided the answer to her question. "Oh, Christian. Why?"

He didn't answer her. Instead, he said, "You never took lovers in your past lives. Why now, Aja? Why this time?"

Her mind reeled. She sat up. "This is a different time, Christian. People have sex more freely, without the repercussions imposed by society. And I was… lonely. I thought they could fill the void I felt—the void I've always felt since I lost my powers…" She added in a quiet voice, "And you."

She could tell that he was trying to understand, but the wound was obviously deep. She had betrayed him.

"Christian," she said as she stared deep into his eyes. "They meant nothing. I didn't fall in love. I've never fallen in love. In five hundred years, you are the only man I have ever loved. You know that."

He nodded. But his jaw did not unclench.

"You're the only one, Chris." Her hand moved along his temple to his cheek. "I belong only to you," she whispered. "Forever."

Finally, his muscles relaxed a bit. He reached for her and pulled her into his arms.

"I love you," she told him. "I would never intentionally hurt you, Christian. I didn't know I belonged to you, I didn't know we'd end up together."

He let out a long sigh as he gently stroked her hair. "I know, Aja. It's not your fault. It's just…"

Painful.

He didn't have to say the word. She knew the damage she'd unwittingly inflicted. It broke her heart. But she would make it up to him. She would prove to him that he was the only man for her—that she loved him more than anything.

Snuggling close to him, she said, "You have to forget about the past, Christian. Our circumstances are unique and there was no way to predict how any of this would turn out. All that matters is that we're together now."

He kissed the top of her head. "It seemed like such a valiant notion when I agreed to protect you." His voice was low and strained. "I remember thinking that we'd be together forever. So at first, the fact that you didn't know who I was when you were reincarnated didn't seem so difficult to deal with. As long as I could still see you, still speak with you from time to time, I figured I could handle it. But…" He shook his head and let out a sharp, hollow laugh. "I was wrong. It's been much more difficult than I imagined. It's been pure torture, Aja."

Her heart constricted, as though it were shriveling up in her chest. "I'm so sorry, Chris. I've asked so much of you—"

"No," he whispered. "I wanted to do this. I agreed to it. None of it is your fault, Aja." He was quiet for a long spell, then said, "You should sleep. You'll need your strength to find Maylar."

Aja wanted to continue talking, but she knew he was right. The fatigue had crept up on her again and she knew she needed to rest. She closed her eyes and tried to find solace in the fact that she and Christian had been reunited, tried to find comfort in his arms. But her heart still hurt over the betrayal. The last thing she ever wanted to do was torture Christian. Knowing he harbored pain broke her heart.

"Sleep, Aja," he said, as though he knew the thoughts that plagued her. "Sleep."

And she did, albeit restlessly.

Chapter 11

Sunlight streamed through the partially opened drapes in Aja's kitchen. She didn't bother skirting the edges of the shimmering rays. She wouldn't burst into flames if sunlight touched her skin. It would singe Christian if he lingered too long in it, but it wouldn't kill him, either. In fact, his body composition had always fascinated her. He had breath in his lungs and blood flowed through his veins, but he had no heartbeat. Rather, the Elders had once explained that the blood was circulated via skeletal muscle. Christian's heart had ceased to have a purpose when he'd become a vampire.

Though Aja had vampire blood coursing through her veins, she was still a witch first and foremost. Still human. Unfortunately, she didn't posses her full strength or power. That would come in time, she was sure. For now, she relied primarily on the boost given to her by being part demon. It was an odd existence, this half-witch, half-vampire combination. She could sense her biological chemistry attempting to reconcile the changes and make adjustments to her skewed insides. She lingered between two worlds.

She craved blood, which was the most significant internal change she felt. The thought repulsed her, so she avoided thinking about it. She still required food for sustenance, which quelled her aversion to the blood a bit.

She settled herself at the table in the formal dining room and opened the paper. Her eyes scanned the headlines, but her thoughts were on Christian.

Aja frowned. For several lifetimes, her desire for Christian St. James had been seemingly unrequited. She realized it must have been hell for Christian to maintain his distance. She hoped it had eased his longing to know she'd never married another.

Her frown deepened. Unfortunately, she'd taken lovers in her current lifetime.

"That could drive him insane, you realize."

The deep voice filling her dining room didn't surprise Aja. She peered over the top of her newspaper. Draken stood in the far corner, watching her with a smug smile on his handsome face. She'd sensed his evil presence even before he'd appeared.

Tall and golden, Draken was Adonis personified. But his angelic, sculpted looks were deceiving. He was evil, pure and simple. He was possessed by greed and dark intentions.

"What are you doing in my house?" She eyed him with suspicion, wary of his presence. "More importantly, what the hell do you think you're doing tapping into my thoughts?"

Draken's smile was confident and... vile. "We share the same powers, Ajana.

I discovered how true that was when I redirected your teleport yesterday, as an experiment. We're connected now. Just like you and Christian."

"You and I share nothing remotely similar to what I share with Christian. Don't ever delude yourself into thinking we do."

Draken merely shrugged.

"What do you want?" she demanded in a quiet voice.

"The same thing I've always wanted, Ajana. You."

Aja's anger ignited. "How can you be so warped? You stole part of my powers, you arrogant ass! I want them back."

Draken crossed the room and sank into a chair across from her. "Sorry, sweetheart. But that's one request I can't fulfill."

Aja's eyes narrowed as she glared at him. "Don't ever call me that."

Draken let out what sounded to be a long-suffering sigh. "I see this is going to be a challenge."

"What's going to be a challenge?"

"Bringing you over to my side."

Aja laughed. "Oh, please." She stared at him a moment. His confidence didn't waver. Realization dawned on her, chilling her insides. "You're serious."

"We belong together," he told her in a matter-of-fact tone.

Draken had been her childhood nemesis, always taunting her to participate in one of his crazy schemes and teasing her for being so strait-laced. As they'd grown up, he'd pursued her romantically. Even after she'd met Christian. She couldn't believe he still held out hope—after five hundred years, no less—that she'd have a change of heart.

But his admission answered some very important questions for Aja. She had wondered why Draken would put the spell to return her powers into motion. He'd started the incantation and called forth the spirits. He'd been the one to release her powers from the medallions, when it should have been her. The Elders had provided a few pertinent pieces to the puzzle—Draken obviously needed her substantial powers to bring Kabore into their realm.

But there was more to the story than that. She could feel it. Gaining a portion of her powers hadn't been his only intent. Aja's stomach turned as she realized Draken had participated in the return of her powers because he knew it would bind them together.

Her anger escalated. She opened her mouth to tell Draken exactly what she thought of him. But he shocked her into silence with his next words.

"I intend for us to rule the Elders' realm, Ajana."

For a few moments, all Aja could do was stare at Draken, her mind reeling. Finally, she said, "I think that bolt of lightning scrambled your brain."

He chuckled. "We have more power than anyone else in that world."

"The Elders have more power in their pinkies than we have combined. They'd never let you rule," she said, her voice laced with disgust.

"They won't have a choice, Ajana. Not when I'm done." The evil practically dripped from his lips.

Aja regarded him with a mixture of loathing and caution. "Just because you're more powerful now than ever before doesn't mean you can abuse the gifts given to you. Or the ones you've stolen, I might add."

"Spare me the lecture, Ajana. I have a very simple proposition for you. Would you like to hear it?"

Something about the wicked glimmer in his gold eyes told her she definitely didn't want to hear his proposal. But she knew she had no choice.

She crossed her arms over her chest. "Whatever it is, I'm sure I'm not going to like it."

Draken did not seem to notice her irritation. "I meant what I said earlier. You're going to rule with me, Ajana."

She stared at him, wide-eyed, mouth gaping open. When she regained her composure, she said, "You're out of your sorcerer's mind."

He continued on, as if she hadn't spoken, as if he didn't comprehend her disbelief and incredulity. "The time has come for change, Ajana. I *will* rule the Elders' realm, and you will sit by my side."

She shook her head, fought for a coherent thought. When one finally formed, she voiced it. "Even if I were to agree to this lunacy, Draken, which of course I never would, what makes you think Christian would let you get away with this?"

"That's another thing, Ajana," Draken said as if they were engaged in an amiable negotiation he was confident of winning. "I won't share you with the vampire."

Anger seared her insides, chasing out the chill she'd felt earlier. "You won't have to share me, Draken, because I would never accede to your desires. So why don't you just teleport yourself out of my house? And my life?"

He let out a low groan. As though she taxed him unnecessarily. "I know this is difficult for you, Ajana. But once we're together, you'll see it's all for the best. It's destined to be."

"No," she said. "My destiny is to stop you from hurting the Elders, from wreaking havoc in their world. My destiny is to destroy Kabore. My *destiny*," she said, her voice gaining strength, "for as long as it exists, is to be by Christian's side."

"While we're on the subject," he said, again as if her words didn't even register. "You're to stay out of his bed... and keep him out of yours. Do you understand me, Ajana? You are not to join with Christian again. Ever."

Aja had been stunned by all of his previous revelations, but the words Draken spoke now did more than stun her. Incensed, she said, "You're completely insane!"

"I mean it, Ajana," he said, his expression deathly serious. "You are not to make love with the vampire again. You belong with me. I won't allow him to touch you."

The angles of Draken's finely sculpted face turned hard and a dark look entered his usually bright, luminous eyes. "You must do as I say, Ajana. You can't defeat Kabore on your own—you'd be a fool to even try. The time has come for the Elders to step aside. We will rule. We're young and we're powerful. We are the future, Ajana."

A chill ran through her. "I will never agree to this. You know that."

Draken nodded. "I understand it might take some persuasion on my part. I'm prepared to do what I must to ensure our future."

She didn't like his words any more than she liked the hard glint in his eyes. "There's nothing you can do to persuade me, Draken."

He leapt out of his chair and leaned over her, bracing a hand on the table. He gave her a long, menacing look. "You will do as I say, Ajana, or I will make Christian's life a living hell."

Ice coursed through her veins. She scarcely had the breath to ask, "What do you mean by that?"

Draken's look did not waver. He said, "Every time you disobey or betray me, Ajana, I will torment Christian." He crooked a golden eyebrow at her. "I know his greatest weakness. I know the one thing that will drive him mad."

And with lightning-quick speed, he projected erotic images into her thoughts, filling her mind with an endless stream of her naked limbs and sensual moans. Like a movie playing in her head, Aja saw herself making love with the two men she'd taken as lovers in this lifetime.

She jumped out of her chair and it fell backward, hitting the hardwood floor with a resounding thud. She stared wide-eyed at Draken.

"Stop that," she hissed. "Stop playing images in my head that don't belong there. I knew nothing of Christian when I dated those other men. You can't use those memories against me. Against *us*."

"Oh, I can," Draken assured her. "And I will. Trust me, Ajana. They'll rattle around inside his head long enough and the demon in him will take over. He'll snap. He'll either go mad or he'll unleash his own brand of vengeance. He'll hunt the men who touched you and he'll kill them. He'll become the demon you've always loathed."

"No," she said with conviction. "Christian isn't like those demons. He's not evil. He's not like you or Kabore or any demon I've slain. He would never kill innocent people."

"He won't be in his right mind, Ajana. Not when I'm through with him."

She stood her ground. "He's too strong for you, Draken. He can overcome anything you try to do to him."

"Not this. His love for you is his greatest weakness. He was jealous of those men, Ajana. Jealous and outraged they could touch you—make love to you, make you moan in ecstasy—when he could not." He gave her a long, contemplative look. "He lived through it once. You don't want him to suffer an encore performance, do you?"

Aja couldn't believe what she was hearing. She did not want to aid Draken in advancing himself in the Elders' realm, in viciously usurping them, but she wasn't sure she was capable of stopping him. "The Elders won't let you get away with wielding this power so recklessly and selfishly. They won't let you torment Christian."

Draken looked supremely confident when he said, "The Elders can't stop me, Ajana. I operate in this world, where they have no power, no authority. And now that I possess half of your powers, I can rule their realm." He gave her a serious look. "The time is drawing near for the Elders' reign to end. Those with a better understanding of today's modern world must step in. It is time for new blood. We're it."

"You're crazy," she said on a soft rush of air. She shook her head, amazed at the direction in which Draken's evil plotting had turned.

"You've been gone a long time, Ajana. You don't know anything about our world—but you will learn."

She eyed him across the room, understanding he had become more than a pest or an annoying presence in her life. He'd become the enemy. An adversary who dared to come between her and Christian.

"Do we have a pact?" he asked in a quiet voice.

Aja's mouth gaped open. How was she to answer that? Even as they argued, Kabore's power continued to multiply and soon he would unleash his evil on innocent people. Of course, Aja couldn't allow that to happen.

But to agree to Draken's terms?

The thought of putting any sort of distance between Christian and her was too painful to even consider. Yet, what choice did she have? Above all else, the Elders had taught her not to put her desires ahead of the good of her people.

As painful and frustrating as it was to agree to what Draken requested, Aja knew there was no alternative.

Her heart tormented and twisted, she said, "I will do as you ask where Christian is concerned. For now." She gave him a hard, level look. "Make no mistake, Draken. I will find a way to defeat you."

She turned away from him and headed toward the doorway. She looked at him over shoulder before leaving the room and added, "You won't come between us, Draken. What Christian and I share is even more powerful than you."

Chapter 12

That evening, when Christian waltzed through the front door of Aja's house, he knew exactly what she was up to. The smell of herbs permeated the hallway and the air grew more aromatic as he headed toward the kitchen. He found a pot on the stove, with water in it that had boiled over. Christian chuckled. Aja had never been much of a cook, and concocting brews and potions had always ended in a big mess they'd cleaned together.

He wandered into the living room and found her sitting cross-legged on the sofa. Before her stood an enormous globe and her hands rested on its smooth surface. Aja's eyes were closed and her body was perfectly still. She was in the room physically, but her essence was somewhere else.

Christian frowned. She shouldn't have started looking for Maylar without him. Astral projections left her vulnerable. It was his duty to protect her body when her spirit lingered elsewhere. But her soul was also under his protection, and he couldn't guard it during astral projections while watching over her physical being.

He wondered how long she'd been gone, how far she'd traveled.

He checked the tall French doors and the windows, making sure they were all locked. Then he settled into the sofa next to Aja and waited for her to return.

Three hours passed before Aja's eyes fluttered open. She let out a long sigh and slumped back against the plump cushions on the sofa. Christian eased an arm around her neck and she snuggled close to him.

"I'm exhausted," she said. "I can't find her anywhere. I don't detect her presence in our world and I know she's not in the Elders' realm—it would be too dangerous for them. Where else could she be?"

"Hell of a big solar system out there," Christian said.

Aja grinned up at him. "Cute. But I don't think she's communing with the Martians." She rested her head on his shoulder and sighed again. "She's hiding somewhere. I just can't fathom where."

Two nights later, Aja wandered around Christian's enormous office, hoping some of his artifacts might spark her imagination and help her come up with more clever ways in which to find Maylar. She'd been drawn to his office, really. Something lingered here. Elusive, yet powerful.

"I told you I read the story of Ajana and the Corte Terre *Roma* tribe when I was in junior high," she began, her gaze connecting with Christian's. He stopped working on final exams, focusing his attention on her. "I was always fascinated by the adventures she and her companion undertook in order to protect innocent people from demons—not knowing it was us, of course. But I remember reading one passage over and over again. It was a section you wrote on our first trip to Paris. That was such a peaceful time for us. There were no demons to slay in the countryside and no evil touched us. For the briefest period of time, we weren't demon hunters, we were simply two people who'd fallen in love."

Christian grinned at her. "I remember."

"It was the happiest time of my life," Aja told him. "When I read that passage in *this* lifetime, I thought it was incredibly beautiful and romantic. I wanted to visit that very place you wrote about, and I wanted to stand in the tall green grass that ran alongside the pool of water from the waterfall and feel the presence of the two people I'd read so much about."

Christian's eyes suddenly lit up. "You believe Maylar knows the story as well?"

She nodded. "How could she not? She's a descendent of the Corte Terre tribe. I'm one of her ancestors. I'm sure she's heard the tale, perhaps the Elders have even read it to her as a bedtime story."

Christian retrieved a large book from a nearby shelf and placed it on his desk, in front of Aja. She opened the old volume and flipped through half of it before she selected the page she wanted. She tapped the vellum paper and said, "Don't forget that Maylar is not your typical six-year-old girl. She is a very clever and powerful witch. And she possesses talents other children her age do not. For instance, she likely would have taken to reading long before now, at the Elders' insistence and tutelage so that she could read the spell book."

Aja trailed the pads of her fingers over the page she had turned to and closed her eyes. She pulled in a deep breath and held it for a brief bit of time. When she felt Maylar's presence, she opened her eyes and gave Christian a satisfied smile.

"Clever girl, indeed. She's read this passage. And this is where I'll find her."

Christian's dark brows knitted together. "I don't follow you."

"Maylar is inside the book. Inside the story, actually. At the very place where you first declared your love for me."

"But how…?" Christian began to ask. He quickly swiped a hand through the air to dismiss his skepticism. "Dumb question. You said yourself she's incredibly powerful."

"Enough so to trick Kabore and hold him captive. But for how long?" Aja sighed. "That's our million-dollar question."

She lifted her eyes from the book and gazed at Christian. She couldn't help but smile, so wonderful was it to be with him again. Even having her doorstep darkened by Draken could not take away the sheer delight and pleasure that built inside her at the mere sight of Christian. Her beloved. The one man she would love the rest of her days.

"What are you grinning at?" he inquired as he came round the desk and slipped his arms around her.

"You, of course." She let him hold her, despite Draken's words. They had not made love the past two nights because Aja was drained physically from searching for Maylar. She had yet to tell Christian about Draken's lunacy and hoped she wouldn't have to. If she could locate Maylar today and coax the little girl out of hiding, then visit the Elders once again to solidify a plan to vanquish Kabore—and stop Draken's reign of terror—there might be no need to mention the sticky situation to Christian.

Aja frowned as she gave further consideration to her predicament. Of course, Draken knew she would go to Cassius and Vassar and tell them about his rantings. Why was he so confident he could conquer them? Did he really believe she'd side with him in the end, helping him to usurp the Elders? Did he really believe she'd leave Christian for good?

"What is it?" Christian asked, apparently sensing her tension.

Aja slipped from his arms. "Nothing."

She was not ready to share with him the conversation she'd had with Draken and the ultimatum he'd issued. It would no doubt send Christian into a fit of rage. Plus, Aja simply didn't have the heart to say the words out loud. To tell the man she loved and craved that Draken was in the position to command her in such a way. She wanted a chance to fix the problem first, and hoped it would be left at that—something Christian need never know.

To cover her own unease and frustration, she forced a smile to her face. She ran a finger along Christian's furrowed brow. "It'll be alright. We'll find a way to win this battle, Christian. As always."

He drew her into his embrace again and kissed her. Aja wrapped her arms around Christian's neck and let him hold her for a few moments, knowing it was dangerous. But Draken did not interfere, and she breathed a sigh of relief at that.

When she pulled away, she forced herself to concentrate on the task at hand. She had to retrieve Maylar from inside a storybook.

"I need my spell book," she told Christian. "So I need to go back to my house."

He nodded. She knew he sensed something was amiss, but he didn't press her. He merely turned off his desk lamp and followed her out of his office. They drove home to conserve Aja's strength. Once there, she concocted a special spell for what she needed to accomplish. As she sat before the open storybook, she pushed all thoughts from her head and concentrated on reciting her incantation.

Chapter 13

Christian paced the floor in front of the tall fireplace. Once again, Aja sat cross-legged on the sofa, although it was only her body that remained. Her essence had left the room several hours ago, in her hunt for Maylar. He turned to face her physical being and frowned. Something was wrong. Aja was keeping something from him, he could feel it. They were too connected to successfully keep secrets from each other. But Aja was trying to do just that.

Christian rubbed the back of his neck and tried to ascertain when, exactly, the wall had gone up between them. He'd continued his bodyguard gig by prowling the garden late at night, while she slept. During the day, she searched for Maylar. The effort left her so exhausted, Christian simply tucked her into her bed and stood guard over her while she slept. This evening, she'd insisted they go to his office and they rushed out without making love.

His frowned deepened. What had happened to make Aja withdraw from him? What was making her so tense? And why was she blocking him from her thoughts?

Had she given further consideration to the way in which he'd altered her biological composition and was now angry at him for it? Was that possible? Was she upset because she was now part vampire?

Christian continued to pace as the questions mounted. He couldn't stand being in this state of restlessness and anxiety. He needed to speak with Aja, to find out what she was feeling, what she was keeping from him. But he could do no more than wait. She was obviously having a hell of a time coaxing Maylar out of the storybook, if that was, in fact, where the little girl was hiding.

Christian sank into the sofa beside Aja's still body. Her eyes were closed and her head hung forward. He reached a hand out to her and stroked a fat auburn curl. Her hair felt like silk between his fingers. He lifted the long strands and rubbed them against his cheek, loving the feeling of all parts of her against his skin. He sighed in frustration, gently dropped the curl so it bounced back into place, and then stood. He resumed his pacing in front of the fire, wondering anew why Aja had become so distant.

⁂

Aja returned, with company. She unfolded her legs and stretched her body. She glanced over at the little girl who'd teleported herself into her living room. Maylar was adorable. She had springy blonde curls and large, intelligent, amber-colored eyes, a Corte Terre attribute. She was petite and delicate, but also very clever and resourceful. Convincing her to return had been quite a chore, but she'd consented after Aja had found her weakness.

Maylar had heard much about the children of this world and their love of the circus. Aja had bribed her with a trip.

Now Maylar stood in the center of the living room, her inquisitive gaze surveying her immediate surroundings until it landed on Christian. Her already enormous eyes widened.

Aja laughed. "Don't worry. He only looks intimidating." She stood and crossed the room to where Maylar stood, the little girl's gaze still locked on Christian.

He moved slowly toward her and went down on one knee in front of the tiny witch. "I'm Christian."

"Maylar." She held a small hand out to him and gently smoothed his furrowed brow, as though she could sense something was amiss with him. Aja watched the exchange with interest.

Several moments passed. Maylar dropped her hand and Christian gave her a warm smile. "It's a pleasure to meet you, Maylar."

Aja had always wanted children with Christian. She'd sensed he would be a wonderful, caring, protective father. The bond that had just formed between he and Maylar confirmed her suspicions.

A familiar emptiness consumed Aja. It was unfortunate they would never have children together.

Christian stood to his full, imposing height, but the easy grin remained on his face. "I'll make dinner."

Maylar brightened. "I have heard the children of this world like cheese that is melted on bread."

"Easy enough." Christian cast a look toward Aja. She forced a smile to her face, not wanting to draw his suspicions as to the direction in which her thoughts had just roamed.

The look he gave her conveyed a message she dreaded receiving. He wanted some answers. Luckily, he didn't press her now. Instead, he wandered off to the kitchen.

After he'd gone, Aja returned her attention to Maylar, who frowned at her.

"What's wrong?" Aja asked, instantly alarmed.

"You love him and you want to have children with him."

Aja shrugged. "That's all very irrelevant right now."

Maylar seemed to contemplate this. "You are sad, are you not?"

Aja knew Maylar's mystical abilities mirrored her own. So, too, did her intuition. It would be pointless to lie to the little girl or withhold the truth. "I suppose I am. But I'm happy I found you."

She let Maylar explore the house, curiously inspecting items of interest and inquiring about this or that. Explaining the television to the little girl proved to be difficult, but Christian stepped in and gave an explanation Maylar easily understood. They sat at the dinner table together, like a family, and enjoyed grilled cheese sandwiches and chips.

Later, Aja tucked Maylar into the bed in the guestroom. Aja asked if Maylar would like her to read a bedtime story, but the little girl was already asleep.

Aja flipped off the light, but left the door cracked, in the event Maylar needed her in the middle of the night. She found Christian in her bedroom, sitting on the bed, his elbows resting on his knees. His dark green eyes followed her as she entered the room and crossed to the closet. She stepped inside and changed into a nightgown. She removed her makeup and jewelry in the adjoining bathroom, then returned. Christian's gaze did not waver—she felt it on her the entire time.

Aja's insides twisted. She stood in front of Christian, knowing she had to find some excuse as to why he couldn't stay with her tonight. He reached for her hand and pulled her to him so that she was wedged between his powerful thighs. Her heart fluttered as his hands held her hips, keeping her in place. He leaned forward and his mouth grazed her stomach. The thin material of her nightgown seemed to not even exist as his touch seared her skin.

Aja's fingers twined in his thick, lush hair as his mouth moved higher. His tongue flicked over a hard nipple. Aja bit back a moan. She needed to stop Christian from going any further. She needed to tell him the threat Draken made against them. She needed...

Christian.

He eased back onto the bed, pulling her down on top of him. Heat and desire coursed through every inch of her. Christian grabbed fistfuls of her nightgown and raised it up to her waist. His hands moved under the silk and caressed her bare skin. His mouth, warm and greedy, slid over her neck and collarbone. She felt his erection pressed against her and longed to have him inside her.

"Christian," she whispered. She knew she had to put an end to this, but couldn't find the strength to do it. Her hands roamed his hard chest, her fingers worked the buttons on his shirt. His skin was warm and his breath came in hard pulls. He nipped at her neck, his fangs grazing her sensitive flesh.

Aja felt a wave of excitement wash over her. He rolled her onto her back and settled between her parted legs. She pushed the dark blue material of his shirt over his shoulders and down his arms. He wiggled out of the garment and her hands continued to explore his smooth flesh and taut muscles.

Christian let out a low groan. His hands cupped her breasts and Aja was lost.

"I love you," she whispered. "So much."

His mouth moved down to the tight center of one breast. "I love you, too, Aja." He laved a nipple with his tongue, sending exquisite jolts of electricity directly to the heart of her.

"I want you, Christian. More than ever," she panted. "*Desperately.*"

"I'm all yours, sweetheart."

"And I belong to you, Chris. Only to you. Forever."

He lifted his head and his eyes locked with hers. A slow grin spread across his lips. But in a heartbeat, his eyes clouded and he jumped off the bed.

"What the *hell*?" he shouted. His hands clutched at his head and he closed his eyes tightly.

Aja's breath caught. She knew exactly what had just happened. Christian shook his head violently, as though attempting to shake out the mental images and sounds. She knew what plagued him.

He let out a low curse then dropped his hands. His eyes flew open and he glared at her. A sharp, primal growl fell from his lips.

"Chris," Aja said in a tentative voice. She climbed off the bed and went to him. She gripped his upper arms and held his gaze. "Listen to me. I can explain."

His eyes narrowed, his jaw clenched. "Explain what, Aja?"

"What you just saw. It's my fault. I should have stopped you sooner. I'm so sorry." Christian's muscles tensed beneath her fingertips.

"What the hell is going on, Aja?"

She swallowed hard. "It's Draken. He's torturing you because I disobeyed him."

"Since when do you answer to Draken?" His voice was strained, as though he were holding onto his composure by a very thin thread.

"I don't. Except... well, I'm sort of in a bind with him right now. One I'm trying to work my way out of." She rolled her eyes. Christ, how was she supposed to explain this? How was she supposed to tell him they couldn't be together?

"Aja," Christian said in a low tone that conveyed a hint of warning. "I need to know what the hell is going on and I need to know *now*."

She pulled in a full breath and nodded. "Draken doesn't want us to be together, Chris. He has this insane notion that he's going to usurp the Elders and rule their realm. With me by his side. And he doesn't want to *share* me with you. I made a pact with him a couple of days ago. I told him I wouldn't make love with you. In return, he wouldn't torment you with images of me and... my other lovers."

In an instant, it felt as though the air had been sucked out of the room. The hairs on the back of Aja's neck stood on end as Christian's eyes darkened to black. The soft light caught the edge of a fang when Christian's lips parted to let out another low growl.

Okay, this is bad.

Aja's heart hammered in her chest and she began to tremble. "Christian," she whispered.

"I will kill him for this."

Her fear intensified. "You can't kill him, Chris," she said, the panic rising quickly inside her.

"Why the hell not?" His fists clenched and unclenched at his sides.

Aja swallowed down a lump of emotion. She could feel his tortured soul, could feel his pain. It brought tears to her eyes. "Chris, please. Listen to me. I'm going to work this out with Draken. He won't win. I just need to find a way to stop him. But first, I have to destroy Kabore."

"No, Aja. This can't wait. How *dare* he try something like this!" He pushed her out of his way and stalked toward the French doors that led to her balcony. "Enjoy your last few breaths, Draken," Christian called out in a menacing tone.

"Chris, no!" Aja flew across the room and grasped his arm. Though her strength was no match for his, she was able to latch onto him and hold on tight. He dragged her toward the doors as his long strides carried him across the room. "You can't kill Draken. The Elders won't allow it. They'll punish you! Please, Chris! You have to stop. Let me handle this!"

Christian stopped abruptly and turned to her, causing Aja to lose her grip on him. She stumbled backward and fell squarely on her backside. She stared up at Christian, knowing there was fear and dread in her expression.

Christian's features instantly softened. His eyes changed from black to green as he dropped to a knee beside her. "I'm so sorry, Aja. Are you okay?"

Aja's heart broke a little more. "Don't look at me like that. You didn't hurt me."

Christian smoothed a hand over her cheek. "I never would. Not intentionally."

She stared at him, incredulous, shocked she would have to reassure him. "I know that. Christian, I trust you with my life. I always have."

He closed his eyes for a moment, let out a long sigh. Then he focused on her again, a gentler look playing on his face. He carefully helped her up. He brushed back wayward curls and then cupped her face in his hands. "I love you, Aja. I would do anything in my power to keep from breaking your heart. But I'll be damned if I'll let Draken place any restraints on us."

"I know," she said in a soft voice. She drew in a long breath of air, let it out slowly. "There's something you need to know. Something else I haven't told you about."

"What?" he asked, his handsome features turning dark and ominous as though he knew—just knew—she had kept something from him that she shouldn't have. "What is it, Aja?"

"Draken and I are bound together because of the powers we share. Our lifelines have joined, Chris. I can't kill him, nor can you. If you do… I'll die, too."

Christian's hands fell away from her face. He turned on his booted heels and reached for the antique brass levers on the French doors. He pulled them open, stepped outside and slammed the doors so hard behind him the glass panes rattled.

Aja's heart constricted over the torture he endured. Because of her. Because of his love for her.

It wasn't fair. He was selfless. He'd made more sacrifices than even she could fully comprehend. He didn't have to be a part of this—it had never been his destiny. It was hers. But he loved her enough to play this important role. And where had it gotten him? What reward had he ever gleaned by helping her? For helping the Elders, whose realm Christian didn't even come from?

He didn't deserve this torment. Aja had to find a way to stop it.

But what if she couldn't persuade Draken from further tormenting Christian? What if she couldn't destroy Kabore? What if Draken found a way to bring the demon into the Elders' realm?

Aja had never felt this hopeless. It wasn't in her nature. Even when her father had been murdered, she had forged on, knowing how important it was to continue to hunt and slay demons. She had always known her purpose in life, had always had a bit of control over the outcome. But not this time. Now she felt weak and insignificant. Wholly incapable of saving the people she loved. Incapable of protecting Christian's heart, not to mention his sanity.

Tears crested her eyes and streamed down her cheeks as she collapsed into a chair and sobbed.

In the wee hours of the morning, Aja opened the French doors and stepped out onto her balcony. A warm, gentle breeze ruffled her silk nightgown. Silvery clouds shrouded the near-full moon. The scent of magnolias lingered in the air.

"I know you're out here," she said in a quiet voice. "I can feel you."

"Go to sleep, Aja." Christian's deep voice slid over her like a warm caress. "We'll find a way to deal with Draken. He won't win. Ever."

She stared at the long shadows in the far corner of the balcony. She knew

Christian stood there, though he did not step into the light so she could see him. His watchful eyes were likely focused on the courtyard below. Christian would sense if demons lingered close by. He would protect Aja from anything evil. But she knew it vexed him—tortured him, even—to know he could do nothing about Draken. At least, nothing that would be acceptable to him without destroying Aja.

"Somehow this will work out," she assured him. "I'll find a way, Christian. A binding spell maybe…" Though she wasn't entirely sure that would work on Draken. He was now as powerful as she was. It would be difficult to overpower him. But she would try anything to put a stop to this. "I won't let you continue to suffer like this, Chris."

"I can't take much more, Aja."

In that instant, she knew Draken had been right. As strong as Christian was, five hundred years of watching over her had taken its toll on him. She feared what he would do if Draken pushed him to the edge of sanity.

"I'm so sorry," she whispered, the tears building in her eyes again. "I've asked more of you than I should have. More than I had a right to."

"I knew what I was getting into, Aja. And I would do it again because I love you. But I won't let Draken dictate what we can and cannot do. Nor will I let him stand in the way of us being together. We don't have much time as it is, Aja. Every minute we're not together is wasted."

"I know." Her voice cracked as a sob lodged in her throat. She wrapped her arms around herself and shivered, despite the warm air that blew through the tall foliage on her balcony. She sniffled loudly. "Please forgive me."

She turned away and went back inside. Climbing into bed, she pulled the covers up to her neck. Aja closed her eyes, though she knew she wouldn't sleep.

Chapter 14

Aja entered the Elders' realm much easier this time. Her strength had increased ten-fold over the past few days and she was becoming much more accustomed to her skewed chemistry. But she was still mad as hell at Draken.

She stalked into the private chambers of Cassius and Vassar. She stood before them, hands planted on her hips. "Can you alter what Draken has done—joining our lifelines? Is it possible to change this?"

Cassius shook his head. "He possessed the power to do as he pleased when he invoked the spell with the medallions, Ajana. Sharing your powers now is what makes him such a threat to our world."

"He's torturing Christian. How am I supposed to stop him?" She knew the Elders would give her advice. They were like fathers to her, the only family she'd ever really had. But they were also powerful deities who could help her.

The Elders, who rarely ever showed emotion, looked deeply disturbed.

"You must keep Christian away from Draken," Vassar said. "In a fit of rage, he may lose touch with his good sense and do something... regretful."

"Fatal," Cassius added.

Like kill Draken... and, consequently, her.

"I understand that. Convincing Christian is another story."

"His intention may be to threaten Draken or to forcefully persuade him to stop antagonizing the two of you, but, Ajana, you must remember that Christian is a demon. He does possess a dark side. Once tapped into, well..." Cassius' voice trailed off.

"He may not be able to stop himself from killing Draken," Vassar finished the sentiment none of them wanted to hear. But it was the truth. Aja knew it in her heart.

"I need to bind Draken," she said. "I need to bind his powers so that he can no longer use them. It's the only way I can think of to stop him without ending my own life."

Vassar looked instantly stricken. "You cannot even consider that as an option, Ajana! You cannot take your life, nor can Christian end it. Not even to stop Draken from entering our realm. Do you understand?" He sat forward in his chair, imploring her with his intense gaze. "Ajana, there is so much more to your destiny than you know. More than we are at liberty to divulge to you at this time. Not even for our sakes, Ajana, can you sacrifice your life in order to keep this realm safe. You will find another way!"

Confusion swirled around inside her, but the conviction in Vassar's eyes and the disconcertment in Cassius' features told her she must heed their warning.

She nodded to indicate she understood, though she really did not.

Despite the fact that she would be risking her powers, she had to face the inevitable. "The binding spell is my only option."

The Elders exchanged looks. Cassius' expression was grim when he said, "You must be very careful. If Draken overpowers you…"

"Yes, I know," she answered in a quiet voice. It would be the end for them all.

"You will need more than a typical binding spell for this task, Ajana." Vassar stood. He began to pace in front of his chair, which both startled and alarmed Aja. She'd never seen the Elders in such dismay. "You must be sure of the action you intend to take. Draken has the ability to turn the spell. He could fight it and force it back onto you."

She nodded. "How am I supposed to defeat him if he's as strong as I am?"

Vassar came to an abrupt halt. His eyes glowed brightly as some sort of realization seemed to dawn on him. "Draken is as *powerful* as you are, Ajana. You must never forget that. But he is not as *strong* as you are. He does not possess the kind of physical strength you do. *Vampire* strength, Ajana. You have Christian's blood coursing through your veins and you possess a superhuman strength that Draken does not."

Hope began to build inside of Aja, chasing out the dread. She smiled at the Elders. Her mentors, her family. "You're right. Of course."

Cassius stepped down and took her hands in his. "You must draw upon that strength, Ajana. We will give you the spell to bind Draken, but you must rely on the strength Christian has given you in order to make it work. Do you understand?"

She could see by the grave expression on his face and the compelling look in his eyes that this was a dire situation. A matter of life and death. Hers. Theirs. The people of this realm.

She nodded her head, this time knowing exactly what she must do.

"If you fail," Cassius said, "There will be no one else to stop Draken from unleashing Kabore in this realm. We will all die, Ajana."

"I know," she said in a quiet voice. "I won't let that happen. I promise you."

Vassar said, "You must first bind Draken from using his powers. If he is not able to command Kabore, you will have a better chance of destroying the demon. He will be disoriented when Maylar releases him. You will only have seconds to use that to your advantage."

Cassius released her hands. He whispered a short incantation and a scroll materialized in his hand. He passed it to Aja as he explained the binding spell. He urged her to commit the incantation to memory. The potion she would need to concoct was a simple one. She would need to drink it before she could surround the evil sorcerer with the binding energy force. Cassius also gave her very specific instructions about the potion and spell she would need to defeat Kabore.

"The responsibility you bear is great, Ajana," Vassar said. "You alone have the power to save this realm."

Aja felt the pressure, knew the severity of the situation. But she believed in her powers, believed in the strength Christian had given her. "I haven't been lingering about for five hundred years to botch this, Vassar. I *will* bind Draken, and I *will* destroy Kabore." She heard the conviction in her voice and was rewarded with a smile.

Vassar's grin warmed her insides. "You *can* do this, Ajana. You *must* do this."

"I know." She wanted to hug the Elders, just in case this was the last time she saw them. But since they generally frowned upon displays of affection such as that, she opted instead to teleport out of their realm, before her emotions got the best of her.

Christian spent the afternoon with Maylar, while Aja visited the Elders. He did his absolute best to bury his anger and be as amiable as possible. He didn't want to frighten Maylar with the intensity of his emotions. He fixed her breakfast and lunch. He taught her to play Go Fish. Unfortunately, Maylar knew every card he was holding before he revealed them. They tried Chess, but considering they both had the gift of reading minds, they knew each other's moves before they were made, and ended two games at a stalemate.

Christian was just about out of clever ideas. So he selected a book from Aja's home office and began to read to the little girl. He quickly learned she was fascinated by sixteenth century Europe and wanted to know every detail of the world in which Christian and Ajana had lived. She asked intelligent questions and listened closely to everything he said. Hours passed, and yet she still sat there next to him, as though mesmerized by his words.

In the late afternoon, she stifled a yawn. She curled up on the sofa next to Christian and rested her small head in his lap while he continued to read.

Christian wasn't sure what to make of the gesture. He had no idea how to treat a small child—or a small witch. But Maylar seemed comfortable with him, happy to be in his presence. Something loosened in Christian's chest. The tension gripping his body eased a bit.

Maylar was an exquisite child. Beautiful and vibrant. She filled the house with a wonderful energy that brought a measure of peace to Christian. He and Ajana had discussed having children, long before the Elders had revealed her destiny to her. Christian had not cared whether they had boys or girls, all that had mattered to him was that their home be filled with laughter.

He had not forgotten that dream. And though he'd never had children of his own or been around small children, he felt incredibly paternal with Maylar in his care.

He couldn't help but rest a hand on her tiny shoulder, wanting to convey that he would protect her as he did Aja. She would always be safe in his charge.

Maylar stifled another yawn. "She wanted children, too."

Christian closed the old volume of Shakespeare's plays he'd been reading to her and set it on the end table. "Did she tell you that?"

"Ajana longed for a family because she'd never had one. Not really. She hadn't belonged to the Corte Terre nor had she belonged in the Elders' realm."

"She's always been between worlds," he mused.

"She prefers this one, I can tell." Maylar sat up. She gazed at Christian, her big amber eyes alight with warmth and happiness. "We could be a family. The three of us."

If Christian had a beating heart, it would have swelled to twice its size, he was sure. As it was, he felt a curious tenderness for the miniature witch. He mussed her bouncy blonde curls and gently coaxed her to return her head to his lap. "We'll see what the Elders have to say about that."

Christian found himself hoping they would approve. For a moment, he considered the possibility of which Maylar spoke. The anger he'd felt so sharply last night had suddenly vanished.

Oh, he was still determined to rise above any threat Draken threw his way, but he no longer felt like strangling the sorcerer with his bare hands. In fact, his rage had turned more toward pity. He pitied Draken.

The powerful wizard had pined after Aja for half a millennium. And though they were bound in some mystical way because of the spell he'd invoked, she would never be his. She didn't love him. She didn't desire him.

She loved Christian. He knew it deep in his soul. And that love was unwavering and everlasting. She hadn't known she'd loved him when she'd taken lovers in this lifetime. And though it still rubbed him raw to think about it, he knew he couldn't blame her. Or the men she'd been with.

It occurred to Christian that perhaps his territorial nature had gotten the best of him. Five hundred years was a seriously long time to be without the woman he loved. It was possible, he conceded, that his jealousy wasn't really a valid emotion. Aja had not betrayed him. Ever.

And never once in their first lifetime together had she ever given him reason to doubt her love for him or loyalty to him.

Hadn't he written about how strong and pure and loyal Ajana had been?

Why had he doubted her last night?

He hadn't, he realized. He'd doubted himself.

While Maylar slept in his lap, Christian forced himself to admit the truth. He wasn't as powerful as Draken. He was a vampire, and he was immortal, but he did not possess the kind of power Draken, Aja and Maylar had. But it was more than that. He wasn't truly a part of their world. Yes, he operated within the established laws set forth by the Elders, but he did not truly belong in their realm. Draken and Aja shared similar powers and they shared a connection to the Elders and that world.

In addition to feeling pity toward Draken, Christian also had to admit that he was jealous of the sorcerer. Jealous that Draken had a special connection to Aja.

He raked a hand through his thick hair and let out a puff of air. How utterly foolish of him. She belonged to him, not Draken. She loved him, not Draken. His jealousy was completely unsubstantiated.

"Yes," Maylar whispered in her sleep.

Once again, Christian knew he'd become a part of something bigger than himself.

Chapter 15

"I'll no longer allow you to torment Christian," Aja said as she paced the elaborate stone floor of Draken's castle. "I will not let you use the power you stole from me for evildoing. I will not let you usurp the Elders. And I will not let you destroy the peaceful world in which they live."

Draken crooked a golden eyebrow at her. He stared at her from his spot in a tall, uncomfortable-looking wooden chair, which gave the disturbing illusion of a throne. His elbows rested on the arms of the chair and his fingers were tented together just under his chin.

"You visited the Elders today. Whatever spell they gave you to defeat me won't work. I'm just as powerful as you are, Ajana. You can't win against me."

Aja pulled up short and glared at the wizard. "You are damn lucky to be alive this morning, Draken. Christian's temper nearly snapped last night, but he held himself in check because he now knows the consequences involved. But that doesn't mean he won't find some way to get even with you."

"I'm immortal, or have you forgotten?"

Aja crossed her arms over her chest and narrowed her eyes. "It's possible to kill an immortal being, Draken. Or torture him. There are ways to make your eternity a living hell. But that won't be necessary if you stop tormenting Christian."

"But I so enjoy it."

"What *is* it with you?" she snapped, her anger instantly sparked. "Why are you so greedy? And why are you so determined to make my life, and Christian's life, miserable?"

Draken's jaw clenched. "I don't like the vampire, Aja."

"He's none too fond of you, either, Draken. So you're even."

"*No,*" he all but spat as he shook his head. "He still has you."

Aja wanted to throw something at him. "Five hundred years have passed, Draken. I love Christian more now than I did in our first lifetime together. I will always love him." She took several steps toward him, narrowing her eyes at him to emphasize her words and the anger she felt. "And even if Christian died tomorrow, he would still be the only man I would ever love. There will be no other, Draken. Not now. Not ever."

The sorcerer seemed to consider this for a moment. He pressed his fingertips to his pursed lips. Finally, he said. "He's not like us, Ajana."

"He doesn't have to be, Draken. I don't care if he doesn't have our powers. I don't care if he's not from our realm."

Draken pressed his palms against the arm of the chair, as though trying very hard to contain his mounting frustration. "You and I will be together, Ajana," he said through clenched teeth. "It's as simple as that."

"Did it ever occur to you that I don't want to rule with you? Did it ever occur to you that I just want to live a normal life with Christian until I die?"

"That's what I'm saying to you!" Draken said in an exasperated tone. "You *aren't* normal, Ajana. You never will be."

The words he spoke struck a sour chord, though she refused to let Draken know how deeply he'd wounded her.

"If you'll just stop fighting me, you'll see how easy this all is. The two of us, ruling the Elders' realm. You'll be fully immortal."

"And what good would that do me?" she challenged. "If I can't be with Christian, what good is immortality? I don't want it, Draken, unless I can spend eternity with the man—the *vampire*—I love."

Draken hissed under his breath. "How could you throw away such a priceless gift?"

"How could you think I would choose *you* over Christian?" Anger flashed in Draken's eyes. Aja ground her teeth. "I choose Christian, Draken. Not you. And together, we will defeat you. You won't rule the Elders' realm. Ever."

Reasoning with him, trying to sway him from his dark, evil plotting, was clearly not going to work. Aja had hoped he would give up on his plan if he knew she wouldn't concede, if he knew she'd choose Christian over him. Apparently not. He'd make her rule with him by threatening her or blackmailing her, she was sure. He'd devise other ways to torment Christian until she consented.

There was nothing left for her to do. As dangerous as it was to attempt the binding spell, Aja knew she had no choice. She had to try it. Even if it meant losing her own powers, she had to do *something* to stop Draken and his reign of terror.

She stood not more than six feet from him. She closed her eyes, delved deep inside herself, summoning her mystical powers.

"What are you doing?" Draken asked in a curious tone.

Aja did not answer him. She slowly, softly began to chant the words the Elders had asked her to memorize.

"Ajana?" Draken said, trying to break her concentration, to no avail. She heard him climb out of his chair. "What are you up to?"

She continued to chant until she felt the energy building within her. She opened her hand, held it palm up. Her eyelids fluttered open as the power coursed through every inch of her, making her body vibrate and hum with life and the magical energy she possessed. A small yellow orb began to form, hovering above her palm.

"You can't use your magic on me," Draken scoffed. Though his words sounded forceful, his tone held a hint of doubt. "I can counter anything you try, Ajana. We are equals."

"No," she said in a quiet voice. "We are not. And I'm going to prove it."

With great force, she twisted her arm and sent the ball of energy sailing through the air, toward Draken. He held his hand out to stop it from hitting him. A continuous stream of bright yellow light arced between them. He fought her energy back with all his might, keeping the light from reaching him.

Draken's smile was sinister. He said, "You see? You can't defeat me. There's nothing you can do, Ajana, that I can't counter. I'm just as powerful as you. You can't win against me."

Aja chanted louder in an attempt to force the energy past Draken's hand. Instead, he lifted his other hand and managed to channel the energy between the two without it entering his body. The energy deflected from one palm to the other. And with that second open hand, Draken redirected the energy, sending it back to Aja. She held her other hand up, keeping the returning stream of light at bay.

Draken began some chanting of his own. Aja felt her arm weaken. As forcefully as she tried to send the energy to him, he was sending it back with great strength. Her arm began to quiver. She tried to focus, concentrating all her efforts on fighting him off while still trying to overpower him. They reached an impasse, but Aja felt her own power weakening.

Draken's determined look and fierce chanting began to take a toll on Aja. She couldn't force the energy toward him while deflecting what he was sending her way. She felt her muscles tighten, saw her arm shake violently as she fought off the ray of energy. If it reached her, it would render her powerless. Draken could do as he pleased during that lapse. Whether he bound her powers or commanded her to join him, she would have no way of countering him. She would be completely at his mercy.

Aja could not let that happen. Too much was at stake. Maylar, the Elders. She had to fight for them.

And for Christian.

Thinking of him, Aja felt a spark of hope. She possessed something Draken did not. Though their powers were similar in nature, Draken was not a demon. He was a sorcerer.

Aja recalled the Elders' words. She was stronger than Draken because of Christian. She needed only to summon that strength. She needed to tap into it, draw it out, use it against Draken.

Christian was strong by nature, ever more so because he was a vampire. If he were in this situation, he would not lose. Christian did not know how to lose. Though she'd tied his hands recently, she knew he was working on a way to overcome the threats against them. Christian would never give up.

Nor would she.

As her arm began to retract of its own accord, inching closer and closer to her chest as Draken overpowered her, Aja closed her eyes and reached inside herself once again.

Her strength lingered there, waiting for her to call upon it. She did so now. She focused on the vampire blood that coursed through her veins, acknowledged and accepted the demon within her. She had feared it, she now knew. She had not wanted to be what she had fought against for so long, did not want to be like the demons that had slaughtered her father and her tribe.

But Aja knew she was not like that. Even the demon within her wasn't evil. It could not overpower her good intentions or her need to help others. Nothing could stop her from fulfilling her destiny. If anything, the demon inside her was just one more strength she possessed that would help her to continue to serve the Elders and her people.

Freed of her inner turmoil, Aja called forth the vampire strength Christian had given her. It swirled around inside her, working its way to her extremities until every fiber of her being pulsed and surged with something she'd never felt before.

She pushed back at Draken's energy, slowly extending her arm away from her, forcing the yellow ray back toward him. Aja ground her teeth, pushed harder. Using all the strength Christian had given her, she countered Draken's energy. When both arms were fully stretched before her and the yellow light flowed in long, steady streams out of her and toward Draken, she felt more powerful than ever before.

Draken fought her. But he started to weaken. Both of his arms trembled. He began to falter. As Aja pushed harder, his arms eased backward, toward his chest.

She chanted louder. Just a few more inches...

When her energy was too much for Draken to fight off, a burst of light exploded at his feet. Then slowly, the long ray of yellow energy began to wind itself around Draken. Starting at his ankles, it circled its way upward to his calves, further north to his knees and thighs. Aja chanted faster, louder.

"What are you doing to me?" Draken asked, his voice filled with fear. The panicked expression on his finely chiseled face told Aja she was now in control.

"I'm taking your powers away from you, Draken. I'm reclaiming them as my own."

A strange hum filled the air, seemingly coming from the energy that continued to swirl around Draken, inching up to his chest.

"You will no longer torment Christian. You will not have powers to use for evil purposes. You will not take over the Elders' world and cause them harm. You will not have any contact with me again."

"You can't do this to me," he shouted. His arms were plastered to his sides and he was unable to move them as the yellow light worked its way up to his shoulders.

"You have no power, Draken. You have nothing."

"No! Ajana, stop this! You can't do this!"

"Oh, but I can. Christian gave me the strength to defeat you. This is *our* destiny, Draken. This moment belongs to me and Christian. You have no power," she repeated. "You have *nothing*."

The yellow energy had raised above his head now.

"I invoke the spirits. I summon the elements of my world. Earth, wind, fire, water and spirit." She felt them converge and surround her. Her hair whipped in the wind. Water rushed through the castle, flames dancing on top of it. The stream split around her and Draken so that it surrounded them.

"I command the spirits. Return my powers to me!" Aja lowered her hands. The energy swirling around Draken flung toward her, hitting her squarely in the chest. She stood still, absorbing the blow. Her entire body vibrated and hummed. Her breath was scarce. Aja felt the new powers mingle with the ones she'd become accustomed to. She felt herself become more powerful. She reveled in the sensations coursing through her, mixing with her vampire chemistry.

Draken dropped to the ground when the last of the energy left him. He was breathing heavily, his chest heaving as he dragged in short puffs of air.

A satisfied smile touched Aja's lips. "I win," she whispered.

Draken lifted his head. "No," he growled. "I still have the powers I possessed before. I'm a sorcerer," he said in a breathless tone. "I still have powers."

Aja's grin widened. "Yes, you are a sorcerer. But I can take care of that, too."

She turned away from him, as if she intended to leave him.

"This isn't over, Ajana. I *will* find a way!"

Aja closed her eyes, summoned the spirits once more. When she felt their presence, she let her power build. Then she turned sharply to Draken. "I bind thee, Draken!"

She pointed a finger at him. A quick bolt of pink light shot across the room, searing Draken, sending him backward until he was sprawled on his back.

"No!" He wailed in a weak voice.

Aja lowered her hand. A satisfied smile teased her lips. "I believe my work here is done."

Chapter 16

"I did it," Aja whispered excitedly as she crept up on Christian and wrapped her arms around his bare waist. He stood in front of the tall fireplace in her bedroom, dressed only in a pair of black jeans. He looked exactly as he had the night her memories had returned to her. His shoulders were squared, his body was tense, as though the few days they'd been forced to keep their distance from each other were as taxing on him as the half-millennium he'd suffered through.

But that was all over. The torment ended here. Tonight. This very second.

Excitement seeped through Aja's veins. The flickering flames in the hearth illuminated the dark room, casting sensuous shadows across the floor and ceiling. The crackle of the fire teased her ears, the warmth emitted caressed her skin. Her arms tightened around Christian's rigid midsection as she snuggled close to him.

He glanced back at Aja, who rubbed her cheek against his shoulder blade and deeply inhaled his crisp, masculine scent. His warm skin felt heavenly against hers. One of his large hands covered hers, locked at his waist.

"Draken?" he asked in a soft voice.

She smiled. "He won't bother us ever again. I stripped him of his powers, Chris. He'll spend the rest of eternity as a powerless immortal. A sorcerer incapable of performing magic." Aja giggled as the delight consumed her. "I was stronger than him. Because of you."

The tension in Christian's body eased considerably as he expelled a long stream of air. He gently pried Aja's hands apart with his and turned to face her. His fingers caressed her cheek then slid deep into her hair. He stared at her, searching her eyes, looking for answers she knew it was time to give him.

"We can be together again, Christian," she told him. Love swelled inside her, stealing her breath. "Nothing can keep us apart. I can defeat Kabore. I know it. I feel it deep in my bones. And then… Everything will be okay, Christian. We'll have the rest of my life together, with no one standing in our way, nothing keeping us from each other."

His head dipped and his lips brushed over her forehead. "That's all I've ever wanted," he whispered. "To be with you."

Tears built in Aja's eyes. "I know. I feel the same. After all this time…" She pulled in a ragged breath. "No one can stop us from being together."

His warm lips swept over her temple, across her cheek. When his mouth settled over hers, Aja felt consumed by love and desire. Her arms wrapped around his neck and she pressed her body to his. Christian's embrace was strong. He deepened their kiss, until it was all Aja could think of. Everything else receded to the far recesses of her mind. She was with Christian, and that was all that mattered to her.

His tongue swept over hers, eliciting a jolt of excitement that targeted the sensitive juncture between her legs. It had been days since they'd made love, and Aja could barely stand another minute of being separated from him. She needed him inside her, needed to feel his strength and his love. The passion he instantly—effortlessly—sparked left her insides burning for him. Pressing her body to his, she rubbed her breasts against his chest, ground her pelvis against his. The erotic caresses spurred her desire, igniting a fire deep within her.

Christian squeezed her tightly, then released her. He broke the kiss and stared deep into her eyes again. "I want you." He all but growled, heightening Aja's arousal.

The possessive look in his beautiful green eyes fueled her lust as much as his words did. "Take me, Christian," she said on a sharp breath as her hands slid over the hard wall of his chest. "I need you."

His eyes darkened and his jaw clenched. "Tell me exactly what you need, Aja."

Her fingers caressed the rigid muscles of his abdomen. She felt a sense of reckless abandon flood her body, consuming her. Inhibitions, doubt, uncertainty all fled in a heartbeat. Hunger overtook her. A raw, fiery, desperate hunger. It seared her insides, stole her breath. Sharp stabs of desire pierced her vagina, causing her pussy to throb and pulse in an almost painful way. Her nipples tightened behind the lacy cups of her bra.

When Aja spoke, her voice was low and throaty. Seductive even to her own ears. "Ravage me, Christian. I need you to tear my clothes off and fuck me. Hard. Like you can't get enough of me. Like we can't get enough of each other."

His eyes blazed with an internal fire that seemed to heat his skin. She could feel the warmth emitted from his body. It made his passion for her almost... *tangible.*

Christian's hands reached for her and Aja let out a soft squeal at his intensity. His muscles were rigid, his body tense. "Say it again," he whispered on a sharp breath.

"Fuck me," she said. "Oh, please, Christian. Please fuck me. Now."

He groaned, low and deep. His fingers curled around the soft cotton material of her blouse, just above her breasts. With one quick yank, he ripped the line of buttons open, sending the small disks flying in all directions.

Aja thought she was going to come right then and there. Christian's intensity made her blood boil and her pulse rage. His hands cupped her breasts and he squeezed them before teasing the nipples with his thumbs through the rough material of her bra. Aja's head fell back as his mouth skimmed over her throat. His sharp fangs grazed the sensitive skin. The erotic sensation jolted her to the core.

"Oh, yes," she said on a sharp breath. "Just like that." She moaned, deep in her throat. This was exactly what she'd wanted when she'd seen him in his office. She'd wanted him to ravage her. To lose all control. To touch her everywhere, to pleasure her in every way. Aja wanted it even more now.

Christian unhooked the front clasp of her bra and pushed the cups aside. His hands moved down her ribcage and to her waist. His warm lips slid over her skin, his tongue sampling her flesh as his mouth made its way to her breasts. He swiped one taut nipple with the tip of his tongue, and Aja came just a little more undone. Drawing the tight tip into his mouth, he sucked hard, pulling her nipple against his teeth.

"Oh, God yes!" Aja cried out. She was a breath away from coming. Her fingers tangled in his hair and she held his head to her breasts. Her pussy ached for him, but she wasn't ready for him to stop pleasuring her sensitive nipples. When he moved to the other one, she moaned again, finding the erotic assault on her flesh to be the most heavenly feeling. Nothing in the world compared to being loved by Christian. As he teased one nipple with his tongue and teeth, his fingers pinched and rolled the other one until Aja was half out of her mind with wanting him. All of him. Inside her, pounding hard. Filling her, quelling the ache inside of her.

"It's time, Chris," she whispered, her lips brushing against the silken strands of his obsidian hair.

Christian relinquished her breasts and backed her up against the wall. The flicker of flames danced across the ceiling. The snapping of the fire filled the quiet room, mixing with their harsh breaths. Christian unfastened his jeans and pushed the material over his lean hips while Aja quickly stepped out of her jeans. Then he had her pinned against the wall. Lifting her up, she wrapped her legs around his waist.

"Now, Christian," she whispered. "Please. Now. I need you inside me. I *have* to have you!"

He didn't hesitate. His thick cock pushed deep inside her. Aja cried out at the erotic invasion.

Christian let out a low, primal growl. "Jesus, Aja. You feel so good." He cupped her ass and drove himself deeper into her. "I love you so much. More than anything."

"Oh, yes." She groaned. He began to thrust hard and fast, causing Aja's pulse to accelerate. She clung to him, clutching at him with her hands and her legs. She squeezed him tight, using her inner muscles to hold him captive inside her as her first orgasm tore through her body. Her eyes closed and she gasped for air as the delicious sensations consumed her. Christian did not let up. He continued to pound into her, unleashing his desire for her, proving she was his.

Aja did not miss the possessiveness of his lovemaking. Not only did it turn her completely inside out, making her hotter and wetter than she'd ever been before, but it also caressed her soul.

"I belong to you," she told him. "Only you. Forever, Christian. I will love you forever."

"And I belong to you, Aja. Forever."

She knew it was true. Even if their eternities weren't the same, she would forever be connected to Christian. He would never forget her. He would carry their love with him for the rest of his existence, immortalizing it for all of time.

"Come inside me, Christian. Please. I need to feel you."

It took no more than her erotic request. He released himself, letting out a low groan as he climaxed. Hot cum flooded her pussy, filling Aja and sparking another intense orgasm. His name fell from her lips as the desire consumed her.

They belonged to each other. Always.

Chapter 17

Late the next night, Christian pulled demon patrol. He had sensed the demons lurking and had left Aja and Maylar in the house to prowl the backyard. While Aja cast the spell to draw out Kabore, Christian would fend off the evil demons and spirits attempting to culminate within Kabore, making him even more powerful. Along with those demons that wanted to destroy the powerful witches.

Christian's shoulders were bunched in knots as he faded into the shadows created by the shrouded moon. He didn't like leaving Aja and Maylar alone. Nor did he like not being there when they exorcised Kabore from Maylar. But if he didn't cover the ground out here, they'd stand no chance when the legion of demons arrived at the door.

Christian tried to clear his troubled thoughts. Aja lingered in them. He loved her so much. He couldn't stand being away from her for a moment. And the thought of anything happening to her wrenched his gut. But she was strong and clever and powerful. He had to believe in her skills and trust she could fulfill her task while he completed his.

Rounding a corner of the house, he pressed his back against the brick wall. He sensed an evil presence. Several, in fact. Christian felt the change in him, felt his fangs protrude, his nails lengthen. He knew his eyes had changed from green to black. He could see everything in the dark shadows with his vampire eyes.

He sniffed the air and caught the direction from which the evil scent came. With quick, stealthy movements, he literally pounced on his prey. His hand clasped a jaw and he gave a powerful twist, snapping the neck. He withdrew a stake from the back pocket of his black jeans and pierced the demon's heart with it.

As he drew back, a second demon attacked him, lunging at him from the side so that Christian landed on his back. He had the stake in hand and took aim. The demon disintegrated. Christian jumped to his feet but remained crouched low. He caught a movement out of the corner of his eye and leapt toward it. He sailed through the air, spike in hand.

On and on it went, slaying demon after demon. Christian had little time to wonder what was happening inside the house. He could only hope the spell to vanquish Kabore worked.

Aja explained to Maylar that once the incantation began, Maylar needed to release Kabore from within her. The little girl was hesitant to concede. With a fearful expression on her angelic face, she told Aja she didn't think she could help vanquish the demon.

"I can handle Kabore, Maylar. You just need to let him out."

"But what if something bad happens?" she asked. "To you or to Christian? To the Elders?"

"We have to try, Maylar." She sat on the sofa and held the little girl's hand in hers. She gave it a gentle squeeze. "It'll be okay," Aja said. "We won't let him hurt the Elders."

Maylar gave a tentative nod of her head, her springy blond curls bouncing on her shoulders. "I believe you, Ajana."

Aja's insides twisted. Her sense of victory, having defeated Draken, was short-lived. Defeating Kabore—who had amassed more evil within him than anything Aja could possibly fathom—was altogether another story. It was, without doubt, the most difficult thing Aja had ever had to do.

Slaying demons roaming the countryside was one thing. Vanquishing a demon of Kabore's magnitude, with young Maylar's life in danger and Christian out of her eyesight, made her anxious and even a bit frightened. But she had to be strong for Maylar. She knew the little witch could read her thoughts, so Aja used her considerable powers to block her out. In doing so, though, she knew it intensified Maylar's trepidation.

"Are we ready?" Aja asked.

Maylar nodded.

Aja retrieved a small vial from the coffee table and handed it to Maylar. "Drink this potion."

The little girl did as Aja asked. Once she'd swallowed half of it, Aja began her incantation. She kept a watchful eye on Maylar, waiting for the most opportune moment. The living room was dimly lit with candles and the flames began to flicker as though a door had been opened. Aja and Maylar exchanged a curious look.

Aja continued her chant. She sensed Maylar was holding Kabore back.

"Now, Maylar," Aja encouraged the young witch. "It's time."

Maylar's little head bobbed up and down. "I know." She closed her amber eyes and pulled in a deep breath.

Aja continued to chant. And wait.

Maylar frowned. Her little face scrunched up tight, her brows dipping in concentration. But nothing happened. She opened her eyes. "I can't do it, Ajana. I had the power to draw him in when he wasn't so evil. But now that he's multiplied, I don't have the power to get him out."

She looked deeply distressed. Aja said, "Just continue to try. I'll help."

Aja reached for the small vial and drained its remaining contents. She sat next to Maylar again. She closed her eyes and concentrated on helping the miniature witch. She chanted softly, until she felt her power grow within her.

When she felt Kabore's presence, she knew she could draw him out. "Are you ready, Maylar?"

"Yes. Um, I think so."

"Okay. Now is the time." Aja reached for Maylar's hand and squeezed it tight. She chanted a few moments more, loud and strong, then said, "I release you, Kabore. *Now!*"

What happened in the next instant caught Aja off guard. Maylar exhaled a plume of black smoke and it filled the living room. Aja lost Maylar in the darkness for a moment. But then her vampire eyes adjusted to the sooty blackness filling the room, and she saw Kabore, more monstrous and menacing than any demon she'd ever encountered, stalk toward her and Maylar.

Aja jumped off the sofa and tried to reach for her crossbow, but Kabore descended upon her so quickly, she couldn't react in time. He swiped a long arm in her direction and sent her sailing across the living room. She hit the far wall and landed in a heap on the floor. She let out a sharp cry of pain. Her vision was momentarily distorted, but then she refocused on the task at hand.

If Kabore was disoriented, as the Elders had predicted, he was merely swiping at any presence he sensed, not sure what he'd hit. She likely only had seconds to respond. Lucky for her, the vampire inside her gave her strength—and the ability to recover quickly from the demon's blow. She got to her feet. She spared a glance at Maylar, who was slumped on the sofa.

She was probably drained physically from the exertion of expelling Kabore. Aja suspected that was a good thing. With Maylar unconscious, she couldn't make any movements that would draw the demon's attention.

Aja began to chant loudly. She only needed Kabore to drop to his knees and she could attempt to spear him. The beast, whose large, egg-shaped head nearly brushed her ten-foot-tall ceiling, swayed from the impact of the spell. Aja conjured her powers and drew forth an electrifying energy that, once it connected with Kabore, had the demon slumping to the floor. She used the opportunity to pierce the demon's heart with one shot from the crossbow.

Unfortunately, Kabore still had the faculties to anticipate her move. He rolled to the side and she ended up spearing the chair instead of him. The beast's enormous, scaly hand reached for her. The seven long appendages protruding from that hand snaked around her neck and her body, instantly immobilizing her. He lifted her up and pinned her against the wall. Aja's feet dangled four feet off the ground.

She choked out a strangled cry. Rendered incapacitated, there was nothing Aja could do to free herself. Kabore was stronger than she was and she couldn't continue to chant, to weaken him, because it was now difficult to breathe. Her body began to tingle as it grew weak and limp. But Aja refused to give up.

She squirmed and writhed within his tight grasp. To no avail. She'd lose consciousness soon if she didn't free herself,

Damn it! The Elders had preserved her spirit for five hundred years and she was going to fail them? She couldn't believe it. *Refused* to believe it. She and Christian had sacrificed too much for it to end this way.

And, as though she'd invoked him with her thoughts, Christian flew through the French doors in the living room, glass shattering and wood splintering in every direction as he surged forward. He landed on his feet, a stake in each hand. Blood and demon dust covered him from head to toe. He looked worse for the wear, but he'd survived the demon attacks.

Relief coursed through Aja. Not only was Christian alive, but he would free her so she could vanquish Kabore.

"When he releases you, go for the fire poker," Christian instructed in a low voice.

A sense of rejuvenation seeped through Aja. She was weak, but she was ready to fight. In the next instant, Christian leaped forward, onto the monstrous demon's back, and drove the two stakes into his thick, greenish-gray, scaly skin. The demon released Aja and she fell to the ground. Pain lanced through her body and stole her breath. Unable to move until the sharp stabs of pain subsided, she watched as the demon reeled from the wounds Christian inflicted with the stakes. He thrashed and bucked, like a bull attempting to dislodge its rider. But Christian held fast to the stakes, which remained embedded in the demon's body.

Now able to speak, though her throat felt raw and tight, Aja began her chant again. Softly at first, but when she saw the adverse effect it had on Kabore, her voice gained strength. He went down on one knee. Aja scrambled to her feet, ignoring the pain that shot through her like a hundred daggers spearing her insides. She made her way to the fireplace and grabbed the poker.

With a tight grip on the large, wrought iron weapon, she moved slowly toward Kabore as she continued to chant. When the demon collapsed to both knees, Aja summoned all the strength and power she possessed and lunged forward, penetrating the demon's tough hide. He let out a loud, piercing squeal that practically shook the rafters.

Aja dug in, bracing her feet on the carpeted floor as she put all of her weight, such that it was, behind the effort, driving the poker deep into the demon's heart. His roar turned into pained whimpers, then angered snarls, then labored pants. Aja managed to just barely get out of the way as the enormous body swayed from side to side, then toppled over. The demon's considerable weight pushed the fire poker all the way into his body, though he was too big for it to run him all the way through. It didn't matter. Aja knew the damage had been done.

Christian released his death grip on the spikes and rolled off Kabore. The demon convulsed and trembled for several moments. Aja watched, wide-eyed and prepared to continue the battle. She dragged in sharp pulls of air, trying to fill her lungs with oxygen. Her body still throbbed with pain and her throat burned.

The demon lying on her living room floor conceded the fight. His body turned gray then disintegrated into a ten-foot-long pile of ash.

Aja slumped into a nearby chair, the adrenaline leaving her. Exhaustion suddenly consumed her.

"That's one hell of a mess," Christian muttered as he crossed the room and knelt in front of Aja. He took her hands in his and gazed deeply into her eyes. "Are you okay?"

She nodded. When her breathing stabilized, she said, "How's Maylar?" Aja's voice was rough and raspy, and it still hurt to speak. She suspected her neck was bruised from Kabore's tight grip.

Christian left Aja to check on Maylar. "She's sleeping," he said. A soft grin touched his lips as he stared down at the small witch, curled up on the sofa, sleeping peacefully. The entire demon-vanquishing ordeal hadn't disturbed her in the least.

Aja's heart constricted at the tender look on Christian's face. He'd fallen in love with the girl as quickly as Aja had.

Christian's gaze shifted to Aja. "What do you say we call it a night?"

"Best idea yet."

He carried Maylar to her bed, then returned for Aja. He scooped her up in his arms and traveled upstairs and down the long hall to her room. Placing her gently on the bed, he did a quick inspection of her injuries. He disappeared into the bathroom for a few minutes, then returned with a warm washcloth. He cleaned the dried blood from the small cuts she'd sustained. His frown deepened when he reached her neck.

"That bad?" she asked in a weak voice.

Christian nodded. "You might want to avoid your neighbors for a week or so. It looks like you've been beaten pretty badly." He forced the scowl from his face and, in a lighter tone, said, "I wouldn't want anyone to think I did that to you."

Aja let out a soft laugh. She reached a hand out to him and skimmed her fingers over his cheek. "You saved me. And the Elders."

Christian eased onto the mattress beside her and pulled her into his arms. "We make a good team."

"The best."

Chapter 18

Knowing it was inevitable, Aja dragged her weary body from her bed the next morning, shuffled down the hallway and then made her way downstairs. Sooner or later, she'd have to deal with the disaster that had once been her living room. She saw no point in putting it off.

Not knowing where Christian had disappeared to this morning, she went straight to the kitchen and made coffee. She took her mug into the living room. Aja drew up short and gasped.

The black soot that had covered her pristine, albeit boring, white walls and the huge pile of demon dust on her floor that had once been Kabore were gone. Her walls were painted a soft, buttery yellow and the carpeted floor had been replaced with polished hardwood. The room was bright and cheery. So unlike the plain, nondescript room she'd lived with since buying the house several years ago.

"Do you like it?"

Aja started. The soft voice that came from behind her caught her off guard. She was still not used to having people in her house. She turned to face Maylar, who wore a hopeful expression on her adorable face.

Aja couldn't help but smile. "Is this your doing?"

Maylar nodded. "Christian helped. But I changed the color on the walls."

"I like it very much."

Relief shone bright in Maylar's large amber-colored eyes. Eyes that matched Aja's perfectly. It occurred to Aja that anyone who saw the two of them together would immediately assume they were mother and daughter. The thought made her heart hurt. Aja would never have a daughter, much less one as loveable as Maylar.

The little girl reached for Aja's hand. "We must see the Elders now."

Aja would have preferred to wait a few days to visit the Elders, knowing that seeing her injuries would trouble them. But she knew they anxiously awaited her return, so she teleported herself into their realm, with Maylar in tow.

The little witch let out a squeal of delight and ran into Cassius' open arms. Aja couldn't help but feel a twinge of regret that Maylar would not be returning with her. In the short amount of time she'd known the petite witch, Aja had grown fond of her. But the Elders, she knew, would want to tutor Maylar, as they had Aja.

"I didn't think you could look any worse than that first time you visited us, after your powers were restored," Vassar said to her. "I was wrong."

Aja self-consciously pulled up the collar of her white, button-down shirt. "He was one bad-ass demon."

To her surprise, Vassar grinned. "Yes, I'm sure he was." He chuckled, a sound Aja had not heard in centuries. "Come," he said as held a hand out to her. "I have something to show you."

They left Cassius and Maylar and entered the private chamber. Vassar sat in his elaborate, ornate chair and Aja stood before him.

"Would you like to see what the future holds for you, Ajana?"

Her jaw fell slack for a moment, but she quickly recovered. "I thought that was forbidden."

"There are exceptions to every rule, Ajana. Surely you know that by now."

Excitement welled inside her, but was quickly tainted by the reality of her situation. As Aja recalled her skewed biological chemistry and the fact that she was now partially immortal, she wasn't so sure she wanted to know what lay ahead for her. What would Vassar show her? A death that was inescapable and the end of her and Christian's love for each other?

"I already know what the future holds for me, Vassar."

His voice was tender and paternal as he said, "You have selflessly served the people of this realm, Ajana, as well as the people in your world. You have made great sacrifices. Never once have you asked to be rewarded. Never once have you asked what's in it for you. The only thing you ever wished for was a long life with Christian, for him not to suffer when your lifetime comes to an end. That, in itself, is yet another selfless act."

Aja fought back the tears that started to build in her eyes. "He's done so much for us. None of this was his responsibility, yet he willingly took it upon himself to help me, to protect me."

Vassar nodded. "He shall be rewarded, too." Vassar's soft grin returned. "I'm offering you an opportunity unlike any other, Ajana. The chance to see what the rest of your life will be like... Will you accept this gift?"

Aja pulled in a full, albeit unsteady, breath. She held it for a few moments as she contemplated her answer, then expelled the air. "Yes."

"Very good." Vassar waved a hand over the prophecy book and it lifted from its eternal perch.

As the book levitated toward her, anxiety seized her insides. Aja nervously wrung her hands. What if her future turned out to be a short one?

The book floated in front of her and Aja stared at it, uncertainty seeping through her veins. A diffused golden glow emanated from the book, surrounding it. The pages made a soft whooshing sound as they slowly turned. Images formed above the book, lingering briefly before morphing into different visions.

Aja saw herself with Christian as they continued to teach at their respective universities over the years. She saw them settled comfortably in her house, with her new butter-colored walls. Images of Maylar followed, and Aja smiled as she watched the little witch grow before her eyes, transforming from an adorable, precocious child to a beautiful young woman.

Aja drew her gaze away from the book and said to Vassar, "Christian and I will be able to visit her, then?"

The images vanished and the golden glow surrounding the book diminished.

"There is more to your destiny than Cassius and I originally shared with you,

Ajana." He gestured toward the book. "Please. Have another look."

The book illuminated once more, and this time, Aja saw Maylar sitting in Vassar's chair. She gasped. Her gaze returned to Vassar. "She is the next ruler of this realm?"

Vassar beamed. "Yes. The time draws near for Cassius and I to relinquish our power, Ajana. It is important that the Chosen One understand everything there is to know about our realm, but also the world in which you and Christian live. It is the only way she can truly become an all-knowing being, and ensure that the decisions she makes are best for her people."

Aja was stunned. She'd had no idea Maylar possessed such power. Vassar stunned her further.

"I have a new charge for you, Ajana. Cassius and I wish you to raise Maylar as your daughter. To teach her everything she needs to know about your world, but also to serve as her mentor and tutor in this realm. She will need to understand her power and how to use it."

A lump of emotion swelled in Aja's throat and tears stung her eyes. "A... *daughter*?"

Vassar nodded. "You and Christian will make exceptional parents, Ajana. Do you accept this charge?"

"Of course, I do," she said, breathless.

"There's one more thing, Ajana."

She brushed away the tears that rolled down her cheeks, but they kept coming. "What?"

Vassar stood. He descended the three steps and joined Aja. He took her hands in his and said, "The reward for your service, and for Christian's, is immortality. I grant it to you, Ajana, hence forth."

Aja gasped. It was more than she'd hoped for, more than she'd dreamed possible. More tears spilled down her cheek. "Thank you, Vassar. You've given me everything I've ever wanted. An eternity with Christian... a family." She choked back a sob, but Vassar didn't seem to mind her display of emotion. He pulled her into his warm embrace and held her tightly.

"You have earned this reward, Ajana. The people of this realm, Cassius and I, are indebted to you and Christian."

"We won't disappoint you, Vassar."

"You never have."

Chapter 19

Cassius and Vassar performed the binding ceremony in their realm. Christian knew he was overdressed in his black tuxedo, but he didn't care. He'd waited five hundred years for his life to be joined with Aja's. It was a day he intended to celebrate. A day he would remember for the rest of eternity.

Aja wore a beautiful white, satin dress with thin straps that sat on her slender shoulders. The wounds on her throat had healed and she wore one of her medallions, recovered from Draken's possession, around her neck. The large ruby in the center of the gold medallion sparkled and winked in the moonlight.

Maylar, wearing a pink satin dress, looked more adorable than ever. She stood by Aja's side as Vassar pronounced them a family, bound together for eternity.

"I love you," Aja told Christian, her eyes filled with emotion, a soft smile on her beautiful face.

"I love you, too. For all of eternity, Aja."

Food and drink were followed by dancing. Christian swept Aja into his arms and held her tightly, only relinquishing her three times during the entire evening. First so she could dance with Cassius and then Vassar, and then a final time so that Christian could dance with his new daughter.

Emotions he'd never experienced before welled inside him. They went far beyond the love and protectiveness he had always felt for Aja. His entire being was filled with hope and optimism for a long, happy future. These new sensations chased out all the old… The dread and the uncertainty and the loneliness that had plagued him for half a millennium were vanquished.

What Christian felt, for the first time since he'd agreed to help Aja fulfill her destiny, was pure and simple joy.

Epilogue

Six months later...

Aja let out a sigh of contentment as she slipped into bed. She snuggled close to Christian, working her way back into his loose embrace. Her head rested on his broad shoulder and one hand splayed over his hard pectoral muscles. She had every intention of letting him sleep. He still pulled demon patrol at night, guarding the house, keeping her and Maylar safe.

But as her fingertips lightly stroked his warm skin, she found herself taking advantage of the situation. Her hand swept lower, over the ridges of his abdomen. Her fingers disappeared under the crisp white sheet that was draped haphazardly over his large body. She grazed his erect penis and excitement jolted her, making her insides coil tight with anticipation. When her fingers wrapped around his thick shaft, Aja's excitement grew.

Suddenly, a large hand covered hers. Aja lifted her gaze to Christian's face. His eyes were still closed, but the hint of a grin played on his lips.

"Oh, good. You're awake."

"What are you up to, Mrs. St. James?"

A little thrill worked its way through Aja's body. She loved when he called her Mrs. St. James. Or when he introduced her as "my wife." Every time he did, she felt the same ripple of exhilaration and joy that she'd felt the night they were joined together by the Elders. Though the ritual in her realm meant the most to her, she and Christian had made their marriage official in this world, with a small ceremony performed over the summer on one of Pembrook's lush lawns. Faculty and staff, along with a few students, from both of their universities had attended.

Their marriage had surprised the hell out of everyone, that was for sure. But not a single person in attendance could doubt their deep love and devotion to each other. Aja knew it was impossible to miss.

She dropped a kiss on Christian's smooth chest as she continued to slowly, languidly, tease his cock. He let out a low groan. Taking that as encouragement, Aja shifted on the bed, pushed aside the sheet and settled between her husband's parted legs. She leaned over him and took his thick rod deep inside her mouth.

Christian's long fingers twined in her hair as she sucked him, then licked him from base to tip, then sucked him again.

"Aja." His groan became a sharp growl. "You'd better stop."

Aja lifted her head and smiled at him, knowing it was a lascivious, mischievous grin. "You don't really want me to stop, do you?"

"Of course not. But..." He let out a sound of discomfort. As though he really needed her to finish the job. "It's Saturday. Maylar will want to watch cartoons."

"Maylar isn't here." Aja went back to work.

Christian didn't stop her, seemingly enjoying her ministrations for a few minutes more. But then, apparently, a thought occurred to him. "Aja, where is Maylar?"

Her head popped up again. "The Elders summoned her about twenty minutes ago."

Christian let out another groan, this one in dismay rather than ecstasy. He gripped Aja's arms and dragged her up the length of his body until she lay on top of him. "What did she do this time?"

Aja couldn't contain her smile. "Seems she tried a spell on Vassar and it went... awry."

"Oh, shit." He rolled his eyes. "What happened?"

"She changed his blonde hair to green."

"Aja!"

"I know, I know!" She laughed. "Casting a spell on one of the Elders is like trying to achieve world peace. Impossible. I know from experience." She'd attempted several of her own spells on Cassius and Vassar as a child. It was, after all, a true test of her powers. "I will admit, though. I'm rather impressed. She nearly succeeded."

He eyed her with a stern look, though the grin that threatened his mouth, making the corners quiver, told her he was just as amused as she was. "What was she trying to do?"

"Change his hair to blue. To match his robe."

Christian attempted to bite back the laugh, but it escaped his lips anyway. He chuckled, low and deep.

Aja changed her position and straddled him, drawing his hard cock into her wet pussy, an inch at a time.

"How long will she be gone?" Christian asked, his voice strained.

Aja settled comfortably over him and sighed contently as his thick shaft filled and stretched her. "All day, I presume." She rocked her hips gently. "My guess is, Vassar will have her polishing his throne and washing his robes by hand. No *magik* allowed."

Christian's hands gripped her hips. He thrust into her, making Aja gasp.

"All day?" he asked between clenched teeth. "This will be the longest period we've had alone since the last time the Elders summoned her. Which was what? Two weeks ago?"

Aja grinned. "We really should teach her better. But... a child in her position of power, with so much responsibility on her shoulders, deserves a little fun from time to time. Besides," Aja said, grinding against Christian, taking him deep inside her body, "I consider it character development. We want our daughter to have a sense of humor, don't we?"

"Call it what you like..." Christian said as he pumped into her, thrusting deeper, faster, harder. "I think they make excellent babysitters."

Aja moaned. "Agreed."

Christian's large hands left her hips and cupped her breasts. His thumbs teased her nipples, making her hotter, wetter. She rode him hard, loving the feel of him inside her, swollen with desire and need. She gripped him tightly as she came, his name falling from her lips. Moments later, he thrust deep inside her and let out a low growl as he came.

Collapsing on top of him, dragging in some much-needed oxygen, Aja counted the moments until they'd both be ready for round two.

"I can read your wicked thoughts, Aja," Christian said in an amused tone.

She lifted her head. "You weren't thinking the same thing?"

He grinned at her. "Every single time we make love, sweetheart. Every single time."

He captured her mouth in a slow, sexy kiss that caressed Aja's heart and soul.

After five hundred years, all of her dreams had finally come true.

About the Author:

Calista Fox is the award-winning author of over 20 novellas and novels with publication dates scheduled into 2009. She began her professional fiction-writing career in 2004, following a successful career in PR, where she specialized in writing speeches and Congressional testimonies. Her books have received rave reviews and she is also the recipient of a Reviewer's Choice Award for Best Erotic Sci-Fi Novella.

Calista is a member of Romance Writer's of America® and two of its Phoenix Chapters, Desert Rose and Valley of the Sun Romance Writers. She has served on the Board of Directors, been the newsletter director and chaired the annual Golden Quill Contest, recognizing outstanding published authors, for the Desert Rose Chapter. She is also a member of Passionate Ink, RWA's erotic romance chapter. In addition, Calista gives presentations and workshops on writing novellas.

Calista attended college on a Journalism scholarship and has worked on newspapers as an editor and reporter. She holds degrees in General Studies and Communications. Calista lives in Arizona, but travels frequently to places like Mexico, Europe, San Diego, and Washington, DC. She has traveled the country by Lear Jet, always with her laptop in tow, and is a spa aficionado!

Reflection of Beauty

by Bonnie Dee

To My Reader:

We never outgrow fairy tales. Maybe that's why there have been more re-tellings of *Cinderella* than practically any other story I can think of. "Poor girl makes good" never gets old. But an equally popular fairy tale theme is found in *Beauty and the Beast*. A scarred man nurtured and saved by a strong woman's love is the sexiest thing imaginable. I hope you enjoy this modern, erotic revisiting of one of my favorite stories.

Chapter 1

"I had the rose dream again last night. The one where I have to tear through all those brambles trying to get to a door that leads through the wall." Chris sipped her morning coffee and stared at the ring the mug had left on the table. "You wouldn't believe how vivid it was. I could actually *feel* the scratching thorns. The brambles were covered with little pink roses, their scent so strong I could still smell them when I woke up."

"Olfactory dreaming. Interesting." Tonya continued to mark the items she needed to order for the shop.

"You don't sound that interested."

"You've been telling me about this Secret Garden dream for months. I passed 'interested' a while ago."

Chris set down her cup. "Well, listen to this. Last night something new happened. I made it through the wall."

Tonya looked up, her brown eyes holding a gleam of curiosity for the first time. "Really? What happened next?"

"Inside the wall was a deserted castle. I walked through an empty courtyard and into the great hall. My footsteps echoing were the only sound. It was really eerie, but I knew I had to keep going." Chris closed her eyes, summoning up the dream that had the technicolor clarity of a movie. "A presence somewhere inside urged me toward it, just like in all the dreams I've been having."

"And did you reach it?"

"Yeah." Chris hesitated. The rest of the dream was too personal. She and Tonya shared explicit details about their sex lives, but the eroticism of last night's dream wasn't something she wanted to share. The almost transcendent nature of the sex would be lost in the telling. "I don't remember much after that, but it was very sexy and intense."

Tonya propped her chin on her hand. "Hot! Tell me about it. I need a dirty story to jump start my day."

Tonya's voice faded away. Chris turned her empty cup around and around in her hands as she replayed every aspect of the previous night's dream.

When she'd finally torn away the curtain of thorns to reveal the door in the wall, her heart pounded with excitement. She held her breath, expecting to wake up, but she turned the knob and the door swung open into a shady courtyard. In the center was a fountain with nymphs swaying in a sensual dance. If water had been flowing, it would've looked like the sprites were cavorting under a waterfall. Instead rust stains made their nude forms bloody and dried leaves collected in whispery pools in the basin.

Weed-choked paths wandered between overgrown garden beds where toppled, vine-covered statues lay. The presence beckoned Chris onward, demanding her attention and she passed through the desolate courtyard to the dark, ominous wall of the castle. She opened massive doors to enter a hall lined with armor. There was no patronizing butler or austere housekeeper to meet her. Her footsteps echoed in the stillness as she walked down the hall and ascended the wide staircase.

She didn't stop to examine the remains of faded luxury in dust-covered rooms. The pull of the entity led her unerringly to a door with wood so highly polished Chris could see her faint reflection in it. *This is how I will look to him*, she thought. *Dark hair. Dark eyes. Dark skin. Short, sharp, intense. That's me.*

In a hurry now to meet the presence that had summoned her for so many nights, she pushed open the door and entered the dark room beyond it.

At last. You're here for me. The voice filling her mind was deeply masculine. It reverberated in her brain cells and throughout her nervous system, making her shiver with need. The presence was overpoweringly male and desperately hungry for her. She could sense it in the dream, feel his desire—a mirror image of her own.

Chris was just as starved for his touch. The feminine, vulnerable aspect of her strong personality rolled over and turned belly up in submission. *Here I am. Take me!*

Her pussy clenching and releasing with each heartbeat, she walked farther into the room. There was a huge four-poster bed at one end. Bookcases and a large fireplace covered one wall. A leather armchair stood beside the hearth, but the owner of the room remained unseen.

She approached a long, oval, wooden frame between two tall windows. Sparkling shards of mirror lay scattered beneath the stand. Her bare feet crunched across them, the pieces slicing her soles just as the thorns had scratched her hands. She stared at the empty mirror frame and one remaining jagged shard dangling there. It reflected part of her shoulder and arm but nothing else. *Where are you?*

Right here. Heavy, warm hands rested on her shoulders, pressing for a moment before sliding down her bare arms to lace fingers with her.

Chris was nude in the dream, but didn't feel shy. She closed her eyes and relaxed into the invisible stroking hands on her breasts, stomach, thighs and sex. His touch was everywhere at once, a subtle tickling like a warm breeze blowing all over her body. It reminded her of the way her brush kissed the canvas when she painted.

She leaned back to find his body, warm and solid behind her. His mouth nuzzled the side of her neck and trailed kisses all the way to the curve of her shoulder. She turned her head to meet his soft, yielding lips. Her eyes may have been open or closed, but it didn't matter which. She knew she wouldn't be able to see him. That wasn't allowed. She didn't care. All she needed was to feel him, clasping her body tightly, exploring her mouth with his searching tongue, pressing his growing erection into the crevice of her buttocks. She turned in the circle of his embrace and her hands caressed his muscled chest and shoulders. Reaching down between them, she grasped his cock. It filled her hand, warm and heavy and solid—too solid to be a mere dream.

Chris stroked up and down the shaft. At the same time, she touched him everywhere at once, just as he was doing to her. It wasn't like the physical world where touch was limited to points of contact between two bodies. In the dream world, she felt him in every cell. Her body was charged with light, her being crackling with erotic energy. The glut of sensation was almost too much to bear. She thought she might come from touching alone before he ever entered her.

This is a good dream. A bubble of laughter escaped her and shimmered in the air around them like dust motes dancing in the sun.

A *very* good dream. The rumble of his voice sent a delicious shiver through her. He was so sexy and masculine and smelled so good. She breathed him in, hot male skin and a subtle, woodsy aroma. He lifted her up with his hands beneath her ass and pushed inside her in one swift, fluid motion.

Chris gasped and held on tight, wrapping her arms and legs around him. His cock filled her completely, satisfying her open, yearning sex. It touched a place deep inside sending waves of pleasure surging through her.

Suddenly they were no longer standing, but stretched out on the silk covers of the massive bed. He rose and fell above her, driving deep inside and hitting that wonderful, magic spot each time. The unfocused sparkles of desire darting through her body coalesced into a strong, steady pulsing whole, like an Impressionist painting in which dabs of color form a complete picture. Her hips lifted to meet each hard thrust of her unseen lover. Her body rose higher each time until she was no longer on the bed, but floating somewhere above it.

The insistent pressure of her growing orgasm suddenly burst, exploding in crystal shards like mirror glass that showered through her entire being, leaving her breathless and exhilarated.

"Hey, Christine! Focus!" Tonia's fingers snapped in front of her face. "Are you even listening to me?"

Chris startled, almost falling off her chair. She quickly covered by standing up. "Yeah. Of course!"

Tonia rolled her eyes. "For those who tuned in late, I said I'm going to take first shift in the studio. I had an idea last night I want to try out on the wheel."

"Sure. Go ahead. I'll open the store for the overwhelming rush of customers."

"Don't joke. I'm too depressed." Tonya went to the peg on the wall, got her smock and tied it on over her jeans and T-shirt.

Chris emptied the carafe from the coffeemaker into her cup and added cream and sugar. By the time she finished, Tonya was sitting at her pottery wheel in the studio. She watched for a moment, enthralled as always by the effortless way her friend could take a gray lump of clay and spin it into a tall, fluted column.

Sipping her second cup of the day, she walked to the front of the shop and unlocked the door. She stepped outside for a moment to watch the neighborhood and breathe in the fumes of car exhaust and city grime—no roses here. Then she sat behind the checkout counter and opened her sketchbook, hoping to jot down a few memories from her dream before they disappeared. She was so engrossed in penciling in the details of rose leaves against rough stone she jumped when the phone rang.

"Good morning, T.S.A. Art Supplies." Chris smiled at the goofy acronym for Two Struggling Artists, which Tonya had insisted on for their store name.

"May I speak to Christina Dawson?"

"I'm Christine. Can I help you?"

"Ms. Dawson, this is Denise Thomas from the Gruen Gallery. We met at Mina Karischnov's party."

"Yes. I remember." Chris's heart began to thump. Meeting Denise Thomas was the biggest thrill she'd had the night of Mina's party, including hooking up with some random guy whose name she couldn't even remember now. "What can I do for you, Ms. Thomas?"

"Please, it's Denise. Christine, I've heard great things about your paintings from a number of people and I'm very impressed with what I saw on your web site. I wondered if I might come by your studio to see your work."

"Of course! Absolutely! Any time that would be convenient for you. My studio is behind the shop and I'm here almost all the time." Chris concentrated on breathing before she hyperventilated and passed out on the phone. She couldn't have been more excited if she'd won the mega-lottery.

"Excellent. I'll swing by around 5:30 today. Will that work for you?"

Chris mentally rescheduled her after-work errands. "Perfect." She thanked Denise then hung up the phone. Whooping, she jumped off her stool and raced to the back room. "Tonya!"

Clay went flying as Tonya's usually steady hand destroyed the vase she'd been forming. "Damn it! You scared the hell out of me. What?"

"I got a call from Gruen—*the* Gruen Gallery."

Tonya turned off the wheel and scraped clay from her hands. "No shit?"

"Denise Thomas. She remembered me from Mina's party. She said 'people have been talking' about my work, and she's coming here today to take a look."

"Oh my God, I can't believe it. You lucky little bitch!" Tonya rinsed her hands in the bucket of water near her wheel and then gestured to the stack of canvases leaning haphazardly against the far wall. "Girl, you've got to get organized. You can't show your paintings like that. Presentation is everything. If you want to be a professional, you've got to look like a professional."

"You're right. We have to clean this place up and hang some of these." Chris went to the paintings and shuffled through them, trying to decide which she especially wanted to draw to Denise's attention. She frowned as she looked at a study of an old man and little boy playing chess in the park. "Will they like my stuff, Tonya? Is it 'artsy' enough for the Gruen?"

Tonya dried her hands on her smock, slipped an arm around Chris's shoulders and hugged her. "They're going to love you. Don't worry."

Chris paused at a painting she'd done shortly after her first rose dream and studied it critically. "What do you think? This one?"

"Definitely."

The two women stood for a long moment gazing at the painting of a mass of pink flowers with vicious looking inch-long thorns and thick vines coiled around a gnarled tree. The leafless tree's branches were twisted and drooping and the stunted trunk was completely bound by the vines. The abundant flowers looked more lethal and sinister than beautiful. The sky in the painting was a stormy gray and the land around the bound tree was barren and ruined.

Chris thought of the breakthrough in last night's dream. She wondered what a therapist would tell her reaching her goal meant. She'd certainly like to know what the male presence in the dream represented—and how she could get in touch with him again, 'cause damn, that had been one powerfully erotic experience.

Eric stared at the numbers scrolling past on the television screen, but his mind was far away from stock reports. He resisted the pull for as long as he could then turned to his computer and clicked the bookmark for Christine Dawson's web site. It took him straight to the artist bio page where Christine's dark, liquid eyes gazed straight back into his.

His need to see her picture was becoming obsessive and more than a little creepy. Yet Eric couldn't stop looking at the beautiful woman and getting lost in her penetrating eyes about a dozen times, or more, a day. Ever since he'd first seen Christine in the footage from her show two weeks ago, he'd been obsessed with her.

In the web page photo, Christine's long black hair was plaited into hundreds of tiny braids that framed her wide, angular face. He wondered how it would feel to touch the braids, to stroke the heavy, bumpy mass or feel them trail over his chest or his groin. How would those full, lush lips feel if he kissed her? How would they feel kissing his chest or wrapped around his cock?

"Jesus!" Eric closed the web page with an emphatic click of the mouse. "You fucking pervert."

He turned his attention back to business, making notations, jotting down percentages and bits of information. But within ten minutes the lure of Christine Dawson pulled him back.

He clicked on the footage of her show, which his assistant Hank had filmed for him. Hank worked as his proxy in a number of situations, including occasionally checking out new artists. Most galleries were willing to suspend rules about not allowing videotaping when they learned it was Eric Leroux making the request. Everyone in the art world genuflected to an eccentric recluse with a seemingly inexhaustible bank account.

Christine's paintings were good, although not Eric's usual taste. He preferred non-representational art. Still, her landscapes and portraits were professionally executed and vibrant with life. She was gifted at capturing the essence of her portrait subjects, the inner joy or sorrow they transmitted through their eyes.

Eric held his breath as the footage of the exhibit ended and Hank's brief interview with the artist began. The film showed a small, compact, African-American woman wearing a long, colorful skirt and peasant blouse that broadcasted 'free-spirited bohemian.' She crackled with energy as she greeted Hank with an outstretched hand.

"Welcome. Thank you for coming." Her eyes cut to the camera and for a moment it was like she was looking into Eric's eyes. His heart froze in his chest.

"And hello Mr. Leroux. Glad you could make the opening." She grinned, a flash of white, even teeth against plum-colored lips. She ran a hand through her hair, arranged in masses of curls rather than braids for the evening. "So, this is my show. What do you think?"

Eric's lips curved to match hers. The woman's smile was infectious, and she was refreshingly unpretentious compared to many of the artists he'd seen. As she chatted in her relaxed fashion about her inspiration for some of the paintings and spoke about her technique, Eric became engrossed in the sexy lilt of her voice, the phrasing of words that was exclusive to her. He was completely enthralled by the way she gestured with her graceful hands, and found the paint stain marking one of them absolutely endearing. Christine Dawson was the most desirable woman he'd ever seen. And Eric had seen, if not actually interacted with, plenty of women.

He'd watched the footage enough times now that he knew exactly when it ended. Before it did, he hit *pause*. The screen froze on an image of Christine laughing, her chin lifted and her eyes sparkling with amusement. She was gorgeous. From the moment he'd first seen her, Eric had experienced a sense of déjà vu. She was so familiar, he thought he must have seen her somewhere before and forgotten it. Although how he could ever forget a face like that, he didn't know.

Staring at her image, he allowed his hand to steal down to his pants and unfasten his fly. He reached inside and grasped the hot, throbbing erection that tormented him. He stroked up and down its length, never breaking the connection between his eyes and the brown, laughing eyes on the monitor. He imagined Christine touching him like this, her hand massaging his cock with firm, steady strokes.

His eyes drifted half-closed as he visualized her straddling his lap, her legs pressed firmly against his hips and her pussy enveloping him slowly, so hot and wet it practically melted him. Her hands would grip his shoulders for leverage as she lifted herself up and down on his cock.

Eric closed his eyes completely, continuing the illusion. His stroking hand moved faster and his hips thrust up. His mouth dropped open as he panted in and out. God, he could imagine Christine pressing her lush lips to his then whispering near his ear. "I want you so much. I've waited for this for so long."

Grunting, he pulled at his cock, hard and rough. The fantasy wouldn't hold. He felt it slipping away and wanted to finish before reality crashed back in. The friction of his palm on the sensitive skin of his shaft built to an unbearable heat. Suddenly his orgasm burst through him, bringing the charade to an end as he spilled over his pumping fist.

Eric opened his eyes and gazed down in disgust at the evidence of his perverted fixation on Christine Dawson.

"You really are one sick fuck." He wiped his hand on tissues he pulled from a box in his desk drawer—and how pathetic was it that he *had* tissues on hand for just such an event.

He stuffed his half-flaccid cock back in his pants and zipped up, kicking the desk drawer closed. With a stab of his finger on the mouse, Eric closed the media program, returning his screen to the hard facts and figures of trading. He stood abruptly, sending his chair rolling back and walked over to the window to gaze out at his garden.

The roses were blooming on the wall and he opened the window to catch a whiff of their rich, sweet fragrance. In the shade, ferns surrounded the pool of koi. Out in the sunlit flowerbeds, a profusion of bright colors and glossy green leaves shone in the sun. The beauty of nature was usually a balm to Eric's soul when his loneliness grew too deep to bear, but today it did nothing to soothe him. He felt desolate and the cheerful flowers only made it worse.

It wasn't enough to look at Christine and indulge in furtive sexual fantasies about her that left him feeling guilty and depraved. He wanted to meet this woman and talk to her in person. He wanted to look into her eyes, listen to her voice and find out if her smile really lit up the room. A thought that had been playing around the edges of his consciousness for the past week suddenly sprang full-formed into his head. There was a way to meet her if he dared.

Eric usually purchased art through a phone conversation and bank transfer, but he could require a meeting with Christine before buying one of her paintings. Hell, he could do more than buy a painting. He could commission one. But it must be something that required meeting with her on a regular basis so a landscape was out. He must hire her to paint a portrait, his portrait. It wasn't outlandish for him to invite her to stay at the house while she worked on it—not if he paid her well enough.

Then he would be able to see her and talk to her and maybe even... maybe even what? Eric let out a disgusted snort at his ridiculous fantasy. He turned away from the garden and returned to his desk. What did he think would happen? That Christine Dawson would have sex with him or even fall in love with him? It was a warped fairytale only a pitiful hermit with way too much time on his hands would invent. Besides, he would never let her see his face, so how could she possibly paint his likeness? The whole farfetched scheme was pathetic.

Eric sat down and gazed at his computer screen, once more filled with the logical sanity of numbers. Facts and figures were decipherable, manageable. They kept a man's mind occupied and didn't nip little bites out of his heart. A productive day of business was what he needed to cleanse his mind of the fantasies he'd allowed to fog it.

Eric logged into his account to begin trading. After several minutes his mind settled and focused, and the daydream of the pretty artist dissipated.

The *You've Got Mail* notice popped up on the screen. He clicked on a message from Hank.

"Anything from the Dawson collection you want? I'll call the gallery and have Denise send the specifics on whatever you're interested in."

Eric gazed at the short message as though at a bomb he was attempting to diffuse. Which wire to cut, the red or the blue? Slowly he lifted his hands and placed them on the keyboard. "I want to talk to the artist directly. I may be interested in more of her work. Get me her phone number from the gallery."

His finger hovered over the button then pressed *Send*.

Chapter 2

"He's weird," Tonya said. "Creepy and weird. Don't do it!'"

"He's rich! I have to," Chris answered.

"I'm telling you, this doesn't feel right. Don't go."

When Tonya talked, Chris usually listened. Tonya was her Jiminy Cricket, the girl who pulled on the reins when Chris's impulsiveness overtook her.

"I know it sounds crazy, driving out into the middle of nowhere and staying with a stranger."

"It sounds like the beginning of a horror movie." Tonya slid the vase of nasturtiums on the counter aside and dusted under it. "And not the kind where the heroine emerges, battered, covered in blood, but alive and victorious. It sounds like the kind where she gets killed in the first half of the movie and her trusty friend has to find out what happened and ultimately uncover her mutilated corpse."

"Well, he didn't sound like a crazy killer on the phone," Chris said.

"They never do. And what are you smiling about?"

Chris wiped the smirk off her face. She couldn't stop smiling every time she remembered the phone conversation with Eric Leroux. His voice was as rich and deep as James Earl Jones's cultured bass. And even though she knew Leroux was white, she thought of warm, dark chocolate dripping over her body when he talked. Before she even knew who he was, before he'd spoken more than a half dozen words to her on the phone, her panties had been wet from the timbre of his voice.

"What?" Tonya demanded again.

"Nothing. I'm just really glad he bought my painting. You know the rose painting was the only thing I sold after the show."

"You've heard the rumors about this guy, right?" Tonya twitched her dust cloth back and forth as she leaned against the display case. "He's supposed to be really messed up, like *Elephant Man* deformed, which is why he's never seen in public."

"Bullshit." Chris affixed price stickers to a line of paint tubes. "It's just something people made up because plain old agoraphobia isn't nearly as interesting."

"What did he sound like when you talked to him?" Tonya asked. "Weird?"

"No." Chris shivered, recalling again how his sexy voice had resonated in the very marrow of her bones, masculine, powerful, aloof yet with an undercurrent of passion that made a woman want to break through the cool exterior to reach the fire. "Polite but businesslike. He offered on the painting, then made his proposal. He sounded like money, like the rent on this shop and my apartment paid up for a while. So I'll paint his portrait—hell, his whole damn house if that's what he wants."

"Point taken." Tonya tossed down her rag, walked over to Chris and gave her a swift, hard hug. "But I'm gonna miss you so much, girl. Seriously, promise me if things are weird there you'll get the hell out immediately."

"Of course. I know you think I'm flaky, but I'm really a great judge of character. If Leroux gives off a serial killer vibe, I'll be outta there in a heartbeat."

Tonya gave her a playful push. "Don't think you've fooled me. I know why you're really taking this job and it's not the money. It's curiosity. You want to see this guy. Deep down you've convinced yourself he's going to be some drop-dead gorgeous Prince Charming."

"Yeah, right. Since when have I been the fairytale type?" Chris messed with the price marker so she wouldn't have to meet her friend's knowing eyes.

"Uh, ever since I've known you." Tonya raised an eyebrow. "Which is why you never hook up with any guy for longer than two minutes. You're always looking for something better, some perfect specimen who doesn't exist in real life."

"Am not."

"Are too. You're too damn picky."

Chris shrugged. "So maybe I'm a little discerning about the qualities I think are important in a man. Why not? Why shouldn't I look for exactly the man I've imagined?"

"I told you. Because he doesn't exist."

Chris couldn't believe Leroux sent a limousine to pick her up from the train station. She didn't own a car, so she'd taken the train from New York to White Plains where Hank picked her up. His presence made her feel a little more comfortable about the whole thing. He'd seemed like a nice guy when she met him at the gallery. Hank greeted her with a friendly smile and neatly fitted her bags, including the case with all her brushes and paints, into the trunk.

"So, does your boss do things like this often, have his portrait painted on a whim?"

He looked up. His eyes, shadowed by bushy eyebrows, were inscrutable. "Mr. Leroux is the least impulsive person I know."

"Why now? Why me?"

Hank removed his cap and ran a hand through his brush-cut gray hair. "Guess he really likes your work. Or maybe he figured it was time for a change."

A change? What did that mean? Chris nodded as if it made sense.

Hank opened the car door for her and she slid into cool, leather comfort. Chris had never ridden in a limo in her life, not even to her high school prom. She checked out the gadgets available in the climate-controlled comfort of the luxurious ride.

The novelty quickly wore off as the car sped silently down the road. Chris's anxiety grew with each mile as she stared out at the forested country of upper New York State. What had she gotten herself into? Who was Eric Leroux?

After Tonya had told her the rumor about his deformity, Chris had done some internet research. It seemed Leroux was generous with his wealth and gave to a number of charitable causes, including an artists' grant and a burn unit at a local hospital.

Looking farther back in the news, she found the names of Eric's parents and brother, Jonathan, at benefits, balls, and social events throughout the seventies and eighties, but there was never any mention of Eric at the same functions. There was an obituary for the Leroux parents in October 1996 and a related article about the car accident that had claimed their lives.

Jonathan Leroux's obituary pre-dated his parents' deaths by almost ten years. He was only seventeen when he died, and there was no explanation of his death. She wondered what had happened and if the loss of his family was what had driven Eric Leroux to seclusion.

Chris looked through the glass panel at the back of Hank's head in the chauffeur cap. She pressed the intercom. "Hi. Not to sound like a little kid, but are we almost there?"

"About ten minutes."

"So, you're a chauffeur as well as personal assistant. Mr. Leroux must go out occasionally."

"Sometimes."

"How long has he been agoraphobic?"

"He's not. He just prefers to stay at home."

"Doesn't that make it kind of hard for him to conduct business?"

"Not really. It's the electronic age."

Chris blew out an impatient breath at his short answers. "All right, Hank. Let me lay it out for you. I've heard rumors Eric Leroux is a recluse because he's deformed or something. What's that about?"

"I couldn't say."

"Well, *is* there something wrong with him?"

"Not that I've noticed."

"If the man never has anyone to his house, why would he want his portrait painted?"

"You'll have to ask him."

"Thanks, Hank, you've been a bundle of help."

"You're welcome." In the rearview mirror, Chris saw him grin.

She smiled too, shaking her head.

As Hank turned the car off the road onto a blacktopped drive through an avenue of trees, another pang of nervous apprehension shot through her. Underlying her fear was an eager curiosity to meet the man who admired her work enough to purchase it. The rose painting was the first piece she'd ever sold and the validation of her talent was almost better than the substantial payment she'd received. Even deeper down in her psyche, swirling around like a vague cloud, was a sense of déjà vu or destiny. Chris couldn't name the emotion, but it had been there since she first agreed to Leroux's proposition. It propelled her inexorably forward into the unknown.

Hank drove down the tunnel of green then stopped at a security gate. Seconds later the gate slid open to let the limo through.

Chris sat up straight and stared through the windshield, awaiting her first glimpse of the Leroux estate. Her sense of expectation grew until the car rounded a bend in the drive and she beheld the house. It wasn't the gothic mansion she'd pictured, but a Frank Lloyd Wright construction of multi-tiered angles and huge panes of glass allowing views of the forest on all sides. So much for a walled castle. The design didn't do much for Chris, who preferred more traditional architecture, but she had to admit the house blended gracefully into the natural setting.

Hank pulled up under a portico.

Chris's heart trip-hammered as she let herself out of the back seat before the chauffeur could do it for her. She drew a deep breath and looked at Hank. "Wish me luck."

A quick frown drew his caterpillar brows together. "Ms. Dawson, be careful."

"What?" Her eyes widened at the warning.

"I mean, be careful with *him.* He may appear aloof when you meet him, but don't let it stop you from getting to know him better."

Getting to know him? I thought I was here to do a job. "Um, okay."

Hank's eyebrows became two again as his frown smoothed out. "All right then. I'll escort you inside then come back for your bags."

As Chris sat on the edge of a chair waiting to meet her new employer, she gazed out the floor-to-ceiling glass at a path leading from the house and down a slope. The walkway was made from great, flat slabs of moss-covered rock and meandered between trees until it disappeared from sight, inviting the viewer to come take a walk in the woods and see where it led. Chris's estimation of the house's architecture and its integral relationship to the woods went up a notch.

She rarely got out of the city. Squirrels were about the most exotic animal she encountered. Here, a wide variety of birds flocked at a feeder and a pair of chipmunks darted around the base, picking up seeds the birds dropped. Chris walked to the window to get a better view of the little striped creatures, which were either fighting or engaged in some really intense foreplay. Her attention was so riveted on the natural drama playing out that when a voice spoke behind her she jumped.

"Good afternoon, Ms. Dawson."

A shiver ran through her at the quiet, husky timber of the voice. It sounded so familiar, probably because she'd talked to him on the phone. Chris turned around.

"Hello, Mr. Leroux. You have such a beautiful h-house." She stumbled over the last word as she caught sight of the man standing in the doorway across the room.

He was dressed in jeans and an untucked, white Oxford shirt. His body was broad at the shoulders, narrow at the hips, with long legs that made the jeans go on forever. However, it wasn't the man's lean build that made her stammer. A mask—not a Halloween horror mask, but a flesh-tone covering—concealed his face. It was eerie since it almost looked like real skin but was clearly not. Leroux's face was covered from hairline to chin. Only his eyes and mouth were revealed. Some scarring was apparent on the left side of his lips. His left ear under glossy locks of black hair was misshapen. The mask ended at his jaw line and scar tissue extended down his neck.

It was impossible not to have a 'what the fuck' moment. She looked away then back again, trying to meet his gaze without appearing to gape at him. It was tricky. She simply couldn't meet a person without looking into his face, yet it was difficult not to be distracted by the mask and figuring out where it ended and real flesh began. Chris felt she was failing miserably in her attempt not to gawk.

Eric Leroux was poised as if ready to bolt from the room at any moment. She decided the best way to show she was unfazed by his unusual appearance was to physically bridge the gap. She walked across the room toward him. She extended her hand toward him, smiling broadly.

"Mr. Leroux, I want to thank you again for buying my painting. It means so much to me that someone appreciates my work."

His eyes were a brilliant, almost unnatural blue shining through the cutout holes in the mask. He looked down at her hand and, after a moment's hesitation, took it. His grip was warm and firm, but the skin felt strange, too smooth and soft. When Chris glanced down, she saw he was wearing a glove—lightweight and peach-colored like the mask on his face.

She looked back up to meet his eyes again. Eric Leroux was watching her process his strangeness. Chris felt a swift stab of anger at him for not warning her ahead of time, for springing this on her then watching her reaction. What the hell did he expect, that she wouldn't be a little taken aback? That she wouldn't wonder why she'd been summoned to paint a portrait of a man who hid his face?

Just when she thought the awkward moment would last forever, Leroux spoke. "You're welcome. Thank you for coming." He released her hand and stepped back.

Chris felt dismissed, like their little exchange was all there was to this trip. She would get back in the limo and be taken away.

"I was just watching your wildlife out there." She waved a hand at the window. "A lot of beautiful birds and some really angry chipmunks."

Her words startled a laugh out of him. For one glimmer of a moment, his teeth flashed and his blue eyes squinted with humor. The rest of his face, of course, remained smooth and expressionless, but it was amazing what a transformation just a curve of the lips and crease at the corners of the eyes could affect. She wanted to see it again.

"So, I guess I've spent way too much of my life surrounded by tall buildings, 'cause I gotta tell you all this natural beauty freaks me out."

She was rewarded by another flicker of a smile. "You grew up in New York?"

"Queens, born and bred. My parents still live there. And you? Is this where you were raised?"

"My parents built this house." He glanced around the room. "Guess I never got up the momentum to move."

"Why would you? It's gorgeous. I bet the scenery is beautiful in every season."

He didn't answer and another silent moment crept past.

Leroux cleared his throat. "I thought you might be hungry after traveling, so there's a light snack set up in the dining room. Or, if you'd rather rest, Hank will show you to your room."

Chris laughed. "Food over sleep every time for me. Can't you tell?"

The quick sweep of his eyes over her body, as though comparing her curvy figure to her words, sent a fine thread of excitement stitching through her. Her nipples grew hard at the quick perusal.

Leroux's gaze snapped back to her face, and Chris imagined a blush behind the mask. He gestured toward the archway at the opposite end of the room. "That way." Leading the way, he walked past her and a subtle, woodsy scent rose to tickle her nose. It was delicious, not too sweet, totally male and very familiar. A strong stab of lust and déjà vu shot through her. The cologne was probably something she'd smelled in one of those scratch'n'sniff magazine ads, Chris decided.

The light snack in the dining room turned out to be a table laden with delicacies—tiny quiches and mini tortes, fresh fruit and crudités, little cakes and exquisite, two-bite sandwiches. Never too nervous to eat, Chris piled her plate with as much as she dared without appearing like a complete glutton.

As they sat at one end of a long, polished dining table, she looked at Leroux's nearly empty plate. "You're not eating."

He glanced down at the few strawberries he'd chosen. "I'm not really hungry."

"Way to make me even more self-conscious," Chris blurted out. "I have to tell you Mr. Leroux, I'm a little—no, make that a lot nervous."

"I'm sorry if I make you uncomfortable. I'm not a very social person, not accustomed to putting people at ease." He picked up a strawberry then set it back down.

Why am I really here? Chris wanted to ask so badly the words trembled on her tongue. There was no way this retiring man wanted his portrait painted. "That's all right. I'm talkative enough for two people," she said. "What do you want to know about me?"

She proceeded to tell, unasked, about her friendship with Tonya, how they'd met in college and opened their shop together after graduation with a huge loan and financial help from both their families. "My parents were dead against me majoring in fine arts. They believed in my talent, but wanted to make sure I had a degree I could use when I finished college. I don't blame them, success in the art world is a hit or miss prospect." Chris popped a tiny quiche into her mouth and savored its cheesy flavor.

"It's admirable that you pursued what you wanted to do." Leroux had been toying with the same strawberry without taking a bite the entire time Chris talked. His translucent eyes watched her, riveted on her every gesture, leaving her feeling warm, as if she had a low-grade fever.

"Tell me about your business," she said.

"It's not very interesting. I trade and invest."

"Where did you go to college? How'd you get to be so successful?"

A hint of smile touched his lips. "I started with money. That helps. Money makes more money." He abandoned the strawberry, resting his hand on the table.

Just eat the damn thing!

"I never went to college," he continued. "I had tutors as a child then taught myself what I needed to know about business. When my parents died, I inherited their estate. All I had to do was manage it."

"Looks like you manage it well." Chris looked around the room at the luxurious furnishings and fine paintings on the walls. His collection was an eclectic mix of classic painters and current rising stars in the art world.

"Would you like to see your painting? It's hanging in my office."

"Yes! Absolutely." Chris's heart beat faster at the idea of seeing her work hung on someone's wall, cared for and wanted, validating her. She followed Leroux from the dining room, down a short hall to his study, aware every step of the way of his tall presence walking beside her, radiating heat that bathed her like sunshine.

As they reached a door of glossy wood, Chris was hit by another wave of déjà vu. This place and moment were so familiar. She searched her mind for a connection and found it—her dream. The similarity was strong enough that she half expected to see bedroom furnishings when he opened the door.

Instead she entered a functional yet plush office. A massive desk with computer terminal sat at one end of the room. A flat screen TV hung on the wall facing it. At the other end of the long room, armchairs and a couch faced windows looking out onto a garden. For a moment, Chris forgot about her painting as she gazed at the riotous color outside the window.

"Beautiful!" Her gaze caught on pink roses climbing the sheltering wall of the garden.

"Here." Leroux pulled her attention back into the room.

Chris turned to the wall near the furniture grouping. Her rose and tree painting hung above a dormant fireplace between tall bookshelves. Her heart swelled with pride. It was perfect. It looked like it had been made to fit in that spot. She couldn't stop the big grin that spread over her face when she saw her baby in its new home. "Nice!"

She glanced at Mr. Leroux and he was smiling, enjoying her pleasure. Another flicker of warmth tickled her insides at the curve of his full lips. At the same time, a strong urge to pull his mask away and see his real face swelled through her. Suppressing it, she clenched her hand at her side. "Mr. Leroux—"

"Eric, please."

She nodded. "Call me Chris. Eric, I need to ask you something."

The smile disappeared from his mouth, and his eyes shifted away from hers. "You want to know why I want my portrait painted."

"Actually, I was going to ask where the bathroom was, but since you brought it up…," she said lightly, trying to ease the tension in the grim line of his mouth.

It worked. Once more surprised amusement lit his eyes for a second before flitting away. "There was a fire when I was young. I was badly burned and scarred. In the years since, I've rarely left this house and grounds except for hospital stays for skin grafts."

Eric paused, tapping his gloved fingers against his thigh as he gazed out the window. "Recently I decided perhaps it was time to confront my issues about my appearance. I've never gone to a therapist, but a friend suggested a portrait as a way to come face to face with myself." He shrugged. "Sounds like psycho-babble to me, but I figured it couldn't hurt. When I saw your work and Hank's interview with you, I knew you were the artist I wanted."

"I'm honored," Chris said. "Really." She tried to picture a whole lifetime spent in this house. It didn't matter how gorgeous the setting, it would be a confining prison for the spirit. "I hope I can help you accomplish what you're trying to do."

His gaze returned to her. "I hope so too."

Chapter 3

After Eric summoned Hank to show Christine to her room, he slumped down on the couch, legs sprawled in front of him. He'd planned this elaborate campaign to get Christine to come to him and now that she was here, he was relieved to have a moment's respite from her company. He hadn't realized it would be so exhausting just talking with someone when he was so used to solitude.

God, she was beautiful, more beautiful in person than he could have imagined. Her vivacious manner, sparkling eyes and teasing smile made him feel warm all over, and not just in a sexual way. The way she glowed was like sunlight touching a shaded patch of garden where light never shone. She overwhelmed him. He felt like he'd been under a microscope or a spotlight, on display for her searching, assessing eyes.

Christine guessed he wanted something more from her than a painting. Eric wondered if the bullshit about facing himself had deceived her. It was the first blatant lie he'd told. The rest was a partial truth. He did want her to paint him, but only because it allowed them to spend time together.

Peeling off his gloves, he tossed them aside then removed the mask. Eric hated wearing it. Although the light material was porous, allowing airflow, having his face covered bothered him, reminding him of the years he'd been requested to wear it in his parents' presence. He never kept it on around Hank or the housekeeper, Carol. Both had known him so long he didn't feel uncomfortable with them.

Eric was aware he had issues stemming from his family's treatment of him and knew most of the problems had been on their part. But understanding his own psychology didn't eradicate the ingrained sense of shame he felt every time he put on the mask.

Leaning his head back against the couch, he exhaled a long breath and stared up at the ceiling. What the hell was he going to do next? How did he think this lame scenario was going to work? Christine might talk to him, even flirt with him in her light, teasing way, but it was never going to go beyond that.

He touched his fingers to his cheek. There was some sensation in the smooth tips of his fingers, less so in the heavier, ridged scars on his face. He couldn't even feel his own touch, yet he craved Christine's. There were plenty of places he'd be able to feel it—on his lips, his eyelids, the right side of his chest and abdomen, his legs and the throbbing, aching muscle between his legs.

His hand drifted down to his crotch, adjusting his erection and pausing to rub it through the stiff denim of his jeans. He half-closed his eyes and stroked a little harder, imagining another hand besides his own touching his cock. It swelled and the hungry need grew more intense.

Eric pulled away with a frustrated curse. God, he should've just hired a prostitute instead of indulging in this travesty of a courtship with a pretty woman who would ultimately, physically have nothing to do with him.

He stood and walked to the sideboard to pour himself a Scotch, just a sip to help him relax and stop acting like a wooden, humorless freak, who couldn't carry his half of a conversation. Very shortly Christine would come down from her room and he would be expected to show her around the rest of the house and property. This time he would try to put her at ease and be a gracious host instead of an overgrown, tongue-tied boy.

✻❧⟨♋⟩❧✻

"Do you have a whole gardening staff to keep this place looking so nice?" Chris asked as she bent over to smell a shaft of yellow snapdragons. "Mm, these are so sweet!"

Eric's eyes zeroed in on her ass, tilted perkily upward, lifting her skirt halfway up her thighs. He swallowed and forced his eyes away. "No. I take care of this garden myself and hire a service to tend the rest of the grounds."

She straightened and looked around at the garden before turning to him. "Really? You do all this?"

He smiled. "I have a lot of time on my hands and I can't sit at the computer all day. The garden is my hobby."

"What else do you like to do?" She frowned at the fountain with dancing nymphs in the center of one of the beds and walked over cup her hand under the splashing water.

"I'm interested in astronomy, literature, history. I'm actually addicted to the History channel."

"Oh, one of those." She laughed. "I dated a guy who couldn't get enough of WWII battles."

A ridiculous little pang went through him, but of course she'd had boyfriends, probably little black notebooks full of them. She was beautiful and amazing and completely desirable.

"Well, I'm more fascinated with ancient history. Greeks, Egyptians, Druids, that kind of thing."

"Me too." She shook droplets of water off her hand then wiped it on her skirt. "It's amazing to think of all the civilizations that have come and gone from this planet. Kind of puts your daily life and all your little hopes and fears into perspective, doesn't it?" She walked the perimeter of the central flowerbed, gazing all around his garden.

Eric was pleased at her admiration of his work. He'd never shown anyone his garden before and it was satisfying to have it appreciated. He understood how Chris felt about her painting hanging in his den.

"You've created a gorgeous place here." She turned to face him. "I should paint you right here in your garden. It's such a part of you."

He frowned. For a little while he'd been able to forget the deception that had brought her here and pretend she was visiting him because she wanted to.

"Or not," she said, noting his frown. "Do you already have something else in mind? Are you interested in a full body pose or head and shoulders?"

Whatever will take you the longest to finish. "I don't know. I guess a full body, and outdoors is fine if that's where you want to work." He thought of the rainy days when the sitting would have to be postponed. Outdoors was perfect.

Chris looked around. "I'll start by doing some quick sketches of you in different poses, different light angles, in various parts of the garden, and see if any of them resonates with you." She walked toward Eric.

He resisted the urge to step back from her. He was torn between wanting to run away or toss her to the ground and ravage her.

She stopped in front of him and looked up into his eyes. Too close. Too nerve-wracking. Too sexy.

He blinked and stared down at her. His body stiffened at her proximity.

She reached up to touch the side of his masked face and he felt her touch through the cotton mask, burning him like a brand. "You know, at some point this is going to have to come off."

"Not yet," his voice cracked a little as it squeezed out of his dry throat.

"No." She took her hand away and stepped back and he could breath again. "Let's start with the sketches right now, okay? I'm psyched! I'll go get my sketchbook."

Before he could delay her or make an excuse to begin tomorrow, Christine was gone. She walked through the French doors leading into the office as if she'd lived here forever. There was never any hesitation in the way she moved, and Eric admired her innate confidence in her body and herself.

"Damn it," he cursed after she'd gone. The charade was starting and he wasn't ready for it. The idea of having Chris examine him from every angle was intimidating. For a man who'd only interacted face-to-face with a few dozen people in his entire life, that scrutiny was too much. He was being pushed *way* out of his comfort zone very quickly. He squatted down and tugged an offending weed from between the flagstones of the path.

"You wanted her. You got her," he muttered.

In a few minutes Chris was back with her sketchbook in hand. "Over here. Let's try one with you sitting on the bench with a backdrop of climbing roses."

Obediently Eric sat on the stone bench.

She gave him a series of further orders. "Now turn toward the left. No, your whole body. That's right. Chin up, gaze across the garden. Too stiff. Relax a little." She began positioning him, pressing his left shoulder back a little, straightening his right leg, taking his jaw in hand and turning his head where she wanted it.

Eric froze while she manipulated him like a mannequin. His pulse raced and his breath grew short. Her touch, so personal and intimate, was killing him, and she didn't even seem aware of it.

"There. More like that." She stepped back and looked at him. "Although you still seem really stiff. Try to hold that pose but relax at the same time." She laughed at the irony of her words. "Or forget posing and just relax. I don't know what I'm looking for, but when I see it, I'll know."

She walked over and plopped down on a flagstone, flipped open her book and began sketching. "Don't think about me. I'm not even drawing you right now. I'm drawing the flowers. Just talk to me for a while."

Eric couldn't think of a thing to say. He was still shaken from her foray into his personal space, the warmth of her hands touching him all over, her scent invading his senses and her body radiating energy like a power line. He was furious with himself for being so aroused and upset by her mere presence.

"Tell me about your family." Her hand moved over the paper, her eyes focusing off to his left.

Eric relaxed slightly, since she wasn't staring directly at him. "There's not much to say. My parents were very busy, very social people. So was my older brother, Jonathan. I wasn't. I didn't have much to do with my family. Then they died." What else could he tell her without sounding even more pathetic than she probably already thought he was? His family barely noticed him. He was a ghost living in their house, a skeleton hidden in the closet. Solitary, isolated, forgotten, until the day Jonathan died.

"I'm so sorry. Losing your whole family like that is terrible." Chris tapped her pencil thoughtfully against the pad of paper. "God, I don't spend enough time with mine. My sisters live nearby, but it's been months since we've gotten together, and my mom keeps asking me to come for Sunday dinner and I put her off. I need to call them all." Her eyes met his again. "So you've lived here alone since your parents died?"

Eric bristled at her sympathetic tone. "It's not much different from when they were alive. I don't mind being alone. Generally I prefer it." He stared at her, daring her to pity him.

Chris dipped her head and started scratching furiously with the pencil. "That's it. Hold that expression."

For several minutes she looked back and forth between him and her sketch. Since his new pose forced him to look right at her, Eric was able to examine her more than he'd dared since her arrival.

The photo on her web page and the video footage from the show didn't do Chris justice. The sun shone on her gleaming, black hair, straightened into a smooth curtain on either side of her face today. It highlighted her bronze features, reflecting brightly off the sharp points of her cheekbones and the bridge of her wide nose. Eric's gaze lingered on her full lips, which looked soft as two cushions a man could sink into. His lips parted slightly, imagining how her mouth would feel beneath his.

Chris wore a simple blue tank top and skirt, leaving miles of bare, brown flesh uncovered. He feasted on her sexy curves, long legs, soft arms, ample cleavage, then quickly returned his gaze to her face.

Her eyes were deep brown and framed in thick, black lashes. A smile curved her lips as she stopped drawing, laid her pencil down and shook a cramp out of her wrist. She studied her drawing then looked at Eric again. "Nice. Very you." She waggled an eyebrow. "Busy eyes, you've got.

Eric felt a burning rush of blood to his face and was actually grateful for the mask that hid his embarrassment. Humiliated that his interest in her was so apparent, he stood and turned away from Chris's teasing smile, folding his arms. "Sorry. I didn't mean to stare."

"Hey, no problem. I was looking at you too." Suddenly she was at his elbow, putting a hand on his forearm.

He looked down at it, intrigued by the contrast of brown skin against the white fabric of his shirt, and frozen by the weight and warmth of her touch.

"We're going to be working together for quite a while," she said. "There's a relationship between an artist and her subject. It's natural if we're both curious as we're getting to know each other. You can look at me all you like."

Eric's gaze rose from her hand to her face. Their eyes locked together for a blazing, hot moment. The look they exchanged was so intense it was like a touch, and in that fleeting sliver of time he realized two things with absolute clarity. One was that he *knew* Christine, actually recognized her spirit on a fundamental level, as if they'd met somewhere before. The second was that he was already halfway in love with her.

Chris squeezed his arm lightly before letting go, the impressions of her fingers lingered. "So what do you think? Shall we try another pose?"

She suggested a different part of the garden, a shaded grouping of ornamental trees in one corner, and had him stand in the shelter of their branches.

"I feel ridiculous," he said, as she moved his body into a shaft of sunlight like a spotlight in the center of the grove.

"You're fine, except, I'd like you to hold this branch with one hand. Like this. Do you think you could lose the gloves?" She held his hand and looked up at him questioningly.

Eric's heart pounded in his chest. Another charge of electricity flashed between them as she held his gaze and waited. He slowly nodded.

Chris grasped the fingertips of the glove on his right hand and tugged.

He wanted to stop her, to tell her to slow down, he wasn't ready. Then the glove was off and his hand was naked to her gaze. He glanced down at the discolored flesh, an unnatural pink mottled with white, but at least smooth, unlike his cratered face.

Chris held his hand, rubbing the back of it lightly with her thumb.

Her touch was like a spark lighting a trail of gunpowder. Fire rushed to Eric's groin and straight to his cock. It rose stiffly. He looked at Chris's eyes, gauging her reaction to the scars.

A slight frown creased her brows. "This doesn't work for me."

He swallowed hard and the rush of blood receded from his dick.

"I don't like the sleeves buttoned at the wrist. It's kinda nerdy." She let go of his hand to unbutton the cuff of his shirt and roll it up a few turns, revealing more of his forearm.

"No. Wait." Eric reached out his other hand to stop her. He felt like a stripper forced onstage for the first time.

"Trust me. This is better." Chris took his left hand, removed the glove and rolled up the shirtsleeve. "See? Much sexier this way."

Jesus, was she making fun of him? His arms were as bad as his hands, mottled in color with the skin stretched unnaturally tight over his muscles. He looked freshly scalded although the fire had taken place over two-dozen years ago. Eric's cock shriveled further, and his soul lay shivering, naked and exposed.

"Now hold the branch like I showed you. Put this hand down by your thigh, like this." After she'd positioned Eric's hand where she wanted it, her fingers trailed up his forearm before she stepped away. Chris looked up into his eyes again. Her tongue ran lightly over her upper lip, a flash of pink. She reached up and combed her fingers through the hair at his temple then nodded. "There. You look really good."

Eric searched for a mocking note in her words and found none. Her velvet brown eyes shone in the shaft of sunlight amidst the dark shadows of the trees and he could see that she meant exactly what she said. She thought he was attractive.

A bubble of laughter rose in his throat and he choked it back. *Just wait 'til you see the rest.*

Chris walked several yards away, took a seat on a bench and flipped her sketchbook to a new page.

As he watched her work, Eric added one more thing to the list of what he knew with absolute certainty. Before this was over, he was going to get his heart broken.

Chapter 4

The tub in the bathroom adjoining her bedroom was about the size of the entire floor space of the bathroom in her apartment. Chris stepped into the huge pool of water and sank down into warmth up to her shoulders. She leaned back against the heated porcelain, closed her eyes and sighed, breathing in a deep lungful of steam.

She hadn't realized how tense she was until her muscles began to unknot and relax in the hot water. Meeting her new employer, adjusting to his appearance then working to put him at ease had taken a lot of energy. She was exhausted.

Eric Leroux was a strange and complex man. And despite the fact that she hadn't even seen his face yet, he attracted her on a fundamental level. His voice alone set her pussy clenching. His clear blue eyes told volumes about his inner turmoil, making Chris want to wrap him in her arms and comfort him. And his masculine presence was so overwhelmingly familiar her body yearned for his.

It was crazy to believe in an instant connection with a man she'd just met, but with her eyes closed, in the privacy of her bath, it was easy to accept the association between her dream lover and Eric. Chris didn't consider herself either a superstitious person or a skeptic, but someone who tried to walk a common sense line between the physical and metaphysical. However, there were too many similarities about this place and this man for her to ignore the link to her dreams.

Chris breathed in the smell of lilacs rising up from the bathwater. It was her favorite scent and she'd been pleasantly surprised to find lilac bath products in the cupboard. It strengthened her sense that Eric knew her well, although they'd never met before today.

Ah, but we have, she thought, once more reliving the dream of making love to the unseen presence. Her hand trailed idly over the surface of the water and came to rest on her breast. She slipped her hand down the wet slope and underneath the water to cup the weight of her tit. Rolling her nipple between her fingers, she twisted and pulled at it, sending pangs of desire shooting down to her crotch.

Chris gave her dream lover an identity. Eric Leroux's voice, his eyes, his smooth, dark hair, his body, his essence created a focus for her fantasy. She imagined him coming to her room at night then slipping into her bed when she pulled back the covers for him. With no words exchanged they would make love, the act more eloquent than words.

Her hands, holding her breasts and tweaking her nipples, became his hands. Chris lifted her tits out of the warm water and let the air evaporate the moisture. Her nipples beaded hard in protest at the sudden cold. She sucked her lower lip between her teeth and whimpered as she continued to squeeze her heavy breasts and tug at her nipples.

The water sloshed as she squeezed her thighs together and wiggled from pleasure. Chris allowed her boobs to settle back into the warmth of the water and slid one of her hands down her stomach to her crotch. She combed through the thatch of pubic hair, like seaweed in her bath lagoon, and fingered her clit. *Mmm. The pirate's treasure chest.* She grinned at the thought.

In her fantasy, Eric touched her there too. With his mouth covering hers, kissing her breathless, his hand slipped down to fondle her pussy. She moaned in satisfaction when his finger found her little nub and teased it erect. He knew just how to move his finger, lightly so she had to thrust her hips up and reach for it.

In a very short time she was moaning for release, but Eric wouldn't give it to her yet. He took his circling finger away, let go of her lips with one last deep kiss then moved down her body until his mouth was poised at her sex.

Chris lifted her hips up and down, a slow pulsing movement, anticipating his tongue. In the bath, her hand abandoned her clit, leaving it aching for the stimulation to resume.

Chris imagined running her fingers through Eric's sleek hair. It would feel so silky between her fingers. Resting her hands on top of his head, she'd push him encouragingly toward her pussy.

He would laugh at her eagerness, a deep, warm chuckle like hot sunlight bathing her. He'd let the moment and her anticipation spin out even longer until she begged for him to continue. Then, finally, he'd lower his mouth and kiss her, just once, right at the crown of her sex.

Chris's thighs squeezed together tight and she shivered in the warm bathwater.

Finished playing with her, he would get down to business, running his tongue up the entire length of her seam then dipping it inside her to taste her juices. He would lap lightly over her clit then tickle it with the point of his tongue until she moaned and thrust toward him. When he'd brought her right to the edge of orgasm, he'd abandon her clit and move to lie between her legs.

Their eyes would meet, ice blue and earth brown, as he reached down between them to position himself at her entrance. With one strong push, he would enter her.

Chris mimicked the movement, moving her hand from her clit to plunge her fingers inside her aching, yearning pussy. The sensation of being filled wasn't nearly enough. She needed a vibrator or dildo to complete the illusion. Or why not the real thing? She smiled at the thought of how shocked Eric would be if she showed up at his bedroom door, dripping wet and horny.

Shifting to this new fantasy, Chris imagined throwing herself at him like a force of nature, tearing off his clothes and pushing him back on his bed. Straddling his hips, she'd pin him to the bed, impale herself on his erect cock and ride him like a racehorse. She'd bounce and toss her hair around and yell as she came.

The wildness of the image seized her. Chris moved her finger rapidly over her clit, her breath gasping harshly in and out. She bucked and jerked, sending the water sloshing dangerously toward the rim of the tub then she came with a long moan before collapsing back into the cooling water.

Resting her head against the porcelain, Chris stared at a flickering candle at the foot of the tub and breathed in the lilac-scented steam. The little release of sexual tension had been nice, but it wasn't enough. Not nearly enough.

And she knew one thing with absolute certainty. Before she left this place, she would know what the real thing was like. She would make love to Eric Leroux.

Chris studied the sketch she'd chosen to use for the portrait. After two days of getting to know Eric better and doing a dozen drawings, she knew this one said the most about him. The pose was a perfect depiction of his interior life.

She faced the primed canvas with its sepia mid-tone base and lifted her brush. It was always at the moment of beginning a new painting that self-doubt surged through her. Was she talented enough? Would this painting turn out to be a pile of crap that let everyone know she was an imposter masquerading as an artist? Chris knew putting brush to canvas was the quickest way to dispel the self-doubting inner voice. She painted a dark sepia outline of Eric's body on the canvas. Working quickly she sketched with her brush, filling the space with an off-center portrait of him in quarter-profile, gazing out the window at his garden.

She didn't need her subject to pose for this part of the painting as she was merely enlarging what she'd already drawn and blocking in shapes. When she was finished, she would have what looked rather like an old-fashioned tintype. Later she would add layers of colors, slowly building the painting from its simplest form to a complex interaction of color, shadow and light.

Chris could already see the finished portrait in her mind; the man standing in darkness looking out at the light. The lighting on his profile was very dramatic and the pose told Eric's story. He was a man shackled by fear and shame, unable to break free of the patterns that held him, imprisoned as surely as if there were locks on the doors of this beautiful house.

During the past two days, Chris had spent much time in Eric's company. They ate meals and took walks together and talked while she drew him. Part of each day, he worked in his office while she enjoyed a paid vacation, catching up on reading, working on new painting techniques, watching daytime TV, working out in Eric's weight room or swimming laps in his indoor pool.

When she was with Eric, she gently probed to learn more about his life and the circumstances that had led him to hide from the world. If her pushing grew too invasive, he drew back like a hermit crab into its shell, changing the subject or discovering an errand he needed to get done. But the previous evening Chris had quite accidentally gotten him to tell much more about his relationship with his brother.

After a long, tense phone conversation with her sister, Rina, Chris had returned to the living room where they were watching a show about Stonehenge. She flopped down on the couch.

"My sister needs to take Valium or Xanax or something. I've never known anyone so uptight in my entire life. We just had a thirty-minute argument about planning my mom and dad's fortieth wedding anniversary. It's not even 'til next year! Rina's already worried about it and she's upset because Lynette and I aren't worried *enough* about it." Chris laughed. "Sisters. You could just shoot 'em."

Her laughter was met by silence. Chris looked over at Eric, sitting in an armchair. He was completely still. It was hard to read an expression from a mouth and a pair of eyes, but Chris had gotten pretty adept at interpreting his body language and felt she'd said something horribly wrong.

Like Legos clicking together, she suddenly knew why Eric's brother had died young. "Oh, God, did your brother...?" There was no way to finish the thought. What if she was wrong?

Eric was silent a beat then cleared his throat. "He shot himself."

"I'm so sorry. I never would have said that." Chris's cheeks grew hot.

He shrugged. "It was a long time ago."

"That doesn't matter. I'm sure it's something you'd never get over. How old were you when it happened?"

"Eleven. I found him in his room."

Chris's hand covered her mouth. "It must have been terrible. For both you and your parents."

"They never got over it. Their lives revolved around Jonathan. His whole life they groomed him for the White House, or at the very least, the Senate. My parents had his whole future planned. It probably sounds crazy to you, but believe me, with their connections, they would have made it happen."

Chris was taken aback. She didn't know how to reply so she remained silent for once and it turned out to be the right thing since Eric kept talking.

"His death devastated them, especially my mom. They lost their golden boy and were left with me." A smile curved his lips. "Hardly candidate material."

"Shame on them for overlooking you and for putting so much pressure on your brother! They sound incredibly selfish to me." The moment her little rant was out of her mouth, she felt like a fool. She'd never been good at heeding her mother's admonishment to think before she spoke. "I'm sorry. I had no right to say that. I know nothing about your parents."

Surprisingly, Eric smiled. "I suppose you're right. I'm far enough away from it all now that I can see their faults. They were pretty fucked up."

Heartened by his smile, Chris took the opportunity to jam her foot deeper into her mouth. "If you know that, why do you still let them control you? Why are you still hiding in this house?"

Eric didn't act shocked or stand up and walk from the room. Instead he shrugged and said mildly, "Knowing something and changing it are two different things. I realize I need to get out of this place, but it's not that easy." He met her eyes with his solemn blue gaze. "I'm trying."

"And that's why I'm here."

"Yes."

Chris pulled her mind back to the present and to her painting. She'd been working on auto-pilot, transferring the sketch to the canvas. She stepped back to survey the rough portrait. It excited her. She couldn't wait to plunge in and add color. She decided to ask Eric to sit for her later in the afternoon so she could block in the areas of shadow. The best part about working with acrylics was they didn't require the drying time of oils, which would have been hard for someone as impatient as she was.

Trailing her finger over the drawing, she traced the mask's edge where it met Eric's hairline. Scarring was visible on his ear, part of his jaw and neck, more gnarled than the smooth, pink-white flesh of his hands and arms. She wondered how bad Eric's face really was and why plastic surgery hadn't improved it. She also had more questions about the fire that had caused his burns and about his bizarre family dynamics. But it would require patience to extract the rest of Eric's story.

Chris brushed her finger over the sepia waves of his hair. When she was finished, it would be sleek, otter brown with gold highlights where the sunlight touched it. She wondered what Eric's hair really felt like and imagined running her fingers through it. She thought she would have a chance soon. Sometimes when their eyes met, energy pulsated in the air between them.

But uncertainty held her back. She was afraid to hurt Eric. He wouldn't be one of her casual relationships, an easy hook-up and a quick discard. If he trusted her enough to reveal his painful secrets and vulnerable heart, she would have to treat his confidence with exquisite care. Was she really ready to deal with what lay behind his mask?

Chris checked to make sure the canvas was dry then spread a cloth over it. She'd already warned Eric he wasn't allowed to see the portrait until it was near completion. He'd agreed easily, clearly not that interested, which confirmed her suspicion that the work was merely a pretext to get her to his house. It should have freaked her out but instead seemed inevitable. Deep inside, she'd known from the beginning, but couldn't resist the pull of destiny or whatever. Since she'd accepted the connection to her dreams, Chris believed she was here for a reason.

Now she just had to decide if she dared take the next step of the journey.

That evening after dinner, Chris suggested they take a bottle of wine and sit out in the garden to enjoy the cool spring evening.

"Tell me about the stars." She leaned back in the rattan chair and looked up at the first twinkling sparks of light in the twilight sky. "I never learned the constellations. Bring your chair over by mine and show me."

The arm of his chair scraped hers and Eric's shoulder brushed hers when Chris leaned close to him. His body heat radiated out, bathing her in warmth. She deliberately pressed her arm against his. "Show me," she repeated in a quiet, intimate voice.

Eric lifted his arm, either to escape her touch or to point at the sky. "See the three stars in a row? That's the easiest constellation to locate, even easier than the Big Dipper. That's Orion, the Hunter. The three stars are his belt, the rest represent his body."

Chris sipped her wine and breathed in the mingled scent of night-blooming flowers and Eric's cologne. She wondered if he wore it because he liked it or if he'd bought it special because of her. Then she wondered if he'd ever worn it for another woman. Just because he was a hermit didn't mean he'd never had a lover.

"So Merope goes with Orion," she said, tuning back into his mythology story.

"That's right."

"And she's way over there with her seven sisters, the Pleiades." Chris leaned her head close to Eric and sighted up his arm, making sure they were looking at the same thing. "Well, that's sad. They have to be apart for eternity."

"Most of the Greek myths don't end well for anybody."

"Gives you an appreciation for modern entertainment like sitcoms where all the problems are wrapped up in a half hour." Chris picked up the wine bottle from the ground near her feet and refilled both their glasses.

She held up hers. "To finding new friends and, uh, taking chances. Sorry, I'm not too good at spur-of-the-moment toasts." She touched her glass to Eric's then sipped the wine before resting her glass on the arm of her chair. "Have you ever played truth or dare?"

He looked at her, his mask a pale blur in the gathering dark. "With who? I never went to summer camp or had parties."

"I don't know." Chris felt bad, but determined to pursue her dark, sinister plan to get Eric to reveal himself to her.

"No. I never played it, but I've seen enough TV to know long-held secrets are revealed or someone dares the pretty girl to go in the closet and kiss the ugly boy," Eric said dryly.

"That's spin the bottle." Chris flinched inside at the word 'ugly.' "Come on. Play with me. I promise you can quit any time if you don't like it."

"I already don't like it, but fine, go ahead."

"All right. To take the pressure off, you can go first," she said.

He refilled his glass then leaned back in his chair, tilted his head up and gazed at the stars again. "Did you have this game in mind when we came out here?"

Chris tsked and held up her hand. "You were supposed to say 'truth or dare' first, but I'll answer anyway. Yes, I planned this."

"To ask me a lot of questions I don't want to answer or to make me take the mask off?"

"You really don't get the rules do you? You can't ask a second question. It's my turn. Now, truth or dare?"

He hesitated, still staring up at the heavens. "Truth."

"Did you really want your portrait painted or did you want to meet me?"

"Christ! Can we quit now?" He took another sip of wine.

"You can switch to 'dare' but I don't think you want to do that."

"You were the school bully growing up, weren't you? The answer is yes. I do like your paintings, but mostly I wanted to meet you and didn't know how else to do it."

"You didn't even know me, except for seeing my picture. What did you like about me?"

"The footage from the exhibit. I liked the way you talked and your smile. Damn it! Now who's asking multiple questions?"

So far, so good. He wasn't happy with her questioning but he wasn't backing down from the challenge either. Chris refilled her wine glass and curled her legs up under her in the chair. "Go ahead. I'll take the dare this time, which means you don't get to ask me anything."

Eric breathed out audibly. Tension held his shoulders taut. He switched his tone from a question to a husky demand. "Would you take off your shirt."

Without hesitation, Chris peeled her t-shirt off in one quick move, leaving her in her lacy bra, low-cut enough to show a curving swell of cleavage. "Now you. Truth or dare?"

Eric's voice was strained. "Truth."

"Have you ever been with a woman? I mean, had sex?" She hoped her intrusive question wouldn't insult him.

"Yes." He drained his glass. "Before you waste more questions, only a few times, with prostitutes, and no, I didn't take off the mask. Truth or dare?"

"Truth."

"How many men have you slept with?"

"A few. Only a couple of real relationships, but some wild flings in my college days. I partied pretty hard."

He nodded, acknowledging it. "Go ahead. Ask your question."

She leaned in close and looked into his eyes. "Do you want to have sex? With me?"

Eric stared right back. Even in the dim light she could see the gleam of his eyes. "You know I do."

The bottom dropped out of her stomach at the huskiness of his voice. If she leaned only a little closer, they would be kissing. Chris imagined touching her lips to his, bringing her hand up to the side of his face and feeling fabric between his flesh and hers.

She sat back on her chair, removing herself to a safer distance. "Give me a dare."

"Take off your jeans," he ordered gruffly.

Chris stood up and unzipped. She watched him watching her as she shimmied her low-riders down her hips and stepped out of them. She stood for a moment so he could look at her in her bra and boy-cut underwear. They had more material than a bathing suit, but she felt completely naked under his scrutiny.

She sat back down in her chair and offered him more wine.

Eric took the bottle, poured and drank.

She held her breath and waited, certain he'd take the dare this time, but he disappointed her.

"Truth."

"Are you angry at your family for the way they treated you?"

"I don't know. I don't think about it. It was a long time ago." His body was rigid, as he sat straight up in his chair, staring at her.

"Dare," she whispered.

"The underwear."

Chris gazed into his eyes as she slowly unhooked and removed her bra then lifted her hips off the seat and took off her panties.

"Stand up so I can look at you." His voice was as harsh as rocks grating together.

She stood. The flower-scented night breeze blew over her skin, bringing her nipples to attention and teasing the curls marking her sex. Although it wasn't cold, gooseflesh rose all over her arms and legs. Her pussy throbbed with arousal at the touch of the air and even more at the forbidden touch of a stranger's eyes. She felt decadent and naughty standing there naked while he was still completely clothed.

And she was horny as hell, ready to fall back into a flowerbed and spread her legs if that's what he asked her to do next.

"Will you take the dare now?" she said.

He shook his head. "Ask another question."

"Do you want to touch me?" She didn't wait for an answer, but moved close so he could reach her body. Her breasts were at his eye level and he stared at them, transfixed. When he didn't move toward her after a few seconds, Chris reached down, took his hand and guided it to her tit. "It's all right. You can touch me."

His fingers glided slowly over the slope of her breast, feeling the shape and weight of it, then finding her nipple and rolling it between his thumb and forefinger.

Chris drew in her breath with a hiss. Her nipple was hot and sensitive and her breast swelled to his touch.

He sat forward on the edge of his seat, both hands fondling her, kneading, stroking her breasts, then trailing down her rib cage and abdomen toward her crotch.

She tilted her pelvis toward him, eyes half-closed in pleasure. "Touch me."

Eric rose suddenly, standing close in front of her. He moved his hands from the sharp blades of her hipbones to cup her face. His fingers roamed the contours like a blind man, feeling the curves of her forehead, cheekbones and jaw, studying her nose and lingering on her lips. He touched the shells of her ears and stroked both hands over her straightened hair, testing its coarse mass.

"I like the braids in your picture," he murmured. "I wondered how they would feel."

She smiled and closed her eyes, surrendering to the sensation of his touch, moving farther down now, to her neck and shoulders, tracing her collarbones then stroking her arms. His fingers twined with hers, holding her hands and Chris felt the hot puff of his breath near her temple. He kissed her there, a quick brush of his lips like a butterfly resting before moving on.

His hands released hers and moved back to her waist, slipping around her back and pressing her even closer to him. The denim of his jeans scraped rough against her crotch and a burst of pleasure shot through her. He stroked his hands up her back, fingering her vertebrae like a pianist playing a keyboard then swooped down her back to hold the round curve of her ass in his palms. He nuzzled the side of her head, kissing her hair.

She lifted her hands and rested them on his chest, feeling his heartbeat and his breastbone rise and fall under the fabric of his shirt.

Eric was wearing another of his long-sleeved, button-down shirts. She unfastened the top button then the second and third. As she started to slip her hand inside, he grabbed her wrists. "No. Don't." He stepped away from her, dropping her hands.

Chris opened her eyes and looked at him from the distance that suddenly separated them. "Is that how we're going to play this? You can see me, but I can't see you. You can touch me. I can't touch you."

"No." Eric's voice was suddenly hard and cold. Like a switch had been flipped, he became a person she didn't know. "No. We're not going to 'play this' at all. I'm finished with your game." He turned and stalked away toward the house.

"Eric," she called after him. "Truth or Dare is never just a game." She watched his rigid back disappear through the doors into the dark office. She waited, but no light turned on inside.

Chris shivered as a sudden, cool breeze swept over her naked, over-heated skin. She bent to pick up her clothes, cursing. "'Truth or Dare is never just a game.' What a fucking stupid thing to say!"

Chapter 5

Eric didn't stop walking until he'd reach his room. He slammed the door closed and leaned against it. His body was drenched with sweat and his heart hammered in a chest so tight he could barely breath. He hadn't had an anxiety attack in years, but this felt like the beginning—or maybe the middle of one.

Damn it! He'd almost gotten what he wanted. The girl of his dreams stood naked before him, encouraging, hell, practically begging him to have sex with her, and he hyperventilated and ran away. What kind of man did that? No man at all, only a half-man freak who didn't deserve a gorgeous woman like that.

But he simply couldn't let her touch him, feel the worst of the scarring on the left side of his chest and shoulder or take off his shirt as she'd been about to do and actually see it. The idea of removing his mask and showing her his disaster of a face was impossible. He couldn't stand to see the shock and revulsion in her eyes.

Chris didn't know what she was playing at. Maybe she felt sorry for him, had some womanly urge to nurture and comfort him. Or maybe she was just curious. Either way, she had no idea how repulsive he really was. And he didn't want her to know—ever.

On some level, he hadn't really believed anything would happen between them. Chris would come to his house, paint his picture and go home, leaving him with his fantasies of 'what if.' To have her actually respond to him, to have the reality of her in his arms instead of the daydream was too much. Eric couldn't deal with it. Not so quickly. Maybe not ever.

He stepped away from the door, running a hand through his hair, and blowing out a frustrated breath. He glanced down. The bulge in his pants persisted despite the fact he'd run away from her. The eroticism of holding her, smelling her, kissing her hair couldn't be dismissed so easily. His cock was hard and demanding an explanation of why it was still in his pants.

Eric ripped the mask off and tossed it aside. He kicked off his shoes, stripped off his clothes and flopped on his back on the bed. His head spun from the half bottle of wine he'd drunk. Closing his eyes, he gripped his dick and moved his hand briskly up and down. He took no pleasure in it, but the punishing strokes and the intense memory of Chris's naked body in his embrace combined to give him a quick, hard release. He shuddered as he came. Warm jets landed on his heaving stomach in pitiful puddles.

He gazed down at the sticky mess in disgust for a moment then grabbed his discarded shirt and wiped his belly clean. Groaning in frustration, he rolled to his side, dragging the covers around him. He wanted nothing more than to fall asleep and forget the whole aborted evening, but the details kept playing over and over in his head. The questions Chris had asked. Her articles of clothing coming off one by one until she stood naked and beautiful in the moonlight. What would have happened if he *had* let her see him? Would she have rejected him or would she be in his bed right now. He could have been with her, maybe inside her right now instead of spending yet another lonely night, whacking off in the never-ending solitude of his room.

He squeezed his eyes tight shut and willed thoughts of Chris away, as he used to will away the memory of Jonathan lying on the floor with half his face blown away. Eric had learned back then how to block the vivid image by putting up a black, blank wall. He used his old defense now until there was nothing of Chris left in his mind except the echo of her voice asking, *Are you angry at your family for the way they treated you?*

And this time he answered, *Yes.*

࿔ৡৢৣৢৣ୧

Eric woke late the next morning with a headache, dry mouth and a heavy feeling weighing him down. It took only a moment to remember why. He cringed at the awkwardness he knew was coming. Facing Chris after last night's embarrassment wasn't going to be easy.

After showering and dressing, he went downstairs. An assortment of bagels, rolls and fruit were arrayed on the dining room table. Chris was nowhere in sight.

Eric poured a cup of coffee and went to the living room to sit and drink it.

Chris was already there, sitting on the couch, watching news on CNN. She looked up when he entered. "Hey. How are you?"

"Fine." He sipped his coffee so he wouldn't have to say anything else and scalded his mouth.

"I don't want things to be weird between us," Chris cut right to the chase in her usual forthright fashion. "I was really pushy last night and kind of drunk. I apologize. You can ask any of my friends or family. I'm impulsive, always acting without thinking first."

"No. I'm sorry. This whole portrait thing was a really bad idea." Eric drew a breath and blurted out what he'd decided to say. "Probably you'd like to go now. I'll pay you for your time. I mean, for all of it, for what the painting would have cost."

"No!" Her eyes widened. "No, I don't want to quit. I want to finish it."

He didn't know what to say. He'd expected Chris to jump at the chance to get away from him and his weirdness.

"I mean, if that's all right with you," she continued. "We'll just keep it profes-sional from now on, okay? But, please, let me finish. I can see this painting when I close my eyes. I've got to do it."

Moving from the doorway into the room, he sat down on the chair across from her. "Is that how you work? You see what the finished painting looks like in your mind?"

"Pretty much. It doesn't always come out exactly the way I expected, but, yeah, it's kind of like a vision. And when an idea gets a hold of me, I can't let it go until I've gotten it down." Chris smiled and all he could see was how she'd looked naked in the moonlight, her dark skin gleaming like polished walnut. "Trust me. This is going to be very good."

Eric didn't see how it could be with him as a subject, but despite the fact that he had absolutely no interest in having a portrait of himself, he still didn't want her to go. "All right then."

They arranged to meet in Eric's office in a couple of hours after he'd done some work. He had a hard time concentrating, but his livelihood depended on paying attention to the ups and downs of the market so he buckled down and focused on his portfolio, managing to shut Chris out of his mind for a solid two hours.

He was in the middle of a phone call when she knocked on the open office door. He gestured her to come in while he finished the call.

"So, what do I do?" he asked as he hung up.

"Over here. Stand just like I had you yesterday," she directed. "It's not the same lighting. I'll need to work again in late afternoon, but for now I'm going to be working on some details that aren't dependent on the exact lighting. I can change things later if they're not quite right."

Eric took his place by the window, staring out at the garden, feeling foolish.

For a while Chris worked in silence. It was a novelty to be in the room with her in silence. She was usually quite a talker. The quiet should have made him uncomfortable, but instead Eric found himself zoning out as he gazed at the garden. He thought about what needed to be done, weeding, transplanting, deadheading the spent flowers, feeding the koi and working on the pump, which had been running loud lately. He was so relaxed he started when Chris finally spoke.

"That's good. You can take a break. This needs to dry, but I'll want to continue later, and remember, no peeking."

"Yes, boss." He smiled at her and for a moment their easy companionship of the first few days was restored. Then he pictured her naked again and knew that friendship wasn't near enough for him.

⁂

Several days passed and they fell into a routine that balanced Eric's work and Chris's painting. They ate meals and walked together as before and worked in Eric's garden for a portion of each day. But their relationship was different since the night of strip Truth or Dare. Beneath their polite veneer was a current of attraction that burned like a fever.

If their hands brushed while passing something at the dinner table, Eric felt a tingle like an electric shock shoot up his arm. He knew it was all in his head, but couldn't stop the constant state of semi-arousal he was in whenever he was around Chris.

Eric thought his feelings would dissipate as days passed and the memory of the way her body felt faded. He thought he'd get used to having her around, but his desire grew stronger every day. It felt like thunderheads gathering on the horizon, the air shimmering with ionization just before a storm burst.

His nights were restless with dreams. Some old favorites he thought he'd put to rest revived to haunt him, like the one where Jonathan's accusing and angry corpse rose from the floor. New dreams were added to his repertoire, erotic meditations on Christine with no particular plot from which he woke with the sheets tangled around his sweating body and a hard-on aching between his legs.

On the third night after the incident in the garden, Eric dreamed Chris was naked and seducing him, leading him into the little grove of trees. She tumbled to the grassy ground beneath him. He pressed into her body, craving her so badly he thought he'd explode. She opened her eyes and looked straight into his, then started to say something he was desperate to hear, but before she could speak the dream shifted. Eric was on a cruise ship with his mother and father. They stood at the railing, dressed in party clothes with cocktails in hand. Mother looked over her shoulder and frowned at him. "Why are you here? Get back inside before somebody sees you."

He retreated below deck where he found himself in a forest. Something dark and huge and ravenous chased him through the underbrush. He could hear it, but didn't want to turn around, knowing what he would see. It was the monster that wore Jonathan's face.

Eric woke with a cry and sat up. His heart raced and he was drenched in sweat as though he'd been running in reality. His hands shook as he pushed back the covers and climbed out of bed.

In the bathroom, he splashed his face and neck with water then stood for a moment, leaning against the sink. He couldn't go back to bed and risk another nightmare. Slipping on his robe, he padded down the hallway and through the doors leading to the second floor veranda.

It was dark and cool outside in the early hours of the morning. He sat in a chair facing east, watching the sky, waiting for the sunrise as he often did when he had trouble sleeping.

"Eric?" Chris's voice came from behind him. "I heard you yell. Nightmare?"

He jumped, practically tumbling off his chair. He automatically started to turn toward her then remembered he was unmasked and put a hand to his face. "Stop! Stay there."

"I can't see your face and I'm not coming any closer, but we need to talk. These past few days, working together and trying to play it cool—it's not working. We both know there's something more between us. I don't want to tiptoe around the edges of it anymore."

Eric drew his robe tighter around him, keeping his head bowed and turned away from her. "Could we discuss this later?"

"No. I think now is good."

He heard a rustling sound behind him. "Don't!"

"Not looking. I'll sit right over here."

He felt ridiculous and childish for not being able to face her like a man.

"I've been thinking about this a lot these past few days and here's what I came up with," she said. "I threw myself at you the other night, pushed too hard and tried to force you into things you're not ready for. So here's my proposition. We try again, but at your pace, on your terms."

Her low, sexy voice reverberated along Eric's spine. He couldn't believe that after the fiasco the other night, she was making him another offer.

"You can look at me, touch me, do whatever you like with me and I won't do anything to you until you give me permission. You can even tie me up if that makes you feel more secure."

The image of Chris's arms stretched over her head, her wrists bound with rope hit Eric with a jolt that set his cock surging. There was a long silence before he realized she was waiting for his answer. "Why? Why would you want to do that?"

"I'm attracted to you. And I'm pretty sure you feel the same, but you're nervous. I understand that." She paused. "Okay, I'm going to tell you something that sounds nuts, but I swear it's the truth. I had dreams about you before I even came here. I feel like our meeting was destined and that I'm meant to be with you—sexually. And, dreams aside, I just enjoy spending time with you."

"How could you possibly be attracted to me? You've never even seen me."

"I see you every day. I know you. The damage to your face is not who you are, Eric, although right now you're letting it dictate your life."

He fell silent, knowing she was right, but she'd also simplified something much more complicated than she could understand.

"What do you think? Do you want to try a physical relationship?"

He'd be a fool to reject her offer twice. Lifting his chin, he looked at the far horizon. As the sun rose, the sky turned from gray to a rosy pink above the line of trees. After a long moment, he answered, "Yes."

Chapter 6

Eric secured the rope binding Chris's left wrist to his bedpost. "Not too tight?"

"No. It's fine. Besides, isn't a little pain supposed to be part of the fun?" She smiled up at him, her dark eyes dancing with mischief. She lay across his bed, arms above her head lifting her breasts so the magenta nipples thrust perkily up from the center of each round globe. Chris seemed to have no self-consciousness about her nudity.

Eric was amazed that she let him, practically a stranger, tie her up. He could be a sadist or a killer. She didn't really know him at all.

She watched with interest as he moved to the foot of the bed and stood gazing at her prone body. Her legs were close together hiding her pussy from his view, but a neat triangle of black marked the spot. Above it her belly rose and fell with her breathing. A ring in her navel winked at him. Her flesh was satiny brown and so smooth and flawless, he could hardly wait to touch it.

Chris's hair was curly tonight as it had been the night of her show. The riot of glossy ringlets fanned around her face like sun rays. She wiggled and arched her chest, testing the ropes by pulling against them. "Wow, this feels sexy! I like it. What now?"

Good question. Now that he had her there, open and vulnerable and at his mercy, Eric wasn't sure what to do next. He rested his hand on her naked foot then trailed his thumbnail up and down the sole. "You're a very trusting person. For all you know I might have plans to tickle you 'til you beg for mercy."

"No!" Her foot jerked away from his hand. "I'm serious. No tickling. Anything but that."

He captured her ankle. "So you wouldn't want me to do this." Again he scraped his thumbnail along the bottom of her foot.

"Agh! Come on, that isn't sexy. It just tickles. You're killing me!" She laughed and wiggled, kicking her free leg out and catching him in the chest.

He caught that ankle too and pinned both feet to the bed. "Okay. No tickling. I promise."

He smiled, loving her laughter and the way she made him feel so at ease. His nervousness was dispelled and he could enjoy whatever came next. He stroked his hands up and down her legs, feeling their perfect smoothness.

Chris settled and stopped squirming once she trusted he wasn't going to tickle anymore. Her eyes drifted half closed as his hands moved up her thighs, nudging them apart when he reached the apex and the dark patch of hair.

The nerve endings in Eric's hands were dull. Over the years he'd learned to compensate for the damaged nerves that made it difficult to pick up small objects or use fine motor skills. But he could feel Chris's soft skin well enough and arousal shot straight to his groin. His dick was already hard just from the erotic sight of her tied up like this. Eric didn't know how long he'd be able to touch and play with her body without losing it.

Her hips lifted off the bed as his fingers moved teasingly up and down her inner thighs, closer and closer to her pussy. She gasped softly when he touched her swollen labia.

Eric met her glittering gaze under the fringe of dark lashes. He licked his lips and breathed out slowly. "Would you mind if I blindfolded you?"

"I told you, whatever you want, whatever makes you comfortable." She smiled again. Once more he was amazed at her complete trust in him. It was empowering to have that kind of control.

He found a silk tie in his closet. He hadn't worn it since his parents' funeral. The way his life was arranged there was little need to dress in business suits. Sitting on the bed by her side, he wrapped it carefully around Chris's eyes.

She lifted her head to make it easier and when he was finished tying a knot, she lay back against the pillow. "This is exciting. What *will* you do with me next?"

Eric removed his mask and took off his shirt before sitting beside her again. He leaned over her and lightly touched his lips to hers. Her soft mouth yielded beneath the slight pressure. He closed his eyes and sank into the kiss.

It wasn't his first kiss. Whores did allow kissing and were paid for the illusion of caring as much as for the sex. But this was Eric's first *real* kiss, the first one that mattered.

Chris made a humming sound down deep in her throat and her tongue flicked out to tickle at his lips.

Eric opened his mouth and met her tongue with his. Sweet and delicate, they danced together. Then a little deeper and harder as Eric's desire grew and he kissed her more aggressively. He pulled away gasping.

"Mm," Chris moaned again. "It's hard to kiss without putting my arms around your neck. You should untie me."

Eric didn't answer. He leaned down and kissed her forehead, her nose, cheeks, jaw and throat—little presses of his mouth and licks with his tongue. He could feel and taste her with his sensitive mouth and she filled his senses. Pausing at the hollow of her throat, he felt her heartbeat thrumming against his lips, strong and steady.

His hands roamed her body, stroking her shoulders and arms above her head then sweeping down to cup her breasts. His mouth followed his hands, kissing her chest and the mound of a breast before settling on one taut nipple. He rolled his tongue over the stiff bud, both hard and soft at the same time. His eyes closed as he suckled one tit and gently kneaded the other.

Eric had purposely kept his jeans on to keep his dick under control. His erection pressed painfully into the zipper of his fly, but he didn't plan to let his cock out to play tonight. He wanted to explore Chris's body slowly and fully before having sex with her. Or maybe he just didn't want to appear as desperate to be inside her as he actually was.

He switched breasts laving his tongue over the other nipple then blowing across it to make it peak even harder. Drawing it between his teeth, he bit lightly.

Chris gave a low groan and arched her back, lifting her chest toward his mouth.

He sucked as much of her breast as he could into his mouth, filling it with her soft warmth. His fingers plucked and twisted her other nipple, drawing another moan of satisfaction from her.

Eric moved farther down, kissing over the soft curve of her stomach. He dipped his tongue in her navel, playing with the silver ring for a moment before moving on. As he approached her pubic mound with his kisses, Chris lifted her hips in anticipation.

"Oh yeah," she breathed, so quietly he could barely hear the words.

He glanced up. Chris's fists gripped the rope binding her to the bedposts. Her head was tilted back against the pillow and her throat exposed. The erotic sight of her pleasure—pleasure *he* had given her sent a wave of delight through him. He brushed his fingers through her curls, separated the folds of her labia and lowered his mouth to her.

He lapped his tongue up the seam of her sex, tasting her musky juices. She was wet and so hot. When he licked the little bud of her clit, it was like pressing a button. She arched to his mouth, moaning. It was so easy to give pleasure. Eric ignored the throbbing pulse of his cock and concentrated on satisfying Chris.

Lying between her warm thighs, he buried his tongue in her pussy and stroked her inside and out while she writhed beneath him. He held her hips to the bed not allowing her to lift them as she wanted to. Teasing around her clit with his tongue, Eric made her whine for his touch.

"Ah, come on. Please."

He smiled as he gave it to her, tickling the sensitive nerve bundle with the tip of his tongue, nipping it then lapping gently over it with broad, flat strokes. He pressed his fingers inside her, moving them in and out as her opening clenched around them.

Her reaction was exciting. She rose and fell, thrusting against his mouth again and again, her moans growing louder and more protracted. Then suddenly she bucked up, arching her back off the bed and crying out.

Eric felt her inner muscles clamp his fingers then release with a wet gush of fluid. He lifted his mouth from her pussy and looked up at Chris, entranced.

Her face below the blindfold was contorted in ecstasy, her mouth open and gasping. Her hands gripped the bedposts and the muscles of her arms were stretched taut. She fell back on the bed, breathing heavily and twitching slightly as aftershocks swept through her.

Eric pressed a kiss to her heaving belly then sat up. He unfastened the top button of his jeans and reached inside to ease the strain on his cock. He only meant to adjust it so it wouldn't press against the seam, but his hand gripped it and began to pull.

"Come on," Chris panted breathlessly. "Where are you? Finish this."

"I thought you came."

"Yes, but I'm not finished. I need you inside me now."

Her arousing words and his own stroking hand almost brought him off right then. "I didn't think you wanted to have sex yet. I thought you'd want to take it slow."

"Do I seem like the type to take anything slow?" She smiled. "But it's your show. You're the one in charge. If you don't want to fuck me...."

With a strangled groan, Eric clambered off the bed and fumbled his jeans and underwear off. He had just enough higher brain function left to remember to put on a condom with trembling fingers. Then he lay on top of Chris's body, nestling between her legs, and pushed inside. Her hot body surrounded him, setting fire to the nerve endings in his straining cock. She was so tight around him, making him feel like his cock was huge and powerful.

She sighed. "That's better. I was aching to be filled."

Her words excited him as much as the sight and feel of her. For a moment as he pushed into her, Eric wondered if Chris could feel the uneven texture of his flesh rubbing against her breasts and belly and if it disgusted her. Then he stopped thinking at all and immersed himself in pleasure.

He drove in and out of her with sharp thrusts of his hips, unable to slow down and savor the sensation. Like a starving man wolfing down a meal, he fucked her hard and fast, grunting with each push and pressing her into the mattress.

Chris let out soft grunts and whooshes of air as he hammered into her. She panted little encouragements. "Oh yeah. Harder. Go on, baby. Like that."

Her words inflamed him. The tension in his cock grew to an exquisite pain, and in a few short moments, Eric's balls drew up tight and ecstasy swelled and exploded through him. He let out a primal groan of release as he came deep inside her, wave after wave bursting through him.

His body shuddered and he collapsed on top of her, turning his face away from her so she wouldn't feel his scarred cheek brush against her. His chest rose and fell as he gasped for breath. Eric ran his hands up Chris's arms feeling her smooth inner arms and the ropes binding her wrists.

"I want to hold you now. Untie me," she whispered against his hair.

He breathed heavily in and out as his heart rate slowed and the last tremors of ecstasy faded away. "Not yet," he murmured.

If you touch or see me, you might not want me anymore. He knew it was true. He would delay that moment as long as he could.

Chapter 7

"Are you crazy?" Tonya's yell shredded Chris's eardrum. "What the hell do you think you're doing?"

"I'm *not* thinking. I'll admit it. I'm running completely on intuition, but I know what I'm doing is right."

"For who? Sounds to me like you're getting your pussy licked and this poor freak thinks you got a thing for him."

"Don't call him that!" Chris felt a rush of anger. "There's nothing wrong with Eric and I *do* have a thing for him."

Tonya snorted. "I've seen your 'things' come and go. You know you've got commitment issues, and a guy like that, he's going to want a lot more from you than you're able to give."

Chris's anger swelled. "How do you know what I'm capable of giving or what I feel for him? This time is different, Tonya. I've never had this connection with any man before."

"But you haven't even seen his face yet."

"So?"

Tonya sighed loudly. "It matters! I'm your friend. I'm not going to bullshit you. When it comes down to it, what he looks like *does* matter. You don't even know how messed up he is yet and you've got him falling in love with you. You're gonna break that poor fool's heart."

"I'm not. I won't!"

"It's too late. You already have. When it comes time to leave and you go back to your busy life and your family and friends, what's Leroux going to have? Just some memories that make it even harder to go back to being alone."

Tonya's words punctured the bubble of joy Chris had been floating in for the past few days. She hadn't thought ahead to her leaving and what that meant for Eric.

"Maybe I'll stay longer. Maybe I'll—"

"How long can you live there? Is that where you want your life to be? What about your career, your life in New York? Do you imagine you're in love with this guy?"

"I might be. I don't know. Jesus, can't you just be happy for me?"

There was a long silence before Tonya spoke again. Her voice was calmer and quieter. "Honey, I'm not trying to badmouth your man or say you couldn't love somebody like that. All I'm saying is it sounds like you're playing with fire, and you need to be careful for his sake as well as yours."

"How do you know *he* won't hurt *me*? Maybe he'll decide I'm too flaky and bossy and tell me to get lost. Maybe I'll be the one to end up with a broken heart."

Tonya's eloquent silence answered her.

Chris exhaled. "All right. I get your point. I'll be careful."

"That's all I'm saying, stop and think a little."

They talked a few minutes longer then Chris found an excuse to end the call. After she hung up, she lay back on her bed and stared up at the pale lilac ceiling of her room. *Her* room. The walls were in complementary shades of purple and blue; a thick oriental carpet covered the floor. The drapes and furniture all exactly reflected her eclectic taste. It was as if she'd designed the room herself it suited her so perfectly.

When she'd first arrived, the fresh smell of the paint and carpet had tipped her off that this room had been decorated in anticipation of her visit. Chris had thought it was kind but a little scary that Leroux had gone to all that trouble for a passing guest. But now she only saw how well Eric knew her before they'd even met. Screw Tonya. There *was* a connection between them beyond the physical.

Although over the past days, the physical aspect had been wonderful enough.

Chris closed her eyes, recalling some of their sexual experiments. Her body still remembered on a cellular level the exquisite torment of the feather torture the other night.

Eric had bound her hand and foot and stroked every part of her body with soft whisks of a hawk feather they'd found while walking in the woods. By the time his meticulous treatment was finished, she was so sensitized that a mere flick of his finger over her clit set her howling and bucking.

Another day, after a long session of posing for her while Chris concentrated intensely on her work, Eric had announced that he was sick of being the model. He said he wanted a turn at painting.

He told Chris to strip and lay face down on the carpet in the office then he painted designs and symbols on her back and buttocks. Even softer than the hawk feather, the paintbrush had tickled delightfully while the rough wool carpet had itched her breasts and stomach. She had rocked her clit against it, seeking relief, but Eric had ordered her to lie still. He was getting damn good at commanding. So, Chris had lain motionless, caught between the twin sensations of prickling on her front and tickling on her back, while sexual tension built inexorably inside her.

When Eric finished his painting, he took her from behind, ramming into her hard enough to drive her across the rough carpet, causing rug burns on her tits and stomach. God, that had been hot! She came so easy with him.

But Eric still hadn't allowed her to see his face or touch the worst of his scars.

Yesterday, however, Chris had made some headway.

She stretched luxuriously on her soft bed and reached down between her legs to touch herself as she remembered the previous afternoon's walk.

They had taken the trail that led down to the pond then hiked around the perimeter of the water. There were twenty acres of land included in the Leroux estate with a number of well-maintained walking trails through both woods and open meadows. The path past the pond was one of Chris's favorites. There were ducks, frogs and fish to look at in the pond and a huge weeping willow shaded part of the walk.

Yesterday Chris had a plan in mind for the secluded spot. She took Eric's hand, which he allowed her to hold now, and pulled him off the path and under the tree. Chris had confidence he would soon let her touch him other places than his hand. She knelt down in front of him and looked up into his eyes.

"Will you let me take your cock out?" She waited for his nod then reached out to unfasten the fly of his jeans.

She pushed his shirt up a little, noting the scarring on his stomach. It was a smooth, mottled pink and white with a kind of shiny, plastic look like his hands. Chris wanted badly to ask more about the fire, but whenever she nudged at that wound, Eric changed the subject. Besides, now was hardly the time. Pushing his jeans down his hips, she freed his cock. It bobbed out erect, like a jack-in-the-box ready to play.

It was thick and engorged. A blue tracing of veins ridged the shaft and the head was an empurpled red. A bead of pearly pre-come oozed from the tiny slit in the smooth cap. Chris took Eric's throbbing staff in hand and stroked up and down.

His mouth opened and his eyes were riveted on her hand encircling him.

Looking up at his face, she leaned slowly and deliberately forward and licked the soft, round head with an elaborate sweep of her tongue.

He sucked in a breath. His stomach twitched convulsively.

She wrapped her lips around the tip of his cock and drew it deep into her mouth, as far as she could swallow without gagging. Eric let out a low, needy groan that sent a hot pulse straight to her crotch. Chris withdrew the long, glistening length of his shaft, allowing a breeze to tickle across it before engulfing it once more. She set up a steady rhythm of stroking and sucking, savoring the musky taste of pre-come on her tongue. Her knees dug into the moist, leafy loam beneath the willow tree and the smell of pond water mingled with Eric's warm, male scent.

As his urgency grew, he thrust toward her. His hands cupped either side of her head, holding it steady and he pumped into her willing mouth. The pace of his thrusts sped up and soon Eric's groans turned to a strangled cry, "Oh God, I'm going to—" He tried to pull away.

She released him from her mouth long enough to say, "Go ahead. It's all right," then continued her rhythm of hard strokes and strong sucking.

His fingers clenched in her hair and his hips pumped very fast, jarring her and almost making her lose her balance.

Chris steadied herself with a hand gripping his flank. She felt his cock swelling even thicker in her mouth then he came with a guttural cry.

"Oh God. Jesus," he panted a prayer as his thrusting slowed then stopped.

She swallowed his warm release then let his cock slip from her mouth. She held it in her hand feeling final tremors passed through it then, tucking it in his pants, sat back on her heels and looked up at Eric. "How's that?"

His eyes were half-lidded and he heaved a deep breath. "Amazing."

Chris smiled in satisfaction as she stood up and moved into the circle of his arms. "Good. There are more rewards like that for good boys who let me touch them." She winked at him, then rested her head against his chest, listening to the vibration of his chuckle.

After the interlude under the willow, they continued their walk, stopping to feed the ducks and check out the progress of a litter of raccoon kits they'd discovered in a hollow tree. It was all very pastoral and fascinating for a city girl like Chris.

And when Eric pulled her off the path again and fucked her soundly up against a tree, she didn't even complain when the rough bark scraped her bare ass. He was so hungry for her, his eyes half lidded and gleaming and his jeans down around his knees.

It was thrilling being bare bottomed, with the hard wood at her back and Eric's hard body pressed against her front. Chris wrapped her legs around his waist and her arms around his neck and held on as he strove for ecstasy. His cock hit her deep inside sending vibrations of delight shimmering through her. And abruptly, unexpectedly, she reached climax, crying out and bearing down hard on Eric's cock.

His orgasm followed hers almost immediately. He made a choked, sobbing sound as he came then buried his face in her shoulder and collapsed against her.

Yes, it had been a very fine and fruitful afternoon yesterday.

Recalling it, Chris lay on her bed, circling her finger faster and faster on her clit. The memory of the feverish intensity with which Eric drove into her, sent a shiver of excitement through her, and reliving yesterday's orgasm spurred her to achieve another. Her breath caught and she let out a little cry as her hips jerked. Pulses of delight radiated out from her clit.

With a final moan, Chris drew her hand away from her crotch and wiped it on her thigh. She gazed up at the pale lilac ceiling of her room and thought about her growing attachment to Eric, and Tonya's scolding on the phone

Tonya, as usual, was right. Chris had to stop thinking with her pussy and use her head about him. She sighed, the pleasure from her orgasm rapidly dissipating as she mulled over the emotional issues she faced. It was hard enough hammering out a relationship in the normal course of things, exponentially more difficult when your lover was emotionally damaged and extremely vulnerable.

Was she in love with Eric? And if she was, could she be happy living out here in the middle of nowhere, hardly interacting with other people? There was no denying her pleasure in his company and in having sex with him, but Chris didn't know if it was real love. She thought it might be. Her heart raced whenever she thought of him and ached at the idea of leaving him.

But as Tonya had pointed out, Chris must find out if she could accept his scarred face before this went any farther, because she sure as hell couldn't live with a masked man forever.

It was time to see all of Eric, to meet him face to face.

"The Power Rangers could kick Ninja Turtle ass!" Chris declared.

"Please! They were just a bunch of kids in rainbow jumpsuits and helmets. The Ninjas were powerful mutants. It's like saying the Power Rangers could kick X-Men ass." Eric half-reclined on the couch, Chris straddling his hips and pinning him down.

"Not the same. You can't compare kid show superheroes to real superheroes." She shoved on his shoulders, pressing him farther into the couch.

"Are you even listening to yourself? Real superheroes?"

"Yeah, comic book types like Superman, Spiderman or Batman."

"How old are you anyway? Weren't the Power Rangers a nineties show?"

"Twenty-six." Chris wiggled on top of him, rubbing against his erection.

"So you were about sixteen or so when the show was on? Pathetic! At least I watched the Ninja Turtles when I was the proper age—a kid."

Chris laughed. "My younger sister, Lynette used to have Power Rangers on after school while I was doing my homework. What can I say? It was strangely addicting in a horrible, cheesy way."

His answering chuckle was rich and deep and vibrated from his chest into her restraining hands. The shiver moved straight up her arms and spread to all her naughty parts. Her breasts tingled and her crotch clenched and ached.

She bent down so her face was inches from his. "I win and I'm going to kiss you now."

"How do you win? We haven't solved the Power Ranger versus Ninja Turtles debate."

"I win because I'm on top and because I say I won," she whispered. Chris touched her lips to his, angling her head to the side and feeling the soft, cotton material of the mask brush against her nose. She settled into the kiss, opening and closing her mouth softly against his.

Eric responded, sweeping his tongue out to meet hers and gripping her hips in his hands.

After several long, searching moments, Chris pulled away, but stayed hovering over him, her face close and her eyes holding his. "You know it's time now, right?"

"Time for...?"

"The mask. It has to come off. Not just because of the painting." She kept her voice quiet, calm and reasonable. "We're past it now, don't you think? We know each other too well to be separated by this piece of material."

His tongue darted out and licked his lips. He gripped her hips even tighter and shifted beneath her.

Chris waited, determined to give him time to respond, praying he would give her the answer she wanted, ready to see and accept whatever he showed her.

The silent moment spun out between them, fragile and tenuous. Chris knew he might go either way.

Suddenly her cell phone rang startling both of them. She sat up, fished it out of her pocket and looked at the caller ID. "Sorry. I have to take this. It's Denise from the gallery."

She climbed off Eric and walked out into the garden to take the call.

"Chris, good news. I have another buyer for *two* of your paintings!"

"Oh my God, which ones and who is it?"

"*Chess in the Park* and *Dog Walker.*" Denise went on to tell about the buyer and the particulars of the sale. "And there's more. I've had two different clients express interest in the *Rose Colored Glasses* painting. I may be able to gently prod them into a bidding war."

They talked for several more minutes with Chris thanking Denise over and over for giving her the opportunity to show at the Gruen gallery, making her success possible.

When she hung up, her pulse was racing, pumped full of adrenaline. Her first impulse was to run to Eric with her happy news. Then she realized her good fortune might not seem so wonderful to him. She would have to go to New York immediately to get the paintings ready to ship, interrupting her progress on his portrait, but more importantly, undermining the confidence he had begun to feel in her.

Chris opened the doors and slipped back into the office, searching her mind for the best way to present her news to Eric.

He was no longer sitting on the couch, but stood before the fireplace, staring at Chris's painting of the rose-choked tree. He turned to her with a smile as she entered the room. Chris was struck anew by how much emotion she could read in only his mouth and eyes.

"Good news?" he asked.

"I sold two paintings and Denise says some people are expressing interest in another." She walked over to him and took his hands in hers.

"See. I told you it's just a matter of time. You're very talented."

She smiled up at him. "Thanks. But here's the thing. I have to go to New York for a while to take care of business.

"Of course. I understand." He squeezed her hands lightly then let go.

"I hate to take a break when it's going so well. Will it be all right if I come back to finish the portrait in a week or two?"

"Sure." His smile remained fixed, but some of the light had drained from his expressive eyes. "And I'll understand if you don't want to finish."

"Of course I want to finish." Chris frowned. "Why wouldn't I?"

"You might feel differently after you're back in the city. You'll be busy with your work." He took a few steps away from her. "As you said, we've gone about as far as we can go."

Chris blinked. "When did I say that?"

"You said if the mask doesn't come off, you're finished painting."

"No. I said we're past the point where you need to hide your face from me."

He walked away from her, toward the window facing the garden and the portrait on its easel. "You're leaving anyway. We both know this affair has no future. It's better you leave with your imaginary picture of my face than the reality."

"I don't think so." She followed him across the room. "Besides, I don't have an image of you in mind."

"Don't you?" He casually flipped back the cloth covering the portrait.

"Hey!" Chris reached out as though to cover the painting then dropped to her hand to her side. "You've already seen this, haven't you?"

"Yeah, I've seen it." He gazed at the picture of a man looking out at the garden, his body in shadow but his face turned toward the light.

Chris swallowed and stared at the portrait, seeing it through his eyes. The man in the painting had Eric's yearning blue eyes and soft, sensitive mouth, but rather than paint the mask, Chris had improvised and given him a generic male face.

"It's just a placeholder," she said, "a template of bone structure and facial muscles covered by skin. It doesn't mean that's how I imagine you look."

He made a scoffing sound. "But I know this is what you'd *like* to see behind the mask." For a moment longer they both stared at the handsome man with the pensive expression staring out the window.

Eric suddenly turned to Chris. "You know, you're right. Maybe we should just clear the air and face up to the truth. Both of us."

Before she could react or reply or even guess what he was about to do, Eric reached up with both hands and removed the mask from his face.

Chris was so startled by the unexpected move that her mouth literally dropped open. With no preparation or warning, she had no time to school her face not to show surprise or horror. She was quite certain that was Eric's intent, to catch her unaware and observe her unguarded initial reaction.

And of course it *was* a shock and it was horrible. She couldn't look at the angry red, raw-looking flesh and not think of how agonizing and frightening it must have been for a poor little boy trapped and burning in a fire. Chris frowned and winced before smoothing her expression into neutrality.

Eric's mouth was a grim line and his eyes narrow. "Is this what you wanted to see? Disgusting, isn't it?"

Chris glared right back at him, refusing to show the least shred of pity because she knew it was Eric's greatest fear.

"It's not disgusting. That was a sympathy wince 'cause it looks like it was incredibly painful when it happened. Give me a break, Eric. You can't expect me not to react. Excuse me if I need a second or two to adjust."

But Eric was busy ramping up from anger into fury. "Go ahead. Take a good look and paint me like this."

He gestured to his face. Despite herself, Chris did as she was bid, gazing at the patchy, discolored pigment of his forehead, nose, right cheek and jaw, and at the ridged folds of scar tissue blazing across his left cheek all the way down his neck, disappearing into the collar of his shirt.

"Want to see more?" He unfastened his shirt, sending a button flying, and stripped it partway down his arms. The worst of the scars were on his left side, covering his shoulder, chest and abdomen in red flesh that seemed stretched too taut. "Makes you sick now to think I fucked you, doesn't it?"

"Stop it. You're the one who can't accept yourself—not me." Chris's throat was tight and she fought back the tears that choked her, struggling to speak without a catch in her voice. "They're scars. That's all. You had a horrible accident."

He laughed harshly. "Yeah, an accident."

Chris wanted to reach out to touch and reassure him, but her instinct told her it would be exactly the wrong thing to do. She clenched her hands by her sides. "There's so much you haven't told me. How did the fire start and how did you get out? How old were you when it happened?"

"I was five and my big brother saved me. Jonathan was a real hero."

His tone was so bitter Chris felt she was missing something. She asked more questions, trying to keep him talking. "How much of the house burned?"

"The fire didn't spread much farther than my bedroom before the trucks arrived. Brand new house—faulty wiring, the inspector said." He snorted as he pulled his shirt back up his shoulders and began to button it. "But my parents never sued the construction company. Isn't that strange?"

He was hinting at something beyond an accident, but seemed to want her to ask the right question to reveal the secret. "So it wasn't faulty wiring."

His eyes blazed bright blue against his red face, but he remained silent, begging her to figure it out.

"You started the fire accidentally, playing with matches or something?"

He imperceptibly shook his head.

Then suddenly the paint daubs came together and Chris saw the entire picture. "Jonathan?"

Eric's slight smile commended her like she was a student handing her work in on time.

"My God. How did it happen?" She pictured two little kids messing around then remembered Eric's brother was six years older. He would've been about eleven at the time. A sick feeling welled in the pit of her stomach.

"It was an accident, right?"

Eric turned away from her and put the white covering down over the painting, arranging it carefully. "For a long time I didn't remember the fire at all, only the aftermath, the time in the burn unit and the skin grafts. By the time I was old enough to ask about what had happened, the wiring story was a fact in our family—when the fire was mentioned at all, which was never."

"Your brother must have felt so guilty. How did the fire start? Was he smoking or something?"

Eric picked up a tube of paint and turned it over and over in his hand. "When I was older, there were a number of times Jonathan got into trouble and my parents had to clean up after him. I only caught bits and pieces, overheard conversations and arguments, but the tension was there all the time. Jonathan was like any teenager rebelling against his parents. He acted out and didn't live up to the image they'd created for him. It wasn't until the day he died I found out the truth."

"What happened?" Chris whispered, afraid she would disturb the hushed atmosphere and interrupt Eric's confession.

"I heard the shot and went to his room. He was lying on the floor." Eric stared sightlessly at the tube of pigment in his hand. "And there was a note."

Chris remained quiet, waiting for him to go on.

"Jonathan wasn't just driving drunk or speeding the last time the cops arrested him. He'd been picked up in connection with a fire in an abandoned building that killed some homeless guy, but my dad's money made the problem go away and kept it out of the media." Eric set the paint back down and crossed his arms over his chest. "His suicide note was an apology for everything he'd done. Seems there'd been more fires than the one in our house or the one he'd been arrested for. Jonathan wrote that he knew there was something seriously wrong with him and he wanted to kill himself before he hurt anybody else."

Chris held her breath. Her chest hurt from holding it and her eyes burned with unshed tears. Her fists remained clenched at her sides.

"The note disappeared. I never saw it again and my parents never mentioned it. We lived with the secret until the day they died, still pretending Jonathan had been as perfect as they wanted him to be."

"Didn't you tell the police about the note when they questioned you?"

He shook his head. "My parents told them I was too traumatized to be interviewed then paid off whoever they needed to. The police never questioned me even though I was the one who'd found his body."

Chris blew out a long, shaky breath. "Eric, I don't even know what to say. 'I'm sorry' isn't nearly enough to cover it." She moved tentatively toward him, reaching out a hand to touch his arm.

He stepped back. "Don't. I don't want your pity."

"Not pity. Sympathy." She stepped closer and took hold of his arm anyway. "I just want to hold you. Won't you let me?"

Eric pulled away. "I'd like to be alone right now. Can you please go?"

Chris wavered, wondering if it was time to press harder or give him space. Finally she nodded. "All right. But I'm not going far. I'll be right in my room. Come to me if you want to."

She hesitated then, before he could stop her, she rose up on her toes, cupped his face and kissed his scarred cheek. It felt pretty much like regular, warm, human skin beneath her lips.

She walked quickly from the room.

Chapter 8

God, he'd been so right when he told himself he was going to get his heart broken. Eric wished Chris would leave now, forever. He didn't want to see her again. He didn't want her to know what she now knew about him and his fucked-up family. Hell, he didn't want to know it himself.

His cheek burned where she'd kissed it. Of course he hadn't really felt her lips. The scar tissue was too thick on the left side for him to have much feeling. But the phantom mark of her kiss burned like a brand in his mind. It would be there always, long after Christine had returned to her normal life.

"Fuck!" He hit out at nothing, bringing his arm around in a wide arc that knocked the portrait and easel over. They fell to the floor with a satisfying clatter. Eric looked at the stand with Chris's paints, brushes, palette and water glass arranged in haphazard fashion. It took every ounce of his self-control to keep from sweeping his arm across the top of it and sending the contents flying as well. He needed to get out of this house, before he destroyed something.

Eric went outside and ran down the path toward the pond. His pumping arms and legs and the air burning in and out of his chest calmed him a little.

As he passed the willow tree, he thought of Chris on her knees before him with his cock in her mouth. Was it only yesterday? He looked away from the tree and pushed the memory from his mind.

Veering off onto another trail, he ran through the deepest part of the woods. It was the longest circuit, a good three miles of winding path that would physically tire him and take the edge off his impotent fury.

The worst part was that he had nowhere to direct his anger. Eric couldn't blame Jonathan for being a screwed up kid whose sick action had nearly destroyed his brother's life. His parents were dead, so what good would hating them do? It would only affect him, not them. He couldn't be angry at Chris for coming into his life like a miracle and shaking him awake, forcing him to face things he'd kept hidden far too long. And he couldn't blame her for leaving him and going back to her own world. He could only rage at vague things like fate and circumstances. Things were what they were and there was nothing he could do about it.

When Eric returned from his run, he slipped in a side door and went straight to his room, avoiding Chris. It was childish. He'd have to face her again before she left, but he wasn't ready yet.

He showered and dressed in sweat pants and a T-shirt then stared out his bedroom window at the trees waving in the wind. The sky was gray and cloudy. Rain was moving in, bringing on a premature darkness. Carol would serve dinner soon and Eric didn't want to sit down to a meal with Chris. He called the kitchen to tell the housekeeper he didn't care to eat, but she should serve Chris in the dining room as usual.

Eric flopped down on his back on the bed, an arm over his eyes, his brain still running a mile a minute trying to process everything. For a man who'd lived an uneventful, regimented life for years, the turmoil of the past month was overwhelming. He couldn't take the ups and downs of his heart. Eric felt he'd lost his sense of himself as an individual. Everything revolved around Chris. His every thought was about her and he didn't know how to stop it. She was inside him now, invading him, even marking him with her kiss that wouldn't fade.

As for today, telling the secret about Jonathan and admitting his anger at his family and the careless action that had shaped his entire life was all too much for Eric to handle. He rolled over on his side and curled his knees up. If he could just shut down for a while, fall asleep and let it all go away, that would help.

He closed his eyes and breathed slowly in and out, covering the jumbled images and emotions in his mind with a soothing black screen. Nothing. He was nothing, just a quiet ghost floating and observing other peoples' lives. It was peaceful and safe in the darkness.

Eric had floated from consciousness into sleep when the sound of the door opening woke him. His head turned toward the quiet click of the closing door. The room was dim; the last orange light had faded from it leaving everything gray.

He knew it was Chris before his eyes focused on her shape. Who else would walk uninvited into his room? He didn't say anything, waiting for her to speak and resisting the temptation to cover his face.

In the muted light, she seemed to glide across the floor toward him. "Are you awake?"

"Yeah." He rolled from his side onto his back.

"Can I sit down?" Without waiting for an answer, she sat on the edge of the bed, her warm weight settling on the mattress by his hip.

"Can I stop you?"

"I know I'm supposed to leave you alone, but I've done that for about three hours now and I have to leave tomorrow and there's no more time to give you space. We have to talk." She paused. "Or, actually I have to talk and you have to listen."

"Okay." Listening was easy. He could do that.

"Everything you told me about what happened to you, that's some heavy stuff. I don't know how you coped without talking about it to anyone all these years. I want you to know I'm here for you and I'm going to continue being here, even when I'm not. I know it's terrible timing, me leaving right now, but we can talk on the phone every day and I won't be gone long, I promise."

Her earnestness was touching and sweet, like a child's pledge, and Eric knew she believed what she said. But he also knew this past month had been magic, a little bubble outside of regular time, and now it was over. When Chris got back to her normal life, he would fade from her consciousness. She'd find things she needed to do, reasons to stay away longer and longer until eventually she couldn't fool herself that she was ever going back. Then maybe she'd call and give him the 'We'll always be friends' speech. And he'd accept her friendship and let her go, because that was best for her.

She reached out and touched his hip, her hand warm through the fleece of his sweats. "I promise," she repeated. "A week. Two at most."

"Okay." It was the only word he was capable of saying.

She smiled, a glimmer of white teeth in the darkness. "Good." Swinging her legs up on the bed, she lay down beside him. "You don't mind if I lie here with you?"

"Can I stop you?" he said again.

She laughed softly and lay on her side, facing him. Resting her hand on his chest, she stroked soothing little circles.

But Eric wasn't soothed. He felt her eyes on his profile and began to tense up. She must feel his heart rate speeding up underneath her stroking hand.

"Hey." She reached to cup the far side of his face and turn his head toward her.

Eric flinched at her touch and grabbed her wrist, pulling her hand away.

"Hey. Look at me." Her voice was louder as she leaned up on one elbow and gazed down into his face. Her brown eyes glittered in the shadow cast by her brow. "Eric, I've enjoyed every minute of these past weeks with you. I want to make love to you tonight before I have to go tomorrow. Will you please relax and let me touch you?"

A *pity fuck,* he thought, but couldn't refuse it. This might be the last time he ever had her and he wanted her so badly. He released her wrist.

Chris rested her hand on his cheek and leaned down to press her lips to his. The tip of her tongue brushed his lips then probed gently into his mouth. It tasted like mint, cool and sharp. He closed his eyes and relaxed into her now familiar kiss, her cushion-soft lips and warm, wet tongue twining with his.

She pulled away and looked into his eyes up close. "See. Nothing's changed. It's just you and me." She leaned to press her lips to his again.

With a low groan, he threaded his fingers through her hair and cradled the back of her head, kissing her harder and deeper. His other hand went around her waist, pulling her on top of him.

They kissed for several moments then Eric surrendered her mouth to coast his lips over the curve of her jaw and the soft plane of her throat.

Chris made the quiet, purring sound in her throat that drove him wild and arched her neck to grant him better access. Her legs straddled his hips and she rubbed her crotch against his erection. After a moment, she pushed his mouth gently away from her throat. "My turn. Let me kiss you. Lie back."

She leaned toward the left side of his face.

His heart beat faster. "No, Chris, you don't have to. I don't have much sensation in that side anyway and it's too—"

She laid a finger on his lips. "Sh. I'm going to kiss you all over."

He swallowed hard, closed his eyes and surrendered to her will. He felt her move against him, her breasts brushing his chest, her lips touching his then kissing his jaw. Her hands framed his face and even though he couldn't quite feel the pressure, he knew she was stroking his cheek. His chest tightened and tears burned his eyes at the gentle, lingering touch of her mouth and hands caressing every inch of his face and neck.

Eric clenched his jaw and swallowed the lump in his throat, unwilling to surrender his last shred of manly pride and bawl like a fucking baby.

Chris kissed her way down his neck to his chest and moved across it, settling her mouth over his nipple and sucking it gently then biting lightly.

A pang of excitement shot from the point of contact down to his groin.

She toyed with one nipple for a while, then moved across to the other. All the while her hands moved across the breadth of his shoulders, down his arms and over the plane of his chest, touching him everywhere.

Eric relaxed and gave himself over to the pleasure of her roaming hands and mouth. His erection pressed into her belly and rubbed against her soft skin.

Chris moved back up until they were face to face once more. She reached down between them and grasped his cock, guiding it to her wet entrance. "No condom," she murmured breathlessly. "Is that okay? I've been tested, and I'm on the pill."

"Yeah," he grated, unable to spit out more than one word. He wanted her so badly he'd say anything to get inside her that instant.

At his consent, Chris sank slowly down onto his cock, her hot depths swallowing him up. She rose above him, bare breasts thrust forward like a figurehead on the prow of a ship. She seemed carved out of the shadowy darkness of the room, but her body was solid and her weight real and heavy on top of him. She moved, rocking back and forth then rising up and down, releasing his cock then drawing him deep inside her once more.

Eric groaned at the exquisite friction and heat on the sensitive skin of his shaft. He grasped her hips and guided her rhythm. His groin rose to meet her downward thrusts. She was slippery wet and hot as burning embers surrounding him.

The hesitation he'd felt about showing his scars or letting her touch them evaporated in the base, animal need that overtook him. He grunted deep in his throat as he pushed into her with hard jerks of his hips.

Chris moaned and rocked her pelvis from side to side, adding a little twist to her rhythm. Her breasts bobbed up and down as she bounced on his cock. She grasped and squeezed them together then toyed with her nipples, pulling and twisting them.

Eric gazed entranced at the erotic sight. She looked like a powerful, sexual, Amazon goddess astride him.

She dropped her hands to his chest, bracing herself as she rode him faster and faster. She drove her body down onto him with aggressive thrusts. Her face contorted in ecstasy as she moaned louder and gasped open-mouthed.

Eric let out harsh breaths as he met every stroke. His balls drew tight and ecstasy raged through his cock. He let out a cry of completion as his orgasm shook him.

"Oh! Oh! Oh!" she cried simultaneously as tremors shook her. Her pussy slammed down on his spasming cock once more and clenched around it in hard pulses. When the last one had faded, Chris collapsed on top of him, panting and sweaty. Her heavy hair fanned over his chest and shoulder, covering him. "Oh my holy God, that was amazing!"

Eric exhaled a deep breath and wrapped his arms around her, holding her burning hot body close. He rubbed his hand quickly across his eyes, brushing away a few latent tears, then closed his eyes. He memorized the weight and feel of her body in his arms, her sweet scent mixed with the musk of sex and the harsh sound of her heavy breathing. When she was gone, he would at least have this memory.

After a long, quiet time, Chris sat up, propped her elbows on his chest and looked into his face. "Are you okay? Was it good for you?"

"Yes." He stroked her cheek, tracing her soft, full lips with his thumb. "It was very good. Thank you for everything you've done for me."

She frowned. "No, thank *you* for everything you've done for *me*. I'm honored that you trusted me enough to show me your face and tell me your story."

Eric didn't know how to respond so he simply smiled.

She touched the side of his face and he still had a quick urge to pull away. "But you're not happy. Eric, I won't be gone long. I'm coming back. This wasn't some impulsive fling. I'm in love with you."

She drew a breath then said it again. "I love you."

Eric's heart hammered in his chest and he was physically incapable of speaking. He couldn't stand Chris's eyes gazing into his a moment longer. He wrapped his hand around the back of her neck and gently pressed her head down to his chest.

She lay, covering him once more with her wealth of hair. Eric stroked the dark mass. The braids were bumpy against his hand as he'd imagined they would be. They felt strong and thick, like rope, like a lifeline you could throw to a drowning person.

Her warm breath blew across his skin. "I really do love you," she whispered. "You have to trust me."

He didn't answer, but continued to stroke her hair, memorizing the texture with his fingertips, sure he would never feel it again.

Chapter 9

Chris smoothed her hand over the shipping label on the flat, rectangular parcel and prayed the painting would arrive safely at its destination. She was sending it express delivery and there was no reason to be anxious, but she couldn't help feeling like she was sending her child off to school alone for the first day of kindergarten.

"Okay. Take it away." She smiled at the carrier and watched him carry her progeny out to his truck. She continued to watch until the FedEx truck drove away then turned from the window and crossed the shop to the checkout counter where Tonya stood, eating yogurt from a container.

"What next?" Tonya asked.

"What do you mean?"

"Your Phantom of the Opera lover. Are you going back?"

Chris frowned. "Please stop teasing about his scars. It's not funny."

"Sorry." Tonya set down the yogurt. "You're really into him, aren't you?"

"Yes, I told you. But it's complicated. Not the scars, but his emotional problems. There's a horrible story connected with the fire, which I can't tell you. And there's the fact that my work is here in the city and he rarely leaves his house."

"That is a problem. So you're not going back?"

"Of course, I am. But I've got things to take care of here. The buyers for my series of sunset paintings want to meet me, and now Denise is talking about a show at the Gruen gallery in Chicago, which would add a whole new dimension of complication."

"Sounds like you're not sure what you want." Tonya leaned against the counter.

Chris thought about that last night with Eric, almost a week ago now. Her skin still burned at the memory and her pussy tingled and contracted. She missed him on a visceral level and each day away from him seemed like a week.

"I think I'm in love with him," she confided to Tonya.

"You what?" Tonya raised her eyebrows. "You've *never* said that about a guy before in all the time I've known you."

"I really think I am. The problem is he doesn't believe me. After I called and mentioned the possible Chicago show, things got weird on the phone. He was quiet and made an excuse to get off the phone as soon as possible. He hasn't answered any of my calls since or returned my messages." She blew out a frustrated breath. "God, Tonya, I know it's not his fault that he has all these issues, but how can I deal with them when he won't even talk to me."

"What does he want—for you to give up everything and come live in his chateau in the wilderness?"

"He wouldn't say that, but I'm sure he'd like it. I try to picture subletting my apartment and moving in with him and I just don't know if I'm ready for that."

"Moving in! Jesus, you really are hooked."

"Then there's the fact that when I told him I loved him, Eric never said it back to me. I'm assuming he loves me, but how do I know?"

"I don't know," Tonya shrugged. "Ask him?"

"Maybe I would if he'd ANSWER MY PHONE CALLS!" Chris was only half joking with her angry yell. "Why does this have to be so hard? And why am I the one making all the effort?"

"One, because he's emotionally messed up, but also because he's a man." Tonya shook her head and grimaced. "Why do men always seem to want a woman to choose between career and love? You should be able to have both."

"I need to find a way to make it all work." Chris glanced at her watch. "And now I'm late meeting my sisters for lunch. I've got to go."

Tonya smiled and reached across the counter to tug one of her braids. "Don't freak out, sweetie. Things will fall into place the moment you stop worrying so much."

In the taxi on the way to the restaurant, Chris dialed Eric's number and got his voice mail again. It was the sixth time she'd called in the past few days. She left a brief message then hung up. "Damn it!"

She reviewed every word of their last phone conversation trying to find the point where she should have said something different. When she'd told him about the developments with the Gruen gallery and that her New York trip was going to take longer than expected, he was silent.

"Eric? Hello?"

"Yeah. I'm still here."

"I am coming back. It's just going to take a little more time. I have to meet with these people who are interested in the sunset paintings then talk to the gallery about the Chicago show."

"It's a great opportunity. I'm proud of you." His words were supportive, but his voice was distant.

"I miss you, and I'll be back soon."

"No pressure. Do what you need to and come to me when you can." Once more his words were right, but his tone sounded like goodbye.

That was three days ago. In her phone messages she continually reassured Eric that she loved and missed him and would be there as soon as she was able, but it was getting harder and harder to say when she got absolutely no feedback from him. She'd begun to dream about the damn roses again, climbing relentlessly over the castle walls and barring the entrance with their dagger-sharp thorns.

The taxi was almost to the restaurant when Chris's phone rang, rousing her from her reverie. It was Rina.

"Chris, I'm at St. Martin's Hospital. Mom's had some kind of episode. We don't know what yet. Maybe a stroke or a heart attack."

"Oh my God! How is she?"

"Stable, I guess. She's still in emergency. Hurry!"

"Should I call Lynette?"

"No. She's already on her way.

Chris directed the taxi driver to take her to the hospital then sat back and stared sightlessly out the window at the passing city streets. She felt sick. Her mother had seemed fine when she'd been at their house for dinner her first night back in New York. She'd bustled around full of energy as always. How could this happen so suddenly and with no warning?

As the taxi pulled up in front of the emergency room, Chris thrust money at the driver and leaped out almost before the car stopped. She raced through the doors and located her sisters in the waiting area.

"Dad's with mom," Rina and.

"What happened? What's wrong with her?" Chris grabbed Lynette's hand and squeezed it, but looked to Rina for information.

"Dad said she felt dizzy this morning and didn't eat breakfast. She went back to bed. When she seemed worse by mid-morning, he made a doctor appointment for the afternoon. Then just before noon she suddenly started convulsing." Rina broke off with a choked sob, covering her mouth with her hand.

"It could be anything. A stroke or heart attack or a brain seizure," Lynette said. "God, she could have a tumor!"

"Don't panic. She'll be all right. She has to be all right." Chris put an arm around each of her sisters and they held each other for a long moment.

Then there was nothing to do but sit down in the waiting area and pass the time until someone came out to talk to them. Chris walked down to a vending machine and brought back coffee for Rina and Lynette. Her own stomach was too jumpy to take the caffeine.

They sat for what seemed like hours but was really only twenty minutes before a doctor came out to tell them their mother may have suffered a stroke but further testing would be needed before he could confirm the diagnosis. She was being moved to the ICU and they would be able to see her in her room soon.

The three women took their seats again and more time drifted past. Chris shifted in her seat, unable to find a comfortable position. After a moment, she rose and went to the window to stare out at the parking lot. It was now late afternoon and the sun reflected golden off the car windshields.

Chris thought about her parents and wondered how her dad would cope if this stroke left her mom incapacitated. Or what if, like Lynette said, it wasn't a stroke but something even worse? The frustration of waiting and not knowing tied Chris's stomach in knots. She glanced behind her at Lynette. A magazine lay open on her lap, but Lynette's eyes were closed and her lips moved soundlessly as though in prayer. Rina gazed blindly at the television mounted on the wall.

Chris pulled out her phone and dialed Eric's number. Once more she got his machine. "I'm at the hospital. My mom's had a stroke or something. They're not sure what yet. Call me back, please." Her voice broke and Chris ended the call without saying goodbye.

A few minutes later the sisters were told they could see their mother. They took turns going into the room so they wouldn't overwhelm her.

When Chris walked in and saw her mom hooked up to an IV drip and a monitor, her heart wrenched in her chest. The indomitable, energetic woman looked diminished and frail against the white hospital sheets. Her gray-streaked black hair straggled across the pillowcase. Chris moved to the bedside and smoothed her hair into place. Mom wouldn't like looking so messy or so weak. When had she developed all those wrinkles? Chris thought as she gazed at her mother's sleeping face.

Suddenly her lashes flickered and her eyes opened. She gazed up at Chris and a faint smile curved her mouth. "Baby."

"Mom." Chris took her hand and bent to kiss her cheek. "How are you feeling?"

"Like crap," she whispered.

"You want ice chips? I can get the nurse to bring some." Chris was pleased that there was no slurring of words and her mom sounded lucid.

She squeezed Chris's hand slightly. "No. Listen."

"Okay. I'm listening, mama."

"So proud of you." She sucked in a lungful of air. Chris wanted to tell her to stop talking and rest, but her mother's intense gaze stilled her tongue. She breathed in harshly then expelled her next words on a breath of air. "You're in love."

Chris started at the unexpected words. She'd told her parents a little about Eric, but hadn't mentioned their romantic relationship. "I think I am," she admitted.

"Not easy. Trust me. Forty years." Her mother continued to speak in short phrases. "Your father." She rolled her eyes.

Chris laughed as she teared up.

Her mom licked her tongue over dry lips. "Won't be easy."

"I know."

"Don't give up." Another hand squeeze emphasized her point. "If you love him, it's worth it. Hear me?" Her voice was louder and commanding.

"Okay. I hear you, mama." Chris's throat was thick with tears. She leaned down to rest her cheek against her mother's. "You're going to be all right."

Lynette entered the room and Chris kissed her mother goodbye and left.

When the girls and their father finally left the hospital, it was late in the evening. Chris's mom was sleeping and a number of tests were scheduled for the following day. Rina went home to her family, but Lynette and Chris went to their parents' home to stay with their dad.

Late that night, Chris finally fell into an exhausted sleep in her childhood bed, surrounded by the paraphernalia and posters of her youth. She slept surprisingly deeply and dreamlessly until early morning when she slipped into a restless doze and had another rose dream. This time the fairytale trappings of a dark castle and ghostly presence were gone. Chris was in Eric's garden, walking the paths, smelling the roses and listening to the tinkling fountain, but despite the peaceful surroundings, she felt a sense of foreboding.

As she came around the edge of one of the flowerbeds, she saw Eric's body sprawled facedown on the ground. She ran to him and turned him over. His face was once more covered with the mask. Behind it his vibrant, blue eyes were open and beseeching.

No words were exchanged. Chris told him soundlessly she was coming back and he needed to trust her and give her time.

Before she could find out what happened next, the shrill ringing of the house telephone woke her. She drifted up through layers of muzzy sleep to hear her father answer it.

His loud cry dispelled the last shreds of the dream. Chris sat bolt upright in bed, her pulse racing. There was only one thing her father's shout could mean.

Chapter 10

Eric stepped out of the shallow end of the swimming pool and toweled dry, then slipped on his robe and walked to the dining room to have breakfast. He looked over the selection of fruit and muffins with disinterest. His appetite was non-existent and he only ate because he had to. As he put a half of a banana and a date muffin on his plate, he resisted the urge to check his phone for more messages from Chris.

His mind was made up. After their conversation the other day about her growing success, he knew he had to push her away from him for her own good. She had a future and he couldn't be a part of it. If he was a real man, he'd have called and told her he didn't want to see her again. Instead he took the coward's way and simply ignored her calls. But just because he wasn't returning them didn't mean he didn't obsessively listen to her voice messages over and over.

Carrying his breakfast to his office, Eric sat at his desk and watched the financial news while he ate. Focusing on his work was the only way he could keep his mind off Chris. But this morning even a sudden surge in the Nikkei couldn't distract him. After ten minutes and half a muffin, he cursed, put down his plate and reached for his phone.

Chris had left voice mail just before one o'clock yesterday afternoon. "Hi, Eric. Just me, leaving another message. Please call back." That was all. Her tone was short and clipped, definitely annoyed. That was good. She was getting his silent memo to leave him alone.

He hesitated before playing the next message. It was only going to be more of the same and he didn't want to hear Chris's voice grow increasingly angry and upset. Swiftly, before he could change his mind, Eric deleted the next message without listening to it. Then he deleted all Chris's saved messages. There. He was finished with his obsession. He should call to tell her she was free of her obligation to finish his painting, but he didn't want to talk to her directly. Later he'd shoot off an email then send her a check in the mail.

Eric snapped his phone shut and went to get dressed. He'd spend a few hours working at his desk then take a long run around the property, maybe swim more laps too. He needed to keep mentally and physically busy. He'd exorcise all thoughts of Chris, what she looked like, felt and tasted like and how her voice sounded when she told him she loved him. He'd keep his mind distracted and his body exhausted, and stop checking his phone for her calls.

Over time he'd forget about their brief interlude. Eric knew it was surprisingly possible to shut memories out of his mind. He'd had years of practice.

Over the next few days, Eric kept up a strict regimen of work and physical exercise. He filled each minute of his long, empty days working around the house and grounds. He drove himself to exhaustion, chopping firewood, laying new shingles on one of the outbuildings and blazing a fresh trail through the woods with his bush hog. He mechanically ate his meals and read a book or watched a program in the evening before falling into a deep, dreamless sleep at night.

Eric had turned his phone off. If Chris was still calling him, he didn't know it.

He took the nearly finished portrait up to the attic, wrapped in its protective cloth and put it in a dark corner.

When he glanced up from his computer monitor and noticed the rose painting over the fireplace, he took that to the attic too, replacing it with the Mondrian that had hung there before.

If all his days were exactly the same, colorless and lifeless, he didn't mind. It was a comfortable routine he'd lived with all his life and could get used to again. And if his daily runs left him feeling like a prisoner jogging in an exercise yard, Eric quickly erased the thought from his mind and went on to the next segment of his day.

He thought he might take a trip to the seashore. A week at a rented cabin on an isolated stretch of beach would be a nice change. He could take his laptop and still get work done. On the other hand, going to the beach would leave him with too many empty hours in which to think. Better to stay in his own environment, stick with his established routine, which seemed to be working fairly well at helping him forget.

The memory of Chris throbbed like the phantom pain of an amputated limb, but he would get used to the loss of her over time.

The night of the fifth day after his new resolve, Eric had a dream.

He was at a beach house, sitting on a deck chair watching the waves sweep the shore in a soothing, repetitive cycle. In. Out. Scouring the sand and leaving the beach smooth and blank in their wake. He gazed at the shoreline in a trance, ignoring the ominous volume of gray waves building up just behind the white, foamy line of breakers.

Something moving farther out in the water caught his attention. He squinted to focus on the floating object thinking perhaps it was driftwood. Instead he saw a woman's nude body tossed on the waves. Her arms waved then a wall of water crashed over her head. He knew the woman was Chris.

Eric raced toward the water, but the sand pulled at his feet, holding him back. He scanned the water, searching for another glimpse of Chris, but the surface remained choppy and dark. There was no sign of her. He slogged endlessly through the sand toward the water. He had to get to her. Just as he reached the water, Chris's body surfaced again. Her mouth was open wide, screaming soundlessly for help. He ran into the churning waves then dove underwater and struck out toward her. But he sunk like a stone even as he tried to swim.

Eric woke gasping for air and soaked with sweat. He sat up and stared around his dark room. The nightmare had been so real it took him a moment to understand he wasn't at the beach or drowning in the ocean. He blinked and breathed out slowly.

By the time he was completely awake, the details of the dream were already fading, but the awareness that Chris needed him remained imperative. Something was wrong with her. He knew it with every fiber of his body. He checked his bedside clock. It was six in the morning, too early to call. If he was wrong and his dream was just a dream, he'd feel like a fool. But he certainly couldn't go back to sleep.

Eric got out of bed and went to the bathroom. He relieved himself then stepped into the shower. The longer he stood under the hot, relaxing water, the more the dream faded and logic prevailed. There was absolutely no reason Chris would need him for anything. It was his own desire to have her back in his life that had manufactured the dream. Chris was busy and happy, living her normal life, enjoying her success. The best thing he'd ever done for her was cut her loose.

Eric turned off the shower and got out, dripping on the bath mat. He ran his hand over his jaw and felt several days worth of stubble in the patches where hair grew. He went to the sink and got out his razor. It was tricky, shaving blind, but he'd had years of practice and the spots that needed shaving were few. When he was finished, he ran his hand over his face, smooth where it should be, ridged everywhere else. He hadn't actually looked at himself in a long time, other than catching a glimpse in a reflective surface like the garden pool. Eric wondered what Chris saw when she looked at him. He was overtaken with a strong urge to know. The only mirror he had in the house was in Chris's bathroom.

Eric put on fresh clothes then went down the hall to the bedroom that used to be his before he'd taken over the master bedroom. When he opened the door, he smelled Chris's subtle fragrance permeating the room. He closed his eyes, breathed in and felt her presence surrounding him. All the memories he'd forced out of his mind came flooding back in. He recalled her laughter and voice and every touch they'd shared. His chest squeezed so tight he felt like he was having a heart attack. *Chris.*

Frowning, he opened his eyes and composed himself. Coming in here had been a bad idea, but since he was here he might as well look at his damn reflection. Eric walked through the bedroom to the bath and faced himself in the mirror over the sink.

Thick, dark hair, still damp and slick from the shower, fell across his forehead. His face was relatively smooth on the right side although the uneven pigment made his skin a patchwork of pink, white and light tan. The left side had sustained the worst damage before Jonathan pulled Eric from the fire and rolled him in a blanket to extinguish the flames.

Eric ran his fingers over the convoluted, red scar tissue that ran from his temple down to where his neck disappeared into his shirt collar. He couldn't really feel his touch, just a faint pressure on his fingertips and cheek. He gazed into the bright blue eyes that looked back into his. Miraculously he'd received only third degree burns on his eyelids and his sight was intact. His brother had stifled the fire quickly or the damage would have been much worse.

Jonathan's suicide note hadn't explained how he'd set the fire. He'd just claimed responsibility for it, saying he hadn't meant to hurt Eric, but the fire spread out of his control quicker than he expected, engulfing Eric's room in flames.

Sometimes Eric thought he had dim memories of the fire, but wasn't sure if they were true or his imagination filling in the blanks. He certainly remembered the pain of the burn treatments. Layer after layer, the damaged skin had to be removed so the new skin beneath it could grow. Painful grafts had shaped Eric's childhood, but the result was no better than this messy collection of features.

He touched his lips. His left upper lip was marred, but the rest of his mouth was intact. Tracing his finger over his lips, he remembered the lingering, warm pressure of Chris's mouth against his.

He dropped his hand away from his face and stepped back a pace, still gazing at his reflection, trying to look through the damage and see what it was about him that had moved Chris to say she loved him. He didn't see much—just a man, who might have been handsome without the scars. It certainly wasn't his looks that had attracted her. Maybe she was simply the kind of woman who had a soft spot for strays and losers.

But that made Chris seem weak or naïve and she wasn't. She was the most forthright, self-possessed, confident person he'd ever met. If she saw something of value in him, there must be something there, although he sure as hell hadn't displayed any admirable qualities over the past week as he'd driven her away by cowardly inaction.

Eric suddenly realized that after his invitation for her to come to his house and paint his portrait, Chris had initiated every step of their relationship. The very first day she'd cajoled him into removing his gloves and telling his story. She'd offered herself sexually and taken it in stride when she saw his scarred face. She'd said she loved him and promised to return then called him repeatedly while she was gone.

Eric had done nothing but take everything she offered and destroy it because he was convinced it couldn't be real. Or maybe he'd thought loving her would require changes in his life that he was afraid to make.

What if Chris really cared for him and he was breaking her heart? Maybe the drowning dream was simply his mind's way of telling him she needed him too. If he'd stop being completely self-involved, perhaps there were things he could offer her: his love for one and financial support for her work and… well, that was about all he had to give her.

Eric turned away from his reflection and walked back to his own room. He got out the cell phone and turned it back on. There was one four-day-old message from Chris.

He played it.

"Eric. It's Chris." Her voice sounded weak and choked. A long pause followed those three words. God, was she crying? "My mom died. We just found out this morning. She was in intensive care at the hospital, but she was supposed to be fine. I guess there was a blood clot or something." Another long pause followed in which he could hear her trying to control her weeping. His stomach clenched. "I'm going to be here a lot longer than I thought. Please call me as soon as you can." Her voice completely broke on her final words. "I need you. Please call."

Four days! She'd called him four days ago, crying, and he'd ignored her.

She'd left no other calls after that one.

He imagined her planning her mother's funeral, dealing with casket or floral decisions and comforting her grieving father and sisters. Meanwhile, he'd been here wallowing in self-pity. Jesus Christ, he was a fucking loser.

Eric took a deep breath then released it. Okay, it wasn't too late to return the call. He pressed Chris's number and got a message saying the customer was out of range then her voice mail.

"It's Eric. I'm so sorry I didn't call back sooner. What can I do to help? Please call me and let me know." He hung up and considered his options. If he couldn't reach Chris on her cell, perhaps he could contact her friend Tonya at the shop to find out what was going on.

He checked the time. It was just after eight, probably too early for the store to be open, but Eric found the number on Chris's business card and dialed it. He was startled when a voice answered. "Good morning, T.S.A. Art Supplies. How can I help you?"

"Hello. Is this, uh, Tonya?"

There was a pause. "Yes."

"This is Eric Leroux. I'm trying to reach Chris, but I think her phone may be turned off. She left me a message a few days ago about her mother's death and I just got it. I wanted to make sure she's all right and find out if there's anything I can do."

"You took your damn time, didn't you? She tried to call you about twenty times since she's been back in New York. What the hell happened to you? She doesn't deserve this bullshit."

Eric was taken aback at her aggressive tone. "I-I know," he stammered. "I'm sorry."

"I'm not the one you need to be apologizing to."

"I know," he repeated. "I thought I was doing the right thing, pushing her away. It was stupid. I'd like to send flowers or—"

"Damn right it was stupid! She's upset. She doesn't need flowers. She needs the people she loves around her. She's burying her mom this afternoon."

Eric cleared his throat. "Can you tell me where the funeral is?"

"One o'clock. Shady Rest Cemetery. If you care about Chris at all, I recommend you get your ass out of your house and be there for her."

He resisted the urge to say, 'Yes ma'am' and instead offered, "I'll try."

Tonya gave him the address of the cemetery so he could get Mapquest directions. "I expect to see you there. You've got that girl's head all in a twist. I've known her a long time and never heard her say she was in love before. Then there's you, some mysterious guy who won't even return her phone calls. I want to see what all the fuss is about."

Eric wasn't sure what to say. Tonya sounded like she might break his kneecaps if he didn't meet her standards. "I'll be there," he said then hung up the phone.

He walked over to his closet and faced a neatly ironed row of shirts. He pushed aside the shirts and the few pairs of dress slacks and reached for one of the few suits hanging in the back of the closet. He'd had rare occasion to wear one to a business meeting. Most of his financial affairs were carried on over the phone or internet.

Eric lifted the hanger on which hung the suit he'd worn to his parents' funeral. It had been almost ten years since he'd worn it, but the cut was classic. It would do. After all, people were much more likely to be staring at his face than a slightly dated suit.

Chapter 11

Chris stood between her father and Lynette staring at the piece of bilious green plastic grass covering her mother's open grave. She listened to the drone of the minister's voice and gazed not at the shiny wood casket but at the fake grass rug. It bugged the hell out of her. Why hide the truth? In twenty more minutes, after the family left, they'd lower the coffin into the ground and cover it up with dirt. Her mother's life was over, her fiery, exuberant spirit, extinguished.

As the group of relatives and friends joined with a soloist in singing *Amazing Grace*, Chris's gaze wandered to the other grave markers lying in flat, neat rows for easy mowing. She hated this place. It didn't have the character of an old-fashioned cemetery. It was impersonal and uniform; the exact opposite of her individualist mother, but it was the plot her father had chosen so here they were.

The day was too bright and cheery. The glare of the sun hurt her eyes and Chris wished it was overcast, gray and somber to match her mood. She knew her mom would want a celebration of her life not a gloomy wailing over her death, but the idea wouldn't take. Chris couldn't shake her sense of despair and impotent fury at God for taking her mother away from her.

A flash of movement caught the corner of her eye. Chris looked to the driveway where the procession of mourners' cars was parked in a long row. A gleaming black limousine pulled up at the end of the line. For a second, Chris thought it was another hearse, some scheduling mistake had been made and another funeral was overlapping with her mother's.

The limo driver got out of the car and opened the back door.

Chris's eyes widened. The driver was Hank and the man in the black suit emerging from the limo was Eric. Her heart woke from its frozen stasis and beat faster as she watched him walk across the grass toward her.

His dark hair gleamed under the bright sunlight. His tall body was austere and graceful dressed in a black suit. He wore gloves and the flesh-colored mask shielded his face once more, but he was here. He'd come out of the security of his house to be here for her.

Eric stopped walking several yards away and stood with his hands at his sides, watching from a distance.

Chris inclined her head and smiled at him, acknowledging his presence.

He returned her nod.

Feeling strengthened by Eric's presence, Chris looked back at her mother's casket and focused on the minister's words about the afterlife.

Soon the service was over and everyone began to disperse. Chris put her arms around her father and hugged him. He had remained stoic throughout, dazed by grief. "You okay?"

He shrugged. "I don't know. I feel blank."

"I know." Chris imagined it would hit him later, as days passed and he came to terms with being a widower.

Rina came up to them. "Come on. Everyone's going to the church for the luncheon. We have to keep moving."

Chris smiled. It was Rina's way of coping, moving people along like a cruise director. "I'll be right behind you." She nodded toward Eric, still standing several yards off to one side. "You don't need to wait for me. Eric will give me a ride."

Lynette raised her eyebrows. "So that's your mystery man."

Rina looked at Eric then back at Chris. "Are you sure you don't want us to wait for you?"

"I'm sure. Go on."

Chris squeezed her father's hands then crossed the manicured lawn toward Eric, drinking in his presence. She stopped walking a few paces from him. "Thank you for coming. How'd you know about the funeral?"

He nodded toward the crowd of people walking back to their cars. Tonya raised a hand and waved her fingers. "I talked to your friend. I'm so sorry for your loss, Chris."

She nodded.

"And I'm sorry I was late for the funeral."

"Well, you're here now." She moved toward Eric and wrapped her arms tight around his waist, resting her head against his chest. His heart thumped steadily beneath her ear and his warm arms enfolded her. She felt his chin resting against the top of her head.

"I'm sorry," he said again. "So sorry I didn't listen to your calls. I thought I was doing the right thing, pushing you away. It was—"

"Stupid?"

"Yeah. Monumentally stupid." He kissed the top of her head. "I'm sorry I—"

"Sh, you can apologize more later. Just hold me now."

He rubbed his hand up and down her back. When she started sniffling, he rocked her gently and kissed her hair over and over.

After several long, precious minutes of reveling in the comfort of his presence, Chris pulled back to look up into his solemn blue eyes. "I meant what I told you. I love you." She paused then added. "This is the part where you say something back."

"I—I love you too. More than you can imagine." His eyes narrowed in a frown. "But I didn't want to say it or even think about it since I knew you were leaving."

She slapped his chest lightly. "I told you over and over I was coming back. What part of that don't you understand?"

He shook his head. "I didn't think you would, at least not to stay. Your life and work is here in the city."

She couldn't deny it. The question of geography had revolved in her mind for days until her mom's death had supplanted it. She sighed. "Well, we can figure that out later. Right now, I'd like you to come and meet my family. I wish you could have met my mom. You would have loved her. Everyone did."

"I wish I could have met her, too. With a daughter like you, she must have been an amazing woman."

"She was." Another wave of sadness swept over Chris. She squeezed Eric's hand tight.

"Are you sure you want me with you? I don't want to be in the way or interrupt things. This is a day for you to be with your family," Eric said. "I could drop you off."

"No, I want you there. Please. I know it's not easy for you being with big groups of people, but I need you." She knew she was asking a lot.

Eric's lips tightened then relaxed in a small smile. "Okay. Whatever you want."

She smiled back at him. "You should practice saying that often."

He laughed, the delicious, rich chuckle that heated her insides. Bending his head, he cupped her face and kissed her. He pulled away and whispered again, "Whatever you want."

※ゝ(ℭℭ)ℯ※

Much later Chris unlocked the door of her apartment and let Eric inside. Glancing around at the shabby hole-in-the-wall, she was a little embarrassed. The worn linoleum couldn't be hidden by colorful throw rugs, and the cheap wallboard she'd tried to disguise with bold paint looked tacky. If she'd known he was coming, she'd at least have cleaned up, although she couldn't do anything about the general air of poverty. It was definitely a struggling artist's home.

She stopped in the foyer to pull Eric into a hug. "Thanks so much for coming today and for meeting my family. They can be overwhelming." He'd actually done amazingly well with Chris's loud extended family, quietly shaking hands and exchanging polite chat with whomever she presented to him. If the curious glances he received bothered him, he hid it well.

"They were nice." He held her close. "I can't believe you introduced me as your boyfriend."

"Aren't you?"

He smiled. "I guess I am."

"Come on." Chris took his hand and led him toward the bedroom. "I'm exhausted. Let's lie down for a while." She cringed when she flipped on the light and saw her rumpled, unmade bed and the piles of clothes tossed all over the floor. She looked up at Eric and grimaced. "All right. My secret's out. I'm a big slob."

"No. It's homey." His eyes glinted with humor.

She smacked his arm. "Shut up." She tugged his jacket down his arms and tossed it across a chair then loosened his tie and unbuttoned his shirt.

When she reached toward his mask, he grabbed her wrists. "Wait."

Chris waited for him to feel comfortable enough to let her continue.

He released her hands. "Sorry. It takes some getting used to."

"That's okay." She shouldn't have expected Eric's years of believing he was ugly and unlovable would be easily eradicated. Chris carefully removed the mask and felt a moment of shock at the ravaged landscape of his face, but it was easier to adjust this time and to simply see the man inside. She wrapped her hands around the back of his neck and pulled him down to her for a kiss.

Their lips pressed together softly and lovingly at first then with mounting intensity. She threaded her fingers through the soft hair at the nape of his neck. Her lips parted and her tongue swept out to meet his. Warm breath combined and the passion of their kisses was searing. When Chris finally pulled away, she was breathless.

She glanced past Eric to the bed. She'd honestly meant to lie down and rest, but now wanted much more than that. Sex was an affirmation of life and right now she needed the comfort and warmth of Eric's body molding to hers. Taking his hand, she tugged him toward the bed.

They both stripped and Chris climbed into bed then held open the covers for Eric to join her. She wrapped herself around him, snuggling into his hard body. "Mm, this is nice."

He gave a quiet murmur of pleasure. "I didn't think I'd have this ever again."

She looked into his eyes from inches away. "I told you I was coming back. Shame on you for not trusting me. I only say what I mean, and I've never said 'I love you' to any man before you." She paused. "Well, there was Ty Barnesdale back in high school, but I was young and stupid and believed it at the time."

"Poor Ty Barnesdale for losing you." Eric stroked the side of her face, his fingers tracing her jaw and her lips then trailing down her neck to rest on the curve of her shoulder. He leaned to kiss her shoulder, her throat and the swell of her breasts. Then he nuzzled her nipples until they stood in peaks.

Chris closed her eyes and reveled in the sensation of his warm tongue lapping over her nipples, his fingers plucking and twisting them. A monofilament of desire shot from her breasts down to her crotch, where the slow, steady glow of yearning flared into aching need. She pressed her thighs tightly together, massaging her clit with the pressure of her own muscles.

Eric's hands slid down her ribcage and his mouth traced a trail down to her navel and below. Her skin electrified at his touch. Each cell responded to his mouth and hands.

Chris lifted her hips, quivering with need, ready for his touch. She savored the feel of his nimble tongue tickling along her pussy lips then delving inside her entrance. Her body rose and fell, responding to his slow laps across her clit. His teeth nipped the delicate bud and she gasped at the unexpected pain intensifying her pleasure.

She writhed and moaned, releasing the tension and anxiety that had twisted her into knots over the past week, releasing her grief and pain with a quiet wail. The force of emotion united with arousal in a potent combination. Deep inside her, glittering sparkles of need gathered and grew then abruptly burst into a fireworks display of light behind her eyelids. Chris cried out and bucked up. She fell back onto the bed as aftershocks pulsed through her in decreasing waves.

"Ahhhh," she sighed, coming down from her high.

Eric kissed her inner thigh then crawled up her body to lie cradled between her legs. He brushed her hair back and gazed down into her eyes. "You're so beautiful when you come. It makes me happy that I can give that to you."

Makes me happy to see you happy, Chris thought, but she didn't say anything just reached down between them and guided his straining cock to her entrance.

Eric groaned softly as he pushed inside, sheathing himself in her heat.

She grabbed his ass and pulled him deeper. Her muscles clenched around his girth, feeling every bit of him filling her completely, nudging against her tender spot deep inside. The lingering remnants of her orgasm gathered there and began to blossom again.

She loved the heavy weight of his body covering her, the quiet grunts he emitted with each thrust, the growing sense of urgency as he pumped faster and faster. She wanted to give him the same pleasure and comfort he'd offered her. Chris stroked her hands from his butt up his back and gripped his shoulders.

Wrapping her legs around his lower back, she clung tight, changing the angle of penetration so his cock filled her even more deeply. She panted words of encouragement. "Come on, baby. Oh yeah. Harder. Deeper."

Eric responded passionately, increasing his pace and groaning deep in his throat. His eyes were closed and his mouth open in rapture.

The deep scars on the left side of his face and the lighter ones on the right barely registered with her now. To Chris he looked beautiful in his bliss and she understood how he could say the same of her.

Eric shuddered and froze. She felt the pulses of his cock as he came and she clenched her inner muscles around him to enhance his orgasm.

Chris was on the verge of coming herself. She closed her eyes and thrust up once, twice, three times, reaching for the brass ring of a second release. It came swiftly and easily, bursting like a geyser and showering down petals of delight. Chris arched off the bed, floating in a dark void filled with exquisite sensations. She heard herself cry out from what seemed like a great distance.

She came back to awareness to find her body trembling and her chest hitching for breath. Eric had collapsed on top of her, breathing just as heavily.

Chris unwound her legs from his back, allowing him to roll off her and lay by her side. For a long time they simply breathed and basked in the afterglow.

Chris lifted Eric's hand and pressed her palm flat against his, comparing the size and color of their hands. Chris's dark skin made a stark contrast to Eric's pink and white flesh. She laced her fingers through his, making one unit of their two hands.

"I've been thinking." His voice was low and soft, the husky bass sending a thrill up her spine. "I was thinking how hard it will be for us to have any time together when I live so far from New York."

"Yeah." Chris prayed he wouldn't ask her to move in with him. She didn't want to turn him down, but his house was so far away from her work and her life.

"It's time for me to make a change. I'll keep the house for vacations and long weekends, but I think I should rent an apartment in Manhattan." He rubbed his thumb up and down the side of her hand. "I know it's too soon to ask, especially considering your mom and everything. You're dealing with a lot. But I wondered if you might move in with me—not right away, but sometime."

"Manhattan?"

"It doesn't have to be up town. Anyplace that's convenient for you would be fine with me. If you'd rather, we could get a place closer to your shop and studio."

"I think I could adjust to a little travel time if I lived in a penthouse." Chris smiled. "Are you sure? I mean, can you afford to have that big house *and* an apartment in New York too?" She glanced up in time to catch his amused smile.

"I think I can afford it."

"Don't make fun. I'm not used to wealth. I come from middle class roots, you know." She unlaced her fingers from his and tickled his stomach.

Eric laughed. "I'll be your sugar daddy and give you everything you want."

Chris leaned up on one elbow and wrinkled her nose at him. "You don't need to spoil me, but believe me, baby, I'm going to be worth every dime. You're going to wonder how you ever got along without me."

"I already do."

She smiled, leaned over to kiss him then snuggled her head down in the crook of his shoulder again. "I love you."

"I love you too." He stroked her hair, fingering the texture of her braids. "You don't think it's too fast? I don't want to do this wrong, rush it and spoil things."

"We'll take our time and think about it. But that doesn't mean we can't see a lot of each other. Just give me space to do my work and the rest of my time is for you."

He stroked her shoulder then traced the curve of her waist, ending with his hand on her hip.

Chris thought how far Eric had come in such a short time. Here was a man who had hidden from life, buried in his tomb of a house with all its dark secrets. For her sake he had come out of seclusion and was now talking about living in one of the busiest cities in the world. She wondered if he could handle such an abrupt change.

"You know, Eric," she rubbed her hand lightly up and down his belly and tilted her head to look up at his face. "Don't take this wrong, but have you ever considered therapy. It might be helpful, considering what you've been through."

His expression gave nothing away. "No. I've never thought about it."

"Would you?"

"I don't know what good it would do. It's all in the past now."

"Not for you. You're still living with your past every day." She rubbed his stomach again and returned her head to its niche in the curve of his shoulder. "No worries. Just something to think about."

"Anyone ever tell you you're a good manipulator?" Laughter shimmered in Eric's voice. "You'd make a fortune in the business world."

Chris smiled. "I have to warn you, my mama always got her way. Dad thought he ruled the house, but she controlled him like a puppet master. Same thing with my sister Rina and her husband. It's in our blood."

"You can manipulate me all you want." He laughed and squeezed her with his arm. "Just as long as I get to tie you up and do things to you whenever *I* want."

"It's a deal."

❧⁂🙶🙷⁂❧

Chris drifted asleep and dreamed of pink, climbing roses. Once more their scent was so strong and real it felt more like a vision than a dream, but this time the flowers and thorny brambles didn't cover a castle wall, barring her entrance.

She stood in Eric's garden with her easel in front of her, looking past the canvas to where Eric was sprawled on a patch of grass near the rose-covered wall. He lay on his back holding a dark-haired baby up in the air and zooming it around like an airplane. The kid squealed and laughed.

Chris thought, "That's mine," and felt a surge of maternal claiming she'd never imagined she possessed. She wasn't really much of a kid person. "And that's mine," she thought, regarding Eric.

She looked at her canvas and saw her painting was complete. Rather than the realism she usually favored, the portrait was a blaze of color and light tempered with darkness that represented everything she knew about Eric. His essence was splashed across the canvas.

She set down her brush.

Eric was suddenly standing beside her, the baby's head resting against his shoulder. He slipped a hand around Chris's waist and examined the painting with her.

She turned toward him, cupping his cheek in her hand and looking into his eyes. "The form doesn't matter, only the substance. Do you see?"

His eyes were bright as stars as he met her gaze. "I see my reflection in your eyes," he said. "I am perfect."

About the Author:

Bonnie Dee writes contemporary, historical, paranormal and fantasy romances. Whatever the setting, she's interested in flawed, often damaged, people
who find the fulfillment they seek in one another—although she sometimes takes
a break from angst to pen a light, frothy comedy.

An avid reader all her life, Bonnie set aside the dream of writing for far too
long. Now with an empty nest and plenty of spare time, she is pursuing her goal
with both hands outstretched to grasp the ephemeral muse. To learn more about
her work, go to bonniedee.com. She's always happy to hear from readers at
bondav40@yahoo.com.

Educating Eva

by Bethany Michaels

To My Reader:

I've always been kind of a nerd—bookish and somewhat of an introvert rather than a gregarious, life-of-the-party type. Some of my favorite romances star similar heroines. The type of lady who is not the belle of the ball and really has no desire to be. She knows who she is and dances through life to her own beat. Her perfect hero loves her for exactly that reason. That's the kind of story I tried to give Eva Blakely, my 19th century sister-nerd. Because as long as I'm behind the keyboard, brains trump beauty and the girl with glasses always gets the guy.

Chapter 1

The next time she eavesdropped at her neighbor's door, Eva Blakely thought, she should remember to bring a blasted chair. Now her bare feet were numb and her knees ached from kneeling on the hard wood floor. And still the enthusiastic couple on the other side of the door continued to copulate, oblivious to Eva's discomfort.

Eva pressed her ear against the slab of oak separating the bedchamber from her own, but all she heard was the same rhythmic thumping, deep grunts and occasional feminine squeals she'd been listening to for what seemed like hours.

She stifled a yawn. Research was turning out to be more exhausting than she'd imagined, since it required her to stay up so late at night. That was when she collected her best research, although in the three days since she'd arrived at the house party, her neighbor had provided her with daytime research, too. And morning research, and tea time research. He was truly a goldmine of carnal data. Now, however, she wished he would get it over with already.

Eva checked her watch. She had to record this newest set of data and outline a new chapter before she crawled into her narrow little bed.

Finally the thumping increased in rhythm, as did the squeals. With one final masculine groan, the creaking stopped. Eva squinted at her pocket watch in the meager candlelight and recorded the time in her research journal.

Then Eva pressed her ear against the door and listened carefully for the conclusion of the mating ritual, the shuffling bedclothes and soft laughter sprinkled with soft words. She couldn't hear the words, only the low, feminine voice, followed by the deeper masculine reply. Specimen B was a talker, she noted in her journal. Unusual for a male. Only 32% of the specimens she'd studied liked to engage in conversation directly after intercourse. But then Specimen B was turning out to differ from her other subjects in a variety of ways, from number of partners, time of day, duration of coitus, and social rituals after the act. He was a fascinating study. Perhaps she should dedicate an entire chapter to his habits alone. Eva scribbled a note about that in the margin and went back to listening.

At last she heard the door leading from Specimen B's bedchamber to the hallway open and close again, leaving only silence within. It was Eva's signal that it was safe to creep back to her small writing desk undetected, and think about her newest set of data. It had been another satisfactory research-gathering mission, even if it had gone on entirely too long.

Eva gathered her journal and tried to rise from her cramped position on the floor. Pins and needles shot through her legs. Numb from the ankles down, Eva lost her balance and crashed against the door separating her bedchamber from her subject's. She let out a small squeak and clapped a hand over her mouth. Eyes wide, Eva held perfectly still, listening for signs of life next door, hardly daring to breathe.

She waited one second, then two, then ten. Finally the clamoring in her veins slowed. She relaxed and allowed herself a deep breath. It seemed both of the subjects had left the chamber to pursue yet more of the pleasure Ivy Hill Manor offered its guests.

Flexing her ankle, Eva smiled, imagining the triumph her book would herald, the day when she and her academic pursuits would be taken seriously. The day she would emerge from the periphery of scientific circles, no longer condescended to with indulgent smiles, and pats on the head, but accepted and respected for her logical and scientific mind. On equal footing with the men. Yes, that would be a glorious day, indeed. Eva couldn't wait.

The feeling in her feet had finally returned. Eva retrieved her scattered things, laid a hand on the door for support, and began to rise. With a sudden whoosh of cool air, the door was gone and Eva tumbled into the softly lit adjoining room.

"Miss Blakely?" asked Subject B, amusement lacing his familiar voice.

Eva squeezed her eyes shut, praying that she was dreaming and was in reality tucked nice and snug dreaming this whole mortifying incident. No such luck.

"It's a pleasure to see you again. Though I'm afraid I'm not quite dressed for callers," he said. Eva could hear his enjoyment of catching her in a less than digni-fied position. As always, he loved to taunt her. Made a point of it, in fact, whenever she had the misfortune of attending the same social event as he.

Before she could frame an appropriate reply, if there was such a thing, Eva was hauled to her feet. Squaring her shoulders, Eva clasped the journal to her chest, and met the amused gaze of Aidan Worthington, Lord Lynnhaven.

Usually so meticulously groomed, now he was in a state of disarray. But that was no surprise, given his recent activities. His midnight black hair clung to his forehead and temples in damp tendrils, his dark eyes glowing black in the soft candlelight. His full mouth was turned up in the same teasing, seductive grin she'd often seen him employ with appalling success on females in ballrooms across London. The expression highlighted that blasted dimple in his left cheek, the subject of many twittering conversations Eva had overheard when forced to attend some silly ball or another in her mother's last ditch attempt to marry her off.

The candlelight made his bare chest, coated in a fine, dewy sheen, gleam like the finest satin, only a few inches from the tip of her nose. Those gushing ballroom debutantes would have need of the smelling salts by now, Eva thought. It was a good thing she had more sense than to be overcome by simple bit of flesh. Well, quite a bit of flesh, actually. And the musky male scent of him that she'd never been close enough to sense before.

Her gaze slipped a little further south to the crumpled bed sheet tucked loosely around his lean hips, his only nod to decency.

"Go ahead, Miss Blakely. Look your fill. I plan to." His gaze traveled over her body. Even though she was covered from neck to toe in a prim, white cotton nightshift, Eva felt naked under his gaze.

Eva felt the blush burn in her cheeks and spread outward across her face. She was hardly a beauty, compared to the stunning young widows and bored wives Lynnhaven usually consorted with. Not that she cared about impressing him or any other arrogant, self-important cad, but she didn't like to be reminded of her shortcomings. Especially by Lynnhaven.

"I assure you, my lord, that I have far more important matters than ogling your person." She pushed her spectacles further up on her nose and glared at him.

"Had you appeared in my doorway a few minutes earlier, you would have had a lot more to ogle," he pointed out, his hand going to where the sheet overlapped at his waist. "But I would be happy to provide an encore."

Eva tamped down the panic. "I am hardly one of your simpering admirers, charmed by your arrogant overtures." There. Hardly even a waver in her voice, Eva thought with satisfaction.

Instead of being suitably chastised, he laughed.

How had Lynnhaven ever managed to charm so many women to his bed? He was rude, assuming, and extremely trying to Eva's limited patience. Even if he did resemble some of the more attractive male nudes she'd studied in the dusty books gathered in the course of her research. Eva glared at him harder.

"I'd never considered you might be the type to enjoy an Ivy Hill house party, Miss Blakely. You surprise me." He stepped closer and slowly traced the line of her jaw with his knuckles. "Did I mention how much I love surprises?"

"I didn't come here for *that*," she said emphatically. But the tingle that raced through her body at his touch made it difficult to concentrate on being outraged. Blast him.

"There is only one thing most people come here for," he said dropping his hand. "That, I can attest to."

"I'm not most people."

"Yes, I've noticed that about you," he said, his carefree grin returning. "So what is it then? Have you come to infiltrate this 'sinful' gathering? Expose us all as shocking libertines? Maybe blackmail one of the guests? You wouldn't be the first to try, you know. And not the first to fail."

"I'm not here to expose anyone's secrets." Not the way he thought, anyway. "And I hardly think anyone would be particularly scandalized to learn of *your* attendance."

"True. But they might take notice if it were to slip out that you, Miss Blakely, had accepted an invitation. By the way, how is your dear mother these days?"

"You wouldn't dare." Though Eva generally did as she pleased, her poor parents would be horrified to return from their latest travels to learn that her only daughter had sneaked off to an orgy in the countryside. And she never would have accepted Lady Kempe's invitation without the assurance that discretion was of the utmost priority here.

He cocked one sable eyebrow and crossed his arms over his damp chest. "Why are you here?"

"If you must know, this is a research expedition," Eva said as haughtily as she could manage.

"Research?"

"An Anthropological Study of the Mating Habits of Civilized Peoples of the Northern Hemisphere." Eva adjusted her spectacles. "The adult male is the subject of Volume 1."

For a moment, Lynnhaven was silent. Then he threw back his head and laughed. "You're writing a treatise on sex." Eva wasn't sure why he thought that was so funny.

Similar studies had been undertaken by prominent anthropologists, though not of the scope and complexity of the project Eva planned.

Eva steamed. "This is a serious scientific endeavor, Lord Lynnhaven. Not some sort of jest." That he didn't take her work seriously raised Eva's ire another notch. If she had not been such a rational, logical individual, she would have hurled the particularly sturdy vase on the writing desk directly at his head. Eva clenched her fists and managed to resist the impulse.

He finally stopped laughing, but the taunting set to his mouth and the twinkle in his eye told her that he still didn't believe she was serious.

"Let me see that," he said, and before Eva could stop him, he plucked the journal from her grasp and began to flip through the pages.

"Those are my private notes," Eva said as calmly as her panic would allow. "Return the journal immediately."

Eva grabbed for the book, but Lynnhaven only held it higher, out of her reach, and continued to read.

"'Subject B'," he read. "I assume that's me."

He clearly wasn't going to return her property until he'd had his laugh, so Eva merely crossed her arms and glared at him. "Yes, you're Subject B."

He flipped through the pages, chuckling occasionally. "I can tell you for certain that the 'session' lasted longer than 47 minutes," he said handing her the journal. "That was just the noisy part." He adjusted the bed sheet ringing his waist, tucking the ends more securely. "Not all aspects of bed sport are audible from the other side of a closed door, Miss Blakely."

Eva frowned. Despite her annoyance, she was curious. "What do you mean?" She was probably more enlightened as to what went on between men and women than any unmarried young woman of quality could be. Her library was full of texts, dating back centuries and describing the human mating ritual in vivid detail. She was very thorough in her research and had spent hours poring over each account. Was it possible that she had overlooked something?

"What I mean," he said stepping closer. "Is that sex is much more than two people coming together physically. It's the anticipation, a touch here, a caress there. It's the subtle, intangible moments that makes the physical part so good. And that, Miss Blakely, can't be found in any book."

Eva blinked at him through her spectacles, ideas churning. None of her books mentioned such a thing. Her own, somewhat clinical encounter had left her with the impression that intercourse was a simple physical function. An urge that must be attended to from time to time. An act with the purpose of procreation. Not the metaphysical exchange Lynnhaven implied. Maybe there was something missing in her understanding, something that was vital to her project.

An idea blossomed. An awful, brilliant idea. It was unconventional. And risky. But then so was her project. She had to ensure that the quality and scope of her data was beyond question if she hoped to distinguish her book from any others. Eva straightened her shoulders and focused on a point just above his left ear.

"You may have a point, my lord," Eva said politely. She prayed she wasn't going to regret her boldness. "What I need is a subject for in-depth research. Someone well versed in the subject, of whom I can ask frank questions. A subject I can observe in his natural habitat, so to speak." Eva forced herself to meet his wordless stare.

"What I need, Lord Lynnhaven, is you."

Aidan liked aggressive women from time to time. Liked it when a woman knew what she wanted and how she wanted it. But a summer breeze could have knocked him over when he heard the words spill from the proper Miss Blakely's full pink lips. Though she made a good effort at hiding her nervousness, her bottom lip trembled slightly and she could barely meet his eye. Her little pink tongue darted out to wet that lip and Aidan felt all the blood rush from his brain to regions further south.

He'd just been propositioned. By the one woman who had rejected his every overture.

She'd caught his attention early in the season, the one spot of color in a sea of debutante white. She did know what she wanted, but had made it clear on more than one occasion that it definitely wasn't him. She was perhaps the one woman who had ever been completely honest with him. He liked that.

And there was the fact that she was one of the most attractive women he'd encountered in his many years of worshipping the female form. Many men in his circle had commented on her high round breasts and what they'd like to do with that lush full mouth of hers. But it was the flash of intelligence in her green eyes from behind her spectacles that prevented them from approaching. Not that she'd pay them any mind.

Aidan suffered from no such fears. He liked her straightforward manner. He liked how she swept across a room with confidence and grace. How she looked a man in the eye and pointed out his character flaws without a hint of artifice. He liked that not a coy bone existed in her luscious little body. And to his amusement, she'd shown absolutely no interest in him.

But she was here now, dressed in nothing but a thin night shift. Her hair, braided loosely down her back, looked almost mahogany in the shadows, but he knew that in the bright light of day, it was the rich red-brown of cinnamon. Her breasts were unbound, and though she tried to hide their fullness with the journal clutched to her chest, he could see the pleasing round ripeness beneath her scant clothing. She was an intriguing, tempting sight standing there in his shadowy bedchamber, alone in a den of sex and decadence, asking for him to be her guide in the erotic arts. Well, sort of.

Aidan smiled, feeling like a hound that had finally run the fox to ground after a long chase. She was finally here within his grasp and with any luck would be in his bed in the next ten minutes. Five if he could manage to pry the damned book out of her hands.

"Lord Lynnhaven?"

Aidan forced his attention away from the naughty things he wanted to do to Eva and back to the women herself.

"I accept." He said quickly, before she could change her mind. He brushed a ginger tendril back from her face. "Shall we begin?" God, he'd be lucky if he lasted seven seconds, even after having slaked the worst of his desire with Lilah only a quarter hour earlier. He couldn't wait to unleash her passionate nature that he'd sensed simmering just beneath that pale silky skin.

"There are some… stipulations." Eva said, intruding on his pleasantly erotic thoughts.

Aidan arched an eyebrow. "Stipulations?"

"Yes." Eva straightened and raised her chin a notch. "This is a scientific endeavor. I won't be participating in these research sessions. Only observing."

Aidan let the silky strand fall and cocked his head to one side, studying Eva. Apparently she was serious about this little book of hers. "If you intended only to observe, you should have taken up birdwatching."

"If you don't want to…" she looked away, frowning slightly.

"I didn't say that," he said, running a hand through his sweaty locks. "Why don't you explain exactly how this… arrangement would work?"

Eva adjusted her spectacles. "I want to observe you. Detail your comings and goings, the sorts of women you… entertain and, umm… how. I want you to clarify the details. I want you to demonstrate and explain this other aspect you think I'm missing in my understanding of human mating rituals."

"And all this would appear in your book."

"Yes. Anonymously, of course."

"Of course."

Eva shifted her weight from foot to foot, not quite meeting his eye. Her chest rose and fell a little faster than was normal. Aidan grinned. She seemed determined to deny the spark that crackled between them. God, how he loved a challenge.

"And what if some of my explanations required a more hands-on approach?"

A slight blush crept up Eva's throat, but to her credit, she met his gaze. "I don't see that such a thing would be necessary. But I will decide that as the situation warrants."

Aidan wanted to howl in triumph. "I promise I won't ravage you, Miss Blakely," he moved in closer so she was forced to look up at him. "Until you ask me to."

She sniffed and raised her chin a notch. "That, Lynnhaven, will never happen."

Though he longed to slide his hands under her nightshift and spend the rest of the night proving her wrong, he forced himself to step back.

Slowly, confident that she was as aroused as he, though she might not recognize it yet, Aidan unhooked the sheet at his waist and allowed it to fall silently to the floor. Had he not been so painfully aroused, he would have chuckled when her gaze dropped to the sight of his cock at full attention.

Let her put that in her journal.

"As you say, Miss Blakely." Aidan turned away and strolled to the washstand in the corner of his room. He dipped a cloth in the water and swabbed his heated body, imagining it was Eva's small hands gliding over his skin. He ran the cloth slowly along the hills and valleys of each bicep down his arms. Rewetting the cloth, he wiped the back of his neck, then his throat, under his jaw and along the tendon that ran along the top of his shoulder, allowing rivulets of clean water to wind their leisurely way south.

Aidan splashed cool clean water on this face and ran fingers though his damp hair, smoothing it away from his face. He looked over his shoulder at Eva to find her as enthralled with his little performance as he'd hoped. He smiled his wolf's smile.

"Be ready tomorrow at midnight for our first lesson."

Chapter 2

Perhaps she'd made a mistake, Eva thought, leaning against the closed the door that now separated her from Lynnhaven. Maybe this time her willful flouting of society's good opinion had finally brought her to the bad end her mother had always warned her about.

Given the amount of research she'd conducted and her own meager experience, Lynnhaven's nudity should not have affected her. Though she hadn't been shocked by his display, it should not have stirred her blood and sent her heart racing.

Reason, logic, intelligence. Those were things one could rely on. Romantic love and even passion were notions contrived by brainless young girls who knew nothing of the world or the men in it. They weren't real. She wasn't irrational enough to believe in them.

But she had not expected her own irrational reaction to Lynnhaven. And there had been a reaction whether she liked it or not. Just a few minutes in his company and a good look at his assets had opened that door to her irrational side, if only a crack.

Eva pushed off the door and crossed to her writing desk where her piles of research were neatly organized. Her palms were damp and her heartbeat hadn't quite returned to normal. She felt anxious. Giddy. She wanted to take a long walk and work off some of the nervous energy that had built inside her belly.

He'd just caught her by surprise tonight. That was all. Next time she'd be ready when he tried to shock her.

Maybe she'd shock him right back.

Eva blew out the candle and climbed in bed. She pulled the covers to her chin, despite the unseasonably warm September night.

Though she was exhausted from her late-night research sessions, she lay staring at the moon-splashed walls, unable to sleep. She tossed and turned, finally throwing the covers off for good.

Giving up on sleep, Eva went to the window and opened it a crack. There was a cool breeze and the scent of the famed Ivy Hill rose garden drifted up to tease her already heightened senses. The night was alive like it never was in the city. The air was thick and exotically perfumed with a tension to it that felt like a storm loomed just beyond the horizon. It played on her already taught nerves instead of soothing them.

From her bird's eye perspective, she could see inside the tight coils of the hedge maze, the centerpiece of Ivy Hill's elaborate gardens. A slip of white within the walls of yew caught her eye and when the full moon emerged from a sheath of clouds, she discovered that the flash of white was actually a piece of discarded clothing. A short distance away was the woman herself. She was quite naked, as was her paramour.

Eva stepped back from the window. Though she should turn away and climb back into her bed, she was mesmerized by what she saw.

The man was sitting on one of the stone benches in a small clearing within the maze, his lady straddling his lap, facing him. Her long, bare legs wrapped around his trunk and her head was thrown back to receive the kisses the man pressed to her pale throat.

Eva felt her pulse quicken and ventured forward again for a better look. Research, of course. She should get her journal and use this opportunity to her advantage. But she couldn't tear her eyes away from the erotic scene unfolding before her.

The man thrust rhythmically upwards, eliciting a small, throaty squeal from the woman with each stroke. Her sable hair swayed with each motion, unbound, reaching nearly to her waist. She looked like a goddess, wild and uninhibited, part of the night.

The man kneaded her backside, jerking her towards him more violently with each thrust of his hips. She raked her nails down his back, though he hardly seemed to notice.

The man dipped his head and fastened his mouth to one of the woman's full breasts. Eva felt her own nipples swell and harden beneath her nightshift. She'd studied countless erotic images just like this one in books. But for the first time, she imagined what it would feel like. Cool night air kissing her bare skin. Hot kisses pressed to sensitive nipples, the light rasp of skin on skin as two bodies moved in one motion. An image of Lynnhaven on his knees, suckling her breasts, swam before her eyes.

Unable to tear her gaze away from the couple, Eva brought her hands up and massaged both breasts, just as the man was now doing to his lover below. She heard a tiny groan and realized it was her own. Biting her lip to stifle the noise, she teased each nipple through the thin shift. She gritted her teeth and longed for more. More what, she didn't know. Just more. Warmth flooded her lower body, tugging low in her belly.

The couple in the garden moved faster now, each straining against the other, their groans and heavy breathing mixing until Eva couldn't discern between the man's, the woman's, and her own.

Eva's breath hissed between clenched teeth. She kneaded her breasts faster, plucking at her tingling nipples. She loved the pleasure-pain that the roughness brought. But she ached lower now, between her thighs where she could feel the dampness gathering.

The man's rhythm increased to a fevered pitch, sending the woman's high-pitched squeals pealing through the still night. Eva slid a hand down her body and pressed it against the part of herself that throbbed. Tingles of pleasure radiated from the center, but it still wasn't enough.

The man in the garden shuddered and clutched the woman to his chest, burying his face in her hair and with a final masculine groan, went still.

Eva's movements slowed, too, and all that filled the room was the sound of breath hissing through her teeth, the beat of her heart hard against her chest. She was drawn tighter than a bow, wanting something more, but not knowing what or how to achieve it.

Eva looked down at her rucked-up night shift, her hands intimately caressing her own body. She stepped back into the shadows, trembling. What was the matter with her? She'd never felt like this before. Never felt compelled to touch herself. Never got lost in a moment of pleasure.

Maybe it was something about Ivy Hill—knowing that people came here specifically for the purpose of engaging in erotic fantasies they couldn't indulge within the constraints of polite society.   They came here for sexual freedom of a kind that did not exist anywhere else.

Or maybe it was Lynnhaven, a small voice in the back of her mind whispered. Could she have been so easily affected by seeing a little skin? Of hearing him talk about the passion missing from her appropriation of the sex act? And if so, how was she to fill in the gaps and still remain a safe, neutral observer?

She frowned and slid back beneath the covers.

If she was as intelligent and as logical as she liked to think she was, she'd march next door right now and inform Lynnhaven that his services were not needed after all. She could carry on as she had before and her project would turn out just fine. That was the logical course of action.

But in a back corner of her sleep-heavy thoughts, Eva wondered what mating would be like with him. Would they dally in his bed? Or in the garden on the cold stone in the moonlight? Would she tremble in his arms and scream her delight as the woman she'd just watched had? Would he?

Eva rolled over and tried to block out the erotic images dancing thorough her imagination. She had to keep a level head. The project depended on it.

Eva could not fail. She would resist Lynnhaven's sensual pull and complete her project as planned.

No matter how much her body begged her to reconsider.

Chapter 3

Eva nearly jumped out of her skin when the light tap on her bedchamber door finally came. She'd been pacing the small room since supper, the tray she'd had sent to her room barely touched. She had alternately longed for and dreaded the time when Lynnhaven would present himself. But now the wait and the wondering were over.

"Miss Blakely? Are you in there?" he called softly though the door.

Eva gathered her writing supplies, straightened her spectacles and strode to the door. This was research, she reminded herself for at least the thousandth time. No matter what reactions the man engendered. She would not let anything or anyone undermine her project.

She opened the door and was almost relieved to find him fully dressed. His hair was freshly combed though it curled slightly at the nape of his neck. He was still dressed for dinner, his snowy white shirt contrasting sharply with the ebony of his waistcoat, trousers and jacket. His signature half-smirk and the twinkle of his sapphire eyes completed the image of the most dangerous man Eva had ever encountered.

"I was beginning to think you had changed your mind when you didn't come to supper," he said, straightening. "Or that you started without me."

"I was working," she said. It came out a little more defensive than she intended. She offered a weak smile.

"Well, let's get on with the work between us," He held out his hand as if they were in a formal ballroom. "Shall we?"

Eva ignored his hand and stepped through the adjoining door to his bedchamber.

She had been too distracted last night to take in much of her surroundings, but tonight the details of his luxurious room were impossible to ignore.

The most dominant feature of the room was the enormous bed. Carved likenesses of faeries and wood sprites peaked around the posts and over the headboard. The massive posts themselves were carved to look like enchanted forest. Intricately detailed leaves and vines wound around them and stretched across the wide plane of the headboard, too. It was sensual and decadent, just like him.

"I think the Kempes have a whimsical side," Lynnhaven said, leading her to a chair near the fireplace. "They tell me this is the fairy bower."

"It certainly is large."

"Yes," he said simply. "It is."

As the previous evening, candles covered every surface in the room, providing a fair amount of light for their activities.

"There's one thing I want to ask of you before we begin," Lynnhaven said, suddenly serious.

"Yes?"

"Call me by my given name. Aidan. Lynnhaven was my brother. I'd much rather you call out my name in your passion than his."

Eva shoved her spectacles high on her nose and glared at him. "Do I need to remind you of the bounds of our professional relationship?"

"I prefer to keep an open mind about that."

"Well, I don't."

Aidan—Lynnhaven—grinned, his left dimple mocking her attempts at stoicism. "Do you always argue with your research partners?"

Eva let out a breath of frustration. "Oh, let's just get started." Eve flipped through her journal to find the next blank page. "Now then, I first must get a detailed sexual history if you—-what are you doing?"

Aidan had shrugged out of his tight-fitting coat and removed his neckcloth. Eva's eyes widened as his long, slim fingers deftly worked the tiny buttons of his waistcoat.

"I'm undressing."

Another button popped free. Eva was mesmerized by the simple gesture, and by the increasingly wide V of skin framed by the snowy white of his loose shirt. Eva swallowed and struggled to drag her gaze back to his face.

"Why?" She was worldly. She was sophisticated. And she could handle the sight of a little male flesh. Or even a lot.

"I thought that getting to know your subject intimately would be a good foundation for future... research." Aidan dropped the waistcoat in the pile of clothing between them.

"I don't think that's necessary." Eva swallowed but continued to stare at his bared flesh, just an arm's length away. "I haven't seen many men in the flesh, so to speak, but I've studied anatomy books."

"Books show you nothing," he said, grasping the back of his shirt and jerking it over his head. "Books don't teach sensation, or texture or scent." He added his shirt in the growing pile of discarded clothing on the floor between them. "They don't teach the tingle of skin on skin contact. Books can't teach pleasure."

Even though she'd seen his chest, and a deal more, the previous evening, there was something very intimate about watching him undress. His eyes darkened, focusing on her face, gauging every reaction. The planes of his chest were fully exposed now and, the muscles of his abdomen formed a double row of hills stretching all the way to the top of his trousers.

Eva blinked before bringing her gaze back to his face. "I'm not here to learn about pleasure. That wasn't a condition of our arrangement."

"Consider it a bonus."

Eva didn't reply, mesmerized by his very nearness. It was dangerous getting sucked into his aura of desire this way. And they'd barely gotten started. But try as she might—and maybe she wasn't trying as hard as she ought to be—she was curious about what he was offering. The pleasure.

"Let me show you what I mean," he cocked an eyebrow. "Unless you're afraid? And you don't trust me?"

Eva shot him a glare that could peel the crimson striped wallpaper off his bedchamber walls and settled back into her chair. Trusting him was the last thing she should do. She re-opened her journal, determined to focus long enough to take notes.

Aidan sat to remove his boots then returned to stand before her. A little too close. "Did you know that a man's nipples are as sensitive as a woman's?" he asked conversationally.

"No," Eva squirmed in her chair, remembering the sensation of stroking herself last night. She scribbled something illegible in her journal.

Chuckling, Aidan gently took the book and set it aside. "You'll gather far more research without that," he said, urging her to her feet.

He had bathed before dinner, she thought. The pleasant tinge of soap was spicy-sweet. But she also detected a hint of the fragrant cigars the men had enjoyed after dinner and Aidan's own unique musky scent. She had the oddest urge to bury her face in the juncture between his shoulder and neck and just inhale him.

He took her open hand and placed it on his chest, and moved it lightly back and forth over his nipple. It hardened immediately.

"See? Just like a woman's."

Aidan dropped his hand, and Eva continued the exploration on her own. She glanced up to find passion already darkening his gaze. When she pinched lightly, Aidan chuckled and removed her hand. "If you keep that up, love, we'll never make it to lesson two," he said in a husky voice.

She lowered her hand, fighting to regain her composure. But she wanted to know more. "Proceed," she whispered. Pleasant tingles raced along her spine as the first spark of heat blossomed low in her abdomen.

He grinned and stepped away from her, and focused his gaze on her face. Her eyes met his briefly, then she watched as his long fingers worked the few buttons of his fall-front trousers. He slid them down and off his long legs and stood before Eva unashamed and completely nude.

He stood statue-still, his arms at his sides, pulse visible at the base of his throat, and let Eva look. She admired the breadth of his shoulders, the perfect proportions, the way his body narrowed at the torso and further to his hips.

And lower.

Her gaze finally settled on the nest of dark hair at the juncture of his thighs from which his organ thrust.

"You're not a virgin, are you?" he stroked himself once, slowly from base to tip.

"No. I'm not," she said firmly.

"Good."

During her one and only sexual experience, Eva hadn't had the opportunity to see her lover's most intimate of appendages. It had all happened in the dark and was over before she could even think about doing any exploring.

But now she had the opportunity to look.

And worry a little.

He was stunning, Eva acknowledged. Like a Greek god come to life. A strong, sensual man at the peak of his sexuality. And he clearly seemed to like it that Eva stared at him.

"What observations would you record in you journal, right now, Eva?" he asked with a low huskiness to his voice. "How would you describe this moment?"

Eva cleared her throat and brought her gaze back to his face. "I would write that you are a... fine male specimen."

Aidan chuckled deep in his throat. "That's all?" He shook his head. Maybe you should come closer. Touch me. Then tell me what you think. What you feel."

Eva didn't need to be prodded. She longed to touch him. But at the same time, she feared she was opening a Pandora's Box. What if she lost herself here with him? Let passion override her logic? Could she afford to take the risk? Could she afford not to?

She tentatively touched his chest with just one finger. His skin was warm and firm and surprisingly soft. She traced his collar bone to the pulse point in his throat, then up over his Adam's apple.

"What do you feel?" he whispered. His breath stirred her hair and his voice reverberated under her touch.

Eva shivered and focused on the sensation. She dragged her fingers up his throat to his jaw. "Your skin is rougher here," she said. "I can't see your beard, but I can feel it just beneath your skin." She stroked gently back and forth, enjoying the tickly friction.

She felt his jaw flex, but he said nothing and Eva couldn't bring herself to look him in the eye. She was afraid she'd break the spell and become too rattled to continue. And she definitely wanted to continue.

She traced the tendon the stretched from his collar bone to just behind his ear. "The cords in your neck are more prominent than a woman's."

She reached up further to thread her fingers though the ebony hair at the nape of his neck. "And your hair is soft and cool compared to the heat of your skin," she observed. "I like how it curls just a bit around my fingers when they slide though it."

Eva cocked her head and played with his curls a moment longer before trailing her hand back down the side of his throat, over his shoulder and down to the flat expanse of his chest once again. She brought her other hand up and lightly brushed his nipples.

"What else?"

"I like the way the hard nubs tickle my palm."

"I, too." It was barely a whisper, but his words were imbued with an abundance of sensuality that made the ball of heat in her belly expand outwards, flooding her senses in a deep, pleasant warmth.

Eva sifted her fingers through the crisp dark hair dusting his chest. "This has a different texture than your beard or the hair on your head," she observed.

The patch of hair narrowed to a line that bisected his abdomen. Eva traced it with her index finger, dropping her other hand to rest lightly on his hip.

Aidan stiffened but remained otherwise still.

Eva slid her hand over his flat belly. She traced the perimeter of his navel. "Here's one part that's almost the same as mine."

"I reserve the right to confirm that claim later on," he said through clenched teeth.

Eva knew she should remind him once again of the professional nature of their partnership, but it didn't seem particularly important at the moment. Instead she glanced lower. She drew in her breath, not quite ready to explore him that intimately.

Yet.

Instead she kept her hand at his waist and circled behind him, dragging her fingers lightly across his ribs.

She reached up to the nape of his neck, and drew her fingers through his soft black hair once again before slowly tracing his spine. Down, down, down, all the way to the top of his buttocks.

"Even your back is muscular." She used both hands to cover the blades of his shoulders. The low flickering light of the fire and shadow made the tone of his skin seem even deeper and for a moment she was mesmerized by the site of her small pale hands on his body.

She paused, then raised her hands again to trace the silhouette of his broad shoulders then skimmed her hands along his sides, over his ribs to rest on his hips. "You're much less curvy than a woman," she said. "Your waist narrows rather than flares, more an inverted triangle than an hourglass. And you're hard everywhere I'm soft."

He let out a short, strained chuckle. "Yes."

"Your backside is round, but more compact than a woman's," she observed. Eva swallowed. "May I.."

"Yes," he repeated through clenched teeth. And the body part in question flexed slightly.

She ran both palms down the plumpest part of his buttocks. She cupped each side lightly, squeezing, then ran both thumbs down the crevice separating the halves. Aidan groaned softly, the first involuntary sound he'd made during her exploration.

Eva drew her hands away and circled to the front. Though he was perfectly motionless, he reminded her of a tightly coiled spring about to explode. His mouth was drawn, the muscles in his face tight. His eyes were darker than usual, the color of the ocean rather than a spring sky and liquid with a glint that made Eva's stomach flutter and sent tingles of awareness racing across her skin.

"Am I hurting you?" she asked softly.

He flashed a strained grin. "No. Not in the way you think."

"May I touch you—" Eva nodded in the direction of his member, unable to finish the rest of her sentence.

"Please," he said in a near groan. Eva wasn't sure if he was begging her to touch him or begging her not to, but since he remained still, she sank to her knees before him.

She touched his thighs. The flesh there, too, was hot to the touch. "Your legs are longer than mine. Your thighs are more muscular." She traced the hollows of muscle. "Your hair tickles," she said, running her palm over the dusting of wiry hair. She slid her hands lower over the mounds of his calves.

"You're muscular here, too. You're muscular everywhere. Not quite the man of leisure you seem to be."

"I ride," he said. "And box. But I never let it interfere with my philandering."

Eva knelt before him. She was face to face with the most fascinating part of his anatomy.

"Go ahead," he ground out, eyes still closed.

Tentatively, Eva ran one finger very lightly up the underside of his cock. It jumped.

She looked up, but Aidan had his eyes squeezed shut, his hands fisted at his sides.

Eva turned her attention back to his cock. She grasped him lightly in her palm. "You're so hot, she observed in a whisper. "And hard. But soft, too. Silky."

Aidan sucked in his breath. His thighs bulged, contracted, as did the muscles of his abdomen.

She released him. "Are you sure I'm not hurting you?" she asked, brows furrowed. She had read that men were quite sensitive there.

"No," Aidan whispered. "You're not hurting me."

She glanced up. He still squeezed his eyes closed, and he was breathing heavily through his mouth. Every muscle in his body was contracted and beads of sweat punctuated his forehead. The veins in his cock shone blue through the nearly transparent skin there.

The lurid image of the couple in the garden sprang to mind and Eva imagined what it would be like if she were to give in to his carnal invitation. Heat exploded low in her belly and her heart pumped a little harder.

Eva traced the cap of his cock again, smoothing his own juices gently over the tip. She had seen pictures of women loving a man with her mouth. It had never seemed especially appealing, until now. "What does it taste like?" she asked in a whisper. "This fluid."

"Sweet Jesus!" Aidan grunted and his hand shot out, arresting Eva's grip on his cock. He was flushed, sweat darkening his hair around his face. His eyes were open now, his pupils deep and black, though his lids were half-closed. He panted slightly.

Eva was mortified. "I'm sorry." She struggled to her feet. Clearly she'd done something wrong. Gotten carried away. Maybe she should call off the whole thing before she embarrassed herself further. "I thought… that was completely unprofessional."

Aidan grasped her wrist and tugged her closer to him. She looked up into his face. "It felt wonderful," he said grunted. "You feel wonderful."

Eva had never seen him anything less than completely composed, totally in control of himself and usually of those around him. Now, to see him this way, so raw, so elemental, more wild animal than man, was intoxicating. She had done this to him. The unsettling feeling he'd aroused in her was reciprocated.

She smiled, enjoying his discomfort. "I like touching you."

"I don't want you to stop," he said, taking a step towards her. "And we don't have to."

Eva wanted nothing more than to slide into his dark gaze and give in to the overwhelming sensations he elicited.

But this was supposed to be about her project. Continuing now would ruin her methodical, scientific approach. She gathered her long-forgotten journal and backed towards the door, unable to resist looking at him a moment longer.

"We can't," she managed to get out. "The project…"

"The project. Yes, of course," he said tightly.

Aidan remained in the center of the room, tense. Coiled. As if he might pounce on her and do all the things she ached for.

She had to leave. Now.

"Eva," he said huskily. The tone with which he spoke her name hung in the erotically charged air between them.

"Yes?"

"Same time tomorrow night?"

She should say no. And run away as if her hair had caught fire.

"Yes. Tomorrow would be perfect."

Chapter 4

The damn woman was going to kill him, Aidan thought, as he watched her pale blue skirts disappear from sight. Love wasn't a word he often associated with women, but he sure as hell loved what Eva did to his body.

The minute the door latched, he stroked himself like he was a boy again. Fast and hard, up and down his shaft until he finally exploded with a burst of pent up energy he didn't know was possible in a man well past the prime of puberty.

Then he did it again.

Eva.

Her touch. Her words as she described his body. What she saw, what she felt.

It had been, without a doubt, the most erotic moment of his life, including the time the Wallingford twins had kept him tied to his bed for three days. This was far better.

Suddenly exhausted, Aidan lay on the bed, looking up at the crimson bed draperies. For the first time ever, he doubted the command he had over his body when it came to desire.

How could he have guessed his reaction to Eva? Her touch had been a sensual torture to him. Excruciating and divine all at once. He could still feel her small, cool hands around his cock, stroking him, teasing him until he wanted to tackle her to the floor and drive into her like an animal.

His cock was stirring again just thinking about it, damn it.

Aidan took pride in the fact that he was known as a man of restraint, a skillful lover, who had iron control over his body and that of his partner's. But with Eva, he wouldn't have lasted more than five seconds, if he'd made into her tight little body at all.

Aidan looked down at his cock, standing straight up once again.

Jesus. He had gotten into more than he bargained for when he'd agreed to be her research partner. The only thing he'd accomplished was the certainty that she had loved touching his body just as much as he loved her hands on him. He'd felt it in the slight tremble of her hands, the catch in her voice as she described what she felt.

She wanted him.

But not nearly as much as he wanted her. Not yet.

He couldn't wait to discover the passion Eva so cleverly hid behind the spectacles and books and research notes. The real Eva. She wouldn't be like the other women, desiring his company only for his title or his wealth or looks. No, she was the only truly honest woman he had met since his older brother had died and made him a lord.

Eva was perfectly clear about what she wanted from him.

And what she didn't.

Not yet, at least.

He threw his forearm over his eyes and tried to clear his mind of all images of Eva. It was all he could do not to jump out of bed and walk—-no, run—-to the mere slab of oak that separated his room from Eva's.

But he couldn't rush her. She was strong-willed and would end their association altogether if he pushed too hard. He'd just have to work harder to make her lose that damned composure of hers. And quickly, before he lost his own mind.

He honestly didn't know how he could be in the same room with her again without giving in to his baser instincts, let alone conduct part two of an experiment that would not end in her being naked between his sheets.

Aidan nearly jumped out of bed when he heard the light knock at his door. She'd come back.

He was across the room with his hand on the knob before it registered that the knock came from the door to the hallway, not the adjoining door.

It wasn't Eva.

"I see you're ready for me," the willowy raven-haired woman purred. She slid past him into his room.

Aidan closed the door, frowning.

"Lilah." He ran a hand through his damp hair.

She sidled up to him, and ran her cold hands over his chest. "Ah, you're already primed," she said. "I do so like it when you have another woman before me." Lilah grinned, her slanted turquoise eyes bright in the paleness of her oval face.

She was beautiful, by any man's standards. Thick waves of ebony hair, high cheekbones, full red lips, slim, but curvy in all the right places. As a lover, she was as inventive and insatiable as any man. She'd even taught him a few things.

But now all he could think of was the woman next door, alone in her room, with any luck as hot and bothered as he.

Aidan felt a tug at his nipple and realized Lilah was kissing his chest. She licked a line down the center then went to her knees. She gripped his cock with practiced hands and stroked him expertly. "You're still tense. I can fix that." She looked up at him and licked her lips.

Most men in his position would wrap their fists in Lilah's loose, thick hair and let her sweet mouth take them to heaven. Hell, he would have been that man an hour ago. Her ministration was just what he needed.

But not what he wanted. Not after getting a glimpse at what bedding Eva would be like.

He disengaged her hand and backed away.

Lilah frowned up at him. "What's the matter?"

"Nothing," he said, swiping a hand though his hair. "I'm just, um, tired." He shrugged into his dressing gown that had been laid out on his bed and tied it securely.

"Tired," she said disbelieving. Lilah rose gracefully to her feet. She smoothed her gown and patted her hair, all the while her keen eyes evaluating him. "I've never known you to be... tired." She smiled seductively and sidled up closer to him. "That must have been some first round." She brushed his nipples. "Want to tell me all about it?"

"You know I'd love to," he lied, grasping her wrists lightly and removing them from his body. "But not tonight." He kissed the knuckles of each hand and tried to grin at her.

Suddenly an idea popped into his head. The perfect solution to his little control problem with Eva.

"Tomorrow night," he kissed her left palm. "In the maze," he kissed her right palm. "Ten o'clock."

Lilah's pouting frown turned into the seductive smile that had brought many men to their knees. Literally. "That's better."

She reached up on her tiptoes and kissed Aidan hard, open-mouthed, her tongue slithering into the recesses of his mouth. He kissed her back, but it didn't bring the usual thrill. He just wanted her to leave, so he could lie on his bed and think about the woman he couldn't have.

Lilah broke the kiss and sauntered to the door. She glanced over her shoulder and smiled. "Don't be late." She didn't bother to close the door behind her.

It was a brilliant plan. He would master this uncontrollable lust with Lilah, then go to Eva more calm and in control than he had been tonight.

Then he'd slowly drive her out of her mind with desire.

It was foolproof. Absolutely, positively 99.3% foolproof.

Chapter 5

In the daylight, Ivy Hill was as dull as any other country house party. The ladies slept in, rising sometime after noon to chat, have tea and perhaps stroll the gardens on a mild day. The men rose early, and spent most of the day outdoors attempting to hunt down and shoot whatever type of small mammal or bird presented itself. It was only at night that the difference in this house party became obvious.

In the darkness, couples roamed the manor in various states of disarray, without any attempt at subtlety as to their activities. Typical parlor games became a whole new type of entertainment when the guests played in the nude. And though she hadn't seen it herself, Eva had heard whispers about special rooms within the manor that were tailored to fit any carnal fantasy a guest might harbor. There truly seemed to be no desire too peculiar here.

But the grounds seemed innocent enough when Eva ventured out after breakfast. She found Lady Kempe seated on a garden bench amongst the roses, still lush and fragrant in the early fall. Glad for a friendly, clothed person to talk to, Eva approached.

Lady Kempe had attended many of the same lectures and scientific talks as Eva. She was a supporter of Eva's project and in fact had suggested Ivy Hill might be just the place to conduct her research.

"Eva. I was just wondering if you had arrived. I haven't seen you at supper all week."

"I've been working," Eva said. "I had a tray sent up."

"Ah, I see," Lady Kempe nodded, a slight smile playing at her lips. "I was just thinking going for a stroll in the sculpture gardens. Won't you join me?" Lady Kempe rose and shook out her skirts.

"Of course." It was nice to be out of doors and in friendly company. Eva hoped it would take her mind off Aidan. As if she could forget with the constant barrage of erotic images skipping though her brain and the warm scent of Aidan's skin seeming to linger on her hands. Still, Eva tried to focus on the day and on her companion.

Lady Kempe was not the sort of woman Eva imagined to host the types of activities that went on at Ivy Hill. A seemingly respectable widow, she was still very beautiful, through old enough to have grown children. Her honey-colored hair was still thick, her figure trim and always displayed in the height of fashion. Her skin was as smooth and unlined as it was when she had been a debutante herself. But there was a subtle sadness in her blue eyes that never went away, no matter how brightly she smiled.

"Have you found Ivy Hill to be a fruitful source of research?"

"Yes. I've been able to gather quite a bit of data that would have been impossible to come by any other way." Eva stroked the crimson petal of one of the lush roses. "Lord Lynnhaven has agreed to assist." She said it casually and without blushing. Almost.

Lady Kempe smiled. "I'm not surprised. He's had his eye on you all season."

"He's had his eye on everything in skirts all season," Eva said, dropping the petal. "Though I think he was a bit surprised at my proposition."

"I imagine he was. Coming from you." Lady Kempe led the way through the arch that signaled the entrance to the sculpture garden. Their heels crunched the gravel of the path that snaked its way thorough the immaculately groomed gardens.

Eva inhaled the fresh clean scent of the country morning.

The day was quiet with only the occasional twitter of birds and the light buzz of insects, as attracted to the roses as the women were.

"It's a pity that such a beautiful setting should only be shown once a year," Eva observed.

Lady Kempe smiled. "Yes. It is very beautiful here and the guests never have any complaints, but I find I enjoy my privacy. I come here whenever I can."

Eva didn't look at Lady Kempe as she asked, "Does Lord Lynnhaven come every year to the party?"

"Well, let me see. I believe it was right after he came into his fortune that he first accepted my invitation. The year his older brother died. Four years, now, I think." Lady Kempe strolled to the first sculpture, hands clasped behind her back. "He's very popular here. Hearts would be broken if he skipped a year, I think. Or if he married."

No surprise there. He was clearly the ladies' choice in ballrooms as well as boudoirs. Women flocked to him like flies to horse dung. And Eva couldn't really blame them for it. He was handsome and even charming when he so chose.

Lady Kempe bent to pluck dead leaves from the base of the sculpture, then stood admiring the piece. The statue was a life-sized replica of a young man stretched out on his side. He leaned on one elbow and was so life-like, Eva swore she could smell the warmth of his skin. He was also completely nude. He had a curious grin on his face, Eva thought, cocking her head. Content but also a little nervous, too.

"It's very... life like," Eva observed.

"Yes," Lady Kempe said, smiling. "But let me show you my favorite. Ah, here we are," she said, stopping before a particularly large statue. "I believe this one is called *The Tempest*."

The artist had captured the subject in the act of tearing the shirt from his body. He had a wild look in his eye. Primal. Untamed. Pure masculinity. The man exuded an overwhelming sensuality, just barely leashed, though he was merely stone. It made Eva a little uneasy, like watching a caged lion pace back and forth just beyond his tenuous barrier.

"I confess I've spent hours gazing at this piece," Lady Kempe said. "But every time I see it, I'm seduced by it all over again."

"I—I understand," Eva said. And strangely, she did. She understood this statue in a way she might not have just a day ago. "He looks very... wild," Eva said.

"He was," Lady Kempe said, a small smile playing across her lips. "But wildness the best part. Losing yourself in the moment. Diving right in without fear, without regret, without thought of what tomorrow might bring."

Eva frowned. She'd never understood how a person would want to get so swept up in an emotion that reason would fall by the wayside. Intercourse was, after all, a biological function, not an emotional one. She eyed the statue again.

Lady Kempe was watching her. "Haven't you ever wanted to do something that made absolutely no sense whatsoever? Take a walk in a rainstorm? Take off your slippers and feel the cool grass between your toes?"

Succumb to Aidan's undeniable sexual magnetism, Eva thought. And ruin whatever objective research she hoped to glean from him? Hadn't she learned her lesson once, long ago when she'd been much younger and much more naïve?

"No," Eva said quickly, looking away.

As if Lady Kempe could read minds, she turned back to Eva and smiled brightly. "I think Lynnhaven is the perfect choice for your project." She settled on a stone bench facing the statue. "You won't be disappointed."

Disappointment wasn't what Eva was worried about. It was the sense that she since she set the acts in motion, she was no longer the one in control. Already her thoughts had strayed far from pure research. And that was the one thing she couldn't afford if she wanted to achieve her dream of academic recognition. Still, she couldn't help but be curious about her newest research subject.

"I'm surprised Lynnhaven isn't already wed," Eva said as casually as she could manage. "He must be in his mid-30s by now."

"He was betrothed once."

Eva turned to stare at her. "What happened?"

Lady Kempe shrugged. "It was the classic dilemma. He fell hard in love with a beautiful debutante and became utterly devoted to her. But she wanted a title, not a younger son. She married his brother the following spring."

"Oh."

"Since then, there has been no one to catch Lord Lynnhaven's particular interest. Until you."

Eva felt the blush creep up her neck, "If he is interested in me, it's only because I'm the only woman who doesn't prostrate herself at his feet. He only wants what he can't have."

"Perhaps." Lady Kempe looked past Eva and nodded towards the house.

Eva turned to see Aidan's long, easy strides carrying him down the slight hill towards them. He smiled brightly and gave her a half-wave. Her pulse quickened a beat.

Lady Kempe smiled at Eva. "And perhaps not."

Chapter 6

"I was hoping to catch you this morning," Aidan said after Lady Kempe had wandered further into the sculpture garden, leaving him alone with Eva.

Eva looked up at him and blinked. "Why?"

"You said you wanted to take my sexual history. We didn't quite get to that last night."

"Oh. Of course." She seemed just slightly disappointed.

Good. Maybe she had spared him a thought or two after their 'lesson'. Lord knew he had tossed and turned all night tormented by a single desire—to see Eva. He certainly didn't trust himself to touch her. He knew he'd end up pushing her too hard and then she'd find herself another research subject and go back to looking down her nose at him as if he was a lecherous poltroon.

But now he could talk to her. Tease her until she smiled. He didn't remember ever having such fun with a woman, not a woman fully clothed, anyway.

He'd spent the night wondering how he was going to get through a full day until he saw her again. Around dawn, he realized that her research provided the perfect excuse to seek her out before that evening's lesson. He shouldn't, but he couldn't resist.

"There is a particularly nice bench in the labyrinth. I thought that would be the perfect place for you to carry out your inquisition. We shouldn't be disturbed at this time of day."

Eva wasn't having it. "I don't care for labyrinths."

He cocked his head, undaunted. "Why not?"

Eva straightened her spectacles. "With each intersection, one only has a 50% chance of choosing the correct path. Multiply that by a dozen intersections and one could wander around for hours without ever finding the center of the maze or her way out again. I don't care to be lost without a solution."

Aidan took her arm and gently tucked it in the crook of his elbow. "It's fun to get lost once in a while. And I'll promise to hold your hand, should you become frightened."

"That's the problem." She stopped, forcing him to stop walking as well.

"All right. No maze today. How about the lake, then? There's a bench there as well. Acceptable but not nearly as fine a bench as the one in the labyrinth."

A hint of a smile played across her lips and they started walking again. "I didn't realize there was a lake on the property."

"There are two. One on each side of the house. Well, they're more like ponds, actually. But the east lake does have ducks."

"They're probably cowering in fear as much as the gentlemen guests seem to relish the hunt." She looked over at him. "Why aren't you with them?"

"I'm not much of a hunter, I'm afraid. And you? What do you do when you're not… experimenting?"

She replied haughtily. "Lately I've been putting most of my time and energy into my project."

He had a sharp desire to know how she really spent her time—what she liked. What she did. What she thought about. "What else do you do?"

"I also read and attend lectures now and then."

"And attend balls," he said, looking over at her.

"Only when I can't think of a good excuse to decline."

"Most young ladies your age can't get enough of the social life," Aidan said, smiling down at her. "What do you find so offensive?"

"Not offensive so much as dreadfully boring. I'd rather curl up with a good research volume than stuff myself into a gown and parade around looking like I'm trying to attract the attention of a potential husband."

"You're not looking for a husband?"

"No."

"Never?" He couldn't imagine Eva spending her life alone, forever concealing her passion and fire behind a stack of dusty tomes.

"Perhaps I thought about it when I was younger," she said softly, biting her lip. "I thought I might like to marry. But now I find that I prefer my independence." They reached the edge of the lake and Eva tugged her hand from Aidan's arm.

"What do you mean?"

"I go out when I want to go out and stay in when I want to stay in. I manage my own funds, read whatever I choose, associate with whomever suits me. In short, I am my own person, not a shadow of my husband."

He doubted Eva could ever be a shadow of anyone. "I don't blame your wanting to remain unattached if you carry that bleak outlook on marriage."

"I don't see you running full tilt for the altar, either."

Aidan gestured towards the bench at the edge of the lake, and put a hand at her back, guiding her. "Hmm, good point. My only defense is that I just haven't found the right woman yet."

"I think the problem is that you've found too many."

"That, too."

Eva settled on the bench and Aidan sat next to her, careful to leave a small, respectable space between them. He was man of control. Usually, anyway. But there was no use testing his limits more than necessary.

She opened her journal and licked a finger before turning each worn page. "Ah, here we are." She frowned at the page a second before looking up at him again. "These questions should give me some background on you as a subject." She paused and flushed just lightly. "Some of the questions are of a very personal nature."

"Yes, I expect so."

"Let's begin, then."

Despite her best efforts to keep her mind firmly in the realm of science, Eva really didn't know if she would be able to get through all 147 carefully crafted questions about Aidan's sexual history. Just looking at him made the blood rush to her face. Grilling him about the minute details of his sexual past was likely to cause some kind of spontaneous combustion.

But she had a book to write and Aidan had agreed to be her research subject. She would plow through it as the logical scientist she was, instead of some lust-stuck girl.

"Your age?"

"32."

"Do you have any diseases or infirmities?"

"No. I definitely do not suffer any infirmities."

Eva detected a note of amusement in his voice, but scribbled down his answer and pressed on.

"Age at first sexual encounter?"

"What exactly do you consider a sexual encounter?"

Eva looked up at him. "Isn't that obvious?"

"No. Do you mean the first time I kissed a girl? Or when I first held a breast in my hand? Or maybe the first time I—"

"Kiss," she said quickly. "At what age did you first kiss a girl?"

"Ten."

"Ten?"

"Well, I was no Cassanova, but Becky Bolton didn't seem to mind."

Eva shook her head. "Proceeding on. When did you first have intercourse?"

"Fifteen."

Eva's head snapped up. "That is quite... young."

His easy grin was gone. "Is it?"

"Betsy again?"

"My stepmother." Aidan looked out over the lake, more serious than she'd ever seen him. "Anne married my father for his title and was faithful to him all of about two weeks."

Eva shook her head. "But you were just a child. Her stepson."

He focused on Eva once again. "Yes."

She had the sudden urge to reach out to him. To touch his hand. To soothe the man who had learned at such a young age to distrust.

He shrugged. "Of course, my father was no more faithful to her."

As quickly as it had come the shadow over his features lifted and the mischievous glint in his eye returned. "What about you? Who was this mysterious lover of yours who left you in need of research subjects to learn about passion?"

Stiffly, Eva said, "I'm not the subject of this study."

"You could be."

"It wouldn't be proper."

Aidan laughed. "I think we left propriety in the dust the moment you pressed your ear against my door. Don't you?" His gaze never left her face. "Tell me about this despoiler of yours."

Eva recognized the stubborn tone in his voice. He wasn't going to leave it alone until she fully humiliated herself.

She let out a breath and rolled her eyes. "He was a young assistant to my father. A fellow academic. Father gave him a room in our house."

"He was so overcome by your beauty he couldn't resist?"

"Hardly."

"Well, then, how did it happen?"

Eva adjusted her spectacles. "If you must know, he wanted to marry me."

"You turned him down?"

She shook her head. "No, I accepted." Eva closed her journal and swallowed. "But a few weeks later, my best friend got married. She told me all about the pain and the humiliation involved in the wedding night ritual. I wanted to see for myself what I was getting myself into by agreeing to be his wife. So one night, when the house was asleep, I went to his room."

"I wager he wasn't expecting that."

"No. But when I explained to him my purpose, he was good enough to acquiesce."

"Damn charitable of him." Aidan looked at her. "You hated it then. The way he made love to you."

She shrugged. "It all happened so quickly and was over so fast, I really didn't have time to judge whether it was awful or not. Painful, yes. But there were good parts."

"All of the parts can be good ones with the right man."

Eva looked away. "Yes, well, he evidently was not the right man. The next morning he said that he didn't believe I had been an innocent. That no virgin would come to a man in his rooms as I had, only a woman of questionable moral character."

"What a self-righteous prig."

"He did allow me to break the engagement and save us both a lot of humiliation."

"And that's when you decided not to marry at all."

"I suppose so, yes. I don't want to give a man the power to judge me that way. And—" she took a deep breath. "And it wasn't as if his lovemaking was so compelling, I had to seek a repetition."

Aidan smiled slowly. "Well, here you can learn what can happen between two lovers when the man has more sense than God gave a goat."

"I came to Ivy Hill to gather research. I'm not here for... carnal indulgence."

"That's the most insipid word for fornicating I've ever heard," Aidan stopped walking and faced her. "And I don't believe it for a minute. I think you are indeed here for the... indulgence."

"I said—I didn't come here to indulge myself."

Aidan stepped closer. "I think you came here to satisfy a hunger for more than just knowledge."

"You're wrong." Despite her annoyance as his presumption, her pulse quickened, and it suddenly became difficult to focus on anything other than Aidan. He took up her entire field of vision and her entire train of thought.

"Am I? You certainly enjoyed touching my body last night. Did you think about me after you went back to bed all alone?"

"Of course not," she lied. "Touching you was purely research."

He shook his head slowly, a dangerous glint in his eye belying the hint of a grin. "I'm afraid a logical, intelligent woman such as yourself will settle for nothing less than hard evidence."

Before Eva could comprehend his meaning, he pressed her body to his from breast to toe. She saw his mouth descending just as her eyes fluttered shut.

The jolt of pure desire when his mouth met hers came swift and hard. She'd been kissed before, but never like this. It wasn't so much a kiss as an invasion, and though she would rather be tortured than admit it to Aidan, it was a welcome one—one she had thought about and craved as she had run her hands over his hard glistening body only a few hours earlier.

"Eva," he breathed, breaking the kiss. "You are the most sensual woman I've ever known. You've just spent much too much time denying it."

And for a moment she forgot who she was, who he was, and the project and all the other reasons she shouldn't indulge in this.

She raised her head, opened her lips slightly, and he deepened the kiss, caressing every corner of her mouth. His fingers threaded through her thick, upswept hair, holding her tight as if she would bolt at the first opportunity.

Sensation clouded any sort of logical thinking. She was operating on pure sensation now. Eva wound her arms around his neck and allowed the silk strands of his hair to slide between her fingers just as she had the previous evening.

He groaned. "I love it when you do that," he whispered. "Actually I love everything you do." He took her mouth again briefly, then coaxed her wrists from behind his neck.

He covered her hands with his larger, warmer ones and slid them down the hard planes of his chest. "I love it when you touch me here," he whispered.

Even through his clothes, Eva could feel his muscles twitch and the steady thud of his pulse.

"And here," he whispered as he guided her hands down his torso, over the hard ridges of his abdomen. Eva's breath caught as warmth blossomed deep in the pit of her stomach. She met his dark gaze with her own.

"Here." He slid their palms further downward to his muscular thighs.

"And here," he breathed. He took her mouth more gently this time as he led her hands to the placket of his trousers, where he was already hard and straining against the buttons.

She moaned softly into his mouth. When his hands came back up to cradle her face, hers stayed right where he'd put them, tracing the length of him, absorbing his heat, exploring gently through his clothing.

Eva leaned into him and wished that she could see more of him, that she could touch him as she had the previous night and be touched by him in return.

Kisses came faster now. He nipped at her bottom lip before soothing it with a softer caress, then diving inside for another taste. If he kissed every woman like this, it was no wonder they fell so easily into his bed. If this was the drug he was peddling, it was amazing there was no line outside his door.

Eva didn't realize her breasts were so sensitive until Aidan cupped one, then teased the hardened nipple through the thin fabric of her walking dress. She groaned again at the sensation the zipped through her body to the pulse between her thighs.

She had visions of the maze and the couple she'd seen there. She stroked his cock harder, wondering if she dared open the placket so she could take him in her hand.

Aidan groaned deep in his throat. He broke the kiss and looked at her with a passionate intent that turned her knees to jelly. He was out of breath, too, and a tendril of his midnight hair had fallen across his brow.

"I want you, Eva. More than I can say. Say you want me, too. Say yes," he leaned in for another lingering kiss. "Please." He searched her eyes for the answer he sought.

Eva blinked once. Twice. Her mind was fuzzy.

"You won't be sorry. I swear it."

Her gaze slid away.

She would be sorry. She'd be sorry the instant she said yes. Well, maybe not at that precise instant. But once it was over, she couldn't go back. Then she'd be sorry.

The logical part of her mind reengaged. She wanted him, she acknowledged. And she wanted to finish her research project and write a book that would establish her career as an academic. And getting involved with a research subject, losing the scientific objectivity, would wreck all of that. She couldn't say yes to Aidan and have the life she'd always wanted. The life she'd worked so hard to build. She had to choose.

Eva swallowed and slowly removed her hands from his body. She stepped back, putting space between them. His hands fell away, too, and he sighed deeply, her actions louder that any words could ever be.

Eva straightened her spectacles and cleared her throat. "The project—"

He shoved a hand through his damp hair, disheveling it further. "Yes, I know. The Project trumps all."

There was a hard edge to his voice she'd never heard before. "If you don't want to participate any longer—"

"I do," he said straightening his clothing. "Believe me, I do."

"Then we'll just look as this little… interlude as what it was," she said adjusting her spectacles. "A mistake."

He turned his head to look at her, arching one black brow.

"Two healthy, unattached adults succumbing to… a moment," she explained.

"It was more than a moment."

Eva glared at him. "A moment that got out of hand. But it won't happen again," she said to reassure herself. "So there's no reason we can't continue on in a professional capacity. Correct?"

"No reason at all."

"Then I'll see you tonight as planned?"

"Yes." He looked out over the lake, his answer curt.

She started up the hill. "Are you coming back to the house?"

"In a bit," he said, still looking out over the lake. He had a fierce expression on his face. Not quite angry. Disappointed, she supposed. Disgruntled. Out of sorts. Wishing things were different.

Eva looked back at him once more, sitting alone on the bench.

She knew exactly how he felt.

Chapter 7

As he walked to the maze that night, Aidan reflected on the "moment" by the lake. It proved to Aidan that his plan to meet Lilah before continuing the next lesson with Eva was not only brilliant, but necessary. He'd been hard as a post all afternoon and had ended up going for a swim with the ducks just to gain a measure of cold comfort, however brief.

It had been a long time since he'd been this worked up over one woman. And that little previous "moment" had ended ... not well. But he was older now, and wiser. Or at least older.

Now he was experienced enough to know what to do with unwanted feelings—divert them.

Eva did that too—in a different way, he realized suddenly. But it was her passion that she was trying to divert after being burned the one time she dared let it out. But he was just the man to show her that feeling and fulfilling passion was entertaining—as long as it was with him.

Still he must be cautious. She was so skittish she might bolt if he didn't proceed carefully. He knew that, yet his body wasn't getting the message. He prayed that his interlude with Lilah would give him the necessary control to seduce Eva by inches. He knew it was the only way she could be coaxed from her shell.

The moon high overhead cast just enough light to see the trail to the maze. This was one of his favorite aspects of Ivy Hill, Aidan thought as his boots crunched the white pebbled path. There was the faintest hint of a nip in the fall air, but it was still warm for September. The hedges were tall, towering several feet over his head and cast deep shadows in narrow corridors.

Eva was right—one could easily become lost in the twists and turns, the shadows and alcoves the maze offered. But Aidan knew exactly where Lilah would be waiting for him, willing and ready. She was just what he needed to take the edge off of his irrational desire for Eva so that he could keep his head and continue the slow, seductive game they were playing with one another. And that was a game he intended to win by coaxing her to his bed where he'd give her firsthand knowledge of his "mating habits".

The sounds of other guests enjoying the maze carried easily on the clear night. He heard giggles, the occasional squeal as games of erotic hide-and-seek were played out among the fragrant yew. Aidan quickened his step and entered the maze. A few more twists and turns, a quick shuffling of clothing, and he would be inside Lilah's luscious body. Sated at last.

Aidan frowned. For some reason, the prospect of being with Lilah didn't have its usual appeal. He couldn't help but wonder what Eva was doing right then. Was she preparing, too? Making notes? Pacing her room, waiting for him? Plotting how she was going to steal a little more of his sanity, all in the name of science?

Was she even now sitting in her room alone thinking about his hands on her body—or had she recovered her academic detachment, and writing some damn scientific account of an encounter that had left him spinning?

She was unlike any woman he had ever known. Beautiful, whether she acknowledged it or not. Intelligent, without a doubt. She didn't hesitate to speak her mind. Direct. He smiled to himself. He never knew what would come out of her mouth next.

He just knew it would never be some insipid social nicety she didn't really mean.

He glanced back at the house, and a light in a window upstairs caught his eye. All the guests were out making the most of the warm evening. There was only one person holed up in her room.

Waiting. For him.

Aidan paused on the trail, just before making the final turn into the clearing where he knew Lilah waited for him. She was probably already nude. He could still remember the look of pure, unapologetic need on her face when she had caressed him intimately. The darkness of her eyes, the soft flush in her cheeks. The way she looked up at him with hot smoky passion simmering just beneath the surface. The way Eva should—

Suddenly Aidan was striding back the way he'd come, away from Lilah, out of the maze. He ran shaking hands though his hair. He couldn't wait another minute. To see if he could bring the same response to Eva's body, possess her senses as she had his.

He slipped back inside the mansion and took the stairs two at a time. He had his hand on her doorknob before rational thought returned.

Aidan drew a deep breath. This was no good. He ached for her and had for days despite his best efforts. He couldn't very well rush into Eva's bedroom in this state. If he went in now, he'd push her too far. She'd push back. Then she'd take it in her head to find a new research subject and he'd never have her. He wondered just how lenient visiting hours were at Bedlam.

Aidan snatched his hand from the doorknob as if it was on fire. He would march right back down the stairs, fuck Lilah until he was as limp as a noodle and then, and only then, would he consider allowing himself to be alone with Eva again.

Eva's door opened a crack.

Bloody hell.

"Aidan? Is that you? I didn't expect you so early."

He wasn't about to confess that, like a lovesick youth, he just couldn't wait. Instead he said smoothly, "I knew you'd want to get started on the next ... lesson."

"Oh. The next lesson."

He'd planned to cover foreplay in this lesson, but with his cock at full attention and his nerves drawn as tight as a drum, he knew he wouldn't even be able to say the word "breast" without exploding.

No, he had to maintain control of the situation. Ease his desire.

There was just one solution.

Aidan smiled down at Eva.

Her hair was drawn into the usually tight chignon. Her breasts bloomed above the square neckline of her simple blue gown and his cock twitched. He forced his gaze to her face. Her features were arranged in their normal fashion, but the hint of roses in her cheeks gave away her true state of mind. She adjusted her spectacles under his examination.

"I thought we would do some more… exploring tonight," Aidan said. "If that's agreeable to you."

"Yes, of course. That would be nice."

"I have a special room to show you, he said, picking up a candle, then taking her hand and leading her out in to the hallway.

"A special room?"

A hint of uncertainty caught her voice.

"Not to worry. I promise you'll enjoy it."

"Where is this room?"

"Just around the corner." He was walking too fast, and tried to consciously slow his pace. But he held on to her hand. Just in case.

He located the room easily and noted the crimson ribbon tied to the knob with more than a little relief. Finally a piece of luck. It was empty.

He tugged the ribbon from the handle, opened the door and guided her inside with a hand at her back. Then he set the candle down on a side table, and its light flickered across the walls. "May I present the Toy Room."

꧁ᨰ꧂

Eva's eyes widened as she took in the room around her. She'd though Aidan's bedchamber was decadent, but it didn't even come close to this ballroom-sized space.

A large chandelier suspended from the ceiling illuminated the dozens of erotic paintings and sculptures that adorned the room. There were portraits of nudes, both male and female and pictures of couples engaging in various intimate acts. Sculptures of the same were posed in the corners of the room. The styles were eclectic, some very old. It must have taken the Kempes years to collect these risqué objects of art.

Beneath her feet was a deep, soft rug in rich reds and golds. An enormous bed was situated in the center of the room on a platform. The sharp scent of sandalwood wafted from an incense burner perched on the mantle over and enormous marble fireplace.

And then there was Aidan. He had already removed his coat and waistcoat and his shirt hung loose on his body, doing very little to disguise the wide expanse of tawny skin. He was staring at her, taking in her reaction to her erotic surroundings. A small smile of amusement and something more played over his lips as he leaned against the mantle. Watching her.

Eva felt warm under the spell of his gaze, as if she was standing there bared though she was completely clothed. She turned to study a painting of a particularly well-endowed medieval lady and cleared her throat before speaking. "Why do they call this the toy room?"

"You can see, surely, that this chamber is all about self-pleasure," he said.

Eva turned back to face him just as he reached for the hem of his shirt. She watched every movement of his fingers, every slight contraction of muscle as he disrobed before her. When his hands went to the placket of his trousers, her eyes followed. She was exasperated to find that she was fixing her gaze on him like starving woman on a roast goose. She cleared her throat. "What do you mean by self-pleasure?"

He didn't answer until he was nude. "I'm going to let you in on a little secret, Eva," he said, sauntering slowly towards her. "Once a lad discovers his male parts and how nice it feels to handle them, he never forgets."

Her throat was dry, but she forced the words out. "That's not a secret. It's been the subject of much research."

"But has any researcher studied this so closely?" Aidan stroked his cock slowly, up and down.

It was so close that she could reach out and—she snatched her hand back. "I was able to study this quite closely last night."

"I remember," he said. "But have you ever stroked a man like this? Until he climaxed at your touch?"

Eva's mouth was suddenly dry, and she wet her lips before answering. "No." She didn't look away from Aidan touching himself. She barely even blinked.

"It mimics actual intercourse. And achieves the same result."

"One strokes faster and faster until climax," Aidan kept the same slow, steady pace. "Of course, it's always better if there's a partner performing the service," he said arching an eyebrow. "Are you interested in researching this?"

Eva approached him as if in a trance. Oh, she wanted to touch him again, she admitted. She'd thought of little else all day. Whether she was nibbling on tea cakes or viewing the erotic sculptures in the garden, the only images that danced before her eyes were Aidan's golden flesh, his flashing blue eyes, the dimple in his left cheek, the way his mouth seemed to mold perfectly to hers when he kissed her.

When she stood before him, the male, slightly musky scent became intoxicating. He smelled of the outdoors. Of the nighttime breeze and the gardens heavy with the remnants of summer's rich perfume. She tilted her head up to meet his gaze.

Flecks of gold candlelight danced in the deep blue depths. His black hair was tousled and fell across his forehead in gentle waves. Eva had the sudden urge to trace his jaw from just below his ear to the point of his chin. But before she could act on it, he caught her hand gently in his and led it to his cock.

"Like this." He said this so quietly, she hardly recognized his husky voice. He was as hot as she remembered. She wrapped her hand around his girth and he covered her hand with his, slowly guiding the motion of her hand.

"That's it. A steady rhythm. Up and down, up and down."

His flesh burned beneath her palm. Hot and smooth like a length of the finest silk enveloping a thick hot poker. His big hand engulfed her much smaller one, guiding her, showing her how he liked to be touched. (She had to remember to record this velocity and pressure in her journal.) After a few minutes, Aidan removed his hand from hers and his head fell backwards, his eyes closed.

"That's it," he whispered with a hiss. "A little faster now." The feeling of power was heady, and she gripped a little tighter, more confident. Watching him at his pleasure, knowing she was the source of it, was an exhilarating sensation. And incredibly arousing.

Eva stroked faster. She could feel his elevated pulse right there in his cock. His member throbbed and jumped under her stroke even as her own pulse quickened and her breath became shallow.

"Faster," he ground out.

Eve brushed her other hand lightly over his peaked nipples and stroked faster. He groaned deep in his throat, almost like he was in pain, but she kept going. Every sense was finely tuned to Aidan and Aidan only. She squeezed her thighs together and listed towards him. With the tip of her tongue, Eva tasted the hardened nub.

"Eva," he grunted, wrapping an arm around her waist. Then a shudder wracked his body and he swayed on his feet. His cock pulsed within her palm. Aidan let out a long, low groan. He looked like he was in pain, his eyes squeezed shut, jaw clenched. But after a moment, his face eased back into his familiar grin.

He grabbed a towel and quickly cleaned himself up. "You're a fast learner."

Eva wasn't quite sure how to respond. He might have found his release, but Eva's mind was still clouded with lust, her body aching.

Aidan assessed her with a wicked gleam in his eye. He tossed the towel aside as he stepped closer to her.

"Now it's your turn."

Eva swayed on her feet. "Pardon me?"

"It's your turn." He put his arm around her waist and tugged her against him. The full body contact sent a jolt of electricity skittering up her spine. "You mean—"

"Yes."

The idea of his finally touching her elicited another warm shiver. "You'll touch me... as I touched you?"

"No," he whispered in the shell of her ear. "What you have is much, much more sensitive and complicated. Like a violin whose strings must be plucked in precisely the right order to emit a joyous noise." He nipped her ear playfully before pulling away.

He went to a set of shelves and pulled back a sheath of crimson silk curtains. "This is why it's called the toy room," he said. Eva looked. And blinked. And looked again.

The shelves were full of phalluses in all shapes, sizes and colors.

"Come closer. Have a look."

Eva approached cautiously, footsteps swallowed by the thick rug.

She adjusted her spectacles. In the course of her research, she'd seen many drawings of such things. Cultures all over the world produced some sort of phallic art. But this collection was unlike any of the drawings she studied.

"The Kempes have the most complete collection anywhere in the world," Aidan said, selecting a long thin one made of green jade and carved with cryptic symbols.

"It's... amazing." Eva picked up a shiny black piece with a peculiar pattern of raised bumps for a closer look.

"Is there one you prefer?" he asked looking sideways at her.

"Prefer—?"

"Yes, for your self pleasure."

"No. I don't think so," she set the black phallus gently back on the shelf. But she couldn't take her eyes off the collection.

"Allow me," he said, choosing a thick ivory one that had concentric ridges carved into it. Eva swallowed.

Aidan pulled his trousers on before settling in a wingback chair near the window. "Come here, Eva."

Eva paused. This whole evening had been more than she had expected, even from Aidan. More sensual, more pleasurable, more tempting. And God help her she wasn't ready for it to end just yet.

"Of course, if you'd rather stop for tonight, go back to your room and make some notes..."

"No," Eva said a little too quickly. "I am just trying to determine if this is the best course of action. For the project."

"That's for you to decide, of course," Aidan said, his eyes narrowing. He let his gaze slide over Eva's body and she could feel the hum of awareness between them. "But I won't do anything you don't expressly ask me to. We'll stop whenever you say."

Eva bit her lip. She thought of the sensations she herself had just experienced, the warm tug at the base of her belly, the wetness between her thighs. There was more. She wanted that, she acknowledged.

"All right."

She eased onto his thighs, back straight, hands folded stiffly in her lap. She pressed her thighs together and willed her pulse to slow. She felt like a hare caught in a hunter's snare, though she had chosen to enter. "In my research, I estimate that 22% of women have pleasured themselves," Eva said nervously.

He chuckled and shifted her so that Eva found herself sitting sideways across his lap, her right shoulder and forearm nestled against a hard wall of muscle.

"And what's the rate for males?" he asked.

"98%."

"Umm. I'd say your figures are a bit inaccurate."

Eva sat stiffly in his arms, not knowing what to do with her hands, or where to look.

"Just relax," he said.

She noticed the miniscule crinkles at the corners of his eyes. His full lips. His white teeth. The tiny scar just above his left eyebrow. She could very easily spend an entire day just looking at him, cataloguing every detail. Eva tried to breathe evenly, slowing her raging heartbeat.

"That's it," Aidan whispered. He slipped her shoes off and lightly touched her ankle. She nearly jumped out of his lap. He just snuggled her closer and slid his hand up to her calve, still caressing in small circles over her stockings. "Just concentrate on the sensation and let everything else go."

Up until now, she'd been the one doing all the touching, the one with control over the whole experiment. But now he was taking some of it back. She was letting him... and it felt good.

Eva allowed her eyes to flutter shut.

His hand traveled slowly up her calf, stroking in circles, lightly kneading her flesh. Some of the tension eased from her body and she breathed more deeply, inhaling his seductive scent. Then she felt him edge her skirts up just a bit. Cool air kissed the delicate skin of her calves, even as his large, warm hands traced the slow circles higher and higher.

She let her head fall to the side, resting on his shoulder. The heat was building again, slowly this time, but more intense. His warm strokes inched higher and her thighs fell open to allow him more access.

His knuckles brushed the curls at the apex of her thighs and Eva's breathing hitched.

"You're wet for me already," he whispered. His breath tickled her closed eyelids and she arched just a little, craving more contact. He complied, lightly tracing the slick seam of her sex.

"Do you like this, Eva? Do you want more?"

Eva moaned softly and squirmed in his lap. He was driving her mad with his taunting little strokes.

"Tell me."

She arched again, seeking his touch.

"Tell me, Eva," he insisted again softly. "Tell me what you want."

"Yes. More."

He nuzzled her cheek and she was sure she felt him smile.

Aidan pressed a finger into her warmth just slightly, just enough to tease, then withdrew.

Eva almost groaned. Warmth radiated from her center. Desire, sharper than before, tugged low in her belly and between her thighs. She held her breath, anticipating his next stroke.

"More," she breathed finally. She shifted on his lap, opening her thighs even further. She was past caring about things like composure or control, about what she needed for her research. Now every thought, every breath, every nerve ending anticipated his next touch. "Please," she groaned.

Finally his long finger plunged inside her. She gasped at the gentle invasion and arched into it.

"You're so sensual, so responsive. So beautiful. I didn't know...."

Aidan used two fingers to plunge into her body, deeper and deeper. The stretching, the friction, the sensation of his strong warm hands on her body, in her body—it was too much. But still not enough.

Her hands wandered to her own breasts, kneading the ache away through the fabric of her gown, plucking at her tingling nipples.

"Oh, my God, Eva," Aidan groaned out. Eva opened her eyes to find his gaze riveted on her hands, watching her stroke herself. His eyes had gone dark, hooded, smoldering with a heat that both frightened her and excited her. She was beyond mortification she may have otherwise felt. Only the pleasure mattered now.

She could feel the heat of his bare chest burning through her clothing, feel his heart beating a rapid pace against his ribs. He shifted slightly, and Eva felt his erection press into her hip. Suddenly she had the urge to touch him again. She wanted to hold him and stroke him again. She reached between their bodies and stroked his hardness through the fabric of his trousers.

"Sweet Jesus," he grunted. Eva gasped when his hand left her body, and groaned in pleasure when it returned a mere second later.

"Touch me, Eva. Touch me. Please."

She reached between their bodies once again to find he'd undone his trousers. She wrapped her hand around his cock and began to stroke him as he'd shown her earlier.

She felt a cool hardness at her opening and realized it was the ivory phallus. She squirmed, nervous and excited all at the same time. She let her thighs fall open once more and struggled to slow her breathing relax a bit.

"I want to give you the same pleasure you've given me," he whispered dragging the phallus through the moisture at her opening. He eased it inside just a bit so that the cool smooth head teased all the nerve endings he'd already set on fire with his fingers. "Is that good?"

She groaned and arched her back.

"I'll take that as a yes."

His thumb teased the sensitive nub just above her opening, sending a new wave of pleasure coursing through her already over sensitized body. He eased the phallus in inch by cool inch until she was full and gasping at the new sensations. Then he began to move. Slowly at first, the smooth ridges of the phallus taking her by surprise and pleasure with each stroke. It felt like her body was on fire, each muscle clenching, waiting for more. Eva gasped and stroked Aidan's cock faster. Harder. Told him what she wanted by acting out her desires on his body.

Aidan matched her stroke for stroke, his head thrown back against the chair, jaw tight. The musky scent of their mingled arousal swirled though Eva's senses as her breath caught and she begged Aidan not to stop.

The pressure built, burning white hot where he touched her. It was too much. She gritted her teeth and stroked him faster.

She barely registered his deep groan and the rush of warmth as her own release overtook her. Waves of pleasure radiated from her center as her muscles contracted around the slick phallus. She knew she cried out, heard it echoing off the walls of the decadent bedchamber. But she was beyond caring. She just wanted to ride the crest of pleasure wherever it might take her.

Finally the waves eased to a gentle hum and she collapsed against his chest, sweaty tendrils of hair clinging to her forehead, her breath ragged.

Aidan withdrew the ivory phallus and tugged her skirts down with shaking hands.

She opened her eyes to find him staring down at her, still nestled against his chest. His eyes blazed, his breathing erratic.

"Well?"

She struggled to sit up, but he held her tight. She gave up and snuggled against his chest.

"What did you think?"

Thinking? No, not quite yet. Eva smiled to herself. She had to stifle the urge to giggle.

"It was nice," she said as casually as she could.

He arched a brow. "That's it? That was some volume for 'nice'."

"Very nice, then." So nice she wanted to stretch out on the bed and beg him to play her body again. And again. She smiled. "Though you said this room was about self-pleasure… and I had very little to do for myself."

Eva looked up and found Aidan's stare focused on her lips. He lowered his head and without thinking, she raised her mouth to his.

Just as his lips brushed hers, there was knock at the door. "Aidan? Are you in there? You were supposed to meet me at ten."

It was a woman's voice.

Eva scrambled off his lap, feeling slightly dizzy, as if she was emerging from a dream. She glanced down at her wrinkled gown, her bare feet, at the ivory phallus Aidan still held in his hand. She smoothed her hair as best she could without a mirror. She must look like... well, a woman well-pleasured.

Frowning, Aidan handed Eva the toy and stood to refasten his trousers. He opened the door enough for Eva to see it was Lilah, Aidan's frequent lover.

"Someone said they saw you headed this way. Oh. You're busy," she said with a sly grin. Her wide green cat's eyes focused on Eva then flicked away dismissively.

"My apologies, Lilah. I got distracted." He shoved his hands through his hair.

"Yes, so I see. That's been happening a lot lately, hasn't it? No matter." She went up on tiptoe and kissed Aidan on the mouth, angling her head and opening her mouth. Her eyes remained open and fixed on Eva as she kissed Aidan thoroughly.

A wave of anger rushed over Eva. But she forced herself to dismiss it. Aidan could kiss whomever he wanted. It was of absolutely no concern to Eva as long as he fulfilled his role of research subject for her.

Eva turned away from the spectacle Lilah seemed determined to make and concentrated on repinning the frayed tendrils of damp hair back where they belonged.

"See you soon, Aidan," Lilah purred before Eva heard the door shut.

Aidan turned around and Eva pasted a bright smile on her face.

"Eva, I..."

Eva held up hand to stop his words. "No need to explain," she said. "You have only one week a year at Ivy Hill. Why should you deprive yourself just because you're helping me with my project?"

Eva strode to the door with as much confidence as she could muster, journal clutched to her chest. She handed him the phallus. "Well, thank you for a lovely evening. That was very... educational."

Aidan wore a confused frown. His own hair was mussed and damp along his forehead. Eva felt that disconcerting pull of desire once again and knew that if he so much as crooked his little finger, she'd be right back in his lap, head thrown back, thighs opened, wanting more. She swallowed. She had to leave now, while she was still in control of the situation.

"So our next lesson is scheduled for tomorrow night—unless you have other plans," Eva said, indicating the closed door to the hallway.

"No. No plans." He said following her to the door. His eyes still shone bright. He opened the door for her, but caught her arm before she could slip out, back to the cool darkness of the corridor.

He pressed the ivory phallus into her hands with a wink. "Tomorrow. Until then—"

Chapter 8

"You're a fine mess," Will observed, reining up beside the black stallion on which Aidan was perched. "Something the matter?"

"Nothing a couple bottles of whiskey and three French whores wouldn't solve," Aidan said, frowning. In truth, French whores wouldn't do the trick. There was only one woman he contemplated—the one who'd kept him awake all night, aching. He couldn't count the times he'd thrown off the covers and strode to the door, ready to grab Eva up out of bed and pound into her until they were both sweaty and sated. Then, perhaps then he could get on with his life. And get some sleep.

"I've never seen you this way," Will said, leaning forward on the pommel of his gray. The thick waves of Will's golden hair shone in the sunlight. His perfectly sculpted jaw and blue eyes made him almost too pretty for a man. But the ladies didn't seem to mind.

"I've got this under control."

"Yes, I can see that," he said, kicking his mount to a trot to match Aidan's gait. "Another one of your fleeting obsessions?"

Aidan shot his oldest friend a dark look. "Why would you say that?"

"I know the signs. And because you've been noticeably absent from the festivities. Poor Lilah caught up with me in the garden last night, quite piqued about you're spending all your time with a certain young woman, apparently kept locked in your room, since nobody else has even had a chance with her."

"She's free to seek out whomever she wants," Aidan said even as a boulder settled in the pit of his stomach at the idea of some other man putting his hands on her.

Will grinned wider. "Well, at least you're finally doing something about it. Watching you make a fool out of yourself over Miss Blakely, who clearly wanted nothing to do with you, was amusing at first, but grew quite tiresome by the end of the season."

"Sorry to bore you."

"Oh, I'm not bored. Not anymore. I've got a reluctant lady of my own in my sights." Will reined in and leaned forward on the pommel. "So tell, me, what's next? You must have some scheme planned to lure the poor girl to your bed."

"No. No scheme." He just wasn't in the mood to discuss Eva or his odd reaction to her with anyone. Not even Will, his oldest friend and compatriot in all of his most interesting escapades. The stories he could tell about some of the nights they spent working their way through the loose women of London. Those he could remember anyway.

"You're looking a little green around the gills," Will said, his astute green eyes missing nothing. "Perhaps you should retire to the house and catch a little nap before this evening's festivities."

Aidan thought of Eva alone in her rooms, and wondered what she was doing, what she was thinking about. "That's a capital idea," Aidan said, and without even bidding Will goodbye, turned the stallion towards the house and Eva.

Eva tossed down her pen, splattering ink across the pages of her journal. It was impossible to record what had happened the previous evening. Every time she tried, she got, well, caught up in the moment again. Flashes of Aidan's dark eyes glowing as he stroked her, the memory of how her body burned for him. Anticipating what he would do tonight. It was all getting quite in the way of her scientific endeavors.

He was becoming a distraction. Things were getting messy. Out of control.

Eva sank down on the side of her small bed, giving up on the writing for the afternoon. Why was she pretending that she was still just doing research? She knew that Aidan's lessons had gone far beyond clinical the moment she'd allowed him to kiss her by the lake. And again last evening. Well, all thoughts of the project had slipped from her mind as soon as he touched her that first time—and she'd enjoyed it. She'd enjoyed it and wanted more.

This was no good. For the project or for her. All she thought about now was Aidan—his body, his touch, his kiss. But somewhere in the throes of passion, Eva had glimpsed another side of Aidan from that she thought she knew. He was generous, just as concerned about her pleasure and her comfort as with his own. Gentle. Sweet, even, at times. That she hadn't expected. If he'd been the cocky, self-indulgent man she'd seen in ballrooms all season, this wouldn't be an issue.

She lay back on her bed, late afternoon sunshine lighting her room. Was she becoming... entangled? Or was the draw of lust so powerful as to be confusing the matter? Maybe she should leave Ivy Hill, just pack her trunk and choose a new subject who didn't muddle her thoughts her as Aidan did.

She closed her eyes, remembering his hands on her body, so warm and sure. Aidan was an incredibly sensual being and she had no doubt he'd be an excellent lover. He would take his time. He'd stoke her desire slowly. Make her hot until she was begging for his touch again. Begging him to give her satisfaction.

Without realizing it, Eva had begin to stroke her breasts through her gown. She was startled, but it felt too good to stop. Her eyes opened. Maybe that was it. This need was a biological function. Maybe once a woman was introduced to sensuality, she could never go back again. Why should Eva fight this desire now? After all, he'd shown her how to take care of it herself.

Eva slipped her dress over her head with shaking hands. Could she really do this? Be that kind of woman? The familiar tug of desire when the cool air touched her skin made her breath catch. Yes, most certainly. She could, and she would.

Eva draped her dress on the end of the bed, and lay down once again. She shut her eyes and allowed her hand to drift down her body.

The afternoon sun filtered through the curtains as Aidan lay on his bed. He was contemplating how, exactly, he was going to get through another night of "lessons" with his sanity intact, when he heard her deep moan in the adjacent room.

Aidan cocked his head. Was she doing research with someone else? The idea was disturbingly unpleasant. Who? Granville? Peaksley? They'd certainly jump at the chance to tumble a gorgeous woman like Eva.

Aidan crept to the connecting door and gently laid his ear to it. Her deep throaty groans sent blood rushing to his cock. He listened intently, frowning, for a deeper male answer. It didn't come. Only Eva's breathy groans and small gasps.

Realization finally dawned. When he pictured the solo act going on in the next room, his heart skipped a beat.

Unable to tear his ear from the door, he listened harder, resisting the urge to free his cock and give it a good stroke himself. Her breathy moans grew louder. He recognized them from last night's lesson—and from the lurid fantasies that had plagued him all night.

He stood and turned the knob slowly, praying it was well-oiled and silent. He just wanted a peek,that was all. He just wanted to witness Eva touching her own sweet body.

He opened the door a crack.

She lay on her bed, fully nude, save for her white stockings and garters, her pale green gown crumpled beneath heels that dug into the mattress as she arched against her own hand. He could see nearly her whole body in three-quarter profile, the sun splashing through the window to blanket her body in late afternoon amber. Her cinnamon hair was loose, spilled over the snowy pillow and the side of the bed, wavy from the tight plaits she normally wore.

Her dusky pink nipples were tightened, and he was close enough to see the gooseflesh that covered them as she kneaded and plucked at the peaks.

Her other hand was occupied lower on her anatomy, buried in the wet curls at the apex of her splayed thighs. As he had predicted, Eva was a fast learner. The heel of her hand applied pressure while her fingers plunged inside.

Suddenly the wrongness of what he was doing struck him. He shouldn't be watching. What the devil was the matter with him? Had he been reduced to some kind of voyeur? He had every intention of leaving Eva to her pleasure, of closing the door and hobbling back to his own room. Really.

Then he heard it.

"Aidan." She groaned his name softly, her lips barely moving. "Aidan. Oh. More."

His head throbbed. Both of them.

She called out his name softly over and over until she was chanting it though clenched teeth, eyes squeezed tightly shut.

Aidan longed to answer her plea. Longed more than anything to burst into her room and give them what they both wanted.

But he stood rooted to the spot, mesmerized by the flush of her skin, the gentle sway of her breasts as her body writhed in pleasure.

With a long low gasp of his name, Eva stiffened then was still, her eyes closed.

He wanted to stay all afternoon and watch her. But she wouldn't be pleased to know he'd been watching a very private moment, even if he was involved indirectly.

Aidan closed the door without a sound and retreated to his own room. His breathing eventually slowed as he sat on the edge of his bed, incapable of coherent thought.

He'd witnessed women pleasuring themselves before, and two women touching each other. But he'd never seen any woman so fully engrossed in the act, as uncensored, unbridled, completely caught up in her own pleasure.

His erection throbbed. It was going to take more than a swim in the pond to solve this problem.

He lay back on the bed. Will was right. He was a mess. The woman was driving him crazy.

He had to have her. Tonight.

He would do his utmost to push her over the edge and into his bed before the night was over.

But he had to be careful. He couldn't assume that Eva, the scientific journal-keeper, was like the women who fell so easily for him. She would give—and take—as much as she chose.

So he would just have to figure out how to make her choose. Aidan thought of Ivy Hill and all the pleasure it offered. What would Eva like? What would push her to the edge?

Aidan smiled. He had it. He knew enough of her to guess at her pleasure even if she didn't yet know herself. He'd be willing to wager that she'd never touched herself intimately before he introduced her to the pleasure.

And now he had another pleasure for her, one that would push her right over the edge, and with any luck into his bed for a good long time.

Chapter 9

Eva was eager for Aidan to arrive that night, but worried, too. Her little interlude earlier in the afternoon only served to plant him more firmly in her mind. She knew she'd blush when he finally appeared. He'd know she'd been thinking about him, and as more than a research subject. He was fast becoming an object of obsession for her. That was why she'd decided that tonight would be their last research session.

She should leave Ivy Hill now, before he got to her room. But she wanted just one more taste. Just one. Then she'd go home and write her book.

At last the tap on the adjoining door came. Eva smoothed her hair, willed her hands not to shake, pasted on a bright smile, and opened the door.

He leaned against the door frame in his typical, relaxed pose, but tonight the gesture was imbued with a languid sensuality she knew must be a product of her own earlier fantasies.

She cleared her throat and tried to clear her mind of the lurid images.

He pushed off the door frame and reached for her hand. She clutched her journal in one hand, but allowed him to take the other and ease her closer.

"Good evening, Eva. Did you have a…pleasurable day?" He stared into her eyes, as if searching for something. He must not have found it, because after a moment his gaze dropped down to her lips.

Without looking back at her eyes, he said, "I thought we'd do a bit more field study tonight. If you're in agreement, of course."

"Field study?" It sounded so… scientific.

"There's another room I'd like to show you," he said, now looking full at her.

"What exactly do you have in mind?"

"You can trust me," he said, tucking her hand in the crook of his elbow.

"Perhaps." Unwisely, she did actually trust him to a degree. He would never do anything to hurt her, of that she was certain. He was not spiteful or mean. He'd demonstrated just the opposite by being such a good sport and participating in her project, though such an experienced man must needs find it frustrating.

Aidan led her out through her bedroom door and down the long, darkened corridor. "Ivy Hill has numerous rooms that have been specially modified to accommodate guests' most decadent pleasures and most secret fantasies."

"Like the Toy Room."

"That's just the beginning." He stopped beside a door at the end of the long hallway. He grinned as he tugged two crimson ribbons from the knob and entered the room. "This is a viewing room."

Eva stepped inside the dark room. The drapes were open, though and the moon cast its pale, bluish light across the floor. She could tell that the room contained a bed, but not much other furniture.

"Over here," Aidan whispered in her ear. He tugged her hand to the left side wall.

She heard a sliding sound and a rectangle of light opened in the wall.

"Take a peek," he whispered in the shell of her ear. She shivered. "Here. Stand on this stool."

He grasped her waist and lifted her to stand on the stool so that she could see through the opening.

All she saw was a bed. A very large bed, without any hangings or curtains. It was more of a padded platform than a bed. Like a stage. And it was covered in white furs.

"All I see is a very odd bedchamber." Eva asked, pulling back to look at Aidan, "What am I supposed to be viewing?"

"Just wait. The show is about to start. I know it will help with your research."

Before Eva could inquire just what sort of show they would be viewing, the door to the next chamber was flung open and a giggling couple tumbled inside.

"Watch," Aidan said softly in her ear. He had sidled closer, his spicy musky scent already working on her senses. His breath stirred the hair at her nape. His body molded to hers from hip to shoulder.

Eva peered through the opening in the wall, determined to ignore the physical reaction of her body to Aidan's mere proximity and concentrate on the scene unfolding before her. For her research, of course.

She didn't have to wait long. The couple was kissing and touching, moving ever closer to the massive bed.

The woman's emerald green gown came off with a few tugs and in a blink, the man's evening attire had been reduced to a crumpled pile of black on the crimson carpet beneath their bare feet.

Aidan moved behind her, putting his cheek right next to hers so that they were both looking through the opening into the room beyond. His scent was crisp like soap and starch with a hint of male muskiness that always affected her. She should tell him to back away, to stop standing so close. But the truth was, she liked the warmth of him at her back, his breath stirring the tiny hairs on the nape of her neck.

Besides, the activities she was witnessing next door were truly… intriguing.

Now the couple was completely nude, bodies flush, front to front. They were kissing, his hands tangled in the woman's hair. Eva felt the growing tug low in her belly and familiar little thrill of anticipation. She shifted.

"Do you like this, Eva?" Aidan whispered in her ear. Shivers skittered down her spine. "Watching, I mean."

"Don't they mind?" Eva asked, evading his question.

Aidan chuckled softly. "No. In fact they like it. Did you notice that two ribbons were tied to the door? One ribbon would have merely meant that this room was available. Two means that they wanted an audience. It adds another dimension to their lust knowing that someone is watching."

A shiver of anticipation skated over Eva's skin. Would she do such a thing? Would Aidan? A deep groan brought her attention fully back to the room beyond the opening.

The man was holding the woman, with her legs wrapped around his waist. Eva's fists clenched in her skirts, a hot rush of warmth filling her belly. Her mouth went dry as she focused unblinking on the naked couple.

Aidan shifted behind her, moving closer. His chest was pressed against her back, his cheek still pressed to hers.

He whispered, "He's inside her, now. Sliding in and out of her."

Aidan's hands went to Eva's waist, pulling her more snugly against him. Even through the layers of skirts, Eva could feel the heat of his erection pressing against her backside. She swallowed, watched the couple grunt against and writhe against each other.

The man walked the woman back to the bed and slid her off his erect member. She didn't protest as he positioned her on all fours facing away from him. He stroked her backside lovingly before giving it a sharp smack.

"He's going to enter her from behind now," Aidan whispered.

Eva watched entranced as he did just what Aidan predicted, sliding his long member into her with a loud groan. Eva couldn't see the woman's face, as it was buried in the bed coverings, but she heard the gasp of pleasure that escaped her lips once the man was fully seated inside her.

As if this gave him a new notion, Aidan pushed more insistently at her back and she couldn't help arching backwards just a little to feel him more fully. Her nails, she found were now clutching the sides of his trousers, rather that her own skirts, urging him even closer. She burned between her thighs, longed to touch herself, to build toward the release she'd experienced earlier.

The man leaned forward over the prone woman and reached under her body to fondle her breasts.

Eva gritted her teeth. Her own nipples were puckered with anticipation beneath her clothes.

Then Aidan's hands were there, warm, gentle but firm, deftly stroking her breasts through the fabric of her gown.

"Many women like it from behind," he whispered. "It's a whole different sensation as you can see, gives the man a lot more room to maneuver. It's a deep penetration. Hot and wet and deep." He punctuated each of those last words with a light nip at her earlobe.

Then Aidan found her nipples and plucked at them lightly through her gown. His voice was velvety in her ear. "You like that. You have sensitive breasts. I want to lick them, Eva. To suck them until you're screaming for me. Then I want to nibble them gently and send you right over the edge."

He kissed her neck then, leaving hot trails down the side of her neck to the neckline of her disheveled gown. "Would you like that, Eva? Would you like me to love your breasts like that" He rolled the anatomy in question between his fingers while nipping lightly at her exposed neck with his teeth.

"Yes," she breathed. It came out a moan.

Eva opened her eyes to find that the man was kneeling on the bed, now, the woman's hips grasped roughly in his hands as he pounded into her with more force. The rhythmic slap of flesh on flesh matched the pulse pounding though Eva's ears. She was burning up, Aidan's heat overwhelming.

Aidan ground against her backside in deep, slow circles while continuing to tease her erect nipples.

"I want you, Eva. I want to be buried inside you, pleasuring us both." One hand slid out of her bodice and moved to the juncture of her thighs. He put his hand over the ache and rubbed her though her dress. "You've possessed me. I can't think of anything but your sweet scent, your body's reaction to my touch...." He growled low in his throat and nipped her neck a little harder, stroking her faster with his hand.

Somewhere in the deep recess of her foggy mind, Eva knew she shouldn't be enjoying this so much. She should have her mind focused on finishing this and escaping Ivy Hill with her project intact. But she'd always been an observer, an outsider, watchful of intimate human contact. She'd never sought it. But she wanted it now. It was vital that she have it, and savor it—with Aidan.

She arched into that wonderful hand, welcoming the hot liquid sensation flooding her body, turning her knees to mush.

Aidan's hand left her then, circling her waist and spinning her to face him. His pupils were huge black pools in his dark eyes, his breathing erratic. He kissed her then, hard, and her arms immediately went around his neck, clinging.

Something was different now. He wasn't seeking just a taste this time, but total surrender. He'd tempered his desire in previous kisses, but now it was open, a roaring inferno that threatened to engulf her. And she wanted it. God help her, she wanted to be swept away on his tide.

She opened her mouth slightly and allowed him entrance. She kissed him back desperately, ineptly, she was sure, but the low growl in his throat told her that he didn't mind.

She slid her fingers through the thick silky hair at his nape, loving the sensation of the cool strands slithering between her fingers.

"I want to see you, Eva," he whispered when he came up for air. He was breathing hard. His eyes were wide, searching her face desperately for the answer he wanted. He looked down into her upturned face. "I want to taste you everywhere. Tell me you want me, too. Tell me you'll let me make love to you. To show you all the pleasure there is to give. And receive."

There was no hesitation in her mind—or body. "Yes."

He groaned "Thank God." He kissed her a moment longer. "My room. Now."

"Mine's closer," she said, pulling his mouth back to hers.

"Good point," he said when he came up for air. And with that, he scooped her up in his arms and strode out of the room and down the hallway.

Chapter 10

She wrapped her arms around his neck, urging him to hurry to her room. They could have just stayed where they were, but Aidan knew once wouldn't be enough to satisfy the lust he'd suffered the past week. He'd much rather find a bed now where they could remain until daylight. And beyond. Eva's door was only a few steps closer than his, but knowing he could have her in the same exact spot where she'd been fantasizing about him earlier was too tempting to pass up.

Aidan kicked the door open and tossed her on the narrow bed—the same bed where only hours before she'd touched herself, imagining it was him, calling his name.

This time she would be screaming his name.

Aidan attacked her mouth, kissing her hard, fast. Deeper. He had to be deeper. He buried his hands in her hair and showed her everything her wanted to do to do with his tongue, his lips. He nipped lightly at her lips before moving to her sensitive earlobes and throat. She smelled of lavender, he registered on some level. Sweet and feminine. Luscious.

Eva made tiny mewling noise in his ear as he licked her throat, dropping little light kisses, then nipping gently. She arched beneath him, clearly as aroused as he. He had only one thought, one drive. And that was to be in her as quickly and as deeply as possible.

He pulled back and sitting on his knees over her, practically ripped off his coat, his waistcoat and finally his shirt.

She ran her cool hands over the planes of his chest as he undid the fastening of his trousers. It was dark as pitch here, but he could imagine how wide and dark her eyes must be if she was any where near as aroused as he.

"I want to see you," she said in a husky whisper.

Aidan climbed off the bed and made his way to the window. He jerked open the curtains and the full moon above illuminated the room. Eva lay sprawled on the bed, her hair a hopeless tangle, her dress crumpled and rucked up to the tops of her thighs. She lips were deep pink from his hard kisses and her eyes were as dark as he'd imagined. She sat up and tugged her gown off over her head.

Aidan was mesmerized by her sheer eroticism. She was no missish girl, but a woman with full-blown passions. Unashamed. Uninhibited. And it was all directed towards him. He was torn between wanting to worship her beauty for just a moment longer, and wanting to bury his cock in her.

His cock won out.

"You are the most beautiful woman I have ever seen," he breathed, and meant it. She took his breath away. And she was about to become his. She wouldn't regret choosing him. He'd make sure of it.

Aidan pushed his trousers down and off and started back to the bed before he noticed her trunk, situated by the door. It was fully packed. He looked about. Her possessions were neatly packed and ready to go.

"You're leaving." It wasn't a question.

Eva's eyes closed for an instant. "Yes."

His jaw clenched.

"When?"

"Tomorrow at first light," she answered sitting up.

"You are going to give up on your project?"

"I have all the data I need. Or I will… after." She reached her arms towards him, but he stood firm, his arms crossed over his chest.

Suddenly the desire that had raged in his veins cooled. A new and most unpleasant emotion surfaced.

"After we make love."

"Yes."

He refastened his breeches and reached for his shirt.

"Wh-what are you doing?" she asked, sitting up.

"Leaving."

"Why?" She got out of bed and approached him. "I thought—"

"You thought I'm some specimen you can just manipulate to satisfy your curiosity."

"Aidan—"

He couldn't bear to hear any more. Aidan stomped out of the room, slamming the door behind him. He strode down the hallway, down the stairs, and out into the cool fresh night air.

A brisk walk and a dip in the pond might cool his ire, and his desire. But he doubted it.

He still wanted her. But he wanted her to want him with same intensity. Not for mere research. Not because she was conducting an experiment. But because she wanted him. Aidan.

That was damn disconcerting. He'd always taken sex where it was offered, had never even conceived of that not being enough.

Until Eva.

Aidan circled round the rear of the house and strode past the maze without even a thought of seeing what sensual delights might lurk inside. There was only one woman he wanted. And she was leaving Ivy Hill.

The moon was a bright golden orb above him in the black sky. He strode toward the path that would lead him through the woods to the pond when he heard a rustling in the grass.

"Aidan," a feminine voice called out. Lilah's flowing form floated over the dark landscape towards him like a specter.

He frowned.

"I've been looking for you," she purred, pressing her breasts against his chest.

He was shocked that not one drop of desire was stirred at her closeness. Eva had ruined him for any other woman.

She looked up at him with an expression he recognized. It was a look that used to bring him to his knees. Ignite a burning desire in him.

Now it seemed calculated. Fake. Cold.

"What is it, Lilah?" he asked, jaw clenched. He just wanted to be alone with his thoughts. Take a long cold swim. Forget.

She grinned, her hand moving towards the front of his pants.

"You're a hard man to find, these days," she said squeezing him with enough pressure to make him wince. "But now that I've managed to track you down...,"

She leaned in, turning her perfect face up to him, anticipating his kiss.

Instead, he grasped her wrist and removed it from his crotch. "Not now, Lilah," he said with as much restraint as he could muster.

Her eyes went wide.

"What's the matter. Are you tired again?" She teased, snaking her hand to his privates once again. "Your reputation will be in shreds."

Aidan stepped back, breaking contact with her.

"I can't do this anymore, Lilah. Not tonight, not ever. I'm sorry."

Lilah opened her mouth to say something, but Aidan had already disappeared into the woods, alone.

⁂

How dare he deny her, Lilah thought watching the broad retreating back. How dare he turn her down, her of all people? Men lusted for her, but she only took a select few to her bed.

Aidan was one of them. He had an impressive cock and knew what to do with it, certainly. But so did many of her other lovers. He had wanted her like all the rest—before Eva Blakely had entered the picture.

Lilah didn't mind sharing her lovers. After all, she herself refused to be tied to just one man. She refused to be at a man's mercy when he cared to grant it, and his wrath when he didn't.

She didn't even mind ending this tryst with Aidan. But she would be the one to end it when she was ready. Not him.

It would be easy to remedy the situation, though, she thought with a sly grin. Men were easily led by their cocks and Lilah was an expert trainer.

Chapter 11

Just as Eva thought she had Aidan understood, he did something to surprise her. First when she had been sure he was nothing but a self-centered wastrel, he was kind and generous. Now that she'd agreed to sleep with him, he'd fled.

It just didn't make sense. According to her research, 62% of all men preferred a one-night affair with no ties and no repercussions. Did Aidan fall into the minority then?

Eva sat on the side of her bed. She could have told him her plans to leave, she supposed. But what reason could she give?

The truth? a small voice hinted. But what was the truth? That he frightened her?

Yes.

That she wanted him for more than just an aid to her project?

Yes.

That no man had ever made her feel so desirable and smart and worthy?

Yes.

Eva went to window and saw Aidan striding across the lawn towards to small wood that bordered the property to the west. Her heart clenched and her body throbbed just looking at him.

She should take his exit as a sign. She should crawl in bed, go to sleep and wake early in the morning, and set out for home.

She should—But her life was full of shoulds. Just this once she wanted to do something just for the enjoyment, just because she wanted to and it felt good, even if it wasn't logical or part of a bigger plan. That was what she should have told Aidan, instead of making him think bedding him was only part of her project.

She wanted Aidan in her bed. Now, tonight. And she'd squandered her opportunity by making him think research was the only reason she desired him.

Before she could think about the consequences, Eva was in motion. She pulled on her stockings and gown and grabbed a shawl on the way out the door, not even bothering with her slippers.

Eva flew down the stairs and out into the night. The cool breeze caressed her skin and the cold damp grass tickled her stockinged feet.

She followed the path she'd seem him take. The patch of trees and undergrowth was dark. Insects hummed deep in the shadows and vines tripped her as she hurried towards where she'd seen Aidan disappear.

Around a bend in the trail, she saw him. His back was to her and he was standing on the edge of a small pond. Then he began stripping off his clothes.

Eva held her breath at the sheer male beauty of him. He carried so easily his power and strength, leashed until he willed it loose.

He flung his clothing in the general direction of a large boulder at water's edge and waded into the pond. He ducked under the surface, and when he emerged on the far side of the pond a moment later, he stood, flinging back his hair, the arc of water glittering in the moonlight.

Eve was torn between going to him immediately and watching a bit longer. She shifted in the underbrush and the crack of the twig beneath her heel echoed in the silence of the dark forest.

Aidan's head snapped around. His eyes narrowed as he caught sight of her. "What do you want?" he asked.

Eva swallowed. The time for games was over. She stepped from the underbrush. "You. I want you."

Aidan's jaw tightened. "Go back to the house, Eva. Find some other hard-on for your experiments."

She'd never seen him angry. Teasing, laughing, irritating. Maybe even frustrated, but never angry. Eva stepped forward. "I don't want anyone else. I want you, Aidan. Just you."

Aidan looked at her, head cocked. His chest and torso rose out of the water, his dark hair slicked back against his skull.

"Do you?" he asked. "Will you take notes in that bloody journal while I'm fucking you senseless?"

Eva swallowed. "No notes." There was only one way to convince him she was serious. She unbuttoned her gown, letting it slip down her body to pool at her feet. Aidan's gaze slid down her body. He slowly began to wade towards her.

"No timing the sweaty parts?"

She could see the lines of anger fading from his face. She smiled and pulled the chemise up over her head. It, too, joined her gown on the ground. "No pocket watch."

Her nipples puckered at the cool air, even as the familiar burning tug in her belly began to build. Aidan's torso emerged from the pond, rivulets of water streaming down his chest.

"Stay with me all night," he insisted.

When the dark thatch of hair and his full erection emerged from the water, she rolled one silk stocking down her leg, then tugged it off. The other followed. "All night?"

"There's a lot I plan to do to you."

Aidan approached slowly, intently until the water pooled around his ankles.

He paused, looked at her, his eyes glowing. "And not one mention of the word 'project' while we're in bed."

Eva smiled. "Agreed."

Then he was on her, his cool wet skin pressed against her burning flesh.

He kissed her hard, possessively, his hand tangled in her hair, plucking at it until it fell free down her back.

"I've imagined you like this. Coming to me. Naked. Hungry." Each word was punctuated by more probing kisses.

Aidan's hands slid down her arms, gathering her closer to his chest. Eva wrapped her arms around his neck, determined to think of nothing else but this moment. This man.

She kissed him back eagerly, matching his hunger with her own. She ran her hands down his chest, stopping to brush her palms over his flat male nipples. He sucked in his breath and pulled away to look at her.

He grinned for half a second before recapturing her mouth. "I love the way you touch me."

The night was alive with sound, the gentle lapping of water of the pond, insects in the dark weeds making their own love calls, and the wind rustling through the canopy of dry leaves overhead. But most of all there was Aidan. The sound of his voice when he whispered naughty things in her ear, the feel of cool wet skin against her burning flesh, his big warm hands roaming all over her body, overwhelming her senses, making her forget everything else.

"I want you, Eva. Since the first moment I saw you at the Nottingham ball, I've wanted you." He trailed kissed own her throat and went to his knees.

"I didn't like you," she breathed as he traced the nipples of her bare breasts. His warm hand on her bare breasts sent shivers rippling through her body. When his mouth fasted on one nipple, teasing, tempting, she buried her hands in his hair and drew him closer.

"And now?" he asked, looking up at her.

Eva smiled down at him, this man who made her feel so... significant. She brushed a stray lock of damp hair off of his forehead. "I find you more appealing now."

Aidan grasped Eva's hips and drew her closer to him. Before Eva could even imagine what he was about, he'd fallen to his knees, and his face was buried between her thighs. She gasped and slid her fingers in his hair, holding on for dear life as ripple after ripple of sensation, almost too much to bear, shuddered through her body.

Aidan used his fingers to part her gently before lapping at her opening. Her belly clenched with the violent eruption of desire. Her erect nipple tingled, aching, while the low pull in her belly became almost painful.

Aidan thrust inside her with one long finger and moved his mouth further up to tease the sensitive spot he'd played so expertly the night before. Fire raced through her veins, and she threw back her head. Then he began to move his finger in and out of her slick body, sucking gently at her clit at the same time.

On some level, Eva knew the screams that rang out through the dark woods were hers. But as the pressure and wetness built between her thighs and Aidan thrust more quickly, sucked a little harder at the apex of her desire, she just didn't care.

Eva squeezed her eyes shut, bit her lip. Her hands fisted in his damp hair as she strained forward. His mouth made her feel feelings she didn't know were possible. She had never imagined this—never imagined the pleasure one man could bring one woman.

The pressure built until Eva was sure she was about to rip in two. Finally it exploded in waves of pure joy that rippled throughout her body and left her weak, slumped against him.

Aidan steadied her when she would have lost her balance and as the ripple subsided, she heard him whisper.

"How about now? Has your opinion of me changed at all?"

She opened her eyes just a slit to peak down at him. "Yes. Most definitely. I was wrong to ever think badly of you."

He smiled up at her for a long minute before his expression became serious once again.

The low thrum of desire began anew in her veins. His eyes darkened as he rose to his feet, sliding against her body as he did. His cock pressed into her belly, his warmth engulfed her.

Her lips parted slightly and he threaded his fingers through her hair, gently tilting her face up to his.

"This won't be gentle." His soft voice belied his warning.

A shiver raced up her spine and she felt her pulse quicken. She wanted him as he wanted her. Rough, raw. "Good."

Aidan crushed her to his body, wrapping both arms around her. His rock-hard erection pushed at her belly. She ground against him harder, wanting to feel all of him, on her, in her, all around her.

"I won't be able to wait very long," he said, nipping her bottom lip.

"Then don't."

It was all the encouragement he needed. With a low growl deep in his throat, he jerked her off the ground, wrapping her legs around his waist.

Eva wrapped both arms around his neck and kissed him deeply, using her tongue to tease and caress his mouth just as he had done to her. She thrust with her tongue, showing him what she wanted.

Eva had the vague sensation of motion but still gasped when her bare backside brushed the large boulder at the water's edge. Aidan grasped her backside, making a barrier between her bare skin and the rough cold stone.

He lifted her slightly. "Help me, love."

She shifted until she felt the head of his cock at her slick entrance. She pressed down slowly, drawing him inside inch by slow inch.

He was burning hot and she didn't know how she'd bear the pure pleasure of it.

"You're so tight," he whispered through clenched teeth.

"It's been a long time." She shifted, taking more of him. "And it wasn't like this."

At last he was fully seated. He kneaded her backside gently but she could feel how tightly strung his muscles were, how much it cost him to be still inside her.

She kissed him then and raised herself slightly, showing him what she wanted. Then he was in motion, thrusting slow but deep, his hips making tight circles designed to give her the maximum pleasure of his body.

Her nails dug into the flesh of his shoulders and he buried his head at the side of her throat.

Eva tilted her hips to give him even better access and a deep groan escaped him as his tempo increased. Pleasure radiated from her center, out to tease each nerve in her body, from the tips of her hair to the toes that curled into his backside with each thrust. The friction of the light hair on his chest rubbing at her sensitive nipples sent a new set of chills racing down her body.

Aidan raised his head and stared into Eva's face. His eyes were black shiny pools, his face creased with need and the strain of holding back. She stroked the damp hair back from his forehead.

"Let go," she said and kissed him deeply.

She felt the instant he followed her advice and sent his restraint flying to the four winds. He grasped her hips and increased his tempo, plowing into her harder and faster. His strength took her breath away, and she gasped in surprised delight.

Pressure built almost painfully in her belly and between her thighs where he slid in and out of her in an ever-increasing rhythm.

Then she was sailing through the night, his name on her lips as she cried out her pleasure. His deeper grunts of release mingled with hers as he thrust a final time and stiffened, clutching her to him.

He leaned his forehead against hers, eyes squeezed shut and as Eva's pulse began to slow to a normal rhythm, she knew she'd never be the same.

Chapter 12

Making love to Eva brought a lightness to Aidan's mind, he thought. Her dark lashes were spayed across pale cheeks, her hair a riot of ginger on the white linens. The sheet wrapped around her slumbering body had slipped a little so that the rosy tips of her breasts were visible.

The familiar stirring of his cock began again and he smiled. Finally having her in his bed was a mission accomplished, though he oddly was never quite sated. The more he had had her during the past four days, the more he wanted her.

Eva, for her part, had matched him desire for desire. He'd been right about her passionate nature. Once she had decided to free it, they had explored many exotic rooms in the manor house, and with each new experience, Eva's delight became more and more important to him.

She stirred, a small smile playing on her swollen lips. It was a wonder she could move, he thought. His own muscles ached from all the activity they'd enjoyed the past few nights. And mornings. And evenings, he though with a grin. She, too, it seemed, was as insatiable as he.

She came awake slowly, finally opening those amazing eyes to look at him.

"Morning, love," Aidan said, stroking her hair from her face. "Sleep well?"

"No," she said as she sat up and stretched. "Not at all."

Aidan's gaze was automatically drawn to her high round breasts, and he reached out a finger to trace her nipples.

The spark instantly flooded Eva's eye once again and the sensual tug at his groin increased.

"You're going to kill me, woman." He said reaching for her.

But she lurched back, out of his way.

"I just might," she said, smiling. "Lie back."

A little thrill of pleasure rippled though him. So far she had been open to whatever he wanted to show her, but she'd never yet taken the lead.

He did as she requested and lay back on the pillows, eyes never leaving her face. "Just what do you have planned, love?' he asked, not really caring, as long as it was what she wanted.

She smiled at him and flipped her hair over her shoulder. "Research," she said. "You are still my specimen after all."

"That's true. Well, never let it be said that I didn't do my part for science," he grinned. "Experiment all you like with my poor man's body."

"I intend to."

Eva rose from the bed, naked and unashamed. He loved her like this. Sensual and confident in her own woman's power.

She plucked something off the floor then climbed back into the massive bed. She crawled over to him on all fours, threw back the covers that covered his growing erection, then smiled up at him.

"This may be a short experiment."

"I'll do my best to maintain, Miss Scientist."

"See that you do."

Eva crawled over his body to straddle his waist. His cock poked at her backside, but she ignored it. He could feel her cool woman's flesh against his belly, the beginnings of moisture wetting her curls.

"You are not to touch me until I say," she said, holding a discarded cravat.

"Not even a squeeze?" he asked gently grasping one golden globe, tweaking the nipple.

She leaned backwards, out of reach. "No."

Aidan dropped his hand and groaned. He might explode now of he didn't touch her. Or even if he did. He eyed the cravat, wondering just what she intended.

"If you comply, I promise you will be rewarded."

Aidan grinned and placed his hands behind his head. "You've talked me into it."

"Good."

Eva leaned forward. As her breasts swayed above his mouth, he managed to catch one nipple. She had sensitive breasts, he'd learned. Just massaging and suckling in the right way was enough to make her climax. She let out a throaty groan and allowed his tongue to tease her for a moment. Then she sat upright and tied the cravat securely around his eyes.

Beneath the blindfold, the room became as black as night. This was a new experience for him. He wondered where Eva had learned it. From one of her research books, no doubt.

She leaned forward pressing her breasts against his chest to whisper in his ear. "You are not to touch. Or speak or make a noise in any way."

He opened his mouth to argue, but she silenced him with a finger on his lips. "Nothing. Or I stop. Understand?"

He nodded.

Eva sat up again and he was painfully aware of the wetness that now seeped from her onto his belly.

She stroked him slowly, beginning with his chest. She teased his flat nipples with the palm of her hand before leaning forward to nip them with her teeth. Her breasts were flattened against his torso. He squirmed, each sensation heightened with the absence of sight.

She kissed his chest and worked her way downward over his torso and around his navel. She climbed off his body and settled on her knees between his splayed thighs.

Aidan breathed heavily, clenching his teeth against the strong pull of sensation centered wherever she happened to be touching him. His body was tight, his cock throbbing.

He could feel the lightest brush of her fingers, the stir of her hair across his belly, the warmth of her body nestled between her legs. He could smell the musky warmth of her skin, his own scent on her.

It was amazing. She was amazing.

She trailed wet kisses down his torso, then paused. He held his breath, bit his lip against begging her to continue.

Then she touched him. She ran one finger gently up one side of his cock, then the other. She shifted forward and he could feel her breath on the tip of his cock. God, he was going to explode before she even managed to....

He stifled the groan deep in his throat as her tongue finally darted out to taste him. He flexed, using all his power and restraint to keep from wrapping hands in her hair, forcing her to take him fully inside.

She took her sweet, torturous time, laving him up and down while gently fondling his sac. Her hair brushed against his belly and thighs as she pleasured him until he was nothing but a ball of pulsing awareness. He gritted his teeth until his jaw ached but still she continued.

Aidan struggled to hold on, to think of anything else besides this beautiful amazing woman pleasuring him so thoroughly. He thought of the kind and cost of each pair of boots he owned. The color blue. His favorite horse. Anything but what Eva's mouth was doing to him.

Finally she straightened and slid up his body. She kissed his lips, traced the contours of his jaw and whispered sweetly in his ear.

"Did you find that enjoyable?"

He nodded.

He felt her smile against his lips as she ravaged his mouth once more. He was on fire. He had to be inside her. Now.

"Eva," he groaned.

Abruptly she stopped kissing him and straightened.

"Now you know the rules."

Aidan was too far past desire to care about her game. In one movement he was unblindfolded and atop her, hips wedged between her thighs.

He looked down into her surprised face. And grinned.

"Sod the bloody rules," he said and plunged deep into her.

With only a few hard thrusts, he climaxed in tune with her own release.

He rolled to the side, gathering her close. He pushed aside niggling thoughts about how he would give her up when the house party was over, about what would happen when they left Ivy Hill and returned to their real lives. He wasn't ready to give her up just yet, that was certain. With his last conscious thought he marveled at the unexpected treasure he'd found in Eva.

Chapter 13

Eva knew she had to get out of bed sometime. The thought of returning to her room, leaving Aidan's embrace to work on her book was not pleasant. Still, she needed to finish the book, and Aidan had been a more than accommodating research subject, showing her all there was to know about relations between men and women. It had long ago ceased to be research, she allowed. But even so, she intended to finish her project.

She smiled, secretly tickled with herself. She never would have though that she could be so wanton. So fearless. She hardly recognized herself or her thoughts. She never thought she could be brave enough to open herself up to another person,not just physically, but letting him see her interior self, too.

In the deep quiet moments between lovemaking, she'd shared with him her dreams, her hopes for her book, for her life.

And he hadn't laughed. Or told her it was impossible. Or that she was just a woman. Instead he'd actually seemed interested in what she was doing, understood that she had a goal in life, and told her that he admired her will to go after it.

For the first time, here was someone who saw the real Eva—and approved.

Eva smiled and forced herself to disentangle from Aidan. She pressed a quick kiss to his damp brow, and allowed herself to stroke his hair a time or two before sliding down from the massive bed and beginning the search for her clothing. She'd get in a couple of hours of work on her book before Aidan woke. He'd mentioned that he wanted to take her for a picnic at a very secluded spot on the other side of the little wood. She smiled. She couldn't wait for the feast.

She dressed as quietly as possible and sneaked through the door that adjoined Aidan's room to hers. With a final look over her shoulder, and a small smile, she went in to her own room to work.

Aidan awoke from his sated slumber to a familiar warmth in his bed. But her scent wasn't Eva's. His eyes flew open to find Lilah's pretty face not three inches from his.

"It's my turn, now," she purred, stroking his hair back from his face. He tried to lurch back, but found his ankles bound to the foot board, under the covers. One of Lilah's favorite games.

"Let me loose, Lilah."

"Oh, come on, Love. I know you like this little game," she leaned forward and kissed him on the lips. He jerked back and sat up.

Lilah frowned and crawled into his lap. She was naked. Her generous breasts bouncing against him as he leaned forward to untie the ropes holding his ankles.

"I'm not amused. Now get out of here before—"

Lilah's face suddenly turned hard. "Before your darling little Eva finds us together? Come now, Aidan, you were never a one-woman man. Maybe she'd like to join us. Shall I ask her?" Lilah's hands grasped his semi-limp cock and stroked him as he'd once enjoyed.

"No." Panic shot through his brain. He struggled with the ropes, ignoring her touch. It was repulsive to him now that he'd known Eva. He plucked at the ropes, but it was too difficult to get them free with Lilah sitting on him.

He lurched to the side to dislodge her, but she gripped him around the neck and brought him over with her so that he was lying on top of her, between her knees, his ankles tangled in the bed sheets and ropes.

It was then that he heard the click of the adjoining door opening. He tried to scramble off of Lilah, but she brought her lips to his and moaned his name loudly.

"Aidan, I—" Aidan winced at the sound of Eva's voice. He jerked his head back to look at her. Tried to struggle to a sitting position, thrusting Lilah off him.

"Eva, this isn't what it looks like."

Her face was pale, her eyes wide beneath her spectacles.

"We were hoping you'd show up, dear sweet Eva," Lilah purred, sitting up. She ran a finger down Aidan's chest. "He was just telling me yesterday that his fantasy was to have us both. Are you up for a ménage, dear?"

Eva spun and the door slammed shut behind her.

Lilah pouted triumphantly. "I guess that's a no." Aidan quickly untied the ropes.

Though he'd never struck a woman, the urge to throttle Lilah was almost overwhelming.

"Get out," he growled between clenched teeth. "Now."

For once, Lilah listened. Her mask of amused flirtation dropped to reveal pure anger. "Is she worth all that, then? That you would give up what you and I have together?"

"Yes." Aidan grasped her arm and dragged her out the door. He was too angry to speak, too angry to look at her. He just wanted her out of his life, out of his sight for good. He thrust her into hallway, tossed her clothes after her and slammed the door.

Then he went to find Eva. She had to know that he could never want Lilah after what he'd shared with her.

He paused, suddenly alarmed.

Just what had he shared? Sex, certainly. But he'd never felt this way about a lover. Even as obsessed as he sometimes became when getting a new lover, he'd never felt so possessive, so worried about her feelings. He certainly never cared so much about her opinion of him.

He ran a hand through his hair. That was disturbing, damn disturbing. He was nagged by the realization that he wasn't ready to end things. What did he have in mind, exactly? A yearly tryst here at Ivy Hill? An affair carried out beneath the notice of proper society? Nothing seemed to fit, and he didn't know Eva's feelings on the matter, either. Perhaps she would be content to leave here and think of this time they had shared as nothing more than a pleasant interlude. He just didn't know.

All he knew was that he hadn't been with Lilah or even thought of another woman since he'd made love to Eva. And he had to make Eva understand that.

Chapter 14

Eva needed to be moving.

She paced back and forth in her room, willing herself to be calm, to forget the image of Aidan's magnificent body, the body he'd shared with her only an hour before, covering another woman.

Eva stopped, took a few deep breaths and forced the ball of raw emotion to the back of her mind.

Why was she in such turmoil, she asked herself. She had no claim on him. They were not married, or betrothed. They didn't even have an understanding. They'd made love a few times over the past few days. Well, perhaps more than a few times. That didn't signify. To a man like Aidan, it was probably standard practice. He could probably make love to one woman in the morning, another in the afternoon.

But something didn't ring true in that, either. He'd been nothing but attentive to her all this time. Of course until the past few days she'd only seen him for their evening sessions. He could have been going from room to room, making love to whomever he happened to meet for all she knew.

And it was within his right.

What about her? What was she to him?

Clearly she was just another woman to him, despite the intensity of their lovemaking, the spark that sprung between them before and the tender playfulness after.

The pain forced her to acknowledge that she had formed some sort of attachment to him.

It made sense, of course. He had been her first real lover. A connection that intimate was sure to engender an attachment, however fleeting it may be. But she was not *his* first lover. Far from it. Perhaps it was easy for someone with so much experience to move easily from one bed to the next without suffering any sort of emotional attachment.

Aidan had proved that theory quite graphically.

A light knock sounded at her door, and Eva's heart flip-flopped in her chest. She didn't want to see him. She didn't want him to look at her and know her hurt. And she didn't want proof that the attachment she felt was one-sided.

But she couldn't hide in her room forever. It was best if she acted as if none of this bothered her. She took a deep breath, determined that he not see the raw pain that ravaged her.

She stood, smoothing her hair and her skirts. She grabbed the quill she'd been using earlier and went to answer the door.

"Aidan," she said brightly. Her voice sounded false, even to her own ears. "I was just getting some work done." She stepped back to allow him entrance.

He frowned.

He had pulled on some trousers and a loose shirt, though it hung limp and wrinkled, open at the neck. He stepped into the room, and Eva closed the door behind him.

He turned suddenly and stepped closer to her. "Eva, I wanted to explain what you saw. It wasn't—"

Eva held up a hand and forced a smile. "You don't have to explain."

"But I want to. Lilah came in while I was asleep and planted herself in my bed. I told her I didn't want her, but it didn't seem to matter."

Eva smiled again. He was a man with a reputation of bedding dozens of women. Why, she'd witnessed his comings and goings before she ever met him face to face. And the woman in his bed today had been the one she'd heard him with before. She'd recognize the smooth purr of Lilah's voice anywhere. "We're adults, after all, and there was never an understanding between us."

"Eva, you're the only woman I want," he said in a deeper voice. He was getting angry.

"It's fine, Aidan, she said, smiling brightly. "In fact, you've made me think that perhaps I should take another lover myself."

"I—what? What did you say?"

He crossed the room and grasped her arms. She didn't know where that thought had come from. The lie had spilled from her mouth as easily as if it was the truth. And he seemed to believe it. She pressed her advantage. "Well, you've done an admirable job as my research subject," Eva said, gently disentangling herself from his grasp.

"Admirable." He crossed his arms on his chest.

"Yes, you have been most helpful. But I think it's rather like having the same meal day after day. Even if it's pleasant, eventually one longs for something... different."

"You're bored with my lovemaking? That's not what you said an hour ago."

"I—"

He stepped forward, male ire rolling off him in sensual waves.

"Shall I remind you just how admirable my lovemaking can be?" he asked in the low throaty voice she loved.

Eva swallowed. She'd like nothing better than to have him again right now, to erase the other woman's touch from his body and his mind. But that would not salvage her pride, only make her a further slave to her own emotions. No, she needed to disengage completely. For her own good.

"I wouldn't say that I am bored, no. And we can certainly continue with our pleasant little interlude. I just want to experience something—someone—new."

He said nothing, just stared at her, one dark brow cocked, glaring. She was nervous under his intense stare and shifted slightly.

"This is truly what you want."

Eva swallowed and forced the lie. "Yes."

"I'll arrange everything." And he was gone.

Eva sank to her bed and closed her eyes against the pain. Stupid, stupid pride. It always got her in trouble. But at least she'd protected her heart.

And that was the most important thing.

"You want me to what?" Will asked, calmly refilling his tumbler with the rich dark port he favored.

"I want you to make love to Eva. Miss Blakely."

Aidan could barely get the words out through his clenched teeth. He didn't want to be having this conversation, Not with Will, not with anybody. He didn't want to think about any other man taking his place in Eva's bed. But it was what she wanted, clearly.

And she had been right. They had no claim to one another. If this was what Eva wanted, he wanted to get it for her. But he couldn't allow her next lover to be just anyone. Left to her own devices, and as lovely as she was, she would be fresh meat for the more debauched members of the ton here. Aidan had only shown her a taste of what Ivy Hill had to offer. The only man he could trust to treat her as she deserved was his best friend, Will. But it was killing him to ask.

Will took a slow sip and set his glass down. "May I ask why?"

Will's damn composure made Aidan want to punch something. "She wants another lover. Something different," He spat, "A new flavor."

Will chuckled. "Is that what she said?"

Aidan ran a hand through his hair and looked into the fire. "Yes."

"And that troubles you."

Aidan growled an answer.

Will offered, "Someone who hasn't known you nearly as long as I have might say you're in love with the chit."

Aidan narrowed his gaze on his friend. "Well, then it's a good thing you've known me for as long as you have, isn't it?"

Will merely smiled and sipped his drink.

Aidan persisted. "Will you do it?"

Will was silent a moment, just looking at Aidan. "Of course," he said with a shrug. "Anything for a friend."

Aidan let out a breath but didn't feel much better. "You are too kind."

Will ignored his sarcasm. "Besides, she is a lovely girl. Nice, round breasts. I'll bet she's a hellion between the sheets. The quiet ones usually are."

Aidan growled, grabbed the bottle and stomped away.

Chapter 15

Aidan's note was brief and to the point. "Midnight," was all it said.

Eva folded it and tucked it into the drawer of the little writing desk. What had she been expecting? A plea for her to forget the madness? No, not from Aidan. Of course not. Even if he had felt that way, his pride would not have allowed him to express it. Just as her own pride would not allow her to back out of the liaison with whomever he had selected for her.

She had to go through with it, despite her disinterest in doing so. She could chalk it up to research. Human mating rituals were proving far more messy and complicated than she ever would have imagined.

Eva paced the room, stopping before the mirror at least a dozen times to check her hair. To peer at her round, pale face in the mirror. To discern whether she was really going to carry her wounded pride that far.

Eva heard heavy footfalls coming up the hallway of the silent house. It was almost midnight and everyone else was having a stargazing party on the hill. Eva quickly went back to her desk put on her spectacles and pretended to be laboring over her journal, as cool and casual as if she was expecting nothing more than a late supper.

At the knock at her door, Eva bade him enter.

"Good evening, Eva," Aidan said stiffly.

Eva held up one finger and finished writing a sentence in her journal. I can do this, she thought. I can.

She pasted a smile on her face and turned to greet Aidan. And his guest.

She rose from her chair and smiled.

"Aidan. Nice to see you again," she said formally. She could form her speech to treat him as impersonally as he had chosen to treat her, but she couldn't stop the flip-flop of her heart in her chest at the sight of him.

He stood tall, strong, with that one lock of wavy hair splayed across his forehead. But instead of his usual half-grin and relaxed expression, he looked tired. Shadows underlined his eyes and suddenly he looked older than his thirty-two years.

Obviously he'd been up late the previous night. Cavorting with multiple partners all night long, she thought, unfairly, straightening her spine.

"Allow me to introduce William, Lord Northington," Aidan said tightly, indicating his companion. "He's agreed to—"

"Call me Will, my dear," he said stepping forward. He grasped Eva's hand and laid a gentle kiss on her knuckles while meeting her eyes. "A pleasure."

Eva smiled at Will. It was easy. He was handsome with his neatly combed honey blond hair, his sparkling blue eyes, kind and ready smile. She had half-worried that Adian would bring back some troll of a man, big brutish, rough sort to teach her a lesson. But instead he'd brought back a prince straight from a fairytale castle.

"Very pleasant to make your acquaintance, Will," she said politely. She could feel Aidan's eyes on her, hot and piercing, but she refused to give him the satisfaction of meeting his glare.

Eva retrieved her hand. Knowing Aidan was watching, she stepped closer to Will, and cocking her head, give him an assessing stare. "Yes, I think you'll do, Will."

Will grinned and stepped forward to wrap his arms around Eva's waist. He dipped his head and caught Eva's lips in a warm, but fairly chaste kiss.

"Aidan told me you were lovely," he said grinning down at her. "But he didn't tell me you were so delectable." Will stroked her hair and ran a finger down her cheek, tracing the line of her face to her chin.

Eva shivered. The contact was pleasant and Will smelled warm, slightly of brandy and starch. But he didn't melt her insides the way Aidan did with merely a glance.

Stop. Stop comparing Will to Aidan. Forget Aidan, she admonished herself. Forget his touch, how it felt. Concentrate on the physical sensations. Not the emotional.

Eva forced a smile and channeled the vixen she wished she could be. "Why thank, you, Will. Aidan has told me absolutely nothing of you. You'll have to fill me in as we go, I suppose."

"Oh yes," he said huskily. "I'll fill you in on all there is to know about me. Why, by morning you'll be an expert." He stroked her back. "And with much diligence, I'll know just as much about you."

"Diligence?" she said swallowing.

"Oh, yes, I'm a very diligent man when I set my mind to it, I assure you. Especially when it's such a pleasurable pursuit as you, Eva."

Even through all Will's flirtatious words, Eva was aware of Aidan standing just behind Will.

She could feel his stare burning through them both.

Eva glanced up at him. "Thank you, Aidan. You've done a fine job."

She smiled at him, then dismissed him by bringing her gaze back up to Will. Will leaned in for another warm brush of lips.

"I'm going," Adian grumbled. "But I'm warning you..."

"She'll be in good hands, Adian. I promise. Very good hands."

Will gathered her against his chest, and this time his kiss was definitely not chaste. He claimed her lips with more force, more passion, nibbling at her hungrily, his tongue slipping inside for a taste.

Pleasant sensations swept through Eva's body, but not with the same force and abandon she had known with Aidan. Will was warm and strong and, oh, a very good kisser, though. So Eva closed her eyes and concentrated on those things.

Aidan grunted and the door slammed behind him.

Eva could not have chosen a better partner had she picked him out herself, she thought. Aidan had known exactly what type of lover she would desire. Maybe this would be an enjoyable experience after all.

He broke the kiss and nibbled a line to her earlobe. "Now that we're alone, my dear," he whispered. "Let's get you out of this gown so we can really get to know one another."

Chapter 16

Aidan had lost track of the number of glasses of whiskey he'd consumed. And it had only been a quarter hour, according to the blasted clock on the mantle. A mere 15 minutes since he'd left Eva in the arms of another man. Thrust her there, actually, as he'd played the part of procurer.

He poured another tumbler and slung back the burning amber heat like a seasoned inebriate. If he had to help satisfy her curiosity again, he was going to have to contact his vintner and lay in supplies.

He closed his eyes, but all that did was to replay the scene for him, over and over. Will taking her in his arms and doing what Aidan had longed to for two long days. Hell couldn't be worse than imagining Will kissing her, touching her, bringing her to pleasure.

He squinted at the clock again. Twenty minutes since he'd left her. He wondered if they had completed the deed. If so, had she enjoyed it? Had she affected Will the same way she'd affected him?

The door to the study opened, and Aidan stumbled to his feet as quickly as his alcohol-muffled brain would allow.

It was Lilah. Somewhere in the back of his mind, he had expected Eva to come to him and tell him it was all a mistake, that she didn't want any other man.

He sank back into the chair.

Lilah sauntered around the chair to face him. He gathered the strength to look up at her. "I'm not in the mood, Lilah."

She cocked her head, examining him, for once her expression genuine, not some sort of practiced mask designed to get what she wanted.

"I know." She indicated the empty chair next to him. "May I?"

"Be my guest."

He poured another tumbler of whiskey and swirled it in his glass before drinking it.

"Indulging ourselves, aren't we, Aidan? So much drink—that's not like you."

"It has been a rough day."

"I see." Lilah took the bottle gently from his hand and set it aside. "I didn't know she meant so much to you, Aidan. Or I wouldn't have come to your room."

Aidan let his hand drop to the table. "What makes you think that? That she means something to me?"

"Oh, I don't know. Perhaps it's the fact that you're sitting here getting yourself good and drunk while your best friend is having at your girl."

"She's not mine,"

"Ah, the crux of the problem."

Aidan raised his head to look at her.

"What do you know of it?"

Lilah sat back in her chair, a frown marring her perfect complexion. "We're a deal alike, you and I," she said after a long moment. "Headstrong, stubborn," she met his gaze. "We don't let people in, Aidan. We hop from bed to bed looking for whatever it was that we lost somewhere along the way."

He must have had more to drink than he'd realized. Never had he heard Lilah speak about her past, or anything beyond that moment's pleasure.

"So. What do we do about it?"

Lilah leaned forward and put her hand on his. "Go find it, Aidan. What you've been searching for is just up those stairs."

Aidan opened his mouth to protest, but nothing came out.

Instead a warm feeling that had nothing to do with all the whiskey he'd just consumed settled in the spot just above his heart, and he knew Lilah was right.

He loved Eva. Loved her wit, her sense of humor. Loved that she was so open, honest. Loved the way she moaned his name when he was buried deep inside her. Loved the dimple just behind her left knee.

She was his, no matter whether she knew it or not. He had never had such a connection with a woman. He'd never ached for a woman with all his soul, never been tortured by the thought of someone else taking a small piece of what made her so special to him.

He had to convince her what she meant to him.

"I have to—"

"Go," Lilah said, smiling sadly. "Go tell her."

He paused at the door and looked back at Lilah sitting alone before the fire.

"I'll be fine, Aidan," she said. "I always am."

❧❦❧

The effects of the whiskey dissipated as he mounted the stairs two at a time on the way to Eva's room. Would he be in time? He hoped to God that Will was the type of lover to languish and not get right to the business at hand. Thirty minutes. It had been just thirty minutes. Surely the brute would take longer than that to make love to a woman as passionate as Eva.

He burst through her door without slowing or even knocking.

"Ah, Aidan," Will said, rising from the chair near the fireplace. He was just fastening his trousers and Aidan suddenly felt as if he had swallowed a boulder. "I was just finishing up here."

Aidan frowned. "Where is she? Where is Eva?"

Will looked at his friend strangely, then sauntered over, smoothing his shirt back into the top of his trousers. "Resting up for another go, I imagine. I thought we'd try the dungeon for an encore." He frowned at Aidan's expression. "You're welcome to join us, of course. That might be... fun."

"Where is she?" Aidan asked again, teeth clenched.

"She's quite good, you know. You didn't tell me she was a screamer," he said matter-of-factly. "By the way, did she do that thing with her tongue—"

Before Aidan had conscious thought to stop, his fist plowed into Will's grinning face.

Taken completely by surprise, Will sprawled on the floor, blood gushing from his nose.

Will calmly picked himself up off the floor, extracted a handkerchief from his pocket and dabbed at his face.

The adjoining door flew open, and Eva rushed in, concern marring her features. She was repinning her hair, and Aidan's heart ached all over again.

"What the devil is going on in here? Will? Are you all right? What happened?"

Eva looked from Will's battered face to Aidan and back again. "Will someone please explain what's going on?"

Aidan looked awful, Eva though. His hair stood out as if he had shoved his hands through it repeatedly. His eyes were red-rimmed and he smelled like a distillery.

Will grinned, despite the blood oozing from his nose and lip. He sauntered over to Eva and gave her a quick kiss on the forehead. "I was right, my dear. Now I had better be off before Aidan plants me another facer. I wouldn't want to ruin my coat."

Eva waited until Will has left before turning to Aidan. "Have you lost your mind?"

"It's entirely possible," he agreed, crossing the room to her. "Eva, I'm sorry to barge in and ruin your… adventure. But something just occurred to me, something that can't wait."

Eva's heart clattered in her chest and she sat down. "What?"

He took a deep breath. "I—I've fallen in love with you, Eva."

Eva's heart soared for half a second before plummeting. These were the words she'd secretly longed to hear, but now that they had been spoken, she almost wished he could take them back. She could deal with loss more easily than with hope.

"Say something," he said softly.

"Aidan. I don't know what to say."

He frowned and approached her. He knelt beside her chair and searched her face. "Say you love me, too. Or that you can grow to love me. Say you'll stay with me. Be my wife. Share your life with me."

Eva swallowed and looked away. "I told you how I felt, Aidan. I never intended to marry. My work means everything to me. I can't give it up."

"I won't make you, Eva," he said, taking her hand. "I wouldn't ever try to rein you in. It's your independence, your spirit that made me fall in love with you." He looked at their intertwined hands a moment before going on. "You can… experiment with other lovers, if that's what you truly wish," he said so low she barely could make out the words. "Though it would kill me each time. Just as watching you with Will has."

He looked up at her, his eyes bright, and Eva knew he told the truth. Will had been right. Aidan did love her.

"You won't mind my locking myself in my study for days on end while I finish a project?" she asked, hope beginning to spread throughout her body.

"I'll bring you tea and cakes for sustenance."

"You will allow me to lecture in public about my findings?"

"I'll sit in the front row." He grinned slightly.

"You won't mind if occasionally I need to conduct some sort of experiment in our bedchamber?"

"I'll gladly volunteer for whatever you have in mind. Any other conditions?"

"None."

He pulled her to her feet then and kissed her hard, clutching her to his chest. "That's a yes, then."

Eva brushed the limp tendril of hair off his forehead and smiled at him. "That's a yes."

He kissed her again, burying his hands in her hair. Just when Eva thought she'd lose consciousness from lack of oxygen, he pulled away.

"I lied about one thing, however," he said, seriously.

She pulled away a bit, suspicious. "What's that?"

"When I said you could take other lovers, I lied." He tightened his hold on her. "You're mine and I won't share. Your bedding down with Will is what made me realize how much you mean to me. I can't go through that hell again."

Eva smiled and raised on her tiptoes. She whispered in his ear. "I didn't bed with Will."

"What?"

She shook her head ruefully. "I did want to go through with it, if only to prove that you meant nothing to me. But I couldn't. All I kept thinking about was you. You're the only man I want." She kissed his lightly on the mouth. "Will ever want." She kissed him again. "The man I love." This time she kissed him longer, easing into his embrace.

Suddenly he pulled back horrified. "I owe Will an apology."

"Later," she said, tugging Aidan's shirt up over his head. "There will be time to apologize later." She ran her hands over his bare chest until he gathered her in his arms once more.

"You're right." Holding her, Aidan headed towards the bed. "Next Tuesday should be just about right."

About the Author:

Bethany Michaels is a born and bred Hoosier recently transplanted in the South. While she loves her adopted hometown of Nashville, Tennessee, she still misses the winter snow... sometimes. Bethany lives with her husband and four small children and squeezes in writing between nights as a full-time transportation planner and days as a full-time mom. When she has a few minutes, she updates her website at bethanymichaels.com and would love to hear from real live grown-ups.

Men you've been dreaming about!

Secrets

Satisfy your desire for more.

*F*eel the wild adventure, fierce passion and the power of love in every **Secrets** Collection story. Red Sage Publishing's romance authors create richly crafted, sexy, sensual, novella-length stories. Each one is just the right length for reading after a long and hectic day.

Each volume in the **Secrets** Collection has four diverse, ultra-sexy, romantic novellas brimming with adventure, passion and love. More adventurous tales for the adventurous reader. The **Secrets** Collection are a glorious mix of romance genre; numerous historical settings, contemporary, paranormal, science fiction and suspense. We are always looking for new adventures.

Reader response to the **Secrets** volumes has been great! Here's just a small sample:

"I loved the variety of settings. Four completely wonderful time periods, give you four completely wonderful reads."

"Each story was a page-turning tale I hated to put down."

*"I love **Secrets**! When is the next volume coming out? This one was Hot! Loved the heroes!"*

Secrets have won raves and awards. We could go on, but why don't you find out for yourself—order your set of **Secrets** today! See the back for details.

Secrets, Volume 1

A Lady's Quest by Bonnie Hamre
Widowed Lady Antonia Blair-Sutworth searches for a lover to save her from the handsome Duke of Sutherland. The "auditions" may be shocking but utterly tantalizing.

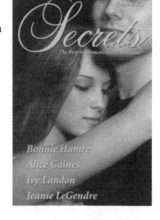

The Spinner's Dream by Alice Gaines
A seductive fantasy that leaves every woman wishing for her own private love slave, desperate and running for his life.

The Proposal by Ivy Landon
This tale is a walk on the wild side of love. *The Proposal* will taunt you, tease you, and shock you. A contemporary erotica for the adventurous woman.

The Gift by Jeanie LeGendre
Immerse yourself in this historic tale of exotic seduction, bondage and a concubine's surrender to the Sultan's desire. Can Alessandra live the life and give the gift the Sultan demands of her?

Secrets, Volume 2

Surrogate Lover by Doreen DeSalvo
Adrian Ross is a surrogate sex therapist who has all the answers and control. He thought he'd seen and done it all, but he'd never met Sarah.

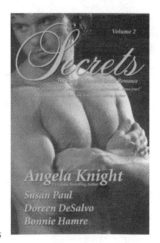

Snowbound by Bonnie Hamre
A delicious, sensuous regency tale. The marriage-shy Earl of Howden is teased and tortured by his own desires and finds there is a woman who can equal his overpowering sensuality.

Roarke's Prisoner by Angela Knight
Elise, a starship captain, remembers the eager animal submission she'd known before at her captor's hands and refuses to become his toy again. However, she has no idea of the delights he's planned for her this time.

Savage Garden by Susan Paul
Raine's been captured by a mysterious and dangerous revolutionary leader in Mexico. At first her only concern is survival, but she quickly finds lush erotic nights in her captor's arms.

Winner of the Fallot Literary Award for Fiction!

Secrets, Volume 3

The Spy Who Loved Me by Jeanie Cesarini
Undercover FBI agent Paige Ellison's sexual appetites
rise to new levels when she works with leading man
Christopher Sharp, the cunning agent who uses all his
training to capture her body and heart.

The Barbarian by Ann Jacobs
Lady Brianna vows not to surrender to the barbaric
Giles, Earl of Harrow. He must use sexual arts
learned in the infidels' harem to conquer his bride. A
word of caution—this is not for the faint of heart.

Blood and Kisses by Angela Knight
A vampire assassin is after Beryl St. Cloud. Her only
hope lies with Decker, another vampire and ex-merce-
nary. Broke, she offers herself as payment for his services. Will his seductive powers
take her very soul?

Love Undercover by B.J. McCall
Amanda Forbes is the bait in a strip joint sting operation. While she performs, fellow
detective "Cowboy" Cooper gets to watch. Though he excites her, she must fight the
temptation to surrender to the passion.

Winner of the 1997 Under the Covers Readers Favorite Award

Secrets, Volume 4

An Act of Love by Jeanie Cesarini
Shelby Moran's past left her terrified of sex. International film star Jason Gage must gently coach the young
starlet in the ways of love. He wants more than an act—
he wants Shelby to feel true passion in his arms.

Enslaved by Desirée Lindsey
Lord Nicholas Summer's air of danger, dark passions,
and irresistible charm have brought Lady Crystal's
long-hidden desires to the surface. Will he be able to
give her the one thing she desires before it's too late?

The Bodyguard by Betsy Morgan & Susan Paul
Kaki York is a bodyguard, but watching the wild,
erotic romps of her client's sexual conquests on the
security cameras is getting to her—and her partner, the ruggedly handsome James
Kulick. Can she resist his insistent desire to have her?

The Love Slave by Emma Holly
A woman's ultimate fantasy. For one year, Princess Lily will be attended to by three
delicious men of her choice. While she delights in playing with the first two, it's the
reluctant Grae, with his powerful chest, black eyes and hair, that stirs her desires.

Secrets, Volume 5

Beneath Two Moons by Sandy Fraser
Step into the future and find Conor, rough and masculine like frontiermen of old, on the prowl for a new con-
quest. In his sights, Dr. Eva Kelsey. She got away before,
but this time Conor makes sure she begs for more.

Insatiable by Chevon Gael
Marcus Remington photographs beautiful models for
a living, but it's Ashlyn Fraser, a young exec having
some glamour shots done, who has stolen his heart. It's
up to Marcus to help her discover her inner sexual self.

Strictly Business by Shannon Hollis
Elizabeth Forrester knows it's tough enough for a
woman to make it to the top in the corporate world.
Garrett Hill, the most beautiful man in Silicon Valley, has to come along to stir up
her wildest fantasies. Dare she give in to both their desires?

Alias Smith and Jones by B.J. McCall
Meredith Collins finds herself stranded at the airport. A handsome stranger by the
name of Smith offers her sanctuary for the evening and she finds those mesmerizing,
green-flecked eyes hard to resist. Are they to be just two ships passing in the night?

Secrets, Volume 6

Flint's Fuse by Sandy Fraser
Dana Madison's father has her "kidnapped" for her
own safety. Flint, the tall, dark and dangerous mercenary, is hired for the job. But just which one is the
prisoner—Dana will try *anything* to get away.

Love's Prisoner by MaryJanice Davidson
Trapped in an elevator, Jeannie Lawrence experienced
unwilling rapture at Michael Windham's hands. She
never expected the devilishly handsome man to show
back up in her life—or turn out to be a werewolf!

The Education of Miss Felicity Wells by Alice
Gaines
Felicity Wells wants to be sure she'll satisfy her
soon-to-be husband but she needs a teacher. Dr. Marcus Slade, an experienced lover,
agrees to take her on as a student, but can he stop short of taking her completely?

A Candidate for the Kiss by Angela Knight
Working on a story, reporter Dana Ivory stumbles onto a more amazing one—a sexy,
secret agent who happens to be a vampire. She wants her story but Gabriel Archer
wants more from her than just sex and blood.

Secrets, Volume 7

Amelia's Innocence by Julia Welles
Amelia didn't know her father bet her in a card game
with Captain Quentin Hawke, so honor demands a
compromise—three days of erotic foreplay, leaving
her virginity and future intact.

The Woman of His Dreams by Jade Lawless
From the day artist Gray Avonaco moves in next door,
Joanna Morgan is plagued by provocative dreams.
But what she believes is unrequited lust, Gray sees
as another chance to be with the woman he loves. He
must persuade her that even death can't stop true love.

Surrender by Kathryn Anne Dubois
Free-spirited Lady Johanna wants no part of the bind-
ing strictures society imposes with her marriage to the powerful Duke. She doesn't
know the dark Duke wants sensual adventure, and sexual satisfaction.

Kissing the Hunter by Angela Knight
Navy Seal Logan McLean hunts the vampires who murdered his wife. Virginia Hart
is a sexy vampire searching for her lost soul-mate only to find him in a man determined to kill her. She must convince him all vampires aren't created equally.

Winner of the Venus Book Club Best Book of the Year

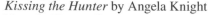

Secrets, Volume 8

Taming Kate by Jeanie Cesarini
Kathryn Roman inherits a legal brothel. Little does
this city girl know the town wants her to be their new
madam so they've charged Trey Holliday, one very
dominant cowboy, with taming her.

Jared's Wolf by MaryJanice Davidson
Jared Rocke will do anything to avenge his sister's
death, but ends up attracted to Moira Wolfbauer, the
she-wolf sworn to protect her pack. Joining forces to
stop a killer, they learn love defies all boundaries.

My Champion, My Lover by Alice Gaines
Celeste Broder is a woman committed for having a sexy
appetite. Mayor Robert Albright may be her champion—
if she can convince him her freedom will mean they can indulge their appetites together.

Kiss or Kill by Liz Maverick
In this post-apocalyptic world, Camille Kazinsky's military career rides on her ability to make a choice—whether the robo called Meat should live or die. Can he prove
he's human enough to live, man enough... to make her feel like a woman.

Winner of the Venus Book Club Best Book of the Year

Secrets, Volume 9

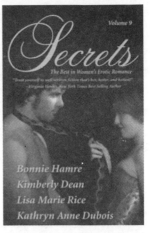

Wild For You by Kathryn Anne Dubois
When college intern, Georgie, gets captured by a
Congo wildman, she discovers this specimen of male
virility has never seen a woman. The research pos-
sibilities are endless!

Wanted by Kimberly Dean
FBI Special Agent Jeff Reno wants Danielle Carver.
There's her body, brains—and that charge of treason
on her head. Dani goes on the run, but the sexy Fed is
hot on her trail.

Secluded by Lisa Marie Rice
Nicholas Lee's wealth and power came with a price—
his enemies will kill anyone he loves. When Isabelle
steals his heart, Nicholas secludes her in his palace for a lifetime of desire in only a
few days.

Flights of Fantasy by Bonnie Hamre
Chloe taught others to see the realities of life but she's never shared the intimate
world of her sensual yearnings. Given the chance, will she be woman enough to
fulfill her most secret erotic fantasy?

Secrets, Volume 10

Private Eyes by Dominique Sinclair
When a mystery man captivates P.I. Nicolla Black
during a stakeout, she discovers her no-seduction rule
bending under the pressure of long denied passion.
She agrees to the seduction, but he demands her total
surrender.

The Ruination of Lady Jane by Bonnie Hamre
To avoid her upcoming marriage, Lady Jane Ponson-
by-Maitland flees into the arms of Havyn Attercliffe.
She begs him to ruin her rather than turn her over to
her odious fiancé.

Code Name: Kiss by Jeanie Cesarini
Agent Lily Justiss is on a mission to defend her country
against terrorists that requires giving up her virginity as a sex slave. As her master
takes her body, desire for her commanding officer Seth Blackthorn fuels her mind.

The Sacrifice by Kathryn Anne Dubois
Lady Anastasia Bedovier is days from taking her vows as a Nun. Before she denies
her sensuality forever, she wants to experience pleasure. Count Maxwell is the perfect man to initiate her into erotic delight.

Secrets, Volume 11

Masquerade by Jennifer Probst
Hailey Ashton is determined to free herself from her
sexual restrictions. Four nights of erotic pleasures
without revealing her identity. A chance to explore her
secret desires without the fear of unmasking.

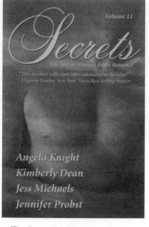

Ancient Pleasures by Jess Michaels
Isabella Winslow is obsessed with finding out what
caused her husband's death, but trapped in an Egyp-
tian concubine's tomb with a sexy American raider,
succumbing to the mummy's sensual curse takes over.

Manhunt by Kimberly Dean
Framed for murder, Michael Tucker takes Taryn
Swanson hostage—the one woman who can clear him.
Despite the evidence against him, the attraction is strong. Tucker resorts to uncon-
ventional, yet effective methods of persuasion to change the sexy ADA's mind.

Wake Me by Angela Knight
Chloe Hart received a sexy painting of a sleeping knight. Radolf of Varik has been
trapped there for centuries, cursed by a witch. His only hope is to visit the dreams of
women and make one of them fall in love with him so she can free him with a kiss.

Secrets, Volume 12

Good Girl Gone Bad by Dominique Sinclair
Setting out to do research for an article, nothing could
have prepared Reagan for Luke, or his offer to teach
her everything she needs to know about sex. Licen-
tious pleasures, forbidden desires… inspiring the best
writing she's ever done.

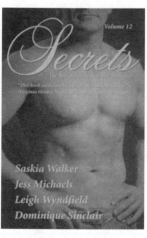

Aphrodite's Passion by Jess Michaels
When Selena flees Victorian London before her evil
stepchildren can institutionalize her for hysteria,
Gavin is asked to bring her back home. But when he
finds her living on the island of Cyprus, his need to
have her begins to block out every other impulse.

White Heat by Leigh Wyndfield
Raine is hiding in an icehouse in the middle of nowhere from one of the scariest men
in the universes. Walker escaped from a burning prison. Imagine their surprise when
they find out they have the same man to blame for their miseries. Passion, revenge
and love are in their future.

Summer Lightning by Saskia Walker
Sculptress Sally is enjoying an idyllic getaway on a secluded cove when she spots a
gorgeous man walking naked on the beach. When Julian finds an attractive woman
shacked up in his cove, he has to check her out. But what will he do when he finds
she's secretly been using him as a model?

Secrets, Volume 13

Out of Control by Rachelle Chase
Astrid's world revolves around her business and she's
hoping to pick up wealthy Erik Santos as a client. He's
hoping to pick up something entirely different. Will
she give in to the seductive pull of his proposition?

Hawkmoor by Amber Green
Shape-shifters answer to Darien as he acts in the name
of long-missing Lady Hawkmoor, their ruler. When
she unexpectedly surfaces, Darien must deal with a
scrappy individual whose wary eyes hold the other half
of his soul, but who has the power to destroy his world.

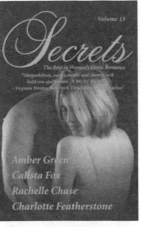

Lessons in Pleasure by Charlotte Featherstone
A wicked bargain has Lily vowing never to yield to the
demands of the rake she once loved and lost. Unfortunately, Damian, the Earl of St.
Croix, or Saint as he is infamously known, will not take 'no' for an answer.

In the Heat of the Night by Calista Fox
Haunted by a curse, Molina fears she won't live to see her 30th birthday. Nick, her for-
mer bodyguard, is re-hired to protect her from the fatal accidents that plague her family.
Will his passion and love be enough to convince Molina they have a future together?

Secrets, Volume 14

Soul Kisses by Angela Knight
Beth's been kidnapped by Joaquin Ramirez, a sadistic
vampire. Handsome vampire cousins, Morgan and
Garret Axton, come to her rescue. Can she find happiness with two vampires?

Temptation in Time by Alexa Aames
Ariana escaped the Middle Ages after stealing a kiss
of magic from sexy sorcerer, Marcus de Grey. When
he brings her back, they begin a battle of wills and a
sexual odyssey that could spell disaster for them both.

Ailis and the Beast by Jennifer Barlowe
When Ailis agreed to be her village's sacrifice to the
mysterious Beast she was prepared to sacrifice her vir-
tue, and possibly her life. But some things aren't what they seem. Ailis and the Beast
are about to discover the greatest sacrifice may be the human heart.

Night Heat by Leigh Wynfield
When Rip Bowhite leads a revolt on the prison planet, he ends up struggling to
survive against monsters that rule the night. Jemma, the prison's Healer, won't allow
herself to be distracted by the instant attraction she feels for Rip. As the stakes are
raised and death draws near, love seems doomed in the heat of the night.

Secrets, Volume 15

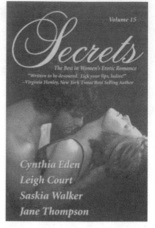

Simon Says by Jane Thompson
Simon Campbell is a newspaper columnist who panders to male fantasies. Georgina Kennedy is a respectable librarian. On the surface, these two have nothing in common... but don't judge a book by its cover.

Bite of the Wolf by Cynthia Eden
Gareth Morlet, alpha werewolf, has finally found his mate. All he has to do is convince Trinity to join with him, to give in to the pleasure of a werewolf's mating, and then she will be his... forever.

Falling for Trouble by Saskia Walker
With 48 hours to clear her brother's name, Sonia Harmond finds help from irresistible bad boy, Oliver Eaglestone. When the erotic tension between them hits fever pitch, securing evidence to thwart an international arms dealer isn't the only danger they face.

The Disciplinarian by Leigh Court
Headstrong Clarissa Babcock is sent for instruction in proper wifely obedience. Disciplinarian Jared Ashworth uses the tools of seduction to show her how to control a demanding husband, but her beauty, spirit, and uninhibited passion make Jared hunger to keep her—and their darkly erotic nights—all for himself!

Secrets, Volume 16

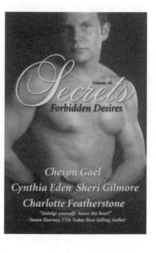

Never Enough by Cynthia Eden
Abby McGill has been playing with fire. Bad-boy Jake taught her the true meaning of desire, but she knows she has to end her relationship with him. But Jake isn't about to let the woman he wants walk away from him.

Bunko by Sheri Gilmoore
Tu Tran must decide between Jack, who promises to share every aspect of his life with her, or Dev, who hides behind a mask and only offers nights of erotic sex. Will she gamble on the man who can see behind her own mask and expose her true desires?

Hide and Seek by Chevon Gael
Kyle DeLaurier ditches his trophy-fiance in favor of a tropical paradise full of tall, tanned, topless females. Private eye, Darcy McLeod, is on the trail of this runaway groom. Together they sizzle while playing Hide and Seek with their true identities.

Seduction of the Muse by Charlotte Featherstone
He's the Dark Lord, the mysterious author who pens the erotic tales of an innocent woman's seduction. She is his muse, the woman he watches from the dark shadows, the woman whose dreams he invades at night.

Secrets, Volume 17

Rock Hard Candy by Kathy Kaye
Jessica Hennessy, descendent of a Voodoo priestess, decides it's time for the man of her dreams. A dose of her ancestor's aphrodisiac slipped into the gooey center of her homemade bon bons ought to do the trick.

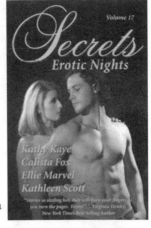

Fatal Error by Kathleen Scott
Jesse Storm must make amends to humanity by destroying the software he helped design that's taken the government hostage. But he must also protect the woman he's loved in secret for nearly a decade.

Birthday by Ellie Marvel
Jasmine Templeton's been celibate long enough. Will a wild night at a hot new club with her two best friends ease the ache or just make it worse? Considering one is Charlie and she's been having strange notions about their relationship of late… It's definitely a birthday neither she nor Charlie will ever forget.

Intimate Rendezvous by Calista Fox
A thief causes trouble at Cassandra Kensington's nightclub and sexy P.I. Dean Hewitt arrives to help. One look at her sends his blood boiling, despite the fact that his keen instincts have him questioning the legitimacy of her business.

Secrets, Volume 18

Lone Wolf Three by Rae Monet
Planetary politics and squabbling drain former rebel leader Taban Zias. But his anger quickly turns to desire when he meets, Lakota Blackson. She's Taban's perfect mate—now if he can just convince her.

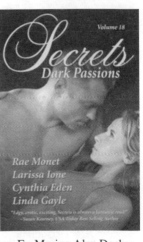

Flesh to Fantasy by Larissa Ione
Kelsa Bradshaw is a loner happily immersed in a world of virtual reality. Trent Jordan is a paramedic who experiences the harsh realities of life. When their worlds collide in an erotic eruption can Trent convince Kelsa to turn the fantasy into something real?

Heart Full of Stars by Linda Gayle
Singer Fanta Rae finds herself stranded on a lonely Mars outpost with the first human male she's seen in years. Ex-Marine Alex Decker lost his family and guilt drove him into isolation, but when alien assassins come to enslave Fanta, she and Decker come together to fight for their lives.

The Wolf's Mate by Cynthia Eden
When Michael Morlet finds "Kat" Hardy fighting for her life, he instantly recognizes her as the mate he's been seeking all of his life, but someone's trying to kill her. With danger stalking them, will Kat trust him enough to become his mate?

Secrets, Volume 19

Affliction by Elisa Adams
Holly Aronson finally believes she's safe with sweet Andrew. But when his life long friend, Shane, arrives, events begin to spiral out of control. She's inexplicably drawn to Shane. As she runs for her life, which one will protect her?

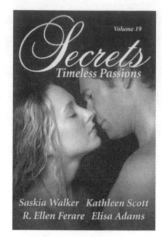

Falling Stars by Kathleen Scott
Daria is both a Primon fighter pilot and a Primon princess. As a deadly new enemy faces appears, she must choose between her duty to the fleet and the desperate need to forge an alliance through her marriage to the enemy's General Raven.

Toy in the Attic by R. Ellen Ferare
Gabrielle discovers a life-sized statue of a nude man. Her unexpected roommate reveals himself to be a talented lover caught by a witch's curse. Can she help him break free of the spell that holds him, without losing her heart along the way?

What You Wish For by Saskia Walker
Lucy Chambers is renovating her historic house. As her dreams about a stranger become more intense, she wishes he were with her. Two hundred years in the past, the man wishes for companionship. Suddenly they find themselves together—in his time.

Secrets, Volume 20

The Subject by Amber Green
One week Tyler is a game designer, signing the deal of her life. The next, she's running for her life. Who can she trust? Certainly not sexy, mysterious Esau, who keeps showing up after the hoo-hah hits the fan!

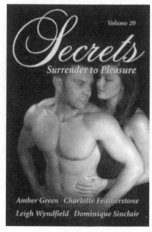

Surrender by Dominique Sinclair
Agent Madeline Carter is in too deep. She's slipped into Sebastian Maiocco's life to investigate his Sicilian mafia family. He unearths desires Madeline's unable to deny, conflicting the duty that honors her. Madeline must surrender to Sebastian or risk being exposed, leaving her target for a ruthless clan.

Stasis by Leigh Wyndfield
Morgann Right's Commanding Officer's been drugged with Stasis, turning him into a living statue she's forced to take care of for ten long days. As her hands tend to him, she sees her CO in a totally different light. She wants him and, while she can tell he wants her, touching him intimately might come back to haunt them both.

A Woman's Pleasure by Charlotte Featherstone
Widowed Isabella, Lady Langdon is yearning to discover all the pleasures denied her in her marriage, she finds herself falling hard for the magnetic charms of the mysterious and exotic Julian Gresham—a man skilled in pleasures of the flesh.

Secrets, Volume 21

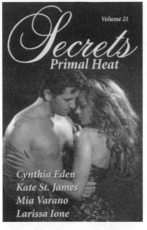

Caged Wolf by Cynthia Eden
Alerac La Morte has been drugged and kidnapped. He
realizes his captor, Madison Langley, is actually his
destined mate, but she hates his kind. Will Alerac
convince her he's not the monster she thinks?

Wet Dreams by Larissa Ione
Injured and on the run, agent Brent Logan needs a
miracle. What he gets is a boat owned by Marina
Summers. Pursued by killers, ravaged by a storm,
and plagued by engine troubles, they can do little but
spend their final hours immersed in sensual pleasure.

Good Vibrations by Kate St. James
Lexi O'Brien vows to swear off sex while she attends
grad school, so when her favorite out-of-town customer asks her out, she decides to
indulge in an erotic fling. Little does she realize Gage Templeton is moving home, to
her city, and has no intention of settling for a short-term affair..

Virgin of the Amazon by Mia Varano
Librarian Anna Winter gets lost on the Amazon and stumbles upon a tribe whose
shaman wants a pale-skinned virgin to deflower. British adventurer Coop Daventry,
the tribe's self-styled chief, wants to save her, but which man poses a greater threat?

Secrets, Volume 22

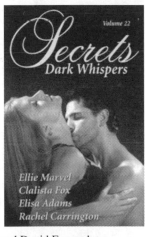

Heat by Ellie Marvel
Mild-mannered alien Tarkin is in heat and the only
compatible female is a Terran. He courts her the old
fashioned Terran way. Because if he can't seduce her
before his cycle ends, he won't get a second chance.

Breathless by Rachel Carrington
Lark Hogan is a martial arts expert seeking vengeance for the death of her sister. She seeks help
from Zac, a mercenary wizard. Confronting a common enemy, they battle their own demons as well as
their powerful attraction, and will fight to the death
to protect what they've found.

Midnight Rendezvous by Calista Fox
From New York to Cabo to Paris to Tokyo, Cat Hewitt and David Essex share
decadent midnight rendezvous. But when the real world presses in on their erotic
fantasies, and Cat's life is in danger, will their whirlwind romance stand a chance?

Birthday Wish by Elisa Adams
Anna Kelly had many goals before turning 30 and only one is left—to spend one
night with sexy Dean Harrison. When Dean asks her what she wants for her birthday, she grabs at the opportunity to ask him for an experience she'll never forget.

Secrets, Volume 23

The Sex Slave by Roxi Romano
Jaci Coe needs a hero and the hard bodied man in black meets all the criteria. Opportunistic Jaci takes advantage of Lazarus Stone's commandingly protective nature, but together, they learn how to live free... and love freely.

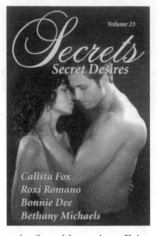

Forever My Love by Calista Fox
Professor Aja Woods is a 16th century witch... only she doesn't know it. Christian St. James, her vampire lover, has watched over her spirit for 500 years. When her powers are recovered, so too are her memories of Christian—and the love they once shared.

Reflection of Beauty by Bonnie Dee
Artist Christine Dawson is commissioned to paint a portrait of wealthy recluse, Eric Leroux. It's up to her to reach the heart of this physically and emotionally scarred man. Can love rescue Eric from isolation and restore his life?

Educating Eva by Bethany Michaels
Eva Blakely attends the infamous Ivy Hill houseparty to gather research for her book *Mating Rituals of the Human Male*. But when she enlists the help of research "specimen" and notorious rake, Aidan Worthington, she gets some unexpected results.

Secrets, Volume 24

Hot on Her Heels by Mia Varano
Private investigator Jack Slater dons a g-string to investigate the Lollipop Lounge, a male strip club. He's not sure if the club's sexy owner, Vivica Steele, is involved in the scam, but Jack figures he's just the Lollipop to sweeten her life.

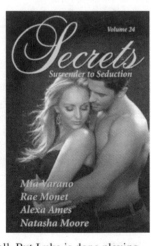

Shadow Wolf by Rae Monet
A half-breed Lupine challenges a high-ranking Solarian Wolf Warrior. When Dia Nahiutras tries to steal Roark D'Reincolt's wolf, does she get an enemy forever or a mate for life?

Bad to the Bone by Natasha Moore
At her class reunion, Annie Shane sheds her good girl reputation through one wild weekend with Luke Kendall. But Luke is done playing the field and wants to settle down. What would a bad girl do?

War God by Alexa Aames
Estella Eaton, a lovely graduate student, is the unwitting carrier of the essence of Aphrodite. But Ares, god of war, the ultimate alpha male, knows the truth and becomes obsessed with Estelle, pursuing her relentlessly. Can her modern sensibilities and his ancient power coexist, or will their battle of wills destroy what matters most?

The Forever Kiss
by Angela Knight

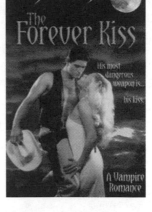

Listen to what reviewers say:

"*The Forever Kiss* flows well with good characters and an interesting plot. … If you enjoy vampires and a lot of hot sex, you are sure to enjoy *The Forever Kiss*."

—*The Best Reviews*

"Battling vampires, a protective ghost and the ever present battle of good and evil keep excellent pace with the erotic delights in Angela Knight's *The Forever Kiss*—a book that absolutely bites with refreshing paranormal humor." **4½ Stars, Top Pick**

—*Romantic Times BOOKclub*

"I found *The Forever Kiss* to be an exceptionally written, refreshing book. … I really enjoyed this book by Angela Knight. … 5 angels!"

—*Fallen Angel Reviews*

"*The Forever Kiss* is the first single title released from Red Sage and if this is any indication of what we can expect, it won't be the last. … The love scenes are hot enough to give a vampire a sunburn and the fight scenes will have you cheering for the good guys."

—*Really Bad Barb Reviews*

In *The Forever Kiss*:

For years, Valerie Chase has been haunted by dreams of a Texas Ranger she knows only as "Cowboy." As a child, he rescued her from the nightmare vampires who murdered her parents. As an adult, she still dreams of him—but now he's her seductive lover in nights of erotic pleasure.

Yet "Cowboy" is more than a dream—he's the real Cade McKinnon—and a vampire! For years, he's protected Valerie from Edward Ridgemont, the sadistic vampire who turned him. Now, Ridgmont wants Valerie for his own and Cade is the only one who can protect her.

When Val finds herself abducted by her handsome dream man, she's appalled to discover he's one of the vampires she fears. Now, caught in a web of fear and passion, she and Cade must learn to trust each other, even as an immortal monster stalks their every move.

Their only hope of survival is… *The Forever Kiss*.

Romantic Times Best Erotic Novel of the Year

It's not just reviewers raving about *Secrets*. See what readers have to say:

"When are you coming out with a new Volume? I want a new one next month!" via email from a reader.

"I loved the hot, wet sex without vulgar words being used to make it exciting." after *Volume 1*

"I loved the blend of sensuality and sexual intensity—HOT!" after *Volume 2*

"The best thing about *Secrets* is they're hot and brief! The least thing is you do not have enough of them!" after *Volume 3*

"I have been extremely satisfied with *Secrets*, keep up the good writing." after *Volume 4*

"Stories have plot and characters to support the erotica. They would be good strong stories without the heat." after *Volume 5*

"*Secrets* really knows how to push the envelop better than anyone else." after *Volume 6*

"These are the best sensual stories I have ever read!" after *Volume 7*

"I love, love, love the *Secrets* stories. I now have all of them, please have more books come out each year." after *Volume 8*

"These are the perfect sensual romance stories!" after *Volume 9*

"What I love about *Secrets Volume 10* is how I couldn't put it down!" after *Volume 10*

"All of the *Secrets* volumes are terrific! I have read all of them up to *Secrets Volume 11*. Please keep them coming! I will read every one you make!" after *Volume 11*

Finally, the men you've been dreaming about!

Give the Gift of Spicy Romantic Fiction

Don't want to wait? You can place a retail price ($12.99) order for any of the *Secrets* volumes from the following:

① online at **eRedSage.com**

② **Waldenbooks, Borders, and Books-a-Million Stores**

③ **Amazon.com** or **BarnesandNoble.com**

④ or buy them at your local bookstore or online book source.

Bookstores: Please contact Baker & Taylor Distributors, Ingram Book Distributor, or Red Sage Publishing, Inc. for bookstore sales.

Order by title or ISBN #:

Vol. 1: 0-9648942-0-3 ISBN #13 978-0-9648942-0-4	**Vol. 10:** 0-9754516-0-X ISBN #13 978-0-9754516-0-1	**Vol. 19:** 0-9754516-9-3 ISBN #13 978-0-9754516-9-4
Vol. 2: 0-9648942-1-1 ISBN #13 978-0-9648942-1-1	**Vol. 11:** 0-9754516-1-8 ISBN #13 978-0-9754516-1-8	**Vol. 20:** 1-60310-000-8 ISBN #13 978-1-60310-000-7
Vol. 3: 0-9648942-2-X ISBN #13 978-0-9648942-2-8	**Vol. 12:** 0-9754516-2-6 ISBN #13 978-0-9754516-2-5	**Vol. 21:** 1-60310-001-6 ISBN #13 978-1-60310-001-4
Vol. 4: 0-9648942-4-6 ISBN #13 978-0-9648942-4-2	**Vol. 13:** 0-9754516-3-4 ISBN #13 978-0-9754516-3-2	**Vol. 22:** 1-60310-002-4 ISBN #13 978-1-60310-002-1
Vol. 5: 0-9648942-5-4 ISBN #13 978-0-9648942-5-9	**Vol. 14:** 0-9754516-4-2 ISBN #13 978-0-9754516-4-9	**Vol. 23:** 1-60310-164-0 ISBN #13 978-1-60310-164-6
Vol. 6: 0-9648942-6-2 ISBN #13 978-0-9648942-6-6	**Vol. 15:** 0-9754516-5-0 ISBN #13 978-0-9754516-5-6	**Vol. 24:** 1-60310-166-7 ISBN #13 978-1-60310-166-0
Vol. 7: 0-9648942-7-0 ISBN #13 978-0-9648942-7-3	**Vol. 16:** 0-9754516-6-9 ISBN #13 978-0-9754516-6-3	**The Forever Kiss:** 0-9648942-3-8 ISBN #13 978-0-9648942-3-5 ($14.00)
Vol. 8: 0-9648942-8-9 ISBN #13 978-0-9648942-9-7	**Vol. 17:** 0-9754516-7-7 ISBN #13 978-0-9754516-7-0	
Vol. 9: 0-9648942-9-7 ISBN #13 978-0-9648942-9-7	**Vol. 18:** 0-9754516-8-5 ISBN #13 978-0-9754516-8-7	

Check out our hot eBook titles available online at eRedSage.com!

Visit the site regularly as we're always adding new eBook titles.

Here's just some of what you'll find:

A Christmas Cara by Bethany Michaels

A Damsel in Distress by Brenda Williamson

Blood Game by Rae Monet

Fires Within by Roxana Blaze

Forbidden Fruit by Anne Rainey

High Voltage by Calista Fox

Master of the Elements by Alice Gaines

One Wish by Calista Fox

Quinn's Curse by Natasha Moore

Rock My World by Caitlyn Willows

The Doctor Next Door by Catherine Berlin

Unclaimed by Nathalie Gray

Red Sage Publishing Order Form:
(Orders shipped in two to three days of receipt.)

Each volume of *Secrets* retails for $12.99, but you can get it direct via mail order for only $10.99 each. The novel *The Forever Kiss* retails for $14.00, but by direct mail order, you only pay $12.00. Use the order form below to place your direct mail order. Fill in the quantity you want for each book on the blanks beside the title.

_____ *Secrets* Volume 1	_____ *Secrets* Volume 10	_____ *Secrets* Volume 19
_____ *Secrets* Volume 2	_____ *Secrets* Volume 11	_____ *Secrets* Volume 20
_____ *Secrets* Volume 3	_____ *Secrets* Volume 12	_____ *Secrets* Volume 21
_____ *Secrets* Volume 4	_____ *Secrets* Volume 13	_____ *Secrets* Volume 22
_____ *Secrets* Volume 5	_____ *Secrets* Volume 14	_____ *Secrets* Volume 23
_____ *Secrets* Volume 6	_____ *Secrets* Volume 15	_____ *Secrets* Volume 24
_____ *Secrets* Volume 7	_____ *Secrets* Volume 16	_____ *The Forever Kiss*
_____ *Secrets* Volume 8	_____ *Secrets* Volume 17	
_____ *Secrets* Volume 9	_____ *Secrets* Volume 18	

Total _____ *Secrets* Volumes @ $10.99 each = $_____

Total _____ *The Forever Kiss* @ $12.00 each = $_____

Shipping & handling (in the U.S.) $_____

US Priority Mail: UPS insured:
1–2 books .... $ 5.50   1–4 books $16.00
3–5 books .... $11.50   5–9 books $25.00
6–9 books .... $14.50   10–24 books $29.00
10–24 books $19.00

SUBTOTAL $_____

Florida 6% sales tax (if delivered in FL) $_____

TOTAL AMOUNT ENCLOSED $_____

Your personal information is kept private and not shared with anyone.

Name: (please print) _____

Address: (no P.O. Boxes) _____

City/State/Zip: _____

Phone or email: (only regarding order if necessary) _____

You can order direct from **eRedSage.com** and use a credit card or you can use this form to send in your mail order with a check. Please make check payable to **Red Sage Publishing**. Check must be drawn on a U.S. bank in U.S. dollars. Mail your check and order form to:

Red Sage Publishing, Inc.   Department S23   P.O. Box 4844   Seminole, FL 33775